SUMMER OF THE MIDNIGHT SUN

Summer of the Midnight Sun

TRACIE
PETERSON

DOUBLEDAY LARGE PRINT HOME LIBRARY EDITION

BETHANY HOUSE PUBLISHERS

Minneapolis, Minnesota

This Large Print Edition, prepared especially for Doubleday Large Print Home Library, contains the complete, unabridged text of the original Publisher's Edition.

Published by Bethany House Publishers
11400 Hampshire Avenue South
Bloomington, Minnesota 55438

Bethany House Publishers is a division of
Baker Publishing Group, Grand Rapids, Michigan.

Printed in the United States of America

ISBN 13: 978-0-7394-6533-2
ISBN 10: 0-7394-6533-3

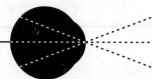

This Large Print Book carries the
Seal of Approval of N.A.V.H.

To Jayce

You inspired the name of
my character and have shown
the light of Christ in your
heart and actions. I'm
proud to call you friend.
May God ever direct
your steps.

Books by Tracie Peterson

www.traciepeterson.com

The Long-Awaited Child • *Silent Star*
A Slender Thread • *Tidings of Peace*
What She Left for Me
*I Can't Do It All!***

ALASKAN QUEST
Summer of the Midnight Sun

BELLS OF LOWELL*
Daughter of the Loom • *A Fragile Design*
These Tangled Threads

LIGHTS OF LOWELL*
A Tapestry of Hope • *A Love Woven True*
The Pattern of Her Heart

DESERT ROSES
Shadows of the Canyon • *Across the Years*
Beneath a Harvest Sky

HEIRS OF MONTANA
Land of My Heart • *The Coming Storm*
To Dream Anew • *The Hope Within*

WESTWARD CHRONICLES
A Shelter of Hope • *Hidden in a Whisper*
A Veiled Reflection

RIBBONS OF STEEL†
Distant Dreams • *A Promise for Tomorrow*

RIBBONS WEST†
Westward the Dream • *Ties That Bind*

SHANNON SAGA‡
City of Angels • *Angels Flight*
Angel of Mercy

YUKON QUEST
Treasures of the North • *Ashes and Ice*
Rivers of Gold

*with Judith Miller †with Judith Pella ‡with James Scott Bell
**with Allison Bottke and Dianne O'Brian

Chapter One

LAST CHANCE CREEK, ALASKA TERRITORY
MAY 1915

"Where is he?" Leah Barringer whispered, scanning the horizon for a glimpse of her brother and his dogsled team. He should have been home weeks earlier, and yet there was no sign of him.

A cold May wind nipped at her face, but it was the hard glint of sun against snow that made Leah put her hand to her brow. They had suffered through weeks of storms, so the sunshine was most welcome, but it was also intense and blinding.

"Jacob, where are you?" Her heart ached with fear of what might have happened. The Alaskan wilderness was not a place to be toyed with, and though Jacob was well versed in the ways of this land, Leah feared for him nevertheless.

Jacob had left nearly two months earlier for Nome. Hunting had been poor in the area and many families were going hungry. He had made the decision to travel to Nome for basic supplies and to replenish the store of goods he and Leah sold from their make-shift trading post. A master with dogs, Jacob figured he could hike out by sled and be back before the spring thaw made that mode of travel too difficult. It was a trip that should have taken two to three weeks at the most.

Storms had made it impossible to send someone out to check on Jacob, and hunger made it unwise. There was nothing to be gained by risking more lives. *Besides,* she reassured herself, *Jacob is as capable as any native Alaskan.* He had the best dogs in all of Alaska too. Leah tried not to worry, but Jacob was all she had. Since their mother died when they were children, they had clung to each other for comfort and support. Their father, a grand dreamer, had dragged them to Alaska during the Yukon gold rush some seventeen years earlier. After his death, Jacob and Leah had made a pact to always take care of each other.

Not that she didn't want more.

Leah was facing the harsh reality that she was nearly thirty years old, and the idea of reaching that milestone was more than she could bear. She longed for a husband and children, but here in the frozen north of the Seward Peninsula, there were few prospects. The natives had little interest in white women. The whites were perceived with skepticism at best and animosity at worst. Most of the natives she and Jacob befriended accepted them well enough, but none had shown an interest in marrying either Leah or her brother.

Leah wasn't sure she could be happy marrying a native anyway. She was not completely comfortable with their lifestyle and interests. Many were steeped in superstitions that she and Jacob could never be a part of. She had shared her Christian faith with anyone who would listen, but traditions and fears were strong motivators compared to white man's stories of a Savior and the need to put aside sinful ways.

And though Nome sported more white men than other areas, most were aging and grizzled, and not at all what Leah perceived as husband material, furthering her matrimonial woes. Added to this, many were just as steeped in their traditions and superstitions as the natives. Most had come up for the gold rush in Nome—hoping against the odds to make their fortune. Few had actually succeeded, and many had lost hope long ago, giving their lives to a bottle or to some other form of destruction.

Ten years ago Jacob and Leah discussed their desires to marry and start families of their own. They agreed if either one found true love, they wouldn't feel obligated to forsake this for the needs of their sibling. Leah had thought they would both find mates and settle down to raise families, but this hadn't happened.

Her guardian after her father's death, Karen Ivankov, understood Leah's distress. The same thing had happened to Karen in her youth. Love and romance had eluded her until she was in her thirties and alone in the wilderness of the Yukon.

Sometimes Karen's long wait to find love and marriage encouraged Leah. Karen often said that when the time was right, God would send a husband to Leah. Leah prayed Karen was right. She prayed for a husband, even as she prayed for Jacob to find a wife. Because, despite their pact from so long ago, Leah knew she would want Jacob to be happily settled as well. But so far God had only sent one person that Leah felt certain she could love.

Ten years ago she had been almost twenty, and Jayce Kincaid had been all she'd ever wanted in a husband. Strong and handsome, brave and trustworthy. At least she'd believed he'd been trustworthy. But what had she known of men at the tender age of twenty? Karen had taught her not to judge men by outward appearances, but rather to test their hearts. Leah had given Jayce her heart, but he hadn't wanted it. He'd actually laughed when she'd declared her love.

"Jayce, I have to tell you something," Leah had told him after arranging to meet him privately.

"What is it, Leah?" he'd asked. "You seem so all-fired serious. Is something wrong?"

"No . . . at least not to my way of thinking."

He had been so handsome in his flannel

shirt and black wool trousers. His dark brown hair needed a good cut, but Leah found the wildness rather appealing.

"So what was so important that you dragged me away from the warmth of the house?"

Leah swallowed hard. "I think . . . that is . . . well . . ." She stammered over the words she'd practiced at length. Drawing a deep breath, she blurted it out. "I think I've fallen in love with you."

Jayce laughed out loud, the sound cutting through her heart. "Leah, it's best you don't do any thinking, if that's what you're coming to conclude."

Leah shook her head, her cheeks feeling hotter by the minute. "Why would you say that? Have you no feelings for me?"

"Well, sure I have feelings for you. You're a sweet girl, but you're way too young to know what love is all about."

"I'm nearly twenty years old!" she protested.

"My point exactly. You aren't even of legal majority. How can you trust yourself to know what the truth of your heart might be?" He picked up a rock and tossed it into the creek that ran behind the Ivankov home. "You're just Jacob's kid sister."

"And you were cruel," Leah whispered, her thoughts coming back to the present. She wiped a tear from the edge of her eye. How long would it hurt? Surely there was someone she might come to love as much as she had loved Jayce Kincaid. But it was always Jayce's face she saw—his voice she heard.

Maybe I'm too picky, she thought as she made her way back into her *inne.* It wasn't a true inne, but it served nearly as well. Instead of being mostly underground, like the native homes, the Barringer inne was a bit more above ground than usual—but not by much; it would have been foolish to have it too exposed to the elements. But to live too far underground would have made Leah feel buried, and Jacob, ever thoughtful of her feelings, had struck this compromise. The log and sod creation also lacked the long tunnel that most innes had. Leah preferred the manner in which they'd built their house but would still navigate the entrances to the homes of her friends. The tunnels were the worst of it, she would say, enduring the two-foot-wide crawling space with her eyes closed most of the time. She just didn't like the feeling of being closed in.

The Barringer house also acted as the trading post, so accessibility was critical. Natives were always coming to trade smoked meats, furs, or finished products. In turn, Jacob would take these things to Nome, where he could trade for supplies that they were unable to glean from the land. With this in mind, Jacob had designed the cabin to be partially underground in order to be insulated from the severe cold of winter, yet simple and quick to get in and out of. He had also managed to put in one window to let light into the room they used for eating and cooking during the long winter months. Of course, in the winter there was no light, so they closed the window off to keep the heat from escaping.

Leah entered her home and made her way down several steps to the first room. She and Jacob had set aside this room for the trading of goods. They carried provisions like salt and spices, sugar, canned milk, coffee, and tools. Of course the natives would have made their way in life without these luxuries, but Leah found that, as word spread, the natives seemed more than content to trade furs for white man's goods. And by operating their trading post, they saved the people from having to travel all the way to Nome.

She looked around the small room. The shelves were pretty much cleaned out—she hadn't even had to worry about keeping shop. There were an unusually high number of tools, however, since people had, as a last resort, traded equipment for food. For the first time, Leah wondered if the village could even survive much longer. Hunger was a constant companion, and although everyone was sharing as much as they could, there had already been deaths. Only the strong survived an Arctic winter.

Leah moved to the right and pushed back the heavy furs that sealed another doorway. Inside was a small room her older native friend, Ayoona, insisted they build when Leah and Jacob had first come to the village nearly ten years ago. They called this the stormy day cookroom, and it held a fire pit and had an opening in the ceiling that allowed the smoke to dissipate. The door was covered with heavy furs to keep out the cold, and when they were cooking here, it was a pleasantly warm room that beckoned them to stay—so much so that Jacob had put in a table and chairs when Leah had complained of being tired of sitting on the floor. It made a nice place to eat their winter meals.

The Barringers also had something that most natives had never concerned themselves with, and that was a stove. Leah liked the stove for cooking and baking. She had learned to do her kitchen tasks in native style over the fire pit, but the stove was a luxury she praised God for on a daily basis.

She checked the stove, making sure there was enough heat to keep the kettle of water and small pot of soup hot. She wanted there to be food ready for Jacob when he returned. If he returned. Again she felt a sinking in her heart.

"He must come back," she murmured, stirring the thin soup. Soon, even this food would be gone. Leah would have no choice but to eat what she had when the time came and hope that Jacob would bring more.

Seeing that everything was as it should be, Leah made her way back to the main living quarters of the inne. Here they had their small table and chairs, their beds, and some chests for storage. It wasn't much, but it had been home for a good portion of Leah's adult life.

"Lay-Ya!"

Leah smiled. It was Ayoona. The old Inupiat woman always called her with emphasis on the "ya."

"I'm here in the back," Leah replied, popping out from behind the hanging fur doorway.

"I brought you food," Ayoona said proudly. "My son was blessed today. He caught a seal. The village is celebrating."

"A seal! How wonderful!" Leah nearly squealed in delight. Seals and walruses had been so scarce she actually feared that something bad had happened to the bulk of the animal population.

Ayoona held a pot out to Leah. "This is for our good friend Leah and her brother, Jacob."

Leah took the offering. "Oh, you have our gratitude and thanks. I know Jacob will be home any day now."

The stocky little woman smiled, revealing several missing teeth. "He will come. I have prayed for him."

Leah nodded. "I have prayed for him too. I spend most all my time praying."

"You should come hunt with my family. I am too old, but you are young and strong. You shoot a bow well—you could hunt for geese with my daughters. When the spring is truly come, they will hunt for squirrel, and you can make Jacob a new undershirt."

"I would have to be a very good hunter to get enough squirrels for a shirt."

Ayoona grunted. "Maybe forty—no more. Jacob is not big man."

Leah smiled. "He's big enough. He eats like he's three men."

"He work like he's three men," Ayoona countered, her grin taking years off her wrinkled face. "I go now. We celebrate."

Leah nodded. "Thank you again. I'll get right to work on cooking this."

"Don't cook too much. You whites always cook too much. Takes flavor out."

Leah laughed and gave Ayoona a wave as the old woman offered her a smile once again. Ayoona had become a dear friend over the last ten years. The old woman had learned English as a child in one of the missions, but she'd never been comfortable with it. She often spoke English in a broken manner, shifting more easily into her once-forbidden Eskimo tongue.

Ayoona had been less suspicious of Leah and Jacob than some—although she had perhaps more reason to fear them because of the misery caused her by other white Christians. Still, the old woman had been kind and offered food upon their arrival. Later when Jacob had sat with the village council, Ayoona had defended them to her son—one of the higher-ranking members. Leah would always be grateful for her kindness.

The villagers had been skeptical and wary of Jacob and Leah when they arrived. Whites generally meant trouble in some form. Either they came bringing sickness or they came demanding change.

Jacob and Leah tried to do neither. Jacob actually had taken a job driving the mail from Nome to other villages where mission workers were desperate for news from home. During the winter, it was impossible for ships to venture north for deliveries, but dogsleds were ideal. The mail runs naturally led to bringing in store goods, and before she knew it, Leah had a job of her own, trading goods. She truly enjoyed interacting with the native people.

It wasn't too long after they settled in Last Chance that missionaries showed up to establish a church and school for the area. Leah felt sorry for these kind people of God. They had an uphill battle to fight against the superstitions the shamans had built into their people.

Busying herself with preparing the seal meat, Leah didn't realize how the time had passed. It was deceiving to try to determine the time by the light of the sun. Some months they were in darkness and other months it was light for the entire twenty-four-hour day. The spring Leah had known in Colorado, where she had lived as a child, was nothing like what she experienced in Alaska. The deadliness of the land seemed even more critical when the seasons changed.

Jacob had hiked out when the ice was thick, able to move the dogs out onto the ice for easier passage to Nome. But that wouldn't be safe now. The temperatures and storms had disguised their effects on the land. Sometimes the snow seemed firm, solid, but as the day warmed it would turn to mush. Night would chill it to ice—but not always in a firm manner. Instead thin crusts would form and give false promises of security to the untrained eye.

"But Jacob's not untrained," she reminded herself, checking the stew she'd made. It was little more than the seal meat and a little salt and flour, but the smell was quite inviting.

"He's capable and he knows the route. Something else must have happened." And that worried Leah even more. Jacob might have encountered a bear or gotten hurt separating fighting dogs. The sled dogs were not always in the best of moods.

"Jacob's back!"

At first Leah wasn't sure she'd really heard the call. She put aside the spoon she'd been using and ran for the door. The native who'd brought the news was one of Ayoona's grandsons. He quickly exited the house after seeing that Leah would follow.

But Leah didn't go far. It dawned on her that Jacob would rather come home to a warm house and food waiting than to have her rushing to him in tears. She would have plenty of time to talk to him, and the natives would see to unpacking the sled. She watched the activity for a moment, then turned back to the house to set the table.

Rushing to the stove, Leah threw in more chopped driftwood, then quickly went to the cupboard and pulled out a large bowl. How she wished she might offer her brother bread or even crackers with the meal. *Maybe he will have brought some of each from Nome,* she mused in anticipation.

Soon the door opened, and the fear that had gripped her for the past weeks evaporated. "Jacob!" she gasped and ran to embrace her brother. "I thought you were gone forever. You really worried me this time." She couldn't see his face for the deep parka hood that he still wore, but his strong embrace let her know he had missed her as well.

"Come over to the stove. I'll help you get out of those wet clothes." She led him across the room. "Don't worry about your boots," Leah said, noticing they were dripping bits of snow and ice, and that they were new—not the mukluks he'd left in.

"There hasn't been too much excitement while you were gone. Just starvation, but of course you already knew about that. Nutchuk cut his hand badly while skinning a seal. I stitched him back up, however, and he seems to be doing fine." She thought of the young native man and how scared he'd been. His mother had told him he would lose the hand for sure unless he allowed the shaman to create a charm, but Nutchuk had just become a Christian earlier in the winter, and he no longer believed such things held power. Leah had been proud of his conviction. "You should have seen him, Jacob. He refused to deal with the shamans because he honestly believed Jesus would heal him. It was a real testimony to the rest of his family."

She stood behind Jacob to help him pull the thick fur parka from over his shoulders. "Oh, and Qavlunaq had her baby two weeks ago. It was an easy birth, and her mother-in-law and grandmother delivered him. It was a boy and his father is quite proud."

The coat finally gave way and Leah hung it on a peg, leaving Jacob to finish disrobing. "I've got your supper on the stove. Are you hungry?" She turned for his answer but stopped in shock when she saw the man before her was not her brother.

"Jayce," she whispered almost reverently. The past had finally caught up with her.

Chapter Two

"I thank you for the warm welcome," he said, grinning roguishly. "I must say you're a sight for sore eyes. And my eyes are definitely sore. The sun against the snow was most blinding—even with our little slitted masks, the sun still made me miserable."

Words refused to form in Leah's mouth. She could only continue to stare at the man before her. How good he looked—strong and capable. Handsome too. She felt all of her girlish dreams and emotions rush to the surface.

Jayce rubbed his eyes. "It was sure my good fortune to meet up with Jacob. Your family in Ketchikan told me you were out here on the Bering Sea, but I really wasn't sure I could locate you. I can't imagine what Jacob was thinking settling out here, but I'm glad he did."

Still Leah simply watched as Jayce stepped forward to warm his hands at the stove. "Smells good, Leah. I recall you were a good cook, even as a kid."

"As a kid." The words stuck in her brain.

"Hmmm, something smells great," Jacob called as he came through the door. He'd already pulled off his parka, so this time Leah was certain it was her brother. "Kimik told me John caught a seal."

Leah finally found her voice. "Yes. Did Kimik also tell you that his wife gave birth to their son a couple of weeks ago?" She decided that, for the moment, ignoring Jayce was the only way she'd be able to compose her frayed nerves.

"Yeah, he seemed mighty proud," Jacob said, hanging his coat near Jayce's. His sandy brown hair fell across his forehead, and he pushed it back. "So I guess you can see my surprise for yourself. Jayce was in Nome looking for good sled dogs, so I thought I'd bring him home with me and show off some of ours."

"Actually, I went there looking for Jacob's dogs. Adrik told me they were the best to be had."

Leah wasn't ready to deal with Jayce just yet. "Jacob, where have you been? What happened? You should have been home weeks ago. We were all terrified, and the people were on the brink of starving."

Jacob frowned. "I know, and I'm sorry. I couldn't help it; I caught the measles and the doctor wouldn't let me leave Nome. I was pretty sick—not to mention quarantined."

"Measles?" Leah questioned.

"Yes, and then the weather turned bad— you probably experienced it yourself. I couldn't even get word to you. I'm sorry if you worried."

"Besides, Jacob's able to take care of himself," Jayce threw in. "You should have known he'd be all right."

Leah felt her anger rise, and she turned abruptly to stare Jayce in the eye. Those lovely dark blue eyes. "I figured Jacob would be fine . . . it was the people here who weren't faring as well." She tilted her chin upward in a defiant pose, just daring Jayce to condemn her thinking. "Jacob is a very considerate man, and he knew the people were suffering. I knew he wouldn't have left them to die and figured something must have happened to him."

"Well, we're here now," Jacob said before Jayce could comment. "And by bringing Jayce back with me, I was able to split the team, borrow an extra sled, and carry twice as many supplies."

"Which reminds me," Jayce said. "I left some things in the sled. I'd better go re-trieve them before they wind up on the store shelves." He laughed and bounded across the room.

"I know the people will be grateful for what you did, Jacob." But Leah wouldn't be among them. She felt the fire leave her and again knew a weakness in her knees that threatened to sink her to the floor. "There's food on the stove. I'll be in the other room putting the things away."

She exited quickly, grateful that Jayce had left the house. She prayed God would help her overcome her shock. She forgot to pray, however, that Jacob wouldn't follow her.

"What's wrong with you? You aren't at all yourself. Did something else happen while I was gone?"

Leah leaned back against the wall and shook her head. "Why did you bring him here?" she whispered.

"Jayce? I already told you."

"Jacob, you know what he did to me. You know how much he hurt me." She looked at her brother as though he'd lost his mind. How could he have betrayed her this way?

"What are you talking about? That was ten years ago. You were just kids then."

"I wasn't a kid. I was nearly twenty years old. In some areas of our country that would be considered almost too old for getting married. Twenty wasn't a child's age, nor was I childish in giving my heart to Jayce. I might have been foolish, but I wasn't childish."

"Whoa!" Jacob said, holding up his hands. "You're really upset about this, aren't you?"

Leah shook her head and hoped her look expressed her confusion. "You really don't understand, do you? It never crossed your mind that his coming here would be a problem for me."

"Well, I guess I figured that everyone would be so happy for the extra supplies, you included, that it wouldn't matter. Look, you aren't the same woman you were back then, and he's certainly not the same man. He even found the Lord, Leah. Isn't that great?"

Leah knew she couldn't protest that bit of news. Jayce's inability to see eye to eye with her on issues of faith had been his one shortcoming. It had also been the one thing she knew would have kept them from marriage, even if he had felt the same way she did.

"I'm glad he's found peace for his soul," Leah said, gazing at the floor, hoping some sort of peace would overcome her anxieties. "But I can't help the way I feel." She sighed. "I can't believe he's here, after all these years."

Jacob came and reached out to touch her arm. "I'm sorry that he still bothers you. I'll ask him to sleep elsewhere if you want me to."

Leah shook her head. "No, I can go stay with Ayoona. But . . ." She lifted her face and saw the compassion in her brother's eyes. He really didn't understand, but he cared that she was hurt. "Jacob, how long will he be here?"

It was Jacob's turn to look away. "I'm not entirely sure. That is to say . . . well . . . he's here to get some dogs. That much you know."

"But what don't I know?" she asked. "What is it that has you upset enough to look away from me?"

Jacob stood and glanced over his shoulder at the sound of Jayce's return. "He's part of a polar exploration group. They want me to join them on a trip north. They want me to handle the dogs."

Before Leah could reply, Jayce shouted from the next room. "Jacob! Where are you? I'm starving."

Jacob looked at Leah and shrugged. "We can talk about it later. I'll go see to feeding him."

Leah watched as her brother started to leave. There was something in his manner—in his tone—that suggested he might really be considering Jayce's proposal. "Wait. You aren't seriously thinking about doing this, are you?"

Jacob stopped midstep but refused to turn. It was enough to let Leah know exactly how he felt. "You are considering it. You're thinking about leaving me to explore the north with Jayce Kincaid." The words were delivered in stunned amazement.

"I'm praying on it, Leah. That's as far as I've gotten. You oughta pray about it too."

He left with those final words still ringing in the air. Leah sat down hard, but she missed the chair. Her backside stung from the impact, but she gave it no mind. Jayce was threatening her security once again.

How can he be here? How could God let this happen? Leah's mind swirled with a million questions. All of which involved Jayce Kincaid.

Her stomach growled in hunger, but she wasn't about to join the men. She doubted she could even choke down food while sitting across from Jayce.

"Hello! I bring the boxes."

Leah recognized Kimik's voice. "I'm coming," she called. "Just put them on the counter."

She got to her feet and dusted off the seat of her pants. There was work to be done. Somehow, someway she was going to have to get a grip on her emotions. But how? How could she exist in the same village, much less under the same roof, with Jayce? If nothing else, his appearance here had taught her one thing.

She wasn't over him. Not by any means.

———

"Leah okay?" Jayce asked. "I know I'm imposing."

Jacob looked at his friend. "She's fine. She's happiest when she's setting the store straight. With all these supplies, she'll be busy for a time. That will help."

"She acted like she was mad at me," Jayce said, helping himself to the coffee Jacob had made.

Jacob shook his head. "I don't know what she's thinking half the time. Women are a mystery." He ladled another portion of the seal meat for Jayce and then for himself, being sure to leave a portion for Leah. Even though he didn't always understand his sister, he was sure she hadn't yet eaten.

"Did I tell you that we're going to have a couple of women along on the trip north?" Jayce said, seemingly unaffected by Jacob's comment.

"Women on a polar exploration team?"

Jacob asked. "That seems a bit strange. What prompted this?"

"Actually it's becoming more typical. Anyway, given that we're only going to do map work on the Canadian islands, it's not deemed quite as dangerous. Of course, you know there are some explorers who claim that there's nothing to surviving the Arctic. Natives do it all the time, after all. So the captain is allowing his wife to join him, as well as some female cartographer. Well, at least she'll be the assistant. Guess she's somebody important from Washington, D.C., and they couldn't get out of it. Even though this is a shared effort, it's mostly a Canadian team. They are, however, trying to earn the respect and interest of the Americans. They want our financial support, you know."

"I'm sure," Jacob said, trying not to think about what Leah's reaction to this trip would be.

"These expeditions are very expensive. I know the team has worked long hours to raise enough money for supplies. We'd have the added expense of a ship, as well, if the captain hadn't volunteered his own. He's an American who's fully sold on the im-

portance of exploring the North. Thinks,
along with others, that Alaska and the Arctic hold promise for many reasons. Military
wants to consider strategic placement in
the North, and I'm sure you've read about
the air flights being made. They want to
eventually put runways up here and fly people back and forth."

"For what purpose?"

"Well, national security for one. Some of
the more innovative men in the govern-
ments of America and Canada see benefit
in the speed and convenience of flight.
Imagine being able to get supplies to Nome
and all points north during the winter. Better
still, imagine being able to get the sick out
to doctors in a timely manner—winter or
summer. It'll just be a matter of convincing
the old codgers who still want to cling to
their horse and buggies."

"But I'm not sure flight will even work up
here, especially in winter. How are you going to keep the planes moving when everything is frozen solid?"

Jayce shrugged. "That would come under
somebody else's department. I'm just in it
for the adventure. You know me."

"Well, I used to. Ten years is a long time. Long enough to change a man or woman from the inside out. You said so yourself."

Jayce nodded. "Seems to have changed your sister. I remember her as a much happier person. Full of laughter and smiles. She seems real serious now."

Jacob drew a deep breath and sighed. "I have a feeling she's only going to get more serious as the days grow longer."

———

Leah finished her inventory, then immediately sent Kimik out with word that the store was open and that they would allow the people to purchase on credit. It was only a matter of minutes before people flooded the place with their requests and demands. Hunger made people feel angry, and no one had any way of knowing when the hunting or the weather would improve enough to see the bellies of the village filled and satisfied.

"It won't be long before the tomcod will be back. Squirrels and goose too," Ayoona said as she arranged her own small pile of supplies. "I dry you many fish, Lay-Ya."

"I know you will," Leah said, putting down the figures in her book. "You and your family have always been very generous with Jacob and me."

"You good people." She leaned closer. "How good is that new man?"

Leah's mouth dropped open. "I . . . what . . . ? You mean Jayce Kincaid?"

"Jacob's new man. The white man."

Leah tried hard not to seem upset. "We knew Jayce when we lived in Ketchikan with our guardians, Karen and Adrik Ivankov. Jayce was a friend to Jacob."

"So he is good man," Ayoona said nodding. "If he long friend of Jacob, he be good."

"I suppose so." Leah put her book under the counter. "I'm closing up now, Ayoona. I wondered if I could ask a favor."

"Sure you ask." The old woman gathered her things in a basket.

"Since Jayce is here, I wondered if I might stay with you for a few days—maybe until he leaves for his trip north."

"You can stay, Lay-Ya." She moved toward the door. "You come before the storm."

"Is there a storm moving in?" Leah realized she'd been inside for several hours without having a clue what was happening outside.

"Yeah, bad storm. You come soon."

Leah nodded. "I've got to take care of a few things; then I'll be there."

Ayoona pressed through the furs just as Jayce came through. "Where will you be, Leah?" he asked as Ayoona left.

Leah tried to ignore him. She figured if she pretended not to hear, maybe Jayce would leave her to her work.

"Are you purposefully ignoring me, or are you just caught up in your duties?" Jayce came and leaned against the counter.

Leah knew there would be no way to avoid speaking to him. "I'm very busy." Leah began to rearrange several items. "What do you want?"

"I asked where you were going. You told that old woman you'd be there. I just wondered where there might be."

Leah shrugged. "Ayoona's inne. I'm going to stay with her for a few days. This place isn't big enough for all three of us."

"Nonsense. You have families in this village who live eight and ten to an inne. You don't need to leave."

She made the mistake of looking into his face. How many times had she seen this same image in her dreams—wished she might once again be reunited with this lost love? She hadn't fully realized until that moment that she was still in love with Jayce Kincaid.

He grinned as if reading her mind. "You don't really want to go, do you? I mean"—his voice dropped low—"we'd miss you."

"You would?" Leah was barely able to form the words.

Jayce's smile broadened. "Nobody cooks as well as you do—especially not Jacob. I've lived with his cooking all this last week, and if you go, I'll be stuck with it again."

The words sobered Leah instantly. "You want me to stay so that I can cook for you? Maybe wash your clothes too?" She fought her anger. "Is that what this is about? I don't see or hear anything from you in ten years and you want me to stay so I can cook?"

"Has it really been ten years?" Jayce asked. He didn't seem to realize how he affected Leah at all.

"No, it's actually been a lifetime," Leah

said, heading for the door. She forced herself to move past him and not give him another glance. If she stopped, she knew it would be her undoing.

Chapter Three

Helaina Beecham stared out the office window. The sight of Washington, D.C., in spring was breathtaking. She loved this city of history and wonder, but it was the abundance of flowers that caught her attention at the moment. Washington was beautiful in bloom. Even the newly planted Japanese cherry trees were doing their best to add beauty to the city, although their blossoms were nearly all gone.

"Sorry to keep you waiting so long, Helaina," said her brother, Stanley Curtis, as he hobbled into the room.

He manages his crutches rather well, she

thought as she swept across the room, mindless of the narrow cut of her skirt, to offer her assistance.

"I'm sorry I couldn't have come sooner. I just arrived home this morning and found your telegram waiting for me." Helaina helped him to a large leather chair before adding, "I came straightaway."

"How was England?" he asked, his voice sounding rather strained.

It was easy to see her brother was in a great deal of pain. And why not? Being thrown from a train had resulted in a broken leg, three fractured ribs, and multiple lacerations and pulled muscles. The doctors all agreed Stanley was lucky to be alive.

"Angry. People are so enraged over the Lusitania being sunk by the Germans that they hardly speak of anything else."

"It's no doubt worse here. A great many Americans lost their lives on that ship. I was terrified to think of you traveling the Atlantic at such great risk."

"Well, it is an unspeakable and inhumane crime to target passenger ships," Helaina said, remembering with great sorrow the stories of anguish and heartbreak she'd heard. "And I was more than a little nervous."

"There is a madness that has overtaken the world," Stanley murmured.

"Let us hope America has the good sense to stay out of it," Helaina said, pushing aside her memories. She detested talk of war and the sorrow it brought.

"England was also beneficial to say the least. I have a feeling you're going to be quite interested in the news I have to share." She watched him struggle to prop his leg on the ottoman, not entirely sure if she should help or let him handle it. When he finally accomplished the deed, she breathed a sigh of relief. Stan could be so independent, and she didn't want to make him feel less of a man just because he was injured.

"So I imagine the news pertains to our Mr. Kincaid."

"Indeed it does. It seems he was involved with a team of experts working at the British Museum in London. While there, he apparently walked away with several prized pieces, including a most valuable gold crucifix, several ornate gold boxes, a half dozen or so odd pieces of jewelry, and a wooden box containing an assortment of gemstones that had yet to be catalogued and valued."

Stanley shook his head and gave a whistle of disbelief. "The British Museum lost all of that to Jayce Kincaid?"

"They aren't proud of the fact, but the man is above average in intelligence and quite cunning. I told them not to feel too bad about it." Helaina offered her brother a smile. "After all, plenty of museums in America have fallen victim to him as well."

"He must have pulled off his thievery there last winter and come straight here to Washington," Stanley deduced. "The agency was on his trail from the start. It was just our good fortune to have a man spot him at a party."

"Too bad he couldn't have been on the Lusitania," Helaina murmured. "It would have saved us all a great deal of trouble."

"If Jayce Kincaid had been there, the ship probably wouldn't have been sunk at all— he probably would have stolen it before the Germans could do the deed," Stanley answered, the sarcasm thick in his voice.

Helaina smoothed the straight lines of her no-nonsense gabardine suit. "He's a master. I'm truly surprised the Pinkertons haven't found a way to secure him, however."

"We've tried. I'm the result of that effort going amiss," Stanley said, waving his arm and wincing. "I thought I had Kincaid for sure. I had no idea he would be able to pick those cuffs." He shook his head.

The look of regret on Stanley's face nearly broke Helaina's heart. Her brother prided himself on his career with the Pinkerton Agency. She gazed beyond him to the company placard behind his desk. *Pinkerton's National Detective Agency* framed the ever-famous watchful eye. Below the eye was emblazoned with their equally famous motto: *We Never Sleep.*

Helaina looked back to her brother. "We can't sit around feeling sorry for ourselves all day. You lost your man and nearly got yourself killed. It's done. If you sit here wallowing in regret, you'll never accomplish anything." She got to her feet as if dismissing any further comment. "England wants him as badly as America, so I suggested we work together. Word has it that Kincaid has attached himself to a joint Canadian-American Arctic exploration team."

"I already know all about that," Stanley

said, seeming surprised that his sister had any idea of this.

Helaina gave him a coy smile. "I have my sources too. After all, that's why you keep hiring me to help you."

While the Pinkerton Agency had used women in its services since before the Civil War, Helaina wasn't truly a Pinkerton at all. Rather she operated more as an assistant— an independent agent helping her brother. When she found her man, or woman as was often the case, there were always regular agents there to make the arrest. But the beauty of Helaina's involvement was that no one expected this twenty-six-year-old woman of social refinement to be working as a bounty hunter of sorts.

Of course, even Helaina hadn't considered such a duty until three years earlier, when a failed kidnapping attempt in New York had left not only her mother and father dead, but her beloved Robert with a bullet in his head. He'd died before she could return from Europe, where she was visiting friends. She'd never forgiven herself for not being at her husband's side—to die along with him that cold February day.

Stanley had been her only comfort, as

had the idea of putting criminals behind bars. Helaina had taken her desire for justice to her Pinkerton Agent brother and begged for a job. In the long run, the agency had found her more useful in a non-official role, and for Helaina, that worked just fine.

"So what are you proposing, Helaina?"

Stanley's voice disrupted her reflective thought. She walked again to the window and looked out on the beautiful spring day. "Probably the same thing you've already come up with, but I'll let you tell me."

"We've arranged for you to join the expedition. Hopefully you can catch up with the team in Seattle before they leave. That is where the American team is gathering. From there they go to Vancouver where the ship *Homestead* is waiting for them. You'll have to leave immediately, of course."

"That's why I have my luggage downstairs," she said, turning. She shrugged. "Although if I'm to go all the way to the Arctic, I'll have to acquire something warmer than gabardine to wear."

Stanley watched her for a moment, then frowned. "I'd rather not send you at all. Jayce Kincaid is not a simple crook or bank robber. He's a killer. He's murdered two of my best agents."

Helaina came back to her chair. "I know." Her tone was rather resigned. "I'll be careful."

"If you get hurt, I'll never forgive myself."

"Look," she said as gently as she could, "I'm a grown woman and am no longer your responsibility. I chose to help. Remember?"

"Don't give me that speech. I've heard it all before, sister dear. You are my only living relative, and whether the law or any other person alive says I have no responsibility to you, I feel I do. I know I do."

He grimaced as he shifted his weight and his train of thought. "The plan is for you to approach him in Seattle," Stanley continued as if trying to set aside his fears. "You'll meet the team and purchase supplies and such. While there, it will be your job to isolate Jayce from the group."

"Do you have a photograph?"

"No. He's never allowed himself to be photographed. However, I helped the agency to put together a sketch. It's over on my desk. I wouldn't count on him to look like this, however. He's a master of disguises. He's even posed as an old man before."

Helaina crossed the room and immediately picked up the drawing and held it at arm's length. She carefully studied the attempt at capturing Jayce Kincaid. He had a lean, healthy look. His hair fell in a rather wild, unruly manner, and his eyes were dark and set in such a way that made him quite handsome. In a roguish way.

"What color is his hair and mustache?"

"Dark brown. He doesn't always have the mustache, but given the nature of the expedition, I would imagine he does. It's also possible that he now sports a beard."

"And the eyes?"

"Dark blue. Very dark—almost appearing black at times."

She never took her gaze from the picture. In her mind the colors came to life. "And his general complexion? Shallow? Pasty? Ruddy?"

"When last I saw him it was a ruddy to tan complexion. He darkens in the summer. I've seen this firsthand. He can look dark—take on an almost Mexican or Indian look."

She could well imagine that. This man could easily fit in different age groups and ancestries. He had a sort of ordinary quality about him, despite his handsome appearance.

"May I have this—take it with me?" she asked, coming back to her chair. She took her seat and only then did she move her gaze from the drawing and return it to Stanley.

"Of course. I had it prepared for you. I also have tickets, cash, and some other things you'll probably need—case file information and background. My secretary has them for you downstairs."

"Good. What is the contingency if this expedition team sets out before I arrive in Seattle?"

Stanley sighed. "I know that the team plans to make its way to Vancouver to pick up the ship they will use. I believe they are boarding a commercial steamer for this purpose. After Vancouver, we have been told the expedition will make its way to Nome, where sled dogs, sleds, and native assistance will be purchased."

"All right, then. I have my first chance in Seattle, the second one in Vancouver, and the last in Nome."

"I hope it won't come to that. I don't know

how much help you'll have if the arrest
takes place in Vancouver or Nome."

She waved off his protest. "But we have
to be prepared. It would be wise if I were to
acquire a bank account in Seattle. There's
always the possibility I will need more supplies than the cash I carry will allow me to
purchase. I'll see to that before I leave
Washington. What time is my train?"

"Five o'clock."

She looked at the clock on the wall.
"Hmmm, well, that gives me two hours to
get to the station. I have a few things to see
to." She got to her feet. "Don't bother to get
up, Stanley," she said as he began to struggle with his injured leg. Helaina walked to
her brother, planted a kiss on his forehead,
and smiled. "And don't worry. I always get
my man."

"But Jayce Kincaid isn't just any man.
Helaina, I'm really worried about you this
time."

She could see the concern in his eyes.
"Don't bother yourself about it." She tried
to sound lighthearted. "Just because he
bested you doesn't mean he'll stand a
chance with me. I'll turn on my womanly

charm and have him eating out of my hand."

Stanley reached out and clasped her wrist. "This man is deadly. It isn't a game. If you suspect that he's discovered who you are, you must get out—and get back here as quickly as possible."

Helaina knew it was futile to argue. "I'll do it. You know I never take chances."

Stanley held her a moment longer, then released her. "Yes, I know exactly how you operate." He gave her a halfhearted smile. "I'll see you soon."

"Hopefully in days," Helaina said, heading for the door. "Shall I bring you anything from Seattle?"

"A new leg," he replied.

"But of course. I hear they sell them wholesale on the docks." She laughed lightly and pulled the door closed behind her before pausing to take another look at the sketch in her hand.

"I'll not be bested, Mr. Kincaid. You've caused harm to my loved one, you've pillaged and robbed, committed murder, and now you're on the run. But you won't outrun me. I always find a way to get my man." She folded the paper and put it into her skirt pocket.

Determination for justice had always driven Helaina Beecham—more so after her family had been murdered, but even as a child Helaina had demanded justice and responsibility from those around her. Her mother had even warned her that she lacked mercy and compassion when it came to forgiving wrongs, but Helaina couldn't help it. If people were going to break the law—do wrong—then there were prices to be paid.

Stanley had once accused her of seeking revenge for the death of Robert and their parents. He had warned her that no amount of service to the agency or anyone else would ever ease that misery, but Helaina knew that doing something was better than doing nothing at all. With each case she told herself the world was just that much safer . . . that other families might never have to know the horror and pain she had endured.

She made her way downstairs, pulling up her skirt ever so slightly. The new war fashions from Europe sported fuller and shorter skirts, but Helaina hadn't yet adapted her wardrobe. In London she had purchased a few older designs by her favorite couturier, Paul Poiret, but most were eveningwear that had been brought into the country prior to the start of the war.

She tried not to even think of the things she'd heard about the war. Cousin fighting cousin, entire countries devoted to the annihilation of another government and people. The labor unions were thriving on the conflict, while the women's suffrage movement in London had lessened their focus on obtaining the vote in order to support the men they loved. They would still be a force to be reckoned with, Helaina believed, but perhaps the day of women voting would be just a little more distant than she'd originally believed.

"Hello, Mrs. Beecham," a young man said, getting to his feet.

"Henry, my brother said you had a packet of goods for me."

"Yes, ma'am. Right here." He handed her a large envelope. "Tickets, cash, and all the information we could get you on Kincaid. We actually have some fingerprint evidence this time. It's not in here, but we'll have it when the time comes for Kincaid's trial."

"I have seen it used," Helaina admitted. "Truly fascinating."

"No two prints are ever alike. Kind of God's way of making sure we were all special, eh?"

She nodded. "Henry, would you be so kind as to arrange for my luggage? I have several stops to make before I head to the station."

"Of course. For you, anything." The tone of his voice and look on his face told Helaina he was still quite smitten with her. Poor boy. He was barely twenty-two, but he'd been more than attentive to her needs since coming on board as Stanley's secretary.

"Thank you, Henry. You're a treasure." She watched him blush and stammer for some sort of reply.

Outside, Helaina hailed a cab. She took a horse-drawn carriage rather than wait for one of the louder, smelly automobiles. Sometimes the contrast still amazed her. The carriages traveled in traffic along with the motorized cars, electric lights had replaced gas for the most part, and there was even talk that soon airplanes would dominate travel and put trains out of business for long-distance journeys.

It was a wonderful time to be alive, Helaina thought. But the shadow of war hung over them. There was no way to tell whether President Wilson would continue to keep them neutral or succumb to the pressures of the so-called civilized world. Helaina wasn't at all sure she wanted America to remain uninvolved. After all, responsible human beings couldn't just turn a blind eye when tragedy and inhumane actions struck another part of the world.

Still, her real concern was Jayce Kincaid. He would now be the focus of her every waking moment—likely some of her sleeping moments as well, for Helaina knew that once she immersed herself in the file on Kincaid, she would even dream about him. Oftentimes ideas would come to her in those dreams, ideas that helped her catch her prey. Her housekeeper in New York would tell her it was God's doing—His way of furthering justice—but Helaina thought such things nonsense and often told Mrs. Hayworth exactly that. The woman was unmoved, however, because of her strong Christian beliefs—beliefs Helaina did not share. After all, if God were really all that Christians held Him up to be, He would have the power to stop injustice and evil. Yet He stood by and did nothing. That didn't sound like the kind of God Helaina wanted to trust in.

Helaina had learned early on that a person had to trust themselves. Trust in their own abilities. That's why she continued to strive toward improving those abilities. She was intelligent, well-read, could shoot, ride, and even play the piano proficiently. Besides English, she spoke several languages fluently, including French, Russian, Spanish, Swedish, and Italian. The latter two were thanks to housemaids who had worked for her family since Helaina was small.

These were talents Helaina had worked to understand and improve. Her abilities weren't God-given, as Mrs. Hayworth would insist; they came instead after hours of hard work. Education was the key, Helaina decided early in life. She was college-educated and widely traveled, and she'd come to realize there was really nothing she couldn't understand or learn if she took the time to do so.

She was a sensible woman, however, and

knew the truth of what her brother had said. Jayce would not be easily fooled or manipulated. It was more than a matter of turning to a textbook or relying on the education she'd collected over the years. Helaina would have to be particularly cunning— even devious. But it was, after all, in the line of duty. Stanley had once told her it all was fair in the service of catching criminals. Lies and manipulation were simply tools they used. Tools that Helaina Beecham used quite skillfully.

Chapter Four

The intensity of the storm took everyone in Last Chance by surprise. By the time Leah finished making preparations for Jayce and Jacob, she had no hope of making it to Ayoona's inne without risking her life. With a sigh, she realized there was no choice but to stick out the storm with Jayce and Jacob. After all, it would probably last only a few hours.

But the hours dragged by, and it became apparent that the storm had no intention of letting up. The wind blew in gale force, driving the dry powdery snow and ice like daggers through the air. Leah tried not to let the walls close in around her, but just thinking about Jayce being in the next room was more than she could bear.

I should have left with Ayoona.

It served no purpose to chide herself on the matter, however. There was nothing to be gained by it. With the wind howling outside, Leah tried to keep her mind on things other than Jayce Kincaid.

At first she tried to focus on some sewing. Leah loved to sew and had learned to work with the many furs and skins that constituted the bulk of their clothes. When sewing failed to keep her mind occupied, however, Leah directed her thoughts to some much overdue correspondence. For several minutes she jotted a quick note to Miranda Davenport. News had come last fall, just before the ships stopped delivering mail, that Miranda's mother had passed away after succumbing to pneumonia.

Miranda had been a good friend to Leah while they were in the Yukon. Sister to the man who had married Karen's good friend Grace, Miranda was as gentle and sweet a woman as Leah had ever known. Miranda had married an Englishman named Thomas Edward, but everyone called him Teddy.

After writing to encourage Miranda and Teddy to visit and explore the vegetation that Teddy so loved to study, Leah picked up another piece of paper. She owed Karen a letter and began to share details of the lean spring and Jacob's long absence. It was hard being away from her surrogate mother. Leah had decided that this would be the year she would journey home to Ketchikan for a long visit, and she wanted to let Karen know well in advance. But before she realized it, Leah was writing of all that was on her heart.

I don't know why he's here now, after all this time. What must God be thinking to bring this man back into my life? I'd like to say that Jayce Kincaid has no effect on me whatsoever, but it isn't true. Every time I look up to find him watching me, my heart nearly skips a beat. I have to admit I still have feelings for him.

She stared at the paper, doing her best to deny the words she'd just written. *But I do have feelings for him.* Feelings that ran the gamut. Leah hadn't expected so many emotions to emerge. If she was honest, a part of her was actually terrified of having Jayce here. She wanted to put him behind her—to forget about him—but he seemed to want things to go on as they had before her declaration of love. He seemed to want—no, to demand—her friendship . . . and Leah wasn't sure she could give that anymore. It was one thing to forgive him, but she couldn't bear to set her heart up for the same kind of misery and pain.

Leah sighed and put down her pen. She couldn't just ignore the way he made her feel. She couldn't deny the thrill that rushed through her when she saw it was Jayce she had embraced and welcomed. Why was he here now—now, after ten years of struggling to lay him to rest in her heart? More important, how could she ever trust him again?

"You're sure quiet," Jayce declared. Leah looked up to find him with two mugs. "I thought you might like some coffee. It'll warm you up—unless you prefer another bear hug like when I first got here." He grinned mischievously and extended the mug. "I know I wouldn't mind."

"Thank you, the coffee is fine." She took

the cup and pretended to refocus on the letter, although her hands were shaking.

"Looks like I got here just in time. You're so cold you're shaking."

Leah kept her head down to keep him from seeing the embarrassed expression she was sure to be wearing.

Jayce sat down opposite her, much to her consternation. "You certainly are more serious than I remember. Seems to me you were a more jovial kid when last we met."

"I wasn't a kid then," she said without looking up, "nor am I now."

He laughed and practically slammed the mug on the table. "You weren't much more than a little girl."

She looked up, barely containing her anger. "I haven't been a little girl since my father died in the Palm Sunday Avalanche seventeen years ago. I was a child of nearly thirteen when it happened—a girl by all accounts—but I grew up that day." The coffee cup shook even more. "I don't know why you insist on remembering me as a child, but I'd appreciate it if you'd stop."

He looked at her blankly, as if stunned by her outburst. "I didn't mean to offend you, Leah. It's just . . . back then you didn't seem to have the weight of the world on your shoulders. You were happier."

"Yes, maybe I was." She realized she'd sloshed coffee all over the letter and quickly picked it up to dry. Ink ran in a blur with the dark liquid. "Oh, bother." She crumpled the paper into a tight ball with one hand, while still holding the coffee in the other. "What do you want, Jayce?"

The bluntness of the question took them both by surprise. He shrugged. "I just wondered what happened to you."

Leah wanted to scream, *"You happened to me, Jayce Kincaid."* But instead she drew a deep breath, then took a long draw from the mug. The hot coffee felt good against the growing lump in her throat.

"I grew up," she finally said rather sarcastically. "If you insist on remembering me as a child ten years ago, then that's what happened. I grew up and saw the world for what it was."

"And what was that?"

"Cruel. Harsh. Deliberate." She had no trouble listing her complaints against life.

"Surely it's more than that. Jacob said you like it here."

"I love Alaska," Leah said without

thought. "I love the people. I'm less impressed with other elements of life, none of which I intend to discuss with you. Why is it you're here and not somewhere else? Why come to Last Chance when Nome surely offers you more opportunity for . . . for . . . whatever."

"Like I said, I needed dogs for the expedition and Jacob has some of the best, or so I'd heard."

"His dogs are excellent, but how did you know he was even here?"

Jayce smiled, lighting up his entire face. Leah swallowed hard and pretended to sip at the coffee. "I went to see your folks in Ketchikan. Adrik was up Sitka way, but Karen told me you and Jacob had moved west. When I caught up with Adrik in Sitka, he told me that Jacob had some of the best dogs in the world. When I mentioned the exploration to the Arctic, he told me that other groups had acquired hunting dogs from your brother. I figured I might as well do the same. All those folks couldn't be wrong, after all." He paused and looked at his cup for a moment. "I had to admit I was stunned at the length of time between visits. I didn't realize nearly ten years had passed since I'd seen you last."

"Time has a way of doing that up here," Leah admitted. Hadn't it taken her by surprise as well?

"Well, I found out where you were and started trekking up this way. It took some doing to get to Nome, but I managed it. When I got there, I was quite excited to learn Jacob was in town. I was prepared to hike out here all on my own."

"You'd never have made it," Leah said, shaking her head.

"You certainly don't have much faith in me."

She looked him dead in the eye. "No. No, I don't."

Jayce appeared taken aback, his dark, blue-black eyes piercing her with their intense stare. It was then that Leah realized how much he'd aged. Despite the fact that he was still handsome, lines of age were clearly visible around his eyes and mouth. *He's only thirty-two,* she thought. *Only two years older than me. Do I look aged to him?* She touched her cheek absent-mindedly.

Jayce opened his mouth to reply, then closed it again. For a moment he simply seemed to consider her words. It was a good opportunity, Leah thought, to escape.

"I need to go. I have things to tend to in the store before bed. I didn't finish my inventory." She got to her feet.

"Sorry I dozed off," Jacob said as he entered the room. "Sometimes the wind just wears me down. The cookroom was plenty warm too." He looked at Leah first, then Jayce. "So what have you two been up to?"

"I tried to write a letter to Karen," Leah said, glancing back at the table. "But I drenched it in coffee. Guess I'll start over later. Right now I'm going to finish my inventory. Then I'll start some supper."

"And I thought I might read," Jayce announced. "Seems like the perfect time for it. Unless, of course, the wind puts me to sleep."

"It's good for little else. There will be plenty of work after the storm. I'm anxious to show you the dogs and see what you think might work for the expedition. And we'll need to build a couple of sleds and make certain we have the harnesses in good order. It was smart of you to buy that gear in Seattle."

"Well, this expedition has been light on

funds, and it seemed the wise thing to do. Although I have to admit, I'm not sure I could even hitch a team these days. But the expedition needs me."

"What exactly is this expedition hoping to accomplish?" Leah asked, wanting to know more.

"Mapping, mostly," Jayce replied. "You know there's a war on in Europe." He frowned. "Or maybe you didn't know. Anyway, you should know about it—after all, it will likely involve us as well."

"We didn't know much," Jacob admitted. "News travels slowly up here—especially in making its way to Last Chance Creek. I brought home some newspapers, Leah. I knew you'd enjoy them."

"Thanks," she murmured. Against her will she turned back to Jayce. "So why should the war concern us if it's in Europe? You don't mean to suggest there will be fighting on American soil, do you?"

Jayce shook his head and toyed with the coffee mug. "I don't believe there will be fighting here, but I do believe we will have to join the fighting if the warring factions don't back down."

Leah came back to the table. "But I don't

understand any of this. What does an arch-duke in Austria-Hungary getting shot have to do with America entering a war?"

"Because whenever there are people who think they are better than others, and willing to shed innocent blood to prove it, bullies will appear to oppress less powerful folk. I've seen the rise of nationalism in Europe. It's fine to be proud that you're French or German, but when you believe yourself to be better than everyone else, it leads to problems."

Leah still didn't see this as a reason to go to war. "But that's their problem—not ours. We're an ocean away."

"Are we?" He raised a brow in challenge. "In case you didn't realize it, Austria-Hungary declared war on Serbia. That brought in the Germans to help the Austrians. Of course, in order to help them, the Germans feel they need to attack France, which in turn brings in Russia, who has an agree-ment with France. One by one, like domi-noes, the countries start falling. Of course, Great Britain cannot stand idly by."

Leah crossed her arms. "That's still Eu-rope and not America. Not even North America."

"But Russia is only a matter of a short distance by ship. Canada is next door. If Great Britain suffers, Canada will come to her aid. Do you not see how intricately we are all connected?"

"I thought it to be one big family feud," Jacob threw in. "Didn't I read that most of the heads of state involved are somehow related to each other? Maybe Leah's right and they should just settle it amongst themselves."

"But it would be no different than if your friends Karen and Adrik began warring with their children. The more intense the fight, the more damage done. Wouldn't you want to help them put an end to their conflict?"

"I suppose, but it's still seems a long way off," Jacob answered, not sounding in the least bit upset by the matter. "By the time it comes to that, the war will be over."

"I wouldn't count on it, Jacob. Some issues—some people—will refuse to just back down and leave well enough alone. I wouldn't count on this being simple. I believe we'll see people fight to the last man if they are allowed to do so."

Leah didn't care for the sounds of such things. "But it would have to take something big to involve America," she said, trying to sound as though she believed it herself. Inside her heart, however, Leah feared Jayce's comments more than she wanted to admit.

"Well, that's part of the reason for the expedition as I mentioned. They are looking to whether we might make more detailed maps of the coast and the islands in the Arctic. We're also to check for the feasibility of creating airstrips."

"That seems out of place up here," Jacob said, shaking his head. "I can't believe it will ever happen. You'll never see planes in this territory; it's too cold. They'd never be able to endure the harsh elements."

"That's hardly what the rest of the world believes, Jacob." Jayce leaned back in his chair. Leah thought he looked rather smug. "Of course, the world also said that flight was impossible—that man was intended to keep his feet on the ground. You'll see, my friend. Air travel will soon be upon us, and Alaska will be no exception. Flight will eventually take over as the main mode of transportation."

"I can only imagine how that would connect us to the rest of America," Jacob said, shaking his head. "Still, I find it impossible to imagine in a place that relies more on boats and dogsleds that airplanes would take over as the main means of travel, but I can tell by your enthusiasm that you don't consider this lightly."

"Indeed not. I'm rarely wrong, Jacob." He laughed and added, "Maybe I should have said I'm never wrong. You'd do well to believe me."

Leah had heard enough. As far as she was concerned, Jayce Kincaid was a visionary with no hindsight or understanding of the past.

You were wrong about me, Jayce. You were wrong about me.

Jayce watched Leah walk away. The long tunic she wore, like a parka made out of cloth, kept her sealskin pants from seeming indecent. Most of the native women wore them, and Leah had apparently adopted the fashion. Jayce thought it marvelous. He'd seen missionary wives along the coast who still wore the cumbersome fashions of American housewives, but they were hardly

appropriate for Alaskan winters or sum-
mers.

"There are some books on the shelf if
you've a mind to read. I brought that stack
of newspapers, too, but I think you've already read them all," Jacob said as he settled into a chair with the Bible.

"Do you enjoy it out here—here at the end
of the world?" Jayce questioned.

Jacob looked up. "It's never seemed like
the end of the world to me. It's isolated, but
the people are good. And it's not as though
we can't move about if need be. I've even
hiked out across the interior in an emergency. There's always a way to get where
you need to be—if you have the Alaskan
spirit driving you."

"I never figured you'd stay. In Ketchikan
you seemed so miserable."

"I guess I was. I wasn't my own man—I
couldn't figure out what I wanted to do with
my life. I was growing up faster than the
ideas would come."

Jayce laughed and slapped his hand on
the table. "And I had ideas faster than the
growing up would allow for. We are a pair to
be sure." He smiled at his friend. "Have you
given any more thought to my proposition?"

"Not much. I haven't had a real chance to pray on it or to discuss it with Leah. I wouldn't want to just up and leave her here—not without giving her some say in it. And I'm not sure it would be safe for her to stay alone."

"So send her back to Karen and Adrik. I know she loves them—probably misses them too."

Jacob nodded. "That she does. We've talked every year about her going for a visit. I think this year might be the best chance."

"See, it would work perfectly. Put her on a ship for Ketchikan and head north with me. It wouldn't take much persuading—I'm sure of it."

Jacob shook his head and put his focus back on the Bible. "I wouldn't bet on it. You think for some reason that you know my sister pretty well—but I've lived with her all of these years and I still can't figure her out."

Jayce said nothing to this. He really couldn't answer without giving away the awkward feeling inside his gut. Seeing Leah had done something to him. He wasn't exactly sure what, but he kept feeling an uneasiness that wasn't entirely unpleasant. In fact, in the back of his mind he wondered whether there might be a chance to rekindle the feelings Leah had claimed to have for him so long ago.

"Has Leah never married?" he questioned, realizing too late that he'd spoken aloud.

"No."

Jacob offered nothing more, and Jayce knew better than to press it further. Instead, he picked up his coffee mug and stood. "You want any coffee?"

"No, I'm fine. Thanks."

Jayce nodded, then spied the ball of paper and mug Leah had left behind. Hoping to be helpful, he grabbed up both and headed to the kitchen. He set both mugs on the counter and started to throw the paper into the stove. He paused, thinking of how Leah had been so absorbed in her writing. *Perhaps some of the letter can be salvaged,* he thought, knowing good paper could sometimes be scarce.

Jayce unfolded the balled-up letter and spread it against the hard surface of the wooden table. The words, for the most part, were blurred. The latter half of the letter, in fact, ran together so badly that it was impossible to really figure out the wording. He began to crumple the paper again until his own name leapt from the page.

. . . Jayce Kincaid has no effect on me . . .

The very presence of his name drove Jayce to better understand. A section of words were mangled in black ink and coffee. It made them impossible to read.

Every time . . . find him . . .

More blurring and run-together swirls before the letter ended with a somewhat promising statement.

I . . . feelings . . . him.

He struggled to make reason of the cryptic message. Did she care or didn't she? Was she telling Karen that she had feelings for him or that she didn't? And why should it matter to him? He held the letter up against the lamp, hoping against all odds that it would reveal the answer to his questions. It didn't.

Jayce glanced up, fearing Leah might walk in at any moment and realize what he'd done. He quickly crumpled the paper and stuffed it into his pocket. Leaning back, he tried to reason what it all might mean.

"You're a mystery to me, Leah Barringer,"

he whispered, "but I intend to solve this before I leave." He smiled and raised his mug.
"In fact, I believe I'll rather enjoy unraveling
this intrigue."

Chapter Five

SEATTLE

Helaina looked at the documents in her hand. "Isn't there a ship heading to Nome sooner?"

"Lady, you're lucky to be on that one. Travel north ain't as easy as it is here," a grumpy old man said from behind his ticket counter. "Ice is breakin' up, but the storms are still a powerful threat. Especially in the Bering. It ain't the kind of place for a lady— if you get my meanin'."

Helaina paid him little attention. She was used to men taking one look at her refined appearance and concluding that she was insignificant or too delicate to handle real-world affairs. "Where might I purchase some supplies?"

The man looked her over with a smirk. "I wondered if you were going to try to make it wearing those fancy city doodads. You'll freeze your backside off, pardon my sayin' so, in that." He sneered down his long nose at the sight of her best traveling suit.

"Well, it's a good thing you aren't responsible for me, then, isn't it?" She gave him a look that froze him in place. "Good day."

She left without getting directions to any reputable mercantile. She knew it would be best to move away from the dock area, but at the same time she felt confident the best supplies for the rugged Alaskan travel would be found here.

Walking to the north, Helaina couldn't set aside her disappointment upon learning that the expedition team had headed to Vancouver the week before. Further investigation informed her that they were already on their way to Nome and would await her there. There was no other word or suggestion as to how she was supposed to get to Nome; rather she was left to figure out everything, including needed supplies, on her own.

Well, it wasn't the first time she'd had only herself to rely upon. The smell of fish and rotting guts mingled with salty air and wet wood assailed her nose, but Helaina refused to react. Her mother had always taught her that a lady of quality might have to endure many hardships. The key to doing it well, however, was in controlling one's reaction. A true lady would keep everyone guessing. And that was something Helaina felt she did quite well.

Helaina spied a sign in a waterfront store that read, *There's still gold to be found in Alaska!* The advertisement further suggested that everything a prospector needed for the frozen north could be purchased inside. She decided the claim merited her attention and pushed open the door.

"Hello, ma'am," a young sales clerk said, seeming quite surprised to see a woman. "Can . . . can I help"—his voice cracked and raised an octave before settling back down—"help you? You . . . lost?"

Helaina surmised the teenager was unused to dealing with women. "I'm not lost. I need to purchase goods for a trip I'm making to Nome in the Alaska Territory."

"You're going north?" He seemed rather stunned.

"Yes. I'm to meet my employer in Nome. I'm a part of an Arctic exploration team. I'll need to have gear that will endure the harsh elements."

The boy studied her a moment, then shrugged. "Most of our inventory is for men. I don't know if we have anything . . . small . . . well, that is . . ."

"Oh, go in the back, Daniel, and let me help this poor woman," a man said as he came from somewhere at the back of the store. The teen blushed furiously and made his exit without another word.

"Ma'am, I'm J. T. Brown. This is my store." He extended a beefy fist in greeting.

Helaina liked his no-nonsense approach. "I'm Mrs. Beecham. I need to purchase whatever might be beneficial to me for a trip to Nome and beyond."

"I heard you tellin' the boy you were bound for the Arctic. It's not an easy place. I've been there myself. Went whaling once." He surveyed her stature. "I think I have some boy's sizes that will fit you, but once you're in Nome, you really should try to get some native-made clothes. See if you can't locate a few of the Eskimo women and get them to sell you some fur pants and such."

"I'll make a note of it. Thank you."

He seemed relieved that Helaina wasn't offended. But why should she be? He was only offering wisdom borne out of experience. He wasn't being condescending in his attitude, nor was he smirking at her as though she had no idea what she was talking about.

The man left quickly and reappeared with a stack of clothes in his arms. He placed these on the counter and went back out of the room once again. Helaina began to search the store for other items that she thought might be useful. She located a sturdy pair of boots that looked to be about the right size.

"You'll want to waterproof them," the man said, holding up a tin. "This stuff seems to work the best."

"Then be sure to include it with my other things," she said, leaving the boots on the counter with the clothes. "I'm also going to need a sturdy bag for packing. Do you have something canvas or leather?"

"I do indeed. I have a pack the sailors like to use. I think it will suit you well." He went to the back shelves of the store and pulled down a large black bag. "This one seems to hold a great deal and endure travel. It's guaranteed to be waterproof—they've put some sort of rubber coating on it. Don't know much else about it."

Helaina nodded her approval upon inspection. "It seems quite sound."

The man nodded. "I'd like to suggest something else. It may sound quite forward, but I've heard good things from the men who've gone north, regarding these." He went behind the counter and pulled out yet another piece of clothing.

"What is it?" Helaina asked.

It was the only time she'd seen Mr. Brown the least bit embarrassed. "Well, ma'am, they are . . ." He looked around quickly and lowered his voice, "Men's theatrical tights."

Helaina wanted to laugh at his whispered words. "Are they woolen?"

"Yes, ma'am. I've been told when worn under your other clothing, they help to keep the chill off better than anything else."

"I can't imagine men being too comfortable wearing these," Helaina said with a hint of amusement.

"They get plenty comfortable when faced with the alternative: freezing. Some even wear more than one pair at a time."

Helaina nodded. "I'll take them. In fact, give me three pair."

Mr. Brown appeared quite pleased with himself. They discussed other items, finally settling the selections and the bill, with J. T. Brown's promise to deliver everything to Helaina's hotel by nightfall.

With this arrangement made, Helaina requested Brown secure her a cab. He was only too happy to help her. After all, she'd made it worth his while to have opened shop that day.

Once she was back at the hotel, Helaina pulled off her kid gloves and tossed them aside. Her hat quickly followed suit. She felt a little hungry but decided against lunch. There was simply too much to plan. While contemplating her schedule for capturing Jayce Kincaid, she disrobed and settled into a dressing gown before spreading out all of her information. The sketch of Kincaid was front and center. She found it helpful to study a man's photograph while in pursuit of him. She wished there had been photos of Jayce Kincaid, but even the English hadn't been of help in this area.

She looked hard at the man's face. The eyes were penetrating—almost hypnotic. This was the face of a killer, she told herself.

Helaina tried hard to imagine what thoughts the man might have—what reasoning he might use to justify his deeds. She'd always wondered what thoughts and planning had gone into the events that had taken the lives of her own loved ones, for surely the men involved had contemplated their actions at length. Kidnapping was not something one did without a plan for victims. Even if that plan was death. She couldn't fathom the mind that perceived such deeds as acceptable.

She thought of her husband and how he might have reacted to the attack. Robert Beecham was no man's fool. Wealth had not been handed to him—he had made every cent by using his brain and brawn. Likewise, her father had also made his fortune. There were no silver spoons to be placed in the mouths of the Curtis children. She and Stanley, and another sibling who had died shortly after birth, had all been born into poverty. But her father refused to be kept down. He created a profitable freighting business, then sold it and bought into an equally beneficial manufacturing company. Little by little, step by step, he had increased their fortunes and had pulled the family from their impoverished circumstances.

Robert had come upon the scene as her father began to seek out investment advice. Robert's ability with figures and reading the market had merited him much success. He had made his first hundred thousand before he'd turned twenty-five and was quite confident in his future. It was one of the things that had attracted Helaina to him.

Of late, however, Robert's image had begun to fade from her memory, and his voice no longer haunted her dreams. She knew she'd not only survived widowhood, but had actually overcome it. Loneliness was no longer an issue. She had systematically driven this, as well as sorrow, away with her focus on righting the wrongs of the world. It was her only defense against drowning in miseries that would never bring her husband or parents back to life.

It was times like this that she could only wonder what the future might hold. She was only twenty-six, soon to be twenty-seven in August. She knew she never wanted to marry again. She didn't want children; the world was much too dangerous to contemplate bringing babies into its threat. But what eluded her was what she did want to do with her life. There were entire volumes of things she didn't want, but coming to an understanding of what was important to have, to hold . . . now, that was difficult.

She looked again at Kincaid. He seemed a perfectly normal man, but she knew he wasn't. His past told a completely different story. He'd killed at least two men—Pinkerton agents who were working to retrieve articles Kincaid had stolen—and he'd nearly killed Stanley. She shook her head.

What caused you to become the man you are? Why did you choose to live a life of evil instead of good?

Stanley had once told her that he was convinced men did not choose such things for themselves, rather those things occurred at random. Rather like a blanket thrown down from the mythological gods of Olympus. It fell on whom it would fall, and from that point on their life would be forever changed.

Mrs. Hayworth had a different view, one taken from her Christian beliefs. *"God has a specific plan for each person's life,"* the woman had said. *"Some men will give in to the devil's prompting. God weeps for them."*

God weeps for them, maybe, but He certainly didn't stop them.

When Robert died, Helaina had been bitter at the platitudes murmured and spoken by all those around her. Even his eulogy spoke of God's infinite wisdom and plan for each man's soul. Helaina had decided then and there that, if this, in fact, was the manner and heart of God, she wanted no part of Him. He was cruel to her way of thinking. A robber of loved ones—unfairly stealing away the very heart of those He called children.

Helaina had rejected any thought of God or His comfort after that. Not that she'd really given Him much thought prior to Robert's and her parents' deaths; but now it seemed it was to be war between her and God. A war that she could only win by altering God's plan—by capturing the evil that He allowed to run free in her world.

"I'll find you, Jayce Kincaid. Like all the others before you. I'll hunt you down and see you pay for the things you've done." She held the sketch with trembling hands. "The law will win out and justice will be done. You will hang for the sins you've committed because whether God will punish you or not—we will. We lowly, puny humans will see it done."

———

Leah felt a deep sense of gratitude when she awoke to silence. The storm had ceased, and the sound of children's laughter could be heard from outside. The missionary school year was completed for the season and the native children, along with the missionaries' kids, were enjoying their freedom.

Throwing back her covers, Leah stretched and yawned. The aroma of coffee and griddlecakes filled the air. She'd overslept, but apparently Jacob had gotten along well enough without her. It was only then that the memory of Jayce Kincaid came back to haunt her.

She grabbed her robe and held it close against her body. Jayce was here. He was staying with them. She found the idea as ludicrous now as when it had first been presented. Jacob had set Jayce up with a pallet in the storeroom. He had teased their visitor that it would be colder than the rest of the house, but that if Jayce was going to explore the Arctic, he might as well get used to it. Then with this arrangement made, Jacob told Leah there was no reason for her to stay with Ayoona.

No reason?

Leah couldn't believe her brother's ignorance. How could he not see or understand the effect Jayce had on her? And how could Jayce be so completely blind to it? As far as either of them were concerned, ten years was long enough to have put the past to rest. Leah sighed. It should have been.

You should just tell him how you feel. The words came from somewhere deep inside. *How can I tell him? It will only serve to embarrass and further hurt me.* But in truth, Leah was already in so much discomfort that talking to Jayce, a man who planned to leave in a matter of days, couldn't be much more painful.

Leah argued with herself for several minutes, but then her gaze fell to the calendar. Jacob had encouraged her to keep meticulous track of the days. With no sun in the winter and no night in the summer, it was easy to lose track of the days unless she kept a ledger.

The day Leah had been dreading had arrived—a taunting reminder of all she had failed to accomplish. May 18, 1915. It was her thirtieth birthday.

Leah stared at the calendar as if to will it to declare a different day entirely. But the truth would win out. She was thirty years old, unmarried, childless. Worse still, there were no prospects of changing any of it.

She went about her duties in a daze. She had dreaded turning thirty. Somehow she could tell herself she wasn't quite so hopeless or destitute while still in her twenties. But this mile marker seemed to make all the difference.

"Well, good morning," Jacob said as Leah came into the kitchen. "I let you sleep on account of your birthday."

Leah looked around frantically. "You

didn't tell Jayce it was my birthday, did you?"

Jacob looked at her oddly. "Of course. Why?"

She sighed. "No reason. Where is he?"

Jacob dished up several flapjacks. "Out with the dogs. Here. I fixed you breakfast and I have a surprise." He pulled a small bottle from his coat pocket. "It's maple syrup. I know you love it and haven't had it for a while."

She couldn't help but smile. "That was really kind of you. Thank you."

"I have another gift for you as well." He left the room and returned with a brown paper-wrapped bundle. "I thought you might enjoy this."

Inside was a new traveling case. "It's wonderful," Leah said, not completely understanding the purpose. "But am I going somewhere?"

Jacob nodded and poured her a mug of coffee. "You and I have talked several times about you going to see Karen and Adrik. I think this year would be perfect."

"And what will you do while I'm gone?"

Jacob looked away. Leah could see he was uneasy with her question, and then it dawned on her that he meant to take Jayce up on the exploration offer. "You're going to go with Jayce, aren't you?"

"I think so. I've been praying on it, and . . . well . . . I think it might be exactly what God wants for me." His expression was one of hopefulness—rather like a little boy asking if he might keep a stray dog.

"I see," Leah said, wanting to be supportive. "I suppose to be honest, I was considering it myself—at least going to see the family. I know Karen would love it."

"Look, just think about it. I need to get out there with the dogs. Jayce wants me to show him the best and help him to train with a couple of teams. I'll be busy all day." He headed to the door. "Happy birthday, Leah."

The words rang in the air long after he'd gone. Leah sat down to the celebratory breakfast but found she wasn't at all hungry.

He's made up his mind to go away with Jayce. The thought left her feeling rather empty. It wasn't that Jacob wasn't entitled to his own life. Goodness, but they'd talked about this on many occasions. Leah had always maintained that she'd go back to Ketchikan if Jacob wanted to set out on his own. They'd only stayed together because neither one had anyone else—at least that's what they told each other.

Leah picked at the cakes, each piece drenched in the precious maple syrup. But even this sweet treat couldn't make the meal more palatable. *He's leaving me. He's leaving and going far away.* But it wasn't Jacob's leaving that held her thoughts captive.

"Knock, knock!" a female voice called out.

Leah immediately recognized Emma Kjellmann's Swedish accent. "I'm in the kitchen."

The blond-haired woman immediately pushed back the fur and stepped inside. "Happy birthday."

Leah smiled. Emma was the only other white woman in the village. She and her husband had come to the Seward Peninsula to bring the Word of God to the natives. While there, she'd given birth to three children, the oldest of whom shared his birthday with Leah.

"Thank you. Are we still planning to celebrate this evening?"

"Oh ja," Emma said with a grin. "Bryce has talked of nothing else."

"Well, turning four is a big event. Would you like some coffee?" Leah asked, getting to her feet. "I'm afraid I'm behind this morning. Jacob let me sleep late."

"Good for him," Emma replied, her accent thick. "It's good for you too, ja?"

Leah laughed. "I don't know about that, but I do feel very rested." She held up the pot, but Emma shook her head.

"I've had plenty. I just wanted to let you know that we'd expect you and Jacob at six. Oh, and bring your visitor too. We'll have plenty of food, thanks to Jacob's trip."

The mention of Jayce caused Leah to consider sharing her woes, for if anyone could advise Leah, it would be Emma.

"Do you have a minute, Emma?"

"Ja. Bjorn is seeing to the children, and the baby is sleeping, so he won't have it that hard. What's troubling you?"

Leah came back to the table and sat down. Emma took the seat opposite her. "It's about our visitor."

"You knew him from before, Jacob said."

"Yes." Leah struggled for words. Emma was such a dear friend, but it was still hard to speak aloud what she'd only dared to admit in her heart.

Emma put her hand over Leah's. "You have feelings for this man, ja?"

Leah looked at the woman in surprise. "How could you know that?"

Emma shrugged. "Why else would you be sitting here instead of helping Jacob with the dogs?"

It was true, Leah thought. She was always outside working with the dogs when there weren't people wanting to purchase something from the store. "I was in love with him once—nearly ten years ago. He spurned me, saying I was too young to know my heart. I was quite devastated."

Emma nodded. "And seeing him now is very hard."

"Harder than I thought it would be." Leah met the woman's compassionate gaze. "I thought I'd put this in the past—dealt with the pain. But seeing him again has brought it all back. I just don't understand why."

"Because you are still in love with him," Emma said matter-of-factly.

The words struck Leah in the gut, but she chose to ignore them. "Why would God do this to me? Why would He allow this man to come back into my life to hurt me?"

"Who can know the mind of God?" Emma

declared. "You know that God has plans we cannot understand."

"I feel so distant from God. I feel so lost. Does that shock you?"

Emma laughed, surprising Leah. "We have all felt that way from time to time. The very nature of God often makes us believe Him to be unreachable. He is, after all, God of the universe—the King of Kings and Lord of Lords. How could He possibly care about the day-to-day issues of our lives?"

Leah nodded. "Yes, I suppose that's how I feel right now. He mustn't care about those details because this has happened. Yet I know that He cares." She bowed her head. "I feel guilty for even questioning Him, but I cannot understand why Jayce is here."

"Perhaps he's here because the time is right to make things new," Emma said softly. She squeezed Leah's hand. "God wants your heart to be whole, Leah. He wants your trust. You mustn't fear. You are poor in spirit right now. You feel depleted of hope and understanding, but God richly offers both. You'll see. Your love for this man has lasted for ten years. Surely God has a plan for that love."

"Maybe that's what scares me the most,"

Leah replied, looking up hesitantly. "Maybe His plan won't be what I want it to be."

"Who can know? But I know whom I have believed in." Emma got to her feet and smiled, adding, "And so do you."

Chapter Six

Jayce washed up for the birthday party. He felt they'd accomplished a great deal, and for that he was satisfied. Jacob had helped him to pick out about twenty good dogs, and given the fact that the exploration team would soon be joining them, Jayce knew he needed to work hard to learn their handling. He also needed to help Jacob finish building two sleds.

Maybe that was why he didn't feel right about quitting early to attend a birthday party. Even if that party was for Leah Barringer—although he seriously doubted that she wanted him at her party. Leah's attitude was a complete mystery to him. At times she seemed congenial, civilized . . . but most of the time she was almost hostile. But why?

Jayce wished he could understand the woman. She was more beautiful than ever— her dark brown hair beckoned his touch and her blue eyes were the color of a summer sky. But it was more than her appearance that seemed to draw him. There was something about Leah that he had never been able to forget.

He had to admit that he'd decided to find Jacob and his dogs mostly because he knew Leah would be here. He'd long ago heard of another man near Nome whose dogs were excellent and very reasonably priced, but Jayce had put that notion aside. He had convinced the expedition leaders that his old friend Jacob Barringer would give them a much better deal and perhaps even consider coming along to handle the animals. Given the fact that the expedition was already facing financial problems, it didn't take much persuasion. And while Jayce knew Jacob would supply only the best animals, his decision was driven by a need to see Leah again.

She'd been on his mind so much over the years. When he'd left Ketchikan ten years ago, Jayce immediately found that he missed Leah. Missed her so much in fact, that he'd temporarily left Alaska in order to forget her. But it hadn't worked, and Jayce had come back to the land he loved . . . but not to the woman who captured his thoughts. In fact, he'd done his best to avoid her. Now the expedition had brought them back together. . . . No, he'd brought them back together.

But why? Why did I come? So much has changed. So many years have passed by. She can't possibly care for me after all this time. But in his heart, Jayce hoped that she did. He hoped that somehow he might be able to get to know her again. The time he'd spend here working with the dogs would allow him to see her every day and that in turn would hopefully show him if he'd ruined his chances ten years ago.

Glancing up from the pan of water Jacob had provided, Jayce squinted against the sun. There were several men down by the water's edge. An *umiak*—a small boat made from animal skins—sat nearby. The men seemed to be asking about something. One man in particular held Jayce's attention.

"It can't be him," Jayce muttered.

He watched the man, being careful to keep out of sight. *Why is he here? Is he looking for me?* It would have taken careful investigation for him to find Jayce. Or was it pure coincidence?

This ghost from Jayce's past life rose up to disturb him like nothing else in the world. This man could ruin everything Jayce had worked for.

Jayce eased around the corner of the inne and fought to settle his nerves. He continued watching as best he could and felt only moderate relief when the man and his companions got back in the umiak and pushed out into the water. As the boat disappeared around the bend, Jayce let out a heavy sigh.

"You coming?" Jayce startled to see Jacob watching him. "What's wrong?" Jacob asked. "You look like you've seen a ghost."

Jayce wasn't about to let Jacob know the truth of it. If it was who he thought it was, Jayce could very well be in big trouble.

"I've just got a lot on my mind. The *Homestead* should be arriving soon, and I need to know my way around handling those teams."

"Well, maybe it won't be as bad as you think. I've decided to come with you."

Jayce forgot about the man and looked at Jacob with a grin. "That's wonderful news, Jacob. I can't tell you how excited I am to have you join us. You won't regret it. The pay's not great, but the adventure more than makes up for it."

"I don't think Leah took the news well, but I did mention having her go see Karen and Adrik. I think she consoled herself with that."

"She's not in charge of you, Jacob. A man can't live his life attached to his sister's apron strings."

"That's not the way it is between us," Jacob snapped.

Jayce waved his arms. "Whoa, now, I didn't mean anything by it. I'm sure you two stick together because you have no one else."

"We also happen to appreciate each other's company. We've been looking out for each other since we were kids, and I don't intend to stop until Leah is properly married to a husband who can take up the job."

"I understand perfectly," Jayce replied, feeling an odd sensation run through him at the mention of Leah marrying.

Jacob leaned in, his tawny brown hair blowing back in the gentle breeze. "I care about what she thinks. You should too."

"I do. Honestly, Jacob. I'm sorry."

Jayce wasn't sure why his friend had become so angry, but he wanted to make things right. "I need to go back to the house and get my gift for your sister. Point me in the right direction for the party."

"It's over there."

Jayce glanced across the way to see a reasonably sized wood house. He could only imagine that it must have cost a small fortune to bring in lumber for such a project. The natives and even the Barringers had houses put together with driftwood, whalebone, and sod. It was rumored that many of the missionaries would not come north without better housing, however. Jayce had read an entire report given by one of Dr. Sheldon Jackson's missionaries that told of the unbearable cold when living in less than a reasonable American house. Jayce had laughed at the situation then, knowing that he would probably live in nothing more substantial than a tent once they were on shore mapping and taking geological samplings in the Arctic.

Still, he couldn't begrudge a worker of God good housing. "I'll be right there."

"Well, hurry it up. We're already late."

Jayce tried not to think about the earlier encounter or of the man from his past. He told himself the sun had caused the man only to look like his old adversary. *He wasn't here. I'm safe.*

He hurried to the Kjellmann's house and knocked lightly before opening the door. Surely they were expecting him, and he knew that no one stood on ceremony north of the fiftieth parallel.

The first sight that greeted him took Jayce's breath away. Leah was standing to the right of the door, her expression one of sheer delight. In her arms she held a baby girl. The child was quite captivated by Leah's attention, and Jayce couldn't help but stare. Leah's face fairly glowed. She seemed so clearly at ease with the baby— so happy.

"She'll make a good mama, ja?"

He looked to find Emma Kjellmann at his side. "I think you're right," he said, shaking off the thought. "Sorry I'm late. I had to go back for her present."

"Not to worry. We do things as they come," Emma said. "Although my son Bryce would rather this party come quickly. Are you hungry?"

"To be sure. Jacob worked me hard today." He couldn't help but say this a little louder than need be, as Jacob approached.

"Oh, quit your complaining. I don't know how such a *cheechako* is ever going to make it up north."

"Don't call me a cheechako. I'm hardly a newcomer. I just need a lot of help," he said, laughing. "That's why I'm taking you with me. Somebody has to look out for me."

Emma chuckled. "Well, there's none better. Our Jacob might as well be native. But what's this about you going away?" she asked, turning to Jacob.

"I've been asked to join Jayce's expedition team to the North."

"Why would any sane man want to go farther north?" Emma asked quite seriously. "I may be Swedish, but this is cold enough for me."

"Me too," a man said, thrusting out his hand. "I'm Emma's husband, Bjorn."

"Jayce Kincaid. I'm glad to meet you and equally glad to be invited to the party. Jacob tells me there is actually to be a birthday cake."

"Can't celebrate a boy's birthday without cake," Bjorn replied.

"Can we eat now?" a young boy asked.

Jayce presumed it was Emma and Bjorn's son. Jacob had already told him the boy shared Leah's birthday.

"Ja. We'll eat now, but you promised to say the blessing in Swedish," Emma reminded her son.

Bryce lit up at this. "I know it all. I can do it." He fairly danced to the table.

Jayce smiled in amusement as the boy took his place and called to everyone else. "Come on. We're going to pray."

Leah looked up to find Jayce watching her. She blushed and clutched the baby close as if to shelter the child from harm. Jayce couldn't help but wonder, however, if Leah meant to protect the baby . . . or herself.

"On the occasion of Bryce Kjellmann's fourth birthday," Emma announced, "he is

going to offer a traditional Swedish blessing."

They bowed their heads and Bryce began. *"Gud, som haver barnen kär se till mig
som liten är."* He paused for a moment, then
added in English, "Bless the food, amen."

"Amen," several people said in unison.

"What did he say in Swedish?" Jayce
asked Emma.

She grinned. "Bryce will tell you."

Bryce nodded and smiled. "God, who
loves all the children, look on me so small."

"Wonderful job, Bryce." Leah handed the
baby to Emma and went to hug the boy. He
eagerly climbed into her arms and hugged
her tightly about the neck.

He whispered loud enough for the entire
room to hear, "I'm glad it's our birthday."

"I am too," Leah replied, giving him a
quick kiss on the cheek.

Several of the natives who'd come to the
party circled round the two and offered their
greetings, blessings, and gifts. It was easy
for Jacob to see that Leah was greatly
loved. But why not? She was kind and gentle with everyone. Well, maybe everyone but
him. For some reason she seemed perfectly
content to make him miserable.

After a dinner of seal, tomcod, and some things unrecognizable to Jayce, Emma produced a birthday cake. He knew Jacob had brought some ingredients with him from Nome, but the cake still amazed everyone. It didn't take long for the dessert, heavier than most of the cakes Jayce had known in the States, to disappear.

Then it was time for gifts. There were many hand-carved trinkets for Bryce, as well as several articles of clothing. Leah received new mittens, a traveling pouch, a fur-lined hat, and a small ivory carving. Jayce felt his book of poetry paled in comparison to the other gifts, but she thanked him for it and seemed pleased.

When they concluded the party at nine o'clock, it was still as light as noonday outside. Jayce loved the long days. He felt they afforded him more working time. He motioned to Jacob as they left the Kjellmanns' house.

"I'm going to work more with the dogs. Would you come and help me?"

"It's nearly time to turn in," Jacob protested, his arms full of Leah's gifts.

"We still have plenty of light."

"We'll have plenty tomorrow, too. Besides, I have to take these home for Leah. I promised I wouldn't get sidetracked."

"I can help you," Jayce offered, "and then we can get back to work."

Jacob stared at him in disbelief for a moment. "I'm tired. I'm going home to clean up and go to bed. You do as you like."

Jayce realized he wasn't going to win the argument. "All right. I suppose it will wait until tomorrow."

"I heard from Ayoona's son John that there has been a lot of fog and storms to the south. Your ship will probably be delayed, so there's no hurry."

"It's your ship too," Jayce reminded him.

Jacob frowned. "I know. I just wish I could help Leah to understand why I think it's so important to do this."

"Let me talk to her," Jayce offered.

"No. You've done entirely enough," Jacob countered and headed for the house. "Just leave her be."

Jayce stood frozen in place. What did he mean by that? What had he done? "Wait up!" he called out. "What are you trying to say?"

Jacob waited, but only for a moment. "I said what I meant to say. Leave her alone.

It's that simple." His calm was more unnerving to Jayce.

"But why?"

Jacob shifted the items and shook his head. "You really don't understand, do you?"

"I don't know what it is I'm supposed to understand. I thought we were all friends here."

"You rejected Leah—why should she listen to you? She was in love with you, and you hurt her badly."

Nothing could have surprised Jayce more than this declaration. "That's what this is all about? She was just a girl."

"Doesn't really matter what her age might have been," Jacob replied. "It still hurt."

"So that's why she's treating me like she is—all fire and spit?"

"What do you expect? You throw her feelings back in her face, disappear for ten years, then reappear as though nothing had ever happened."

"But ten years is a long, long time."

"Not where the heart is concerned." Jacob turned and began walking again.

Jayce followed but waited until they were at the inne to say anything more. "I never meant to hurt her, Jacob. You know that. I never lead her to believe I cared more than I did. I wanted to explore the territory and travel. I wanted to live a life of adventure."

"And that couldn't have included Leah?"

"I . . . I didn't figure she'd stay. I really didn't figure either one of you would."

"Well, you were wrong. We both love this territory. And if you would have bothered to give Leah a chance, you might have learned that for yourself. You might not have had to spend all this time alone."

"What about you? You're alone."

Jacob shook his head. "Not by choice. If I'd had a woman that loved me as much as Leah loved you, I would have married her on the spot. Anyway, just leave her be—I don't want anything to mess up our friendship, but I won't see her hurt. Besides, we'll soon be leaving, and then you won't have to concern yourself with her."

"What if I want to concern myself with her?"

Jacob eyed him warily. "What do you mean?"

"I mean . . . well, I've been thinking about Leah since I first left Ketchikan. I guess I'd like to know if we couldn't find a way to put the past behind us—if she might feel the same for me now that she felt then."

"Are you serious?"

Jayce ran his fingers through his hair. "I think about her all the time."

"Jayce, you'd better think hard before you say a word to her." He took a step closer, as if to reinforce his next statement. "I'll deal with you myself if you hurt her again."

"I promise you, I have only the best of intentions. I don't want to hurt anyone, especially Leah."

This answer seemed to satisfy Jacob, who then dismissed the conversation as though it were nothing more important than detailing the weather. "A bunch of us are going hunting tomorrow. Want to come along?"

"Ah . . . sure . . . I guess so," Jayce replied, his voice sounding distant even in his own ears.

"I'll get you up at three and we'll head out. After we get back we can work the dogs."

"Three in the morning?"

Jacob grinned as though the entire evening had been nothing but carefree. "That's why I'm going to bed now."

Jayce let Jacob go with that. He was still so surprised by the turn of the conversation—surprised, too, by the warning Jacob had given. Walking away from the settlement, Jayce tried to reason through the things his friend had said. He honestly hadn't given any credence to Leah's feelings ten years ago. He had figured her to be a love-struck child—nothing more.

His heart back then had been focused on Alaska, the land being his only focus. Leah had been fun and good to spend time with. Her quick wit and intelligence had helped to pass the time. Her love of God and strength of spirit, however, had been intimidating to the free-spirited Jayce. He hadn't yet come to understand the importance of a life lived trying to please God.

Leah had tried to help him see the truth of it, but Jayce hadn't cared for the truth. He preferred living for the moment—for himself. But things were different now. He had come to accept Christ after spending a long, lonely week in an isolated camp in Canada. Nothing had gone right in his life for months. In fact, he'd gone to Canada after a trip to New York where he'd run into several unsavory characters. Including the man he'd thought he'd seen earlier in the day.

That trip had been a waste of time and energy. He'd hoped to put some things to rest—to mend some fences and see his family's miseries put in the past once and for all. Instead, he'd nearly gotten himself arrested, and all because of . . . him.

He blew out a breath and stared across the vast, open field. The snow was patchy and melting under the intensity of the sun. Would that it could melt the ice around Leah's heart.

He looked back to the house where Leah was now departing with several of her friends. She was laughing and obviously enjoying their company. She didn't see him, and Jayce was glad to be ignored.

"I can't change the past, Leah," he whispered. "I can't right the wrongs of yesterday, but maybe I can make the tomorrows better." But then again, such a thing would require her giving him a second chance, and that might be impossible. Jayce was set to leave for a summer's worth of exploration. Not only that, but he was taking her brother too. She might not see that as an extension of the olive branch.

"There has to be a way," he declared, shoving his cold hands deep into his pockets. "There has to be a way to make this right."

Chapter Seven

Helaina stood on the deck of the *Ally Mae*, grateful to finally be heading to Nome. Her trip had met with nothing but delays: first the train travel west had been slowed by floods and other complications, then there had been problems with her ship passage. No doubt the *Homestead* was already in Nome awaiting her arrival. But would they wait long enough?

Her anxious nature was only heightened by unanswered questions like that. Her worst fears were that the *Homestead* would move north without her, and along with it her chance to catch Jayce Kincaid. She sighed and looked out at the choppy seas. The night had been unbearable with a squall blowing up to send them tossing and twisting on the water. Helaina thought she might very well be thrown from her berth. But at least here she didn't need to worry about the Germans sinking them.

The captain promised them they would dock in Nome in two days if the weather held. But so far rain and fog had complicated the journey and Helaina figured to count on arriving in Nome only after her feet were safely on the shores of that town.

"Ma'am?"

Helaina turned to find an older man of maybe sixty or so. He looked rough, rather worn from life. "Yes?" she asked in her reserved manner. She lifted her chin slightly and eyed him in an almost grave manner.

"Are you married, ma'am?"

Helaina had already suffered the proposals of a half dozen men headed to Nome. "I am a widow."

The man's face lit up. "Well, I'd like to change that for you. I'm looking for a wife."

"But I, sir, am not looking for a husband," she replied flatly.

"But I'm a good dancer—good kisser

too." He grinned and leaned forward. "I could show ya."

Helaina felt sorry for the old man, but at the same time detested his forward actions. "Sir, I thank you for your offer, but I have no desire to marry again." *Or kiss a grizzled old man,* she thought but said nothing more.

She turned her attention back to the water. The old man cleared his throat as if to make further comment, then seemed to think better of it. He sauntered away without another word, for which Helaina was very grateful. She could imagine Robert laughing at the scene. She had always been what he called a "handsome woman," and had known her fair share of attention. In fact, she often used her looks to her advantage. She only hoped that Jayce Kincaid could be swayed by such a simple thing.

The boat heaved right as the waves seemed to increase in size. Once they moved away from the Aleutian Islands, the water and weather were both supposed to have calmed, but so far that hadn't proven true. She'd never traveled to this part of the world, and so far she wasn't that impressed. The cold and isolation weren't at all to her liking.

Once when she and Robert had been courting he had mentioned that he cherished time alone, left to himself in the wilds of the woods in New Hampshire. "I like the solitude, Helaina. There's something refreshing about the silence."

"Maybe for you, but that holds no appeal for me," Helaina had told her husband. "I find being alone like that to be a bore."

He had laughed and hugged her close. "Then you just haven't been alone with the right person in such settings."

The memory made her smile. Despite the grief she'd known in Robert's passing, she wouldn't have traded her marriage in order to have avoided the pain. Sharing the short time they had together was better than no time at all. She had watched other people become consumed by their grief and sorrow. They were unable to be productive—to find a usefulness in life. *Well, not me,* Helaina thought. *I won't be like them.*

A quick glance at her watch confirmed it was well past time to turn in. The lighted skies were deceptive, and Helaina wondered if she'd ever get used to the odd days and nights. Making her way to her cabin, she calculated that, if all went well, she might be able to find Jayce Kincaid and head home within the week. That would be ideal, as far as she was concerned, because already she had been gone from civilization longer than she liked. Even Seattle had paled compared to her homes in New York City and Washington, D.C. Home had always been important to her, even though she traveled many days out of the year away from their comfort. In New York there was always something to do—someone to see—and Mrs. Hayworth to fuss over her. In Washington, D.C., she had Stanley—her last link to family.

For the first time in a long time, Helaina felt homesick. There was a longing deep inside that refused to go away. The only problem was, she was pretty certain it wasn't a place that she longed for. And if not a place . . . then might it be a person?

"What a ridiculous thought. I'm not about to lose my heart—my life—to another person again. I don't want to lose another man as I lost Robert." She looked around, startled to realize she'd spoken the words aloud. No sense in people thinking her daft. Still, the aching persisted. She didn't belong here.

The truth was, she didn't belong any-where. Maybe it *was* a place she was long-ing for. A place where she might belong and feel a sense of security and peace.

————

Two days later, with the storms behind them and calmer waters prevailing, Helaina found herself and her things deposited in Nome. It wasn't much to look at. The dirt streets were narrow, no more than twenty feet wide. Dilapidated buildings lined the thoroughfare—sad reminders of better days gone by. Why, at the turn of the century this city was in its heyday. Gold was found nearby and everyone wanted to be in Nome. Twenty thousand people had called this place home. Helaina remembered hear-ing stories about it from her father. He'd thought every single gold-fevered ninny to be ignorant, ill-advised, and insane.

Now looking at the sad little town, Helaina could only wonder if he hadn't been right. A strong sensation of loneliness washed over her. This was a town of defeat and desola-tion. It seemed appropriate that she should come here to nab Jayce Kincaid.

"Ma'am, can I carry your bag? Where are you staying?" It was the grizzled old man again. Already he was reaching to take hold of Helaina's large black bag.

"I'm not entirely sure," Helaina said, glancing up the street. She allowed the man to make himself useful.

"Well, I know a place not far from here. Just up the way. Couple of native women have rooms. There's also a couple of hotels, but they ain't much better."

"Thank you, I believe I would prefer a hotel." She had no prejudice against the natives; however, she'd learned anonymity was easier to maintain in a crowd. Surely the exploration team would also have rooms at the hotel, making it easier for her to blend in.

The man shrugged and headed toward the town. "How long will you be up here?"

Helaina tried not to be annoyed. After all, the man had been kind enough to carry her things. "I'm to join the ship *Homestead*. Are you familiar with it?"

"No, ma'am. Where's it bound?"

"North. It's an expedition to map the Arctic islands and coastline."

"Seems out of place for a woman like you, if you don't mind my saying so."

"Whether you say so or not, that's where I'm bound," Helaina replied.

The sourdough had been correct in his analysis, Helaina thought as they approached a well-worn building. The hotel wasn't much to boast about. The paint was peeling and the two-story frame seemed to sag as if tired. Still, she wouldn't have to sleep on the streets, and hopefully she'd meet up with her companions.

"Now if they don't have rooms, I'll take you on down to my friends."

"I'm certain to be fine. Thank you." Helaina reached out for her bag. The old man seemed reluctant to hand it over, but he finally let it go.

"You remember, too, my marriage proposal still holds good."

Helaina nodded. "I'll remember."

Inside the dark hotel, a heavy smell of cigar and cigarette smoke nearly choked Helaina. A foursome of men hunkered down in the corner over cards. The smoke was as intense as the expressions on their faces. They didn't even notice her.

Helaina glanced around. There was no

one else in sight; even the front desk was unattended. Moving closer to the desk, however, she spied an open door to the left.

"Hello in back?" she called, presuming there might be an attendant hiding out.

A large man appeared, cigar in hand, frowned, and then glanced around the room. "You here alone?"

Helaina nodded. "I would like a room."

He approached the desk, still acting as though he didn't believe he was really seeing her. "Well, I got a nice one—best in the place. What brings you to Nome? You lookin' for some disappeared husband?"

Helaina smiled. "Hardly that. I've come here to join an expeditionary group. Perhaps you could tell me if the *Homestead* has come in?"

"Come and gone." He looked at her skeptically. "You say you were to join them?"

She felt as though she'd been punched in the stomach. "Yes. I'm to assist the map maker."

He rubbed his jaw and shook his head. "Well, they've gone on without you. Left a few days ago."

Leah gently turned the book of poems over in her hand and thought of Jayce. Why had he given her this volume? Most of the poetry within dealt with romantic notions and love. She felt confident it wasn't his intent to imply a feeling of love for her, so why had he chosen this particular book?

Jayce's continued presence troubled Leah more than she could say. Even more bothersome was that he was taking her brother away. And with their departure looming, the idea of Jacob risking his life chilled her to the bone. She knew Jacob would only tell her that life in general was a risk—that living in this harsh territory was a greater threat than most folks would ever know—but it didn't comfort her. Many men had lost their lives going north to explore the Arctic. That part of the world was unforgiving.

She put the book aside and made her way to Ayoona's inne. The old woman had invited Leah to come and help her cut up seal meat. The hunts over the past few days had been successful. Seal, walrus, and a variety of fish and birds had made themselves available, ensuring that the famine of the winter was behind them.

Leah got down to crawl through the long narrow entrance into Ayoona's traditional inne. The tunnel gave her a sense of being trapped, but Leah pushed through, peeking out as she entered the house. "Hello!" she called.

"Lay-ya, come in and help me," Ayoona called. Her daughter-in-law Oopick was working to boil some seal flippers. They jokingly called them seal's bare feet once they were cooked and ready for eating.

Leah took up an *ulu,* a popular knife with the women. Its curved blade and wooden handle made it easy to use in cutting thick flesh. Ayoona was already hard at work on the blubber.

"I thought you would be working outside today, but then I fought against the wind on my way over here. I hope it won't blow up a storm."

"It won't be bad," Ayoona promised. "But I get too old to fight the wind. Figured it not too hot to work in here."

"How's the baby doing?" Leah asked Oopick, knowing how proud she was of her first grandson.

"He grows strong," she answered, looking back over her shoulder and grinning. "He'll chew the blubber soon."

"No doubt. I saw him yesterday. He looks very strong," Leah said, trying to keep the yearning from her voice.

"You seem much too sad, Lay-ya," Ayoona said. "The days of sun are with us. We can make much work together. The hunts are good again and there is plenty of food. Why are you sad?"

Leah hesitated only a moment before the words tumbled from her lips. "It's about Jayce Kincaid."

"The man who buys your brother's dogs?"

Leah nodded. "We knew him from long ago. . . . I think I already told you that." She toyed with the ulu, forgetting the seal meat momentarily. "I thought he was the most wonderful man in the world. I gave him my heart, but he said I was just a child and that I needed to forget about him."

"But you didn't forget."

"No," Leah said softly. "I didn't forget."

"How do you feel about him now?" Oopick asked.

"I . . . I still care for him. I thought I'd buried all my feelings long ago, but now I realize I care just as much as I did then . . . if not more."

"Then you tell him this," Ayoona stated. Her weathered old face showed no sign of emotion.

"But he hurt me, and I don't wish to be hurt again."

Ayoona shook her head and went back to work. "You cannot hold the man's foolishness against him. Doesn't the Bible say so?"

"I forgave him for what he did."

"How could you and still hold it in your heart?"

Leah swallowed hard. Was Ayoona right? Had she really not forgiven Jayce? "I don't know what to say," she finally admitted. "I thought I'd forgiven him."

"You need to talk to him. See if he still rejects you."

Leah wanted to know the truth, but she didn't think she could bear another rejection from Jayce. Now that she was thirty, and life with a husband and children was becoming more unlikely, Leah felt it difficult to even broach the subject.

"If he say no to you, then you go back to your family in Ketchikan and find a husband. Bring him back here. You let this man go if he say no."

But Leah wondered if it would ever be possible to let go of Jayce Kincaid. He seemed to be imprinted in her heart, and she doubted it could ever be rubbed away and forgotten.

A cry for help sounded from outside. Someone was calling Leah's name. She jumped to her feet, nearly toppling the table. Certain it must be a medical emergency, Leah scurried down the tunnel to the door.

"I'll be back later, Ayoona," she called over her shoulder.

"Leah! Hurry. Hurry fast!" Niki, a young native boy, called. "Jacob needs you!"

Chapter Eight

Leah was directed to her brother's dog kennel. She felt a momentary sense of panic. What had happened to Jacob? Was he all right? The boy sounded very upset, and the dogs were barking and putting up such a ruckus that she feared the worst. Had a bear surprised Jacob? Was he hurt?

She rounded the corner, seeing a man lying on the ground. The man, however, wasn't her brother. It was Jayce.

"What happened?" she asked Jacob as he worked to secure one of the dogs.

"He was in the middle of a brawl. The dogs got a little crazy with each other, and

Jayce foolishly tried to pull them apart. They don't know him well enough yet, and they attacked him."

Leah knelt down and looked quickly at the nasty wound on Jayce's right leg. The blood loss was significant. "Give me your belt, Jacob."

He left the now tied-up dog and quickly came to where his sister worked. He handed her the belt without comment.

"Lift his leg for me," she ordered.

Jayce cried out in pain, his face contorting. Leah quickly slipped the belt up under his thigh and cinched it tightly. "Jacob, make a notch for me to secure the belt."

Jacob worked well at her side, for he had helped her on many occasions. With the belt secured, Leah ordered Niki to run to Ayoona for bandages. She needed to get the bleeding stopped and assess the situation quickly. Leah glanced up to find Jayce watching her. His upper lip was beaded in sweat, even though the temperatures were not that warm.

She assessed his color, noting he was pale. "Try to relax. I know it pains you, but if you fight against it—get your heart rate up—it will cause you to bleed more."

"I feel light-headed," he said in a mumble. "Cold too."

"Jacob, he's going into shock. We need to get his head lower than his heart."

Jacob rushed inside a small shed and came out with an old worn cot. Quickly he positioned it at an angle with the legs at one end collapsed.

"You see to his leg," Jacob told Leah. "I'll take care of the rest."

He lifted Jayce easily, ignoring the man's moans of pain. Leah held fast to Jayce's wounded leg. The movement caused more bleeding, which she knew was bad. Just as they positioned Jayce on the slanted cot, Niki reappeared with Oopick. She carried hot water, while Niki had the bandages. More natives followed after them, eager to know the situation.

Leah and Oopick worked to clean the leg. It was imperative to find if the artery was cut. Assessing the wound, Leah felt confident that, while the lacerations were deep and ragged, the artery was intact. This was very good for Jayce. It would mean the difference between life and death.

Leah's heartbeat pounded in her ears. *He still might die. He might die if you don't do the right things to save him.* Her hands shook fiercely as she wiped bits of cloth away from the skin. Oopick rinsed the wound as Leah directed.

"Let's pack the wound and get him back to the house," she told Jacob. "He'll rest better there."

Jacob called to several men while Leah did her best to secure Jayce's leg with bandages. When she'd completed her task, she stood back. "I'll go ahead and get things ready. Oopick, you come with me."

The native woman was at her side in a moment. They made their way to the inne as Jacob instructed the men to take their places around the cot. Leah left Oopick to hold open the door while she went into their stormy day cookroom. Leah felt this would be the best place to work on Jayce. They wouldn't need it for cooking, and the days were warming up nicely. She stoked the fire in the stove, even as she heard the men making their way down the stairs.

"Just put him in the corner," she instructed the men. "Leave him on the cot."

She could see his color was still bad, and Leah fought to stave off the emotion that was threatening to spill into her voice.

"Jayce, you need to lie still. I want to examine the wound and see about stitching it up."

"I'll lie still. I promise," he whispered.

"I'm going to have Oopick put together some herbs. They'll help you relax—maybe sleep. We can also make a salve that will ease the pain."

Jayce barely nodded. Leah was afraid he might lose consciousness, then wondered if it wouldn't be easier for him. At least that way he wouldn't have to endure every poke and prod of her examination.

Jacob leaned in close. "How's he doing? It's pretty bad, isn't it?"

"It's bad enough . . . but not as tragic as it could have been," Leah added, seeing Jayce frown. "I think the artery is fine. If it had been severed, I couldn't have saved him. I'm not sure how much I can really help him as it is. This is a massive wound, and it really needs a surgeon's touch."

"The closest surgeon is going to be in Nome," Jacob offered. "The hospital's good, but I know a doctor who keeps a small infirmary. He's the same man who fixed me up when I was sick with the measles. He could help us, and Jayce could get more personalized attention."

"That's a good idea. I'm thinking we should stabilize him—get the bleeding stopped—then get him to Nome as soon as possible."

Jacob rubbed his stubbled chin. "Most of the snow is gone or melting at least. It won't be good for the dogs. We'd better go by umiak."

"The waters have been so rough lately and the wind is blowing something up," Leah murmured, thinking of the boats made of skins. "Still, I don't see that we have too many other choices."

"I'll get some of the men to come with us, and we can get more supplies. Anamiaq and his family are back, and they have a great many furs to trade, as well as a long list of desired supplies. We'll see what the weather is going to do and then set out. We can stay close to the coast."

"That would probably be a good idea," Leah murmured, hating to see her brother go away again but also fearing what Jayce's fate would be. She felt overwhelmed by the myriad of emotions within her but knew she was his only chance. If she didn't remain calm, she'd be no good to him at all.

"I want you to come too," Jacob said.

Leah eased the tourniquet pressure enough to see how bad the bleeding might be. Jayce moaned and closed his eyes. The wound only oozed and Leah sighed in relief. Hopefully the bleeding would stop completely.

"Did you hear me?" Jacob asked.

Leah eased away from Jayce. "Oopick, please make a paste with the stinkweed. I have some in the cupboard." The older woman nodded and went to work immediately. Meanwhile Leah motioned Jacob to follow her outside.

"What's wrong?" Jacob asked.

"I'll come with you, but you have to know this situation is grave. The bleeding may start up again. I hate to sew on him and risk the possibility of messing it up. The worst of it will be the bleeding and possibility of infection. Animal wounds are always bad."

"Do what you can for him. I'll have everything ready to go within the hour," Jacob said, then reached out to gently touch Leah's arm. "Look, I know this is hard on you. I know you care about what happens to him."

Leah drew a deep breath and met her brother's compassionate gaze. "I do care, and that's why this is so difficult. I . . . well . . . I feel guilty. I thought I wanted Jayce to know the kind of pain he'd caused me, yet at the same time I wouldn't have wanted him or anyone else to know that kind of hurt. Now he's wounded . . . maybe dying . . ."

"This isn't your fault, Leah. You didn't will it to happen, if that's what you think."

"I know," she said, still trying to convince her heart. "I know I didn't cause it, but I haven't been very nice to him. I could have been a better person—a better Christian."

"Then be one," Jacob said, smiling. "We all make mistakes, take the wrong path— but it's more important that we get turned around and go the right way once we discover the truth."

She nodded. "I'll get my things packed. You see to Jayce's things. He may need to ship back to the States after this. I can't imagine him being able to continue with the expedition."

"No, I can't either." Jacob's voice

sounded distant. "But I wonder if I should go ahead. They'll still need dogs and a handler."

"I wish you would reconsider. I'm not excited for you to go under any circumstances, but at least Jayce was familiar with such trips."

Jacob dropped his hold. "You think I'm incapable?"

"No, it's not that. But I hate to see you head out there on your own, not knowing anyone. You aren't familiar with the territory, and at least if Jayce were on the team, you'd have a friend."

"I can always make new friends, Leah. Look, I know you worry about me, but honestly, we have to go our separate ways at times. You aren't my mother or my wife— you're my sister. You have a life to live as well." Silence surrounded them for a moment. "I'd better go get things ready or we might as well not go."

Leah let him leave, knowing he was irritated with her. She vowed to herself that she'd not bring up the matter again, but in her heart she knew it would be a difficult promise to keep.

———

Jacob was relieved to know that John and Kimik were both willing to put boats together and follow him to Nome. It was always better to travel in groups.

"I'll hunt while we travel," John said. He helped Jacob load the last of the furs on a wheeled sled for hauling to the water. "We might get lucky and find more walrus—even a beluga."

"I'm grateful, John. I don't know how long we'll be in Nome. We'll see what the doctor says, and if we need to stay there, you and Kimik can head back after we get the supplies loaded."

Reaching the shore, Jacob looked out across the sea. To his surprise a large ship sat in the harbor. It wasn't one of the usual ships that came north with mail or passengers. Squinting to catch the name on the stern, Jacob realized it was the *Homestead*—Jayce's ship. Already a small launch was headed their way with half a dozen men on board.

Jacob wondered what the captain would say when he heard the news about Jayce. Surely this would cause problems for the team. The dogs were imperative to the project, and the sleds he and Jayce built were desperately needed for travel over the Arctic snows and ice.

Working to pack the furs—some in John's boat and others in his own, Jacob figured to wait for the men to come ashore. He would have to bear the bad news to the captain, then perhaps escort the man to his home so that he could talk with Jayce. If Jayce was still conscious.

"Hello, *Homestead,*" Jacob said, leaving his umiak as the men approached.

"Greetings. I see you're heading out. I might warn you there's some rough water out there," a stocky, bearded man announced. He came forward and extended his hand. "I'm Captain Latimore."

"Jacob Barringer." They shared a firm shake before the captain turned to the two nearest men. "This is Cliff Cleary and Andrew Johnsson, two of my men."

Jacob shook hands, while the remaining *Homestead* party secured the launch. "I'm good friends with Jayce Kincaid. He asked me to join your expedition as dog handler."

"Splendid," the captain replied.

"Well, not quite so splendid. There's been

an accident, and Jayce is badly hurt. We are just preparing to get him to Nome."

"What kind of accident?" Latimore asked.

"Dogs. I'm afraid they were riled by the scent of something and started fighting. Jayce stepped in, and because they aren't yet that familiar with him, it didn't end well. I'm afraid he'll need to see a surgeon for his leg. I'm doubtful that he'll be able to continue with you this year."

"Now that is a pity. Johnsson here is one of two geologists I was to have on the trip. Kincaid was the other."

"I am sorry. Perhaps you would like to see Jayce for yourself."

Latimore nodded. "Perhaps afterwards you can show me your dogs. We'll still need a couple of teams in order to accomplish all that we have planned."

"I'd be glad to," Jacob said, nodding at the man.

"You other men, stay here. We'll be back shortly."

The team nodded in agreement at this arrangement, taking more interest in Jacob's umiak. "Do you have any more of these skin boats? We'd like very much to purchase at least one more," Cleary called.

Jacob shook his head. "Most of the men are using them to hunt. Winter comes around fast up here and there was a famine last season. We need to lay in a better supply of meat, so I have my doubts anyone will be trading their boats, even at inflated prices."

"Which our expedition cannot afford," Latimore called out as they walked away.

They made their way to the house, where Leah greeted Jacob. "Are we ready?"

"Very nearly. But first, this is Captain Latimore. He's heading up the expedition that Jayce was to have been a part of."

"I see. Jayce is just in here," she said, holding back the fur that covered the stormy day kitchen. "He's quite groggy from the medicine we've given him. He needs to remain calm or the bleeding will start up again."

"Thank you, I quite understand and will give him no cause for alarm." The captain moved past Jacob and slipped into the room.

"Were you expecting him today?" Leah asked.

"No, we weren't exactly sure when he would come. I told him the situation but thought he might want to have a few words with Jayce. How is he?"

"Actually, he looks much better. The shock is wearing off and he's taken some broth Oopick made him. It has some healing properties and will help with the pain. It will also help him to feel relaxed for the trip."

"I'm glad he's doing better. That's an awful wound."

Leah glanced at the fur covering and lowered her voice. "I'm still not sure he won't lose the leg. I'm really very frightened for him."

Jacob frowned. "We will do what we can, Leah. The rest is in God's hands."

"I know, but I can't help but wish I could do more for him."

"You're doing more than most of us even know how. Your nursing abilities have benefited so many here, you just need to have confidence that you'll know what to do— and if you don't, that God will show you." Jacob felt sorry for his sister, knowing how personally involved she got—and with Jayce involved, it was bound to be ten times worse. "He has the best of care in you," Jacob added, putting his hand on

Leah's shoulder. "I know he'd say the same."

Just then the captain came from the room. "He's looking much better than I expected. Very groggy, but the pain seems minimal. He seems to think if he can get proper medical attention, he might be up to joining us in another week or two. I've told him that we'll be in Kotzebue after we leave here. Maybe as long as two weeks. We weren't able to get the native help we wanted in Nome, but one of the men we picked up has relations in Kotzebue, although he calls it Qikiqtagruk." Jacob nodded, recognizing the native name for the town. The captain continued. "He believes he can get us some additional men. Say, you don't have any natives here who would like to come north—maybe help you handle those dogs?"

"I don't know of any, but you could certainly ask around. However, I need to tell you also that I cannot join you at this time. You may purchase the dogs, but I need to help get Jayce to Nome." He looked to Leah and saw her nod of approval.

The captain frowned. "My men won't be knowledgeable with the dogs. We must have them and the sleds, however. Are you certain you can't join us?"

"I have no idea what kind of medical needs Jayce might have. I have to stay in Nome long enough to see him through. Then if he needs to go south to Seattle, one of us may have to go part or all of the way with him." Leah looked rather surprised by this announcement, but it was something Jacob had already considered as a possibility. If they couldn't help Jayce in Nome, he wouldn't just leave him there to die.

"Is there someone who could train my men in your absence?"

Jacob thought about it for a moment. Most of the natives were skeptical of dealing with the whites. "There is a man here in the village who works with me. I'll see if he can help you. If you come with me, we can discuss the payment and the dogs." He looked to Leah and added, "I'll go talk to Anamiaq and send John to help you get Jayce loaded."

"All right."

"Thank you, Mr. Barringer," the captain announced. "This expedition cannot function without the dogs. It is my hope that we can find someone to assist us even yet."

"Most of the natives here are reliable men who know the importance of providing for their family. They won't be easily tempted to venture into the unknown lands with strangers, but you are welcome to try."

———

Leah directed John and the other men as to how to carry Jayce. They were exceedingly careful to follow her instruction. Most of the men were very respectful, almost in awe of Leah. One of the group had even asked for her hand in marriage, although for the most part the natives married their own people. They were fiercely proud of their lineage and saw no good purpose in tainting the line with what they considered a weaker blood. The man in question had been quite desperate, however, finding himself the father of twins after the death of his wife. Leah had rejected his proposal of marriage, but had agreed to work with the other women in the village to see the babies cared for. One of the twins died despite their best efforts. It had been a bittersweet victory to see the other thrive and grow to be a sweet young boy.

Jayce fought to stay awake, but Leah had

given him a heavy dose of stinkweed. She'd boiled the leaves to make a strong concoction that would help with the pain and keep Jayce sedated. Nevertheless, he seemed almost restless to speak—to say something to her. He kept trying to speak the entire time the men were carrying him to the water.

"Leah."

"You need to rest, Jayce. Just be quiet now."

"Leah, I need . . . to . . . need to tell you . . . something."

"It can wait until you're feeling better." Leah put her bag on the rocky shore and moved to the umiak to direct the placement of her patient. "Put him there on the blanket. Yes, that's good," she said as they positioned him perfectly.

Once Jayce was secured in the boat, Leah packed blankets and a down-filled bag around him. She made sure that everything could easily break free in case of capsizing.

As the men walked away, Jayce reached out and took hold of Leah's hand. "I'm sorry, Leah."

"You couldn't help it," she reassured.

"Accidents happen, and the dogs are bad about getting excited."

"No," he said, shaking his head slowly from side to side. "Sorry for the past." He closed his eyes. "I didn't know . . ."

She waited for a moment. "Didn't know what?" She wanted very much to hear what he might say, while at the same time she knew he needed rest.

"Didn't know that I hurt you that bad. Didn't know you really loved me."

She bristled but fought to keep her voice calm. "Had I ever given you reason to doubt my word? Why should you have thought my words less than true?"

Jayce opened his eyes. "I . . . I . . . thought you were too young. Didn't think you knew your . . . mind. I thought . . ." His words trailed off.

The old anger stirred, but she forced it down. "I don't imagine you thought much at all about any of it." She tried to leave, but he held her fast.

"Forgive me, Leah. Please."

She looked at him for a moment, his eyes pleading. She bit her lip and pulled her hand away from him. "I do forgive you, Jayce. I already forgave you long ago." She got up and walked away before he could see the tears that came to her eyes.

"I just can't seem to forget you," she whispered against the Arctic wind.

Chapter Nine

They'd ridden the swells of the Bering Sea less than an hour when heavy clouds formed on the horizon. Leah knew the look of danger. Around these parts bad weather blew up quickly and often lasted for days. And if not storms, then heavy fog could also blind their way. It wasn't a good time to be on the open water.

"We'll have to make for shore," Jacob told her. "I wish we could make it to one of the villages, but I doubt we'll have time. I'll send John ahead to make the best choice."

Leah knew Jacob was right. "I'm sure it will pass quickly," she said in encouragement. Glancing at Jayce, she saw that he slept, despite the situation.

"John!" Jacob called across the water. "Find us a place to make camp. We'll wait out whatever is blowing in."

"Sure. I can do that." The native pushed his men into action.

Leah was amazed at how quickly the umiak pulled away from Jacob and Kimik's boats. John and his men were quite strong, definitely used to battling the sea. In their boat, Jacob had the help of four other men. Leah was grateful for this, because she knew she would never be strong enough to fight the rough water. The men were good friends, but Leah knew they would head quickly back to their village as soon as things were arranged in Nome. As much as they admired and respected Jacob, their own families came first, and this was no time to be slack in hunting and laying up food.

Before long, John directed them to shore. There wasn't a lot in the way of shelter, but Leah knew her brother and the other men would find ways to wait out the storm and keep dry.

"Stay with Jayce," her brother told her as

the men pulled the wounded man from their boat. "We'll put together a safe place for you both." He left the two dogs he'd brought to stand guard.

Leah reached out to pet the two animals she'd helped to raise. Leo and Addy were strong Huskies who took the northern furies in stride. "You're good dogs," she said, stroking the silky fur. The animals seemed to thrive on her attention.

Jayce moaned as he tried to get up. "Are we in Nome?"

Leah left the dogs and knelt down beside her patient. "No, there's a storm blowing up. We'll have to wait it out."

"I'm sorry, Leah," he whispered, still struggling to try to sit up.

"Stay still. I need to look at your leg," she said, desperate for something to do other than converse with this man.

Jayce fell back against the blanket. "Don't let 'im find me."

The statement confused Leah. "Don't let who find you?"

Jayce shook his head. "Can't find me."

The medicine was obviously making it hard for him to think clearly. Leah knew Oopick's stinkweed solution would further the man's confusion, but Jayce needed to rest as much as possible to keep from moving his leg. Leah opened the jar and poured a small portion for Jayce. She thought about the delay with the incoming storm and prayed it would be enough to keep Jayce from misery.

"Jayce, you need to drink this," she said, putting her arm under his neck.

He opened his eyes for only a moment and then closed them again. Leah managed to get the medicine down him—at least most of it. She lowered him back to the ground. She wasn't used to this vibrant, strong, and self-sufficient man being so weak.

She pushed back a bit of Jayce's brown hair. It had a coarse, wild texture to it, but she liked it very much. How often she had wanted nothing more than to run her fingers through the thick mass. She realized she was stroking his head and pulled away.

Don't let yourself be vulnerable. Don't care too much. The internal warning seemed to fall on deaf ears—or at least a deaf heart. The Bible spoke of the eyes of the heart—did the heart also have ears? If so, Leah knew hers weren't listening.

Leah peeled back the bandages and studied the wound. It seemed about the same. An oozing of blood continued to wet the bandages, but Leah knew this was better than keeping a tight tourniquet on the leg. She had been told by a doctor once that such restriction of the blood flow could actually cause the limb to die.

Please, God, she prayed, *help me do the right thing—don't let him die or lose his leg because of my ignorance.*

"How . . . is it?" Jayce murmured.

Leah was surprised to hear him sound so coherent. "Looks like you've been chewed on by a grizzly," she said, trying to sound lighthearted. "I'm sure you'll have quite a scar."

"One more to . . . go . . . with the others," he said, then seemed to drop off to sleep.

Leah rewrapped the leg and pulled a blanket over Jayce. She glanced up behind them and saw that farther inland the men were making good headway in a small cluster of bushy willows. They had taken the umiaks and positioned them in such a way that, when bound together with rope and tarps, they made a shelter. Jacob had tightly bundled the furs and wrapped them in a protective covering of oiled duck canvas. They would make a soft bed for Jayce, Leah thought.

The men came back to shore and motioned Leah away. They picked up the four corners of the blanket on which Jayce slept and carried him to the shelter. Leah followed, bringing her bag of herbs and medicine. Leo and Addy trotted behind her as if tethered. Kimik was the last to join them, bringing their food supply with him. It was a danger to have it inside their camp, but there were no tall trees in which to hang the bag and no time to build a cache. They would simply have to take their chances.

"Maybe a bear will come out in the storm and smell our food," John said, laughing. "He will say, 'Let me come for dinner.' We will let him come—then shoot him. Then we will eat Mr. Bear." They all laughed at this.

One of the other men got a fire going, and only then did Leah see that they had laid in a generous supply of dry driftwood for their fuel. She felt warm and secure—safe with these men and her brother. The only real worry was whether or not Jayce could withstand the delay.

"I'll make supper," John announced. He

unwrapped a pack and pulled out dried seal meat. "There. Supper is ready." The men chuckled again. John always kept everyone in a good mood, and even Jacob couldn't help but join in.

"I'll do the dishes afterward," he said with a quick wink at Leah.

"You are a good man," John said, slapping Jacob on the back.

The storm increased in intensity with a fierce wind that threatened to tear down their little shelter. Kimik sang for them, telling Leah he could make much better noise than the wind. She felt a small amount of comfort in the good nature of her companions. Leo and Addy curled up beside her as if offering her their warmth. Leah gave them each a few affirming strokes before settling down beside them. Before long Leah's eyelids grew heavy, and she no longer heard the wind but rather was mesmerized by her own rhythmic breathing.

In her dreams, Leah was a young woman again. She was taken back in time to Ketchikan and her home in the woods with Karen and Adrik. She had been happy there with Jacob and the rest of her family. Karen had given her husband three beautiful children:

Ashlie, a lovely girl who looked a lot like her mother; Oliver, who definitely took after his father; and Christopher, who seemed a happy blend of both.

Leah loved these children as if they were her siblings. She missed them all so much. Ashlie was now fifteen, nearly a grown woman. She'd been almost five when Leah had left home to help Jacob, and though she'd seen the family several times over the long years, it wasn't the same. Little Christopher hadn't even been born when Leah had left Ketchikan, but Oliver had been a comfort to her. When Jayce had rejected her, Leah had spent a lot time helping care for Oliver. Karen seemed to understand.

"He loves you unconditionally. Babies are like that—men are not," Karen had told Leah. She told her this again now, in her dream.

Leah sat at Karen's table and sighed. "It isn't fair that I should love someone so much only to have him reject me. What's wrong with me? Why am I not good enough for him to love in return?"

"I doubt it has anything to do with you,"

Karen had told her quite seriously. "Jayce obviously has other things on his mind."

"But I want him to have me on his mind," Leah had protested.

She heard the baby cry and started to get up from the table. It was strange, but her legs wouldn't work. Karen only smiled and then faded from view, while the baby continued to cry.

When Leah awoke with a start, she realized it wasn't a baby crying at all, but a combination of the wind and Jayce. She sat up and reached out to touch Jayce's forehead. He was feverish. Leah's chest tightened. The wound was infected—there could be no other explanation.

The heavy overcast skies stole the sun's light, but the small fire allowed her just enough light to see the contents of her bag. Oopick had thoughtfully planned for such a problem. There was willow bark and several other herbal remedies that Leah could use in case of emergency. She pulled a tin cup from the bag and poured water into it before setting it in the coals at the side of the fire. She carefully portioned out some of the willow bark into the water to make a strong tea to fight the fever.

"What's wrong?" Jacob asked, yawning as he sat up.

"He's feverish. I think the wound is infected."

"Can you help him?"

Leah felt her hands shake as she tried to stir the water. "I hope so."

———

Helaina wondered for several days what she should do regarding her situation. No one in Nome knew anything about the *Homestead* except that it had been in harbor, then had left again.

Nothing made sense or offered her insight—no matter how she analyzed the situation. She tried talking to the chief of police, but he had no solution for her. She had posed the possibility of some natives taking her by boat to catch up with the *Homestead.* The man had only laughed at her and told her how ridiculous her proposal truly was, given the fact that the ship could be all the way past the Arctic Circle by now.

Helaina had finally come to the conclusion that perhaps her only hope was to return home and try another time. Maybe she and the Pinkertons could plan ahead and be ready for *Homestead*'s return to Seattle.

Sleep was hard to come by. Her mind was constantly battling to find a better answer to her problems, while the daylight followed them well into what should have been darkness, and totally ruined her routine cycle of day and night. It seemed this foreign and very strange land would offer her no ease.

She had made one friend. When fierce headaches would not leave her, Helaina made her way to a doctor. Dr. Cox seemed happy to meet a woman of social quality and knowledge. He had treated her headaches for free on the condition she share dinner with him that night. It was the first of many dinners, all of which Helaina had enjoyed. The isolation and boredom would have otherwise proved unbearable. At least Cox offered her lively stories and sometimes important bits of information. Tonight's date proved to be no different.

"There was a tidal storm here two years ago. Most of the damage was to the east of us. It fairly destroyed villages along the coast, both east and west."

"How awful. Were many lives lost?"

"Oh yes. It could have been much worse, however. The natives seemed to realize the dangers in some areas. They moved inland and then went to high ground. Of course, the promise of gold in this land has caused white men to come and settle. But they generally are incapable of dealing with the problems and complications of life in the North."

"Did you come for the gold, Doctor?"

He laughed. "In a sense. I knew there would be a need for a doctor, so I came to offer my services. Which I've done. I haven't regretted my choice, but I am thinking of returning south—to my home state of Colorado."

"I'm sure you'll be needed wherever you go," Helaina offered.

"I'm still surprised that you should want to travel into the vast unknown," Dr. Cox said, pouring himself a large glass of port. "Are you certain you won't have any?"

Helaina shook her head. She knew she needed to keep her wits about her at all times. "Thank you, no. As for the travel, what can I say? I have a streak of adventure in me. My husband always told me I was much too wild to tame." It was true, Helaina thought. Although not in the sense of travel, but rather in her craving of big-city life. There was to be no bucolic farms for this woman.

"It has been good to share your company. My own dear wife of twenty years died only last year. But of course I told you that already."

Helaina nodded. The man was twice her age, but she knew he eyed her with matrimonial contemplation. "It is hard to lose those we love, but I find that putting my attention on the life around me has helped me to overcome such loss."

"To be certain, but one cannot discount the possibility of remarriage."

Helaina toyed with her food. "Well, for myself, I do just that. I have no desire to remarry."

"But you are a young woman—only twenty-six. Even the Bible speaks that young widows should remarry."

Helaina bristled at this comment. People always used Bible references as the definitive beginning and end to any solution. "I care not what the Bible says, Dr. Cox. I have not given myself over to worldly religion and spiritualism."

"Nor should you. The Christian faith is neither one."

"I don't particularly care to move forward with this topic of conversation. I have made up my mind that I have little choice left but to return to Seattle and start anew with my endeavors to go north."

"I wish you would stay. At least until I could accompany you south. Your company over supper has given me something to look forward to," the doctor protested.

Helaina shook her head. "I will go tomorrow and book passage on the next ship. I have wasted entirely too much time."

"I'm sorry you consider it a waste," the older man said, looking genuinely hurt.

Helaina had no desire to devastate the poor man. "Doctor, I do not consider our shared meals to be wasted effort or time. I do appreciate the companionship you've offered and am sorry that I cannot remain and share a friendship with you."

"I would like you to consider sharing more than friendship—"

Helaina put her hand up to silence him. "I know what you would have me consider, but I cannot. Please understand; it isn't that you wouldn't make any woman a fine husband, but I will not remarry. I have no heart for it."

"Love would come in time—don't you think?"

Helaina remembered a shadowy vision of her husband lying dead in a pool of blood. She'd not actually seen the scene except in blurry photographs, but many times she had imagined it in detail. "No. Because I would not allow it to. I'm sorry." She got up from the table, most of the food still on her plate. "If you'll excuse me, I must retire."

Helaina sat in her hotel room for hours after that. She thought of the strange land outside her windows. A harsh, unsympathetic land where the men were so very lonely. People here often had both a deep loneliness and an eternal desire for the land around them. It seemed a curse and a blessing.

"I could never love this land—this harsh land of extremes." Conversation with the doctor told her of long winters with darkness. The silence and isolation drove many people insane. She would not be one of them.

Getting up, she made her way to the window and pulled the heavy drapes into place. There were two sets—both designed to block out the summer light. This world seemed so foreign. She honestly wondered how anyone could stand living here for more than a few weeks at a time. Perhaps it was good that she'd missed catching up with Jayce Kincaid.

She was about to change her clothes and retire when a knock sounded at her door. Apprehensive, she went to the nightstand by the bed and pulled out her derringer. "Who is it?"

"Dr. Cox," the man called out.

She frowned. What did he want with her? Had he thought to come here hoping to change her mind regarding marriage?

"What do you want?" she asked, still refusing to open the door.

"I . . . well, that is . . . after you left, a thought came to me. A way to get you to your ship."

Helaina tucked the gun in her pocket and opened the door. Dr. Cox stood there, hat in hand. "What are you talking about?"

"There's a ship that heads north regularly to deliver the mail. It should be making its way in the next couple of days. At least that's the schedule it's supposed to follow. I checked it out."

"Go on." Helaina wasn't entirely sure this would be her answer, but she had no other leads.

"I thought you might catch a ride with them. They could take you along as they make their rounds. You might catch up to your ship and be able to join them."

Helaina considered his proposal for a moment. "It might work."

"There's something else. I heard from someone this evening that the *Homestead* planned to stop for a time in Kotzebue. One of the natives from Nome hopes to enlist the help of his relatives and get them to join the expedition to help with hauling and such things. The mail ship will go to Kotzebue."

This time Helaina smiled. "Dr. Cox, you have given me renewed hope. Thank you for your kindness."

"Perhaps while you are north, you will rethink your position on marriage," he said, his expression hopeful.

Helaina didn't want to encourage the man falsely, but neither did she want to further his pain. "Obviously this is a land of possibilities. One can never tell what Alaska might convince me to reconsider."

He grinned and bobbed his head up and down at least ten times. "Exactly. One can never tell. Why, just look at this town. One day there was nothing here but a small village—then gold was discovered and the place swelled with people and things. It's like that in Alaska. One minute things seem hopeless and without any chance of working, the next they are teeming with possibilities."

"I can see that you are right, Doctor. Tomorrow I shall go in search of information on catching passage on the mail ship."

He looked at the floor. "Well, good night, then."

"Good night, and thank you." She closed the door quickly, unwilling to give him a chance to speak another word.

Leaning back, she sighed. This was better than she could have hoped for. A ride north and the *Homestead*'s delay in Kotzebue just might be her salvation.

Chapter Ten

The storm eventually passed, but a thick fog persisted, keeping the party land bound. It would be much too dangerous to try to navigate the waters in such conditions, but their supplies were running low and Jayce was growing progressively worse. The leg was swelling and had turned red around the wound. Leah feared blood poisoning or worse, knowing gangrene was a threat in an injury like this. Leah knew it would cost Jayce his leg if the infection went unchecked.

During this time, the men often trekked out into the fog to hunt, leaving Leah alone with Jayce. There was nothing anyone could do for him, so it seemed foolish that everyone should sit idle while the camp grew hungry. Leah found that as she sat beside him, the memories poured in.

In Ketchikan, Jayce had been boyish in charm and nature. He had once climbed a spruce just to impress Leah with his ability. She remembered them sitting together talking about the vegetation and nature of this area of Alaska. It was such a contrast to many other areas.

"The Yukon was beautiful," Leah had told Jayce, "but not this lush and green."

"It's all the rain. This area gets so much more moisture through the year. You would think the snow levels would make up for it elsewhere, but it doesn't. It has to snow a great deal, inches and inches, to even equal a single inch of rain."

Leah enjoyed having him tell of places in the interior. "Some people think Alaska Territory, and all they can imagine is snow and ice. But I've seen places where the natives grow vegetables larger than any I've seen in the States. I've spent winters in parts of the territory that were far milder than those I experienced in New York. It's amazing how we convince ourselves that things should be a certain way—when in fact we have nothing on which to base our assumptions."

Like now, Leah thought as she touched Jayce's forehead. *I know in my heart how things should be, but they are not that way at all.*

Jayce's fever raged on, and Leah knew without looking at the wound again that it was festering. She had thought about poking around to dig into the wound for any debris they had missed, but she couldn't bear the thought of causing Jayce more pain. Especially when it might not be that at all. It could just be a poisoning effect on his system from the saliva of the dogs. So as she prayed, Leah made a poultice using the herbs she'd brought along. She could only hope that it would make a difference and draw out the infection.

As the weather settled on the third day and the heavy clouds moved off to the east, Leah happily relished the sun's warmth and light. Jacob studied the seas with less enthusiasm. "The water is still very rough. It won't be easy going, but I don't know what else we can do. Jayce is getting worse," he told John and the others.

"The water isn't that bad," John said. "We need to get him to Nome, so we go."

"It's the right thing to do," Kimik agreed with his father. "If we stay, your friend might die."

Jacob looked to Leah. She felt he needed her approval somehow. "I'm not afraid of rough waters. Jayce needs a doctor and medicine that I do not have."

"Then we'll go," Jacob said, his gaze back on the waters. "But it won't be easy."

"We will pray," John said, coming to put his hand on Jacob's shoulder. "You always say, prayer changes bad times."

Jacob chuckled. "I always say it when it's someone else's bad time. Of course you're right. We need to pray and trust God to bring us safely to Nome."

Although the trip was arduous, they reached Nome without further difficulty. John called it answered prayer, and Jacob and Leah agreed. It seemed that God had created a corridor of protection just for them. He hadn't exactly calmed the seas, but He'd given strength to the men that they might overcome their obstacles.

Leah was relieved to finally have Jayce in the hands of a good doctor—at least she hoped Dr. Cox was a skilled man. She waited impatiently in the front room of the doctor's establishment and paced back and forth several times, often putting her ear to the door of the doctor's examination room.

"I'm sure he'll come talk to us when he knows something definite," Jacob told his sister. "He took great care of me."

She looked to where he sat slouched in his chair, arms crossed and looking for all the world as if he might doze off at any moment. How could he be so relaxed?

"I'm worried that I missed something," she said, looking back to the door. Already it had been an hour. What was taking so long?

"Are you still in love with him?"

The question took her by surprise. Leah thought to quickly dismiss her brother's words, then shrugged. "I care about him. I have to admit that much. I cannot say that it's love." But even as she spoke she knew it was a lie. "All right, maybe I can say it's love. But I don't want it to be."

Jacob narrowed his gaze. It reminded Leah of when he'd assess prey before shooting on a hunt. It made her feel uncomfortable. "Why don't you want it to be love?"

How could her brother be so dense? "Because he doesn't love me in return. I've loved him for over ten years. Ten years when I found it impossible to think of anyone else. Ten years of longing for the one thing I could never have."

"But what if that's changed? Seems to me Jayce was far more worried about whether you would love Alaska as he did and stay in the North. When I talked to him—"

"You talked to him? When?" she demanded.

Just then the door opened, and Dr. Cox's short Eskimo nurse emerged. "You can go in."

Leah forgot her question and rushed past the woman. The doctor stood over an unconscious Jayce, listening to his heart. "How is he?" Leah asked quietly.

The doctor stepped back and pulled the stethoscope from his ears. "I think he'll rest easier now. The leg . . . well . . . only time will tell. It's infected, but there was a broken dog tooth imbedded deep. I'm thinking it might be the cause of all of this."

Jacob came in at this point. The doctor

looked to him first and then to Leah. "Any chance those dogs were rabid?"

"No sir," Jacob said, shaking his head. "No signs of that at all. They were just riled up and didn't know Jayce well enough. He tried to separate them and got himself chewed up."

"Well, I've done what I can. The next few days should tell us a great deal. You did a remarkable job of caring for him," he said, turning to Leah. "Did you train in nursing?"

"Not exactly. I have trained with some missionaries, and when I lived in Ketchikan there was a doctor who let me read some of his medical books. And, of course, the natives have taught me a great deal."

"I see. Well, you probably saved his life. Especially with the onset of the fever. The native willow bark tea is excellent, but I also have some medicine here from the States. I will use it to see which helps him more."

"When will you know if the leg is saved?" Leah asked hesitantly.

"Should see definite signs of healing in the next forty-eight hours. I'd suggest you get a room and get some rest."

Leah nodded, but it was Jacob who spoke. "Keep track of what I owe you. If it's more than this, let me know." He handed the doctor several bills.

"We will settle up when your friend is re-covered," the doctor said, taking the money. "I'll put this on his account. Say, how are you feeling these days? Fully re-covered from the measles?"

Jacob nodded. "Fit as a man can be. The light bothered my eyes for a time, but I did as you suggested and wore the dark glasses. It helped a great deal."

"Good. Glad to hear it. Our epidemic was short-lived. So many have already had measles and some of the other diseases, but you always deal with those who haven't. Especially the children."

"Will you be with him tonight? I could stay," Leah interrupted, concerned that Jayce should not be alone.

"No, my nurse, Mary, will come and be with him. I've sent her home to let her fam-ily know she'll be here through the night. She'll be back shortly. If anything happens, she'll know what to do. I live in the rooms just in back, so she can wake me easily if Mr. Kincaid should have difficulty."

"May I sit with him for a while—just until she gets back?"

The doctor smiled. "Of course you may."

"I'll go over to the hotel and see if there are any rooms," Jacob suggested. "I'll come back for you in a short time."

"Thank you, Jacob." She met his gaze and knew he understood her heart.

Jacob walked the short distance to the hotel. The temperatures were warming up nicely, and he no longer felt the chill he'd known on his journey from the village. He glanced to the skies before entering the Gold Nugget, and as a result walked soundly into another person.

"Why don't you watch where you're going instead of gawking elsewhere?"

He looked at the refined woman and shook his head. "Excuse me, ma'am." He started to walk around her, but she wasn't finished.

"I knew this to be an uncivilized territory, but the rudeness in Alaska rivals any I've ever known."

Jacob stopped and looked at her hard for a moment. "Didn't seem that bad until you got here—maybe you brought it with you."

She reddened. "You, sir, are an ill-mannered oaf."

"And you seem to be a spoiled, insulting ninny," he said, pretending to tip a hat he didn't wear.

The woman's mouth dropped open and her arm shot up to slap him. Jacob merely sidestepped her shot, however. "If you want to be good at that, you'll have to learn not to telegraph your punch."

He walked away feeling rather amused by the stunned expression on her face. No doubt she was some fancy woman from the States, come to Alaska following a gold-sick husband or brother. He'd seen it before, but really didn't care to see it again. He could never really understand why people had to get so riled about little things. He'd meant the woman no harm, yet she acted as though he'd singled her out for an assault.

———

Mary returned shortly and helped the doctor move Jayce to a bed in another room. The infirmary held two other beds besides the one occupied by Jayce. It was a small but sufficient space that seemed much more personal than the hospital. Still, Leah worried that the hospital might have been better equipped to deal with the situation. She prayed they'd made the right decision in coming to Dr. Cox.

Leah remained at Jayce's side while Mary cleaned the surgical area where the doctor had worked on Jayce only moments before. She hummed a tune that Leah didn't recognize, and that, along with her clanking and clunking around, unnerved Leah. Here, poor Jayce was on his sickbed, possibly dying, and somehow it seemed unfair that life would just go on without worry or concern as to whether or not he made it.

She reached for Jayce's hand, then quickly tucked it back under the covers. If someone came in and found her holding his hand, they might think it odd. And if Jayce woke up to such a thing, he would definitely find it strange.

Leah heard the doctor speak to Mary in a hushed manner. No doubt he was giving instructions to her before retiring. Leah then heard commotion in the other room and knew that Jacob had probably returned. She sighed. It was time to go. At least for now.

"How's he doing?" Jacob asked as he joined her. The doctor was right behind him.

"He's breathing evenly and seems to be at rest. I suppose only time will tell the full story. I only pray we might have a happy ending."

"Prayer is a good way to see that through," Dr. Cox said, smiling.

She held his gaze for a moment before getting to her feet. "I'll see you in the morning, then."

He seemed to sense Leah's reluctance to leave. "I assure you he'll sleep through the night. I gave him a heavy dose of medication."

"Come on, Leah. I'm starved. Let's get some supper."

They left the doctor to his business and headed to a restaurant they'd eaten at on several other occasions. The place had been called Lady Luck in the gold rush heyday, but now it seemed the lady had lost her fortune. The structure cried out for restoration and attention, while inside there appeared to be a moderate number of people willing to overlook her dilapidation.

Once they were seated for dinner and had placed their orders, Leah took the conversation back to when the nurse had interrupted them when she opened the examination-room door. She'd been unable to think of little else. "You said you talked to Jayce. I want to know about this."

Jacob's attention was fixed on a caribou steak. Unfortunately for him it was on the plate of the man at the next table. "I don't remember every word, Leah. I talked to him and asked him to leave you alone—not hurt you again."

"What did he say about that?"

Jacob shrugged. "He didn't understand. He thought you were being unreasonable—after all, it had been ten years."

"Time shouldn't matter."

"I told him as much. He said something about how young you were then and how he loved Alaska and intended to stay and explore and he figured we'd both be gone before long."

"I gave him no reason to believe that," Leah said, her anger mounting. No one made her feel more confused than Jayce Kincaid.

"And he figured he gave you no reason to believe there could be anything more than there was between the two of you."

"Of all the nerve. He made me think he cared," Leah said, crossing her arms. That familiar white-hot flame burned somewhere deep in her heart. "He knew how I felt. He had to have known."

"Maybe not," Jacob said, shaking his head. "He really seemed to be genuinely puzzled by your anger toward him."

"So now you're taking his side?" Leah questioned.

"I didn't know we needed to pick sides," Jacob countered. "Look, I came here to eat—not fight. Besides, I think Jayce—"

Leah got up from the table and threw down her napkin. "I have lost my appetite."

She stormed from the room, knowing even as she did so that her actions were childish. Jacob didn't deserve her wrath. Frankly, no one did. It was her fault entirely that she couldn't seem to put the past to rest.

"I don't understand," she muttered. "I don't know why this can't just pass from my heart and leave me alone."

The front door flew open easily as Leah fled the restaurant, ploughing headlong into a woman. "Oh, bother," Leah said, reaching out to keep the woman from toppling backward. "I'm so sorry."

"People here seem to make a habit of

running others over," the woman replied in a refined tone. "But I suppose there's no harm done."

It was then that Leah noticed the woman was white. The revelation seemed to hit the other woman at the same time.

The woman's attitude immediately changed. "You're white. How wonderful to see another white woman."

Leah steadied her emotions. "There are a few of us here in the territory."

"I wasn't entirely sure that was true." She extended her hand. "I'm Helaina Beecham."

"Leah Barringer." Leah was beginning to remember her reason for the rapid departure from the restaurant. She felt rather embarrassed by her escapade. "If you'll excuse me."

"Wait, please. Would you mind telling me . . . do you live here?" Helaina questioned.

"No. Actually I live in a village northeast of Nome. Up on the Bering Sea. We had to bring a wounded man to the doctor. What about you? You sound as though you're new to Nome."

"Indeed I am. I wasn't to be here at all, in fact. I was to join an exploration group in

Seattle, but I missed my boat. Then when I tried to catch up with them here, I was once again too late."

Leah frowned. "An exploration group?"

Helaina nodded and put a hand to her hat. "Goodness, is it on straight now?" she asked, pushing it toward the center of her head.

"Yes," Leah said nodding. "Are you by any chance part of the *Homestead* group?"

Helaina halted her adjustment and looked hard at Leah. It seemed her entire demeanor had changed. "Are you familiar with them?"

"Yes. Some. I know they are heading north to map out Arctic islands and study the geological findings. My brother was asked to join the group because he raises and handles dogs."

"I see." Helaina seemed to relax just a bit, but Leah could tell the woman was still rather stirred up about this news. "I wonder if I know your brother. Why isn't he with the *Homestead* now?"

"Jacob Barringer is his name. He's just inside if you'd like to meet him. We brought an injured man here to Nome. We were having dinner when I . . . well . . . it isn't important. I can introduce you to Jacob if you like."

"That would be wonderful," Helaina said, smiling. She smoothed her beautiful dress.

Leah couldn't take her eyes from the creation. "That's a lovely gown. I haven't seen anything like it in a long, long time, but I can't imagine it lasting long up here."

"Have you lived here long?"

"Yes. We've been up here for what seems forever. We came north during the Yukon gold rush. Our father had gold fever."

"How did you come to be in this part of the world if you were in the Yukon?"

"There were several things. Jacob took a job with the postal service, then later he went into business for himself. We run a small store in Last Chance, a small village on a creek by the same name. My brother also raises sled dogs and makes sleds."

"Seems like there wouldn't be too much demand for that kind of thing."

"Oh, but there is," Leah argued. "He's always selling dogs or trading them to the natives. People come from miles around— sometimes hundreds of miles, to buy his dogs. Then there are the exploration teams like yours. The folks from the *Karluk* came to us a few years back."

"That was a tragedy," Helaina said, showing some knowledge of the event. "I certainly hope *Homestead* does better. Surely this captain knows more about his surroundings and won't get his ship stuck in ice."

"Change happens fast up here. Storms, temperatures, animals—they all can come upon you without warning. I'm sure the captain of the *Karluk* did his best to keep his men safe."

"Well, if I recall correctly, the captain wasn't even with them at the end. He'd gone off to get help. Seems unusual to say the least."

"Sometimes we hear stories that don't line up with the truth. No matter what the captain's actions were, we cannot possibly understand all the details that led to that decision."

They seemed to have reached an impasse, but Helaina was unfazed. "So you mentioned coming north with your father. Is he here as well?"

Leah shook her head. "He died trying to reach the gold, but he had already found someone to care for us before heading up over the Chilkoot Pass. We were well cared for after his death. We eventually left the goldfields to settle in Ketchikan. My guardian's husband was part Tlingit, so he wanted to be around his people."

"I see," Helaina replied as though she were trying to put all the pieces together. "Well, I'm quite delighted to have run into you, Leah Barringer."

Leah smiled. "Well, I was the one doing the running, but no matter. Come on inside. I'll introduce you to Jacob. If you like, you can share dinner with us."

Chapter Eleven

Helaina had eaten at the Lucky Lady on many other occasions. She motioned to the waitress and ordered a small caribou steak dinner and hot coffee before following Leah to the table. The man seated opposite where she stood seemed the brooding sort. His tawny brown hair fell lazily across his forehead and from the look of his jaw, he hadn't seen a razor in at least a week. There was something familiar about him. When he raised his face, she knew exactly what it was.

"Helaina Beecham, my brother, Jacob Barringer," Leah introduced.

"We ran into each other earlier. Much as our encounter," Helaina said, offering her gloved hand. But Leah's brother was less than receptive. The steak on his plate seemed far more interesting at the moment.

"What's this about?" He looked to his sister rather than Helaina.

Leah took the chair she'd obviously occupied earlier, where Helaina noted that another plate of food awaited. With no other choice, she sat down between the brother and sister and waited for Leah to smooth the waters. She knew her earlier introduction to Jacob Barringer had been an abysmal failure, but given his standing and relationship to her manhunt, Helaina figured she should mend some fences.

"I apologize, Mr. Barringer, for my earlier behavior. I'm afraid the bad news I'd received regarding my ship took away my good manners."

"Helaina was asking about the *Homestead*."

"To what purpose?" Jacob asked, finally looking Helaina in the eye.

She saw in his expression that he wouldn't be easily impressed. The men in Nome had been falling all over themselves for her attention, but apparently not this man. "I'm to assist the cartographer," she told him flatly. "I was unable to catch up with the team in Seattle, and they advised me to come to Nome."

"Well, we just left that ship in Last Chance," Jacob said, turning his attention to a thick crusty loaf of bread. "They're heading to Kotzebue next."

"I wonder if there is any chance of you helping me in that matter."

Jacob shook his head. "None whatsoever."

"Jacob! I honestly don't know what's gotten into him. He doesn't usually act this way."

Leah's tone held admonishment, and Helaina couldn't help but wonder at the pair. Brother and sister they said, but it seemed odd that Leah Barringer should be unmarried and traveling with her brother. Then it dawned on her that they might be two of Jayce's cohorts.

The woman she'd spoken to earlier appeared with a platter of food and a steaming cup of black coffee. She put the plate in front of Helaina and then, still holding the cup, looked to Jacob. "Jacob, do you need anything else?" She smiled sweetly, revealing two missing bottom teeth.

"No, Sally, I'm fine," he said. "Good coffee."

Helaina looked to the woman. "Is that cup for me?"

The woman seemed startled to find the mug still in her hand. "Oh, sure, miss. Sorry about that." Helaina only faintly smiled and took the offered drink. Seeing that perhaps a change of subject was in order, Helaina waited for Sally to leave, then ventured a question.

"Leah, are you married?"

"No," the dark-haired woman said. "You?"

Helaina frowned. This wasn't going as easily as she had hoped. "I was. My husband died three years ago."

Leah winced. "I'm sorry."

Had Helaina not seen Leah with her dander up just moments ago, she might have thought her quite temperate, even quiet. But there was something that spoke of a hard, fighting side to this woman. Helaina had learned to read people well over the years, and she could see for herself that Leah Barringer was a woman with a wounded spirit. It was Jacob, however, who proved the real mystery. Usually she could charm her way out of any situation, but not this time.

"Widowhood has not been easy by any means," Helaina said, hoping to enlist Jacob's sympathy. "The days and nights are so different—so strange after sharing such close companionship." She lowered her head and pretended to dab at her eyes. "Robert was a wonderful man, and a murderer cut him down in the prime of his life. Killed my parents too."

"How awful," Leah said, pausing her fork in midair. "I'm so sorry."

Helaina straightened. "I have found the strength to go on. I've decided to use my education to make Robert proud. That's part of the reason I came here—in honor of Robert."

"Well, people come here for a great many things, Mrs. Beecham. I am sorry for your loss," Jacob said, his tone softer.

Helaina studied him carefully. "What of you, Mr. Barringer? Have you a wife and children?"

"No. I have neither." He cut into the steak again.

"So what brought you to Nome? Leah mentioned you came north during the Yukon gold rush. How did you get from there to here?"

Jacob put down his fork. "Mostly by boat," he answered dryly and grinned.

Helaina didn't care for his amusement at her expense, but she, too, smiled. "I suppose that would be only fitting since there is a great deal of water between here and there."

Leah chuckled. "Jacob, what has gotten into you?" She turned to Helaina. "He's probably worried about our friend."

"The man you brought to the doctor?" Helaina questioned.

Leah nodded and picked at her food. "He was also to have been on your expedition to the Arctic."

"Truly? And for what purpose?" Helaina leaned toward Jacob, hoping to gain his favor with her attention.

Jacob looked at her oddly for a moment. Helaina knew he was trying to guess her game.

"I can't really say what his job entailed. He asked me to come along and help with the dogs. I raise dogs—sled dogs. I was asked to join the expedition as their handler. I've lived on the Seward Peninsula for the last ten years, and I'm well suited to Arctic winters. I seriously doubt you can say the same. Even your manner of dress would suggest you have no knowledge of what it takes to be here in Alaska."

Helaina eased back in her chair. Her initial assessment of the man was correct—he was positively rude. "Well, I believe I do have what it takes. I've trained and studied the territory. I possess mapping skills and feel my company is generally well received."

"Be that as it may, you aren't going far in a flimsy gown like that," he said, pointing to her outfit.

Helaina stiffened. "I didn't expect to find a fashion expert in Nome."

Jacob laughed. "Hardly that. But I do know what works up here. Take the outfit Leah is wearing. She has on thick mukluks—solid, warm, native-made boots. They'll endure just about any terrain and temperature. Then there's the sealskin pants. They offer good warmth, especially when layered. Of course, it's nearly summer now so that's not quite so critical here, but it will be up north. The Arctic is cold, even in

June." He munched a piece of bread and pointed at Leah's top. "That's called a *kuspuk.* It's also native-made. It's put together like the heavy fur parkas, only it's made of cloth for summer."

"Jacob does have a point, even if he presents it in a rather hostile manner," Leah said, looking at Helaina. "If you don't have warmer clothes, I'm afraid you won't be able to endure the desperately low temperatures. Especially if you stay through the winter, as I was told some of the party plans to do."

"Well, I'm not one of them, but I do thank you . . . both." She looked first to Leah, then settled her gaze on Jacob. "I already have an Eskimo woman putting together an odd assortment of travel clothes for me. Although I did come north with boy's jeans and sturdy boots, as well as woolen shirts and heavy undergarments." She smiled, hoping her expression would mask the lie she'd just told regarding the seamstress.

"That will help a great deal. Especially when the seasons change again," Leah said.

"As I said," Helaina began, "I don't intend to stay on through the winter." She really wanted to talk about the injured man and the *Homestead* crew, and a sudden thought sent her in the right direction. "Unless, of course, the injured man—your friend—is the team cartographer. Then I might very well need to stay on and take his place."

"Jayce isn't a cartographer," Leah offered. "He's a geologist."

"Jayce Kincaid?" Helaina thought her heart might stop. "He's here in Nome?"

Leah nodded. "He was working with the dogs, along with Jacob. They got out of control and he suffered a bad wound. It's infected now, and the doctor is fighting to save his leg—and his life. Do you know him?"

Helaina pondered the news for a moment. "Yes." She realized she had momentarily forgot herself. "Well, that is, I know *of* him. I've been told about him."

"You know of him?" Leah asked.

Helaina didn't want to make them suspicious. "Yes, through the exploration association. I've not met him personally, you understand."

This seemed to satisfy the woman. "He's very passionate about Alaska and learning more of what she has to offer," Leah replied. "He's been up here for many years."

"But he's ill now? Maybe even dying?" Helaina hoped her tone betrayed a reasonable amount of worry.

"He's strong as an ox. I'm sure he'll pull through," Jacob replied in a rather clipped tone. "Besides, Dr. Cox knows his medicine well enough. If he can't do the job, I'm sure he'll send Jayce to the hospital or even to Seattle."

The situation was sounding better all the time. Helaina made a pretense at eating but found she was no longer hungry. Jayce Kincaid was right under her nose—and with very little coaxing, she could no doubt convince Dr. Cox to send him to Seattle. Her journey of woes had finally come to an end.

Leah watched the beautiful woman as she ate and wondered at the relationship she shared with Jayce. It almost seemed that she might be lying about knowing him—like maybe she didn't want Leah to know how well acquainted they truly were. She'd stammered over her answer, after all. But Leah tried to push away such thoughts. She didn't want to feel this way. She cared deeply about Jayce, and if someone else cared about his well-being, then she shouldn't be jealous. Especially now that Jayce was so desperately ill.

Leah couldn't put the matter from her mind, however. Helaina Beecham was a beautiful woman, and no doubt she'd treat Jayce with great kindness and a gentle spirit. *Unlike me,* Leah thought.

She considered the way she'd treated Jayce—how she'd done nothing to be kind or friendly toward him. *Why did I act that way? Why didn't I just put the past behind us and start fresh?* She picked at her food, not really tasting any of it.

All through the dinner—in fact, ever since setting out for Nome—Leah had been dealing with a bevy of emotions. Guilt was right there at the top of the list, but now Helaina Beecham had stirred up one more: jealousy. What if there was something more between her and Jayce, but Helaina wanted to keep it a secret? Leah pondered that idea for several minutes.

"When will Jayce be up to having visitors?"

Leah swallowed the bread in her mouth and felt it stick in her throat. Was this woman somehow romantically linked with Jayce? Surely not, for she'd just talked of her departed husband.

Jacob shrugged and pushed his empty plate back. "I guess you'll have to ask the doctor tomorrow. I doubt he'll want Jayce having too much company right away."

"I'm sure you're right, Mr. Barringer," Helaina smiled at Jacob. "I'm equally convinced, however, that people heal faster when they know there are others around who care. Besides, if Jayce isn't improving—if he needs more attention than what he can get here in Nome—I, for one, would be happy to see him through to Seattle. We don't want him to die."

Leah felt her food become an uncomfortable lump in her stomach. "You are a very kind woman, Mrs. Beecham." She followed her brother's example and pushed back her plate. She could see that Jacob was anxious to leave, and frankly, she was feeling more and more driven to check on Jayce—maybe even talk to him and beg his forgiveness for the way she'd acted.

Leah extended her hand. "It was nice to meet you, Mrs. Beecham, but I'm afraid we need to be going. It's been a long day and we're both quite tired." Leah and Jacob stood. Jacob fished out a five-dollar bill and tossed it on the table.

Helaina surprised Leah by getting to her feet. "Are you staying at the hotel?" She opened her small purse and left money by her coffee cup to pay for her meal.

"Yes," Leah answered. "I think so." She looked to her brother.

"Yes, we're staying there. But just tonight. Why?"

Helaina seemed surprised. "Are you heading back so soon? What of Jayce?"

"We aren't heading back just yet," Jacob said, heading for the door. "Hotels are for the rich. We'll camp down by the boats with our friends after tonight. We're just sticking close for now, in case . . . well, you know."

Leah cringed at the thought that Jayce might die without her making peace. She longed to tell him that she was sorry for the anger—sorry for the bitter way in which she'd acted. What if Jayce died and the last thing he could remember about her was how poorly she had treated him?

Ayoona thought Leah should just tell Jayce how she felt, but now she wondered if she'd ever get the chance. *I've been a fool, acting like a spoiled child. Why didn't I just let the past go and smooth things over with Jayce? I'm a grown woman, I should have known better.*

"I find that I'm quite exhausted. If you don't mind, I'd like to walk back to the hotel with you. I realize it's just a short distance," Helaina said, smiling, "but one can never be too careful." She headed for the door without waiting for them.

Leah leaned toward her brother and whispered. "Jacob, why don't you go ahead and walk Mrs. Beecham to the hotel. I'm going to go check on Jayce."

"But it's late," Jacob said, looking at the clock near the door. "It's nearly nine."

"The doctor said they'd be sitting with him throughout the night. I'll just slip in and check on him. You can come for me after you walk Mrs. Beecham to the hotel. I'll sleep better once I know things are going well."

Jacob nodded, his expression softening. "You did a good job, Leah. You can't berate yourself for lack of skills you've never been trained in. If Jayce doesn't make it, it won't be your fault."

Leah nodded very slowly. "I know . . . at least I keep telling myself that very thing."

Jacob and Leah walked out of the restaurant and joined Helaina. "I won't be long," Leah said, and then turned to Helaina. "Jacob will see you to the hotel. I'm going to check on Jayce."

"Well . . . I could come too," Helaina said, seeming suddenly quite excited.

"No, that's all right. You said you were exhausted, and I wouldn't want to cause Jayce too much excitement—in case he's awake."

Helaina opened her mouth to protest, but Jacob took hold of her elbow. "Come along, Mrs. Beecham. I want to get to bed sometime tonight."

Leah thought Helaina seemed quite upset by this turn of events. *No doubt she has some secret interest in him,* Leah thought. *She probably knows him much better than she's conveying.* A million unkind thoughts coursed through Leah's mind.

"She's young and beautiful," Leah muttered. "She's refined and obviously wealthy, given the tip she left Sally just now."

Leah looked to the sky. *Lord, why does this have to be so hard?* With the sun still lighting her way, Leah couldn't even shed a few secret tears. *Help me, Father. Help me to give this all to you.*

Mary greeted Leah at the door. "Come in. He does well."

"Is the fever down?" Leah asked.

"Not so much, but he rest good."

"Can I see him for just a moment?"

"Sure. He won't hear you, though. Dr. Cox give him more medicine. He say the sleep good for him."

Leah nodded. "I know it will be for the best. And I don't need for him to hear me."

Mary led her into the small room where Jayce slept. "You stay as long as you like. I be right here." She pointed back the way they'd come in.

Leah knelt down beside the low bed. She put her hand to Jayce's brow and smiled. The fever was less—she was sure of it. Reaching for his hand, she held it to her cheek.

"Jayce, you must get well. You must."

His rough fingers against her face gave Leah a sense of well-being. "I'm sorry for the way I've behaved. Just when I think I can let go of the past and control my heart, something happens and I act in a way I regret. I don't mean to hurt you with my bitter heart, but I've suffered so long in silence."

She looked at his pale face. Dark circles seemed to engulf his eyes. *Such lovely eyes too,* she thought. "I once loved you with all of my heart, Jayce. And I love you still . . . but I know it's not to be. I'm thirty years old, and I'll never love anyone as I've loved you." She pressed a kiss against his fingers, then gently placed his hand back at his side.

"I know it's too late for us. Your heart is somewhere else—with someone else. But I just needed to tell you that I am sorry." Sadness washed over her, for the moment seemed so final. She was saying good-bye to a dream. A dream she'd held on to for over a decade.

Jacob was waiting outside for her when Leah exited the doctor's place. He immediately saw tears on her face and asked, "He isn't . . . he didn't . . ."

"No, he's not dead. Actually, he's better. I was just . . . well . . . letting go of him."

Jacob looked at her oddly. "Women are strange creatures."

"You call me strange?" she questioned. "You were nothing but odd this evening. You were downright rude to Mrs. Beecham when she asked for help. What was that all about?"

"I had an encounter with her earlier—at the hotel. She was obnoxious and uppity. Yet at the table tonight she seemed all roses and sunshine. I think she's up to something. There's something about her that just doesn't set well with me."

"What if you're wrong? She seemed nice enough, and she's only trying to get to the job she pledged to do." Leah tried hard not to accuse Helaina of anything out of line.

"If she cares so much about that job," Jacob said, shaking his head, "then why was she so eager to volunteer her time to take Jayce to Seattle?"

Chapter Twelve

Helaina hardly slept a wink that night. After tossing and turning for hours, she gave up on any real sleep and got up to rethink her strategy. Although she'd nearly blown her cover by succumbing to anger, Helaina felt confident her mission was safe. The Barringer man didn't like her or trust her, and she feared he wouldn't be persuaded by good works or good looks. She had known men like that, and they were always a difficult thing to factor into any investigation. She would have to be cautious with him.

Leah, on the other hand, obviously cared too much about Jayce Kincaid. In fact,

Helaina was certain that Leah was in love with him. The woman went from weepy one moment to dreamy-eyed the next. Helaina had seen that kind of nonsense as well—especially with weak-minded women. Leah probably had no idea who she was dealing with, Helaina surmised. Men like Kincaid were powerful manipulators with the right women. Helaina could probably use Leah's attraction to her advantage, however. Women in love enjoyed talking about the object of their affections. Perhaps Leah could lend information that might tie Kincaid to other crimes.

But whether Leah cooperated or not, it didn't matter. Jayce would soon be back in custody and headed to the gallows. *Let her love him, but let her stay out of my way.*

Helaina paced the room and tried to imagine a scenario where she could get Jayce back to Seattle with the least amount of resistance. She wondered if her best choice wasn't to bribe the good doctor. At least that way she could arrange to have the Pinkerton men ready to arrest him, and then her job would be done.

"Dr. Cox would do anything I ask. I'm sure of it."

She went to her wrinkled traveling clothes to assess their condition. They were hopeless, but so was the dress she'd worn the night before. She would have to ask Dr. Cox if there was a laundress in town. She considered the storekeeper's admonition to get a native woman to make new clothes. *If I'd had to go all the way to the Arctic to find Kincaid, I would have done just that. But now that the Barringers have brought him to Nome, I won't need anything more than a ticket back to Seattle.* She smiled at the thought.

The thought of Jacob Barringer, however, made her uneasy. The man acted as though he knew who she was and what she was about. She also worried that he would go rushing to Jayce Kincaid and warn him of the strange woman from Washington, D.C.

Taking off her robe, Helaina quickly slipped into her blouse and skirt. *Perhaps Jacob Barringer is also a criminal.* The thought came amidst a dozen other suggestions. *If he's a criminal and suspects that I might be trouble to him, there's no telling what might happen.* But there was no easy way to find out if Jacob was a criminal. To use any kind of communications with Washington would surely give away her position.

So she turned her thoughts away from the Barringers and considered how she might see to Jayce's transfer to Seattle.

"I can tell Dr. Cox that I've received word from the exploration association," she murmured. "I can tell him that they want to personally oversee and pay for Jayce Kincaid's recovery and that I'm to accompany him to Seattle. That's still my best choice. It's the most beneficial for all concerned."

She continued doing up her buttons, wondering just how she might best approach Dr. Cox. It was always possible that he would say no to moving his patient—especially if that man's injuries were too grave for travel. Perhaps she could suggest he accompany them to Seattle. She could tell him that it was her hope they might get to know each other better, in more favorable surroundings. Maybe she could ask him to give her a couple of weeks in order to get to know him, as she reconsidered his proposal.

Thinking of the funny little doctor, Helaina sighed. He had shown her nothing but kindness. It would be cruel to give pretense to feelings that didn't exist. Helaina sat down and shook her head. She'd never worried about such things prior to this moment.

"What's happening to me? I don't even feel like myself anymore. I used to be competent and capable, but since leaving Washington, D.C., nothing has gone right. I can't even think clearly. But why?"

Her state of mind reminded Helaina of the days just after she'd lost her parents and Robert. Nothing had made sense. She had been incapable of making decisions and choices, and all because of the shock she'd experienced. She knew at times like this her housekeeper would tell her to turn to God, but Helaina had no time or interest in that. What would God do about it? If He cared so much about goodness and mercy, then why wasn't Jayce Kincaid swinging from a gallows?

———

Jayce opened his eyes and stared blankly at the ceiling overhead. *Where am I?* He fought against the thick cloud of confusion in his head. *Why do I feel so lousy?*

He tried to turn and only then did the red-hot pain in his leg remind him of what had happened. There had been a problem with the dogs. He could barely remember it, as if it had happened in his childhood instead of only . . . when? How long had he been ill?

"I see you're awake," a man said, coming to stand beside Jayce's bed.

"Where am I?"

"Nome. Your friends brought you here, and just in time, I'd say. I believe you'll recover well, but your wounds were quite deep."

Jayce tried to sit up, and the doctor quickly reached out to stop him. "I'd rather you lie flat. It will help the circulation of blood. That leg needs ample blood to stay healthy. I'd hate for you to lose it."

"Lose my leg?" Jayce asked, his eyes widening. "What's going on?"

"Apparently you were in the middle of a group of ill-tempered dogs. They mangled your right thigh. Had it not been for your friends, especially the woman, you probably would have died."

"Leah," Jayce breathed her name. He'd been dreaming about her. She had come to him in the night . . .

"Yes, that's right. Leah Barringer. She was

here to check on you last night and again this morning. She's been quite worried."

So she has been here. Jayce remembered her touch—at least he thought he did. Had he honestly known her presence, or had it all been a dream?

"So how am I doing, Doc?" he finally asked, pushing aside the memories of Leah.

"It's really too early to tell. The infection needs to clear and healing begin before I can be sure of where we go from here. These things take time."

"How much time? I was supposed to go north with a team of scientists. We were going to map islands in the Arctic."

"Yes, I heard all about your quest. I even met another member of your team. A Mrs. Beecham. She's trying desperately to make her way north—missed her boat, you know."

"Mrs. Beecham." Jayce tried the name. He'd been told there was to be a woman to assist the cartographer. This must be her.

"Are you in much pain?" the doctor asked as he pushed back the covers.

"If I move the leg, it feels like it's on fire," Jayce admitted.

"That's to be expected. I can give you

something for the pain, but it will make you sleep."

Jayce shook his head. "I'd rather clear my mind and stay awake. If it gets too bad, I'll let you know. By the way, where are my friends?"

"They should be here soon. They were already here, but I sent them on to breakfast. I'll bring them back to see you as soon as they arrive. Meanwhile, are you hungry?"

"I could stand something in my stomach," Jayce admitted. He couldn't remember the last time he'd eaten.

"Good. I'll have Mary make you something." He walked quickly from the room, not even bothering to examine Jayce more thoroughly. He paused at the door, however. "I hate to be the bearer of bad news, but I think you must put aside any thought of going north. You will need the next few months to recover, and travel to such a remote and harsh climate would only irritate your condition. Should you get north and have the leg fail you or the blood poisoning return, you'd be sentencing yourself to death." With that he left.

Jayce sighed. Nothing was working out like he'd planned. He wouldn't have another chance to be a part of an exploration team until next year—at least if he followed the doctor's orders. He'd had high hopes of what this expedition might accomplish, and now he wouldn't be there. He balled his hands into fists and smacked them against the mattress, causing pain to shoot down his leg. He winced and gritted his teeth to keep from crying out in pain.

A woman's voice sounded from somewhere in the doctor's house. Jayce strained to listen, and when he heard the woman mention his name, Jayce figured it must be Leah; there was no other woman who knew about him being here. He continued to listen and heard something mentioned about Seattle.

Dr. Cox's voice carried much better. "There's no need to rush the man to Seattle. If I move him now it would be detrimental."

The woman spoke again, but Jayce could only pick up that this was what someone wanted—that they were concerned with Jayce's welfare. But who was she talking about?

He felt helpless to figure it all out and waited, thinking they would come to the room and the woman would reveal herself. By now he was convinced it wasn't Leah Barringer.

But the woman didn't come. Instead, he heard her tell the doctor in a rather agitated tone that he should reconsider what was in his own best interests. It almost sounded like a threat, but that didn't make any sense.

"Why should it make sense?" Jayce murmured. "Nothing else does." He thought about how God was in control, yet with all his plans in disarray, he felt overwhelmed with questions.

Lord, he prayed, *I don't understand any of this. Why would you bring me this far, only to let me be incapacitated? I had a job to do—a job I wanted very much to do—and now that isn't going to happen. I don't understand why things have fallen apart.*

And then without warning a thought came to mind. If he couldn't go north to the Arctic, it might behoove him to go north to Last Chance Creek. There with Leah and Jacob he could spend time learning how to handle the dogs more skillfully. He could also learn more about Leah—maybe even learn enough to tell whether the things he heard her say in his dreams were, in fact, the truth of her heart.

He smiled for the first time. Maybe God had orchestrated all of this in order to give him a chance to make things right with Leah.

———

Jacob was not pleased to look up and find Helaina Beecham entering the restaurant. Only moments ago he'd left Leah with Jayce; she claimed she wasn't hungry and planned to stay and help Jayce in any way she could. Meanwhile, Jacob had hoped for some quiet time with his Bible, but now it didn't look like that was going to happen.

"Hello, Mr. Barringer," Helaina said in a silky tone.

Jacob felt his defenses immediately go into place. She rubbed him wrong—even in her tone of voice. "Mrs. Beecham."

"I wonder if I might join you?"

"I'd rather you didn't. I'd like some time alone."

She frowned and nodded toward the open Bible. "To read that?"

He heard the disdain in her voice. "Yes. Do you have a problem with that?"

"I just find that intelligent men need not lean on superstitions and traditions in order to make their way through life."

"Then we finally agree on something," Jacob replied. He looked at her hard, challenging her to say something more.

"I was wondering how Mr. Kincaid was doing this morning."

"He's doing better. You could go to the doctor's office just a couple of doors down and find out all the details for yourself. For now, however, you'll need to excuse me."

He turned his attention back to the Bible, aware she had not turned to go. What was it with this woman, anyway? Why didn't she just leave him alone? Slowly, he lifted his head to find her watching him. "What is it now?"

"I just wondered what you could possibly find so fascinating about that book. I mean, most of the people I've known who've relied upon the Christian religion were generally weak-willed and rather on the dim-witted side. You strike me as neither one."

"Well, thank you. I think that's the nicest thing you've said to me."

"I haven't intentionally said anything that

wasn't nice," Helaina argued. "I'm sorry if you believed otherwise."

Jacob put his elbow on the table and leaned against it. "What do you want? I mean, I've asked you to leave me alone. I've showed you clearly that I'm not interested in conversation. Is it just that I'm not acting like the rest of the men in this town—falling all over myself to get your attention? Is that what makes me so appealing?"

"I assure you, Mr. Barringer, you are far from appealing to me."

"Good. So leave me alone." He refocused his attention on the Bible.

"I thought Christians were commanded to share their faith."

He sighed and looked up again. "What would you like for me to share?"

She smiled rather coquettishly. "Everything." She pulled out the chair. "I have nowhere to be."

Jacob wasn't about to play this game. He knew she had no real interest in God's Word or God himself. He closed the Bible and stood. "We're all sinners. The penalty for that is death. Jesus came to take that penalty for us. If we accept Him and turn from our sins, we can have eternal life. If we refuse Him, hell is our eternal destination. Would you like to make your peace with God?"

Helaina seemed rather taken aback by all of this. "No, I'm not interested in that, but . . ."

"I've shared the Gospel with you, Mrs. Beecham. You've rejected it, and now I take my leave."

"But aren't you supposed to try to persuade me?" she asked, regaining her composure. She smiled rather alluringly.

"I'll let that be the job of the Holy Spirit," Jacob said. "He's got a much better chance of breaking through your façades than do I."

He left her with that. She was clearly playing a game with him, and he refused to be a part of whatever it was she was trying to accomplish. He walked slowly back to the doctor's office, all the while trying to figure out what Helaina Beecham was doing in Nome. He knew she was to have been a part of the exploration north, but there didn't seem to be any real concern about getting north—not like there had supposedly been when she'd initially met him and Leah.

Jacob opened the door to the doctor's. Mary was there to greet him. "How you do?" she asked.

"I do fine," Jacob said with a smile. "Is Leah still visiting our patient?"

"She help him shave. He not very happy about staying in bed."

"I can imagine. Would you mind if I sit here and read?" he asked, holding up his Bible.

"You read Bible?"

"I do. I love God's Word."

Her smile nearly doubled in size. "I love God's Word too. Only I not read good."

"You should get someone to teach you," Jacob suggested.

"I not go to school. I too old."

"You're never too old to learn," Jacob countered. "There are probably all sorts of people who could teach you to read better. You should start asking at church."

"I do that," Mary replied. "Now I tell your sister you here."

Jacob nodded and settled himself down with the Bible. He read no more than two verses when Leah appeared. "He's doing much better. The leg is already showing signs of healing. Isn't that amazing?"

"And all because something that wasn't supposed to be there was taken out. Seems there are a lot of times in life where you can benefit by removing the offending bit of debris."

Leah looked at him funny. "You're certainly moody today. What's going on?"

Jacob shrugged. "I can't really say. I will say this, however. I've been trying to read the same passage of Scripture for over half an hour. It would sure be nice to get through it."

"You needn't worry that I'll keep you," Leah said, leaning in to kiss her brother on the cheek. "Jayce needs me and you don't. I'll go where I'm needed."

Jacob nodded and waited until she was gone before trying once again to read his Bible. He had just reread the passage from moments ago when Dr. Cox returned from a house call.

"Well, I'm sure you know your friend is doing much better."

"I did hear that," Jacob replied. "Thanks to your sharp eyes and skilled hands, I'd say our friend has a fighting chance."

"Yes, so long as we keep him here instead of sending him off to Seattle."

"Seattle? Why would we need to send him there?"

The doctor handed Mary his bag and turned to Jacob. "Well, according to Mrs. Beecham, that's what the exploration association wishes for her to do. She received word—a telegram, I believe—to have Jayce moved to a hospital in Seattle. I told her I believed it to be a bad idea, however. I have no intention of moving an injured man—at least not at this point of his recovery."

Jacob wondered why Helaina would suggest such a thing. The exploration association had no reason to move Jayce—they had to know the ship was well to the north. "I'm paying for his care, and so long as he improves, I'd just as soon keep him here," Jacob said, sensing that something just wasn't right about the entire matter.

The doctor nodded. "That was my thought exactly."

He left Jacob to sit and wonder at the situation. Mrs. Beecham was definitely up to something, and he knew this for two reasons: One, she acted like a woman with a secret. And two, there was no way anyone could have gotten word to her in Nome re-

garding Jayce's situation. There hadn't
been any delivery of mail, and he'd learned
only that morning that the telegraph had
been inoperable for two days.

Chapter Thirteen

Leah was encouraged by Jayce's recovery, despite his frustration. He was still in a great deal of pain anytime he tried to exercise the leg, but the doctor also reminded him that it had only been two and half weeks since the attack.

Leah had also been happy when Jacob made the decision to send the other villagers back to Last Chance Creek with supplies, allowing him and Leah to stay indefinitely. Kimik had promised to get Oopick to run the store in their absence, and that settled the matter. Mail and other supplies could now be had via the revenue cutter

that regularly headed as far north as Point
Hope. The village wouldn't suffer for the
Barringers' delay with that faithful ship on
duty.

Remaining in Nome had comforted Leah,
and in return for her willingness to help in
his office, Dr. Cox had offered a small room
to her. Leah jumped at the chance to sleep
in a real bed rather than in a tent. Jacob had
been a little harder to convince. Still, in the
end, he had come around to her way of
thinking. When he made himself useful in
collecting driftwood and cutting firewood,
Dr. Cox told him he could sleep in the same
room where Jayce recovered. He would
have to vacate, of course, should they need
the bed for medical reasons, but so far that
hadn't been a problem.

"Leah!"

Leah looked up to find Helaina Beecham
heading her way. Helaina crossed the narrow dirt street, dressed in native style, much
to Leah's surprise. "You look very proper,"
she told the woman.

"I should hope it would meet with your
brother's critical eye for fashion."

"He only said what he did because he
worried you'd die up north," Leah said

frankly. "The Arctic is not forgiving. Which reminds me, we hadn't seen you in some time and figured you'd found a way to reach your ship."

Helaina shook her head. "I received word from the association that Jayce and I were to head to Seattle. They had hoped for us to be there by now, but the doctor didn't feel Jayce could travel."

"He's doing much better now, but I don't think he knows about the association requesting him to come south." Leah felt a tightening in her chest, noting again Helaina's beauty. Her straight blond hair looked quite lovely in the simple way Helaina had tied it back, and her blue eyes seemed a perfect compliment to her peach-colored complexion.

". . . but of course that depends on how well you know him."

Leah realized she hadn't heard what Helaina had just said. "I'm sorry . . . what did you say?"

Helaina laughed. "I was hoping you might help me persuade Jayce to come with me to Seattle. I was wondering how well you knew him."

Leah tried not to let the question bother

her, but it did. "I've known Jayce for over ten years. He stayed with my family for a time in Ketchikan."

"Does he trust you to be honest with him . . . to tell him what would be best for him?"

This question made Leah smile. "No one tells Jayce Kincaid what's best for him— he's a free thinker. He does what he thinks is right and rarely concerns himself with how it will affect anyone else."

"But then most men are that way," Helaina said with a coy smile, "until a woman changes his mind, of course."

Leah said nothing. She'd never had any power over Jayce Kincaid, but it was hard to explain this to the Beecham woman without getting into some of the most embarrassing moments of Leah's life. And she wasn't about to go down that path.

"Well, here's what makes this most critical," Helaina continued. "The exploration association has decided to send a second team north. They believe if they get them in motion immediately, we can be on our way by July. It would mean remaining in the north, but now that I have my Eskimo wardrobe, I don't even mind that idea."

Leah still didn't understand the urgency. "So why can't they pick you up here in Nome? No doubt they will stop for supplies and workers to help on the trip. They could surely pick the two of you up and head out from here. They might even want Jacob and his dogs."

"That would work," Helaina said rather hesitantly, "except for the fact . . . that . . . well, they would like Jayce to hand select the final members of the team. They trust his knowledge of Alaska."

"They should—he knows it better than most people. He's scarcely been out of the territory over the last ten years."

Helaina frowned. "Surely that's not true. I've heard from other sources that he was quite often back east."

Leah shrugged. "He told me he spent some time in Vancouver, but I know nothing about him being back east. In fact, it seems Jacob told me that Jayce had been working at something in the interior of the territory prior to going to Vancouver. He loves this land with such a passion that any person would be hard-pressed to come between him and Alaska."

Helaina was silent, almost appearing to

take offense to Leah's words. Perhaps Helaina knew Jayce much better than she'd let on. Maybe she was in love with him and had planned to convince him to leave the land and settle in the States. The aching returned to Leah's heart. *Lord, please keep me strong. Please don't let this hurt me more.*

"I'm headed back to the doctor's office right now. I've been helping out there in exchange for a room. You could come with me and talk to Jayce yourself. Perhaps if you share this good news of how his superiors want him to pick the team, he would be persuaded to come with you."

Helaina nodded. "I have wanted to visit with him. I've held off, however. I wanted him to feel fully recovered before attempting to convince him to leave. I wouldn't want to be the reason for a relapse."

"Then come along. I'm done with my shopping." Leah held up a small canvas bag. "We might as well see how he's feeling."

"But you will try to talk to him—after I'm gone?" Helaina asked. "Try to help him see how needed he is on this project."

"I can try," Leah said half-heartedly, "but I doubt he'll give my words any weight."

———

Leah and the doctor told Jayce that he was improving with each passing day. His restlessness at being unable to walk long distances caused him to be grumpy, however. The doctor had assured him the stiffness and aching would pass. The wound had been quite deep, after all, and Jayce was fortunate to have a leg to stand on. But even this explanation didn't still the anxiety inside Jayce. He wanted to be back on his own—he wanted to be away from Nome.

"I've brought someone to see you," Leah announced. A woman came in beside her and waited for the introduction. "It's Helaina . . . Helaina Beecham, your teammate."

"My teammate?" Jayce questioned.

"I was to be the assistant cartographer on the *Homestead* expedition," Helaina announced. She moved forward and extended her hand. "Glad to finally meet you. I heard of your injuries when you first arrived but have hesitated to burden you with company."

"I'm grateful for that," Jayce said, giving her hand a brief shake. She looked like a frail thing, much too fragile for life in the north. He doubted if she weighed more than one hundred pounds and surely she wasn't any taller than five foot. And he surmised all of this despite the fact that she wore a loose-fitting native kuspuk and denim pants.

"I heard that your injury was considerable," Helaina continued. "I am sorry for that. Leah tells me that you met your fate while dealing with her brother's sled dogs."

Jayce eyed her warily. Jacob had already warned him about the woman. He was glad to have this advantage, certain that Mrs. Beecham knew nothing of their suspicions. Jacob hadn't even told Leah, for fear that she might let something slip. Jayce watched her for a moment more before finally answering her.

"I was working with the dogs that were to be taken on the expedition. They were spooked, and I, unfortunately, was a stranger in a bad position."

"Well, you appear to have recovered considerably, and that is why I'm here today. The exploration association would like for you to come to Seattle. We are both to travel there."

"For what purpose?" This was exactly the information Jacob had shared. They had both mulled it over for some time, trying to reason what the woman might be about. There was no way she had received word via telegraph at the time she claimed, and there hadn't been time for the mail to reach her from Seattle.

Helaina smiled sweetly and turned to Leah. "Might I have a chair? This will take a little time."

Leah nodded and left to find Helaina something to sit on. When she returned with a wooden chair from the waiting room, Helaina nodded her approval. "Perfect. Now, where was I?" she asked as she took her seat.

"You were about to tell me why I need to go to Seattle."

"Well, here is the wonderful news," Helaina said, looking to Leah as if for confirmation. "There is to be a second expedition. It will leave as soon as the remaining members of the team are handpicked by you."

"By me? Why me?" He looked to Leah. She seemed upset by all of this yet held her tongue, her distress evident in the way she worried the cuff of her sleeve. Had the Beecham woman somehow threatened her or coerced her to remain silent?

"You are the most knowledgeable about the lay of the land. This team will be staying on through the winter," Helaina explained.

Jayce rubbed his stubbled chin. "I have no desire to stay in the Arctic through the winter. I've already promised Jacob to remain with him in Last Chance Creek and practice working with the dogs. We have several important trips already planned."

He could see this news didn't sit well with Helaina, but at the same time he thought a spark of something flared in Leah's eyes. Could it be happiness at this announcement?

"But, Mr. Kincaid, this is a chance of a lifetime. You would be able to handpick the remaining team. The association values your opinion and believes you to be the most capable person to make these decisions."

"I'm sorry, but you must be mistaken," Jayce said, shaking his head. "I have no experience in such matters. They would never ask this of me."

"You're just overly modest, Mr. Kincaid. Your reputation precedes you."

"Truly? And where did you hear of me, Mrs. Beecham?"

Helaina seemed momentarily surprised by this. She quickly recovered, however. "From the association, of course. As well as others. My own brother had heard of you, in fact. He thought you . . . well . . . ingenious."

"I cannot imagine why. I've done nothing to merit such compliments." Jayce made a pretense at struggling to sit up better in the bed. Leah immediately came to his side to assist him. He liked the way she fussed over him and the way her hair smelled of lavender.

"You shouldn't wear yourself out, Jayce. If this is too much, we can go."

"Nonsense. I'm doing quite well. Jacob will be here soon to help me with my walk, in fact." He saw Helaina's mouth tighten at the mention of Leah's brother.

"I am glad that we had this opportunity to chat, Mrs. Beecham. I would be most grateful if you would send my regrets to the association and let them know that I won't be joining them for the second expedition. It might be possible that I could come along next year. But the doctor assures me I would be risking my life to try anything so foolhardy this year."

"I see." Her tone betrayed an obvious displeasure. "I suppose there is nothing I can say to change your mind?"

"Nothing."

"Even if I told you the second expedition would be called off if you refused to join?"

"I find that doubtful, Mrs. Beecham. The men who are funding and overseeing the Arctic exploration are not the type to put all of their eggs in one basket. Certainly not the basket of a lowly geologist. I know them well enough to state quite confidently that if they are planning a second expedition, it will go on without me. Geologists are easy to come by. I met quite a few when I worked in Vancouver for the last year."

"Vancouver?" Helaina asked. "Exactly when were you there?"

"Most of last year. I came north as far as I could get by ship in February, then relied on help from natives to get me to Nome." She frowned only more at this statement. Jayce couldn't quite figure it out. Why should that news upset her?

"You really should tell me sometime how you managed to work your way across Alaska in the dead of winter. I've heard it to be quite impossible."

"For a white woman, it might be, although I'm sure Leah could do it," Jayce replied with a smirk. "I find it hard to believe, for instance, that the exploration team accepted you. You're hardly cut out for living in the north. You're skin and bones. A good Arctic breeze would blow you over."

Helaina's face reddened at this. She clenched her hands together tightly, further amusing Jayce. "I assure you, I am quite strong and capable."

"You've been north before, then?"

She looked to Leah and then back to Jayce. "No, but . . ."

"You have experience in Arctic temperatures of fifty and sixty below zero?"

"No, but . . ."

"Then you probably have firsthand knowledge of winter survival skills?" He arched his brow and stared at her with an unyielding question to his look.

"Mr. Kincaid, I assure you I know very well how to take care of myself in any situation. I am not afraid to listen to the advice of others, but neither do I leave my choices to fate. I am well read on the explorations of other teams who have gone north and failed. I know what is needed and what is expected."

"Ah, but do you know what is unexpected?" He looked to Leah and winked. The action unnerved her completely and thoroughly amused Jayce.

Helaina had clearly had enough. "I will inform the association of your decision, Mr. Kincaid, but I wouldn't plan on being invited to join any future expeditions."

"It's no matter to me," Jayce lied. "I live here year-round. I don't need a sponsorship to study the vast northern wilderness. I make that my life. Unlike some people who must have badgered the association into taking them on this trip, they came to me. They courted and wooed me to join them, much as a man might do when seeking to entice a woman. If they choose not to invite me to another event, I will not be brokenhearted."

Just then Jacob walked through the door. He took one look at Helaina and frowned. "What's she doing here?"

"She came to persuade me to join her in

Seattle. It seems there is to be another expedition north. They are putting together a team and want me to handpick the men."

"That's quite an honor, Jayce. You going?" Jacob asked, as if he didn't already know the answer.

Jayce shook his head. "Nah, I couldn't be bothered. This leg is giving me too much trouble anyway. I'm sure heading home with you is the right choice."

Helaina squared her shoulders and lifted her chin ever so slightly. "Well, I should go send word that you will not be joining the team."

"You do that, Mrs. Beecham," Jayce said, moving gingerly to the edge of the bed. Leah reached out to help him once again. He looked up and smiled at her. "Ah, my pretty nurse has come to see me properly cared for."

Leah halted in midstep, almost as if she were afraid to touch him. Jayce thought her hands trembled as she moved forward to assist him. More and more, he was convinced that the past was not behind them, but rather, it had crept quite intricately into the present. And who could tell what that might hold for the future? Especially after he spent the winter living in close proximity to her.

"Come, Jacob. I'm ready for my run," Jayce said, laughing.

Chapter Fourteen

Helaina couldn't put the thought of Jayce Kincaid from her mind. Things he had said caused her grave confusion. First Leah had told her that Jayce had been in Alaska for many years, with no reason to go elsewhere. Then Jayce himself had said that he'd been in Alaska at the very time he had thrown her brother from a train outside of Washington, D.C. And the ease in which he made the statement indicated he was telling the truth. All the things Stanley had taught her to watch for when people were lying were clearly absent: Jayce looked her in the eye and never looked away, and he didn't stammer or hesitate even once when relating his story.

"But he had to be in Washington," she told herself. "Stanley didn't just throw himself from the train. And he knew Kincaid well enough to have his picture sketched out." Helaina took the picture from her purse and unfolded it. It was clearly Jayce Kincaid.

She spread the picture out on her bed, then gathered her other materials. Everything pointed to the fact that Leah and Jayce were lying. She knew Jayce had been in England from summer through Christmas of 1914. This had been confirmed by the men at the British Museum. He had stolen from them, then returned to the United States. But Jayce said he'd been working in Vancouver with the exploration association. That would be easy enough to prove or disprove.

Helaina continued to study her notes. In February, Jayce had nearly been apprehended by two agents. Instead, he had killed the men and left them bleeding in the streets. Then in April, Stanley had caught up with him again. Her brother had nearly met the same fate as his friends.

But Jayce said he had headed to Alaska

in February. He had gone by boat for as far as he could, then relied on dog sleds and native guides to get him to Nome. It just didn't make sense. Leah had told her at one point that Jayce had come to their village just prior to the eighteenth of May, but that he'd been in Nome for several weeks before that. It just didn't fit what Helaina knew to be true.

So exactly what was the truth about this situation?

There has to be an answer, Helaina thought. She feared that now it would be difficult, if not impossible, to get Jayce to Seattle. She knew she wouldn't find success in enticing him there, and the time for having Dr. Cox insist on such matters for health reasons was clearly behind them. No, short of drugging him and paying thugs to haul him off to some ship for her, Helaina was out of choices.

The other problem was trying to figure out what Jayce planned to do once his leg was completely healed. Would he stay in Nome or return to Vancouver? Or would he go back into the interior, as Leah suggested? Helaina would have to find out, and quickly, if she was to stay ahead of the mastermind.

She tossed the papers back into her large traveling bag and walked to the window. Looking out she could see part of the street. It was such a hopeless little town. Full of all sorts of unfulfilled pledges and dreams. She longed for home more than ever. New York or Washington—it didn't matter. Although at times like this when she was truly troubled, she always appreciated spending time with Mrs. Hayworth. She'd been a source of comfort and care for many years, and her calming presence seemed to reach deep into Helaina's soul. Still, Helaina was convinced that it couldn't be her faith in God that brought this about as much as familiarity.

Jacob Barringer believed in Christian philosophies, and he was anything but calming. In fact, he was quite an irritant. His smug, pompous attitude was enough to make Helaina want to check out his background for criminal activities. Maybe once she returned to Washington, D.C., she'd do exactly that. But first she had to deal with Jayce Kincaid.

She took up paper and pen and thought of the questions she would pose to the Canadian authorities. She needed to know if Jayce was wanted for other crimes during the past year. She would also need to check with the expedition headquarters and find out the truth of Jayce's employment with them. He claimed to have been there for some time; there was no doubt a record of that. Perhaps she could even learn if Kincaid was given over to long absences—which might explain how he could seemingly be in two places at once.

But even as she jotted down notes to herself, Helaina couldn't keep the image of Jacob Barringer from coming to mind. She would have to contact the Yukon and Alaskan authorities and learn about his past as well. No doubt there were things he would just as soon keep buried and hidden away. She smiled to herself and wrote several questions regarding Jacob.

Duty continued to call her back to her scribbled thoughts on Kincaid. At the top of her list was a question she underlined several times. If she could get an answer for it—she just might solve the puzzle.

How could Jayce Kincaid be two places at one time?

"I think you're right," Leah told Jacob as they finalized the shipping arrangements for a load of rice and coffee.

"Right about what?"

"Going to see Karen and Adrik. Despite your plans falling through, I don't think it should stop my trip to Ketchikan. Do you suppose you could get Oopick to continue running the store for a while? I know there will be a lot of work to do to store food for next winter, but perhaps if I promise to bring extra supplies when I return—maybe bring a few things they wouldn't normally have—it wouldn't be so bad."

"I figure there's nothing wrong with just opening the store once a week," her brother replied. "I mean, it's all well and fine to have it open daily when we're there, but I don't see that needs to be the way it is when we're gone. If Oopick only has to worry about doing business there once a week, then I can't see why it would interfere with her preparations for winter."

"That's true," Leah said, nodding. "I could probably stay a couple of months that way."

Jacob signed a paper offered him by the merchant, then turned to Leah with a big grin. "Now you're talking. You can have a great summer together. My only desire is that you'd be back by September. Would that work? I promised Anamiaq to help him with some trapping come winter."

"Of course. I could even be back sooner."

They walked away from the merchant and headed toward the shipping office. "September will be soon enough. Why don't you make your reservation now? Then you won't have to worry about it."

She grinned. "I wasn't intending to worry about it."

Jacob studied her for a moment and laughed. "Well, I guess given everything else you fret over, I figured you might rest easier if the matter was done and behind you."

Leah considered his words for a moment. "I'm trying hard to understand God's will for my life. I think sometimes I know exactly where He's leading, but other times things seem so obscure. Does that make any sense?"

"Of course it does. I often feel that way myself. I remember back to when we were children—the plans I had then, the dreams. I didn't see myself here, that's for sure. Ad-

venture was something our father craved—
not me. Yet here we are."

They began walking again, and Leah
couldn't help but ask, "What about Arctic
exploration? Are you still thinking you'd like
a chance at that?"

Jacob said nothing for several minutes,
just enough time to see them to their next
destination—the ticket office. "I guess I
wouldn't say no to the opportunity. It sure
intrigues me, so I guess there's more of our
father in me than I care to admit." He
grinned at her. "But . . . well . . . I really only
said yes this time because I felt the Lord
wanted me to be there for Jayce. His faith is
just growing—he hasn't really had another
man of God in his life. You know, someone
to share his faith and discuss Scriptures.
With Jayce laid up, we've had some great
times of study and prayer. Sometimes the
doctor even joins us."

Leah had no idea. "That's wonderful, Jacob."

"I see it all as part of God's plan. Jayce
wants more out of life—he needs more. I'm
convinced that what he longs for is a closer
understanding of who God is and what He
wants for his life."

Leah nodded. She knew exactly the meaning of that longing. "I'm glad you've helped him, Jacob."

"I'll tell you something else too." He paused, as if trying to think of the exact words he should say. "I think Jayce is just now coming to realize what he lost when he said no to you ten years ago. I think—and this is just my opinion—that he's sorry for that loss."

Leah thought her heart might skip a beat. She swallowed hard. Could Jacob be implying something more in his words? Could there be a way to reclaim those lost years?

"Why would you say that?" She looked in Jacob's eyes. There was no hint of teasing or exaggeration. His expression, to be honest, was quite encouraging.

"I think he's a smart man—smarter at least than he used to be," Jacob said, looking out at the water. "I know from our talks that he's more compassionate and caring than he was ten years ago. I credit God's touch on his life for that."

Jacob motioned toward the ticket office. "You going to get your ticket or just stand around out here talking?"

Leah wanted to tell him the ticket could

wait, but she didn't. Instead, she marched toward the office, contemplating whether Jayce would be upset to find she'd gone. Perhaps her absence would help him to put things in clear perspective. Maybe it would even give him reason to care.

———

"I can't say I'll be sorry to leave you, Doc," Jayce said, trying to walk without using his cane.

Dr. Cox chuckled. "I'll be sorry to lose you. You're taking the best assistant I've ever had—male or female." He looked to Leah and beamed a smile. "You are a very talented healer, Leah. You should get formal training."

"I'm a little old to be going back to school. Still, I hope the things I've learned here with you help me to help others," Leah replied.

Jayce took several solid steps. "Well, look at me, will you? I'm managing this pretty well, wouldn't you say?"

Leah laughed as Jayce gave a little hop. "You aren't yet up to running behind a sled, but I think once you give yourself a little more time, you'll be fit as the next man. By the time the snows come, you won't even remember this little diversion."

Jayce shook his head. "I'll remember it. I've learned my lesson about wading in to break up fighting dogs."

"So will you leave tomorrow?" the doctor asked.

"Yes. We've been gone long enough," Jacob declared.

"You're welcome in Last Chance anytime you'd like to come visit, Dr. Cox," Leah said, smiling. "I'm sure the people would be glad to welcome a real doctor."

Jacob headed for the door and opened it. "We'll be staying our last night at the hotel just up the street. If you have need of us— you know where to find us."

They parted company and headed to the hotel. Jayce focused on each step, careful not to step into a rut or sinkhole. The leg was much better, but it pained him. Still, he knew he'd probably have nothing more than a stump had it not been for Leah's attentiveness.

He stole a glance at her as she walked just slightly ahead of her brother. She radiated a kind of beauty that other women lacked. He knew confidently that this light came from within her soul. *How could I have been so cruel to her? How could I not have seen the genuineness of her heart?* Once again he regretted the choices he'd made ten years ago.

"I'm so glad to have found you," Helaina Beecham said, greeting the trio at the hotel.

Jayce nearly groaned aloud. What was this woman's attraction to him? She seemed unnaturally intent on keeping track of his health. She constantly asked the doctor about when he might be released and still talked of how she longed for him to join her in Seattle. But he didn't even know this woman.

"What do you need, Mrs. Beecham?" Jacob asked.

"Well, I need your help." She smiled, and Jayce couldn't help but feel that she was yet again up to something underhanded. He and Jacob had talked at length about who she was and why she had attached herself to the party.

Jacob pushed past her and motioned to Leah to go ahead. "I can't imagine that we have anything to offer, but let's go inside so that Jayce can sit, and then you can tell us all about it."

Once they were seated in the lobby, Helaina wasted little time before sharing her needs. "I'd like to come back to your village and learn how to handle the dogs. I've received word that although there will be no second expedition this year"—she looked to Jayce—"there will be another team coming up next year. I volunteered to learn how to handle the dogs and sleds, and the association has granted me several hundred dollars to see to purchases and such."

Jayce noted Jacob's look of annoyance and was surprised when he said, "I suppose we could squeeze in one more person. You will need to bring plenty of winter supplies, however. Once we're up there, I don't intend to be bringing passengers back to Nome."

"I don't mind at all. In fact, I have purchased several pieces from the natives. I have mukluks and sealskin pants, as well as a heavy parka and fur mittens." She seemed quite pleased with herself.

"I'm glad you're finally being reasonable," Jacob said.

"When do we leave?" Helaina asked.

"Tomorrow—midday," Jacob said. "You can sleep late. It'll probably be your last chance for a while."

"That sounds lovely. I'll cherish it." She got up to take her leave. "I'll see you all in the morning."

Leah had refrained from speaking until Helaina was gone. "I thought you wanted to be rid of her. Why did you say yes?"

Jacob and Jayce both leaned toward her at this point. "That woman is dangerous. She's clearly up to something—no good, if you ask me," Jacob said. "I figure it might be wise to keep an eye on her. If you have to have a bear in the house, you might as well determine where he sleeps. Or where she sleeps, in this case. Mrs. Beecham has an unnatural interest in our party—especially in Jayce. We need to know why. Otherwise she could prove to be more dangerous than any of us suspect."

"Well, you are full of surprises," Leah said, shaking her head.

Jayce laughed and eased back into his chair feeling quite satisfied. "You don't know the half of it."

Chapter Fifteen

Leah suppressed a yawn as she prepared to leave Nome. She felt a sense of regret and sadness over leaving Jayce. Yet at the same time, she needed to leave him. She needed time to clear her head and think about the future.

"Are you ready?" Jacob asked.

"I am. I'm tired, so I hope to just go to my cabin and rest. Are you sure you'll be all right with Mrs. Beecham?" She grinned at her brother but just then caught sight of Jayce. "What's he doing here?"

"It's a surprise of sorts," Jacob said. "I hope you won't be mad."

"Mad about what?" Her heart pounded in her ears. Jayce carried a small bag in one hand while balancing his cane with the other.

"He's coming with you."

She looked at Jacob as if he'd lost his mind. "What are you saying?"

"Look, I can't explain it all just now, but we have some reasons to be concerned about Mrs. Beecham's motives for wanting to go north with us. She's lied about several things, including the possibility of a second expedition this summer. She's tried over and over to get Jayce to accompany her to Seattle, but we don't know why."

"I know that much is true," Leah said, remembering Helaina's request that she encourage Jayce to go south. "But I presumed she was merely attracted to him. Why is this going to help?"

Jayce had joined them by now. "Morning, all."

"I was just trying to explain to Leah why you're here," Jacob said. He turned back to Leah. "Helaina has imposed herself on our trip back to Last Chance. Jayce and I are convinced it has to do with him, but we don't know why. If he instead goes with you to Ketchikan, leaving now before she knows what's going on, then she'll be forced to show her hand or come with me."

"But what will that prove?" Leah questioned. She was still unnerved by the idea of Jayce accompanying her on the ship.

"I'm hoping it might prove what she's really up to. Look, I know you didn't plan for company, but it is dangerous to travel alone. I figure Jayce can look after you, and I'll rest a whole lot easier. Please don't be angry with us."

Leah glanced from her brother's pleading expression to Jayce's face. He appeared delighted with the entire matter. "I'm not angry. Just confused."

"If there had been another way, I would have tried it. This seems the only choice other than just calling her a liar."

"And I truly do have business to tend to," Jayce declared. "There are some matters for me to address in Juneau. I can just get transportation from Ketchikan and rejoin you when you're ready to return to Nome."

Leah tried to relax. Jayce wasn't coming to Ketchikan for her company. That much was easy to see. Especially given his last statement. "All right. I suppose the matter is already settled. We'd best be on our way or we'll miss the ship." She leaned over and gave Jacob a peck on the cheek. "Please be careful. She may be dangerous."

Jacob laughed. "More to herself than to me. I plan to put her through the most arduous of trainings. By the time you two get back, she'll be able to run a dog team almost as good as you can."

Leah watched Jacob and Jayce shake hands. "Take care of her," Jacob told Jayce.

"I will. I promise."

The words caused Leah to wince. She turned away. *You'll take care of me for Jacob,* she thought, *but not because you want to. I'm an obligation—nothing more. I have to remember that.*

———

Jacob was glad to see Kimik and some of the other village men. "I wasn't sure if you'd get word or not." He shook Kimik's hand and gave him a hearty pat on the back.

"Icharaq's brother came just in time. We were headed out to hunt. Are these all the supplies?" he asked, looking at the stacks around them.

"Yes. I sent some other things north on

the *Bear.* These were small enough I figured we could handle them."

"Where's Leah?"

"She's taken a ship to Ketchikan to see our family. She'll be back in September—maybe earlier."

Kimik nodded, then called to his companions. "We load now and get home sooner."

"We'll have one passenger. A lady who intends to come north and learn how to handle a dogsled team," Jacob told Kimik.

"A lady? Who is she?"

"Her name is Mrs. Beecham. Ah, there she is now." Jacob saw Helaina walking toward the docks, a young man behind her loaded down with two bags.

When they reached Jacob and the others, Helaina instructed the boy to put her things on the boat. "Just show them which one you want these on," she told Jacob.

Jacob pointed to the nearest umiak. "That one is fine."

The boy deposited the bags and returned to Helaina for pay. She quickly parted with a few coins and dismissed him. "So where are the others?" She looked around, obviously expecting to see Leah and Jayce.

"What others?" Jacob asked, playing dumb.

She looked at him with an expression of great annoyance. "Your sister and Mr. Kincaid, of course."

"Oh." Jacob picked up a piece of rope. "They've already gone." He headed to the umiak, anxious to see what Helaina's reaction would be.

Helaina followed after him, rather breathless. "Why didn't they wait for us?"

Jacob let the matter drag on as long as possible. "Why are you concerned? I'll get you safely to Last Chance."

This momentarily silenced Helaina. Jacob could almost hear wheels turning in her head as she contemplated her next question. He then looked over the remaining boxes, picked up one, and headed to the boat. Before he could return for any more, Helaina was there beside him.

"Good," Jacob said, pointing to the boat. "You can get in and sit there by your bags. We need to balance everything out just right."

"I don't understand why you're being so unpleasant," Helaina said, demanding his attention. "I simply wanted to know where your sister and Mr. Kincaid had gone. You don't have to be mean-spirited about it."

"I didn't think I was being mean-spirited," Jacob replied. "I just didn't understand why their location was of any concern to you." He looked at her hard, daring her to explain.

"I suppose after these last weeks, I've come to care about their well-being," Helaina said sweetly. "They are good people—your sister, especially. I've enjoyed getting to know her and will be happy to know her better."

Jacob decided he'd played around long enough. "Well, you'll have to wait until September to do that. But meanwhile, you'll get the best dog training available. You'll be able to drive a team like a native once I'm through with you."

"I don't understand. Why will I have to wait until September to better know your sister?" Helaina didn't even bother with further pretense.

"Because she's not coming with us. She and Jayce left early this morning on a ship bound for Ketchikan. Leah's visiting family and Jayce is traveling on from there to handle business."

For a moment, Jacob actually thought

Helaina might faint. The color drained quickly from her face as her eyes widened. Then just as quickly as she paled, Helaina's face flushed red in fury. "Why was I not told they were leaving?"

Jacob crossed his arms and looked at her strangely. "Mrs. Beecham, I fail to understand why any of this is your concern. My sister has a life that has nothing to do with yours. Jayce too. You have made yourself a supreme annoyance, as far as I'm concerned, but I'm willing to help you out, given the importance of the situation."

"What would you know of its importance?"

He thought for a moment she might cry. This woman was so strange. She began to pace in front of him even before he answered her. "I know that you said it was critical that you learn how to handle a dog team. You said you were quite happy to spend the winter with us and endure the sub-zero temperatures so that you could better prepare yourself for the exploration planned next year. I've kindly tried to accommodate you on that issue, but now you seem far more interested in something else. What might that be, I wonder?"

Helaina seemed to compose herself. "I simply thought I was to have female companionship, for one. It hardly seems appropriate for me to head north without at least one other woman to accompany us."

"Yet you were prepared to do just that with the Arctic exploration team."

She looked rather stunned at this. It was clear to Jacob that she was caught and had no way in which to escape. He had taken a chance that she didn't know about the captain's wife accompanying her husband. At least he had been right on that account.

"So are you coming with us or not, Mrs. Beecham? I'm going to finish loading the supplies, and then I need your answer." He stalked off, smiling to himself. Let her chew on that fat for a while.

Helaina wanted to throw something at the back of Jacob Barringer's head. She wanted, in fact, to throw him to the ground and beat the smug look off of his face. All of her plans were ruined, and she didn't have the simplest idea of how to resolve the situation. The justice system in this part of the world was so frustrating. Had she felt that the police in Nome would have assisted her properly, she might have engaged them, but her observations had given her little encouragement.

If I tell him that I won't go, it will only make him more suspicious, she thought. Helaina quickly assessed her choices. She could refuse to go to Last Chance, telling Jacob that she'd wait for his sister's return. But she surmised that if she did this, Jacob would probably reject any thought of her coming to Last Chance in the future.

There was a slim possibility that she could catch up to Jayce and Leah in Ketchikan, but she could never hope to maintain her cover under that circumstance. There would be no reason for her to be there, and Jayce Kincaid was not a stupid man. He would easily figure out by eliminating all other possibilities that she was there for him.

If I go with Mr. Barringer, at least I know his sister will return in September. But what of Kincaid? He might not. She had to follow him and not Leah Barringer. There seemed no guarantee that Jayce was coming back to Last Chance Creek.

"So what's it to be?" Jacob asked.

Helaina jumped, not realizing he was standing there watching her. "I must say it's a difficult matter. I suppose I must come with you if I'm to learn about the dogs. I had hoped to further my discussion with Mr. Kincaid about the Arctic as well, but he's not returning until September, I suppose?"

"That's the plan."

She nodded. Since she had no real idea of where Jayce's business would take him, she felt her only choice was to go with Jacob Barringer. "Very well. I suppose my discussions of the Arctic can wait. I'll come with you and learn what I can about the dogs."

Jacob looked at her oddly for a moment. "Are you sure? You're going to be stuck up there for a while. You might be able to get passage on the mail ship, but otherwise—"

"I've made up my mind. This will be fine. I'm sure the experience will be interesting and the time will pass quickly."

Jacob laughed. "I'm sure it will be interesting, but I don't know about the time. If you don't mind, I need you to take your place in the umiak."

She nodded and made her way unassisted into the boat. Her mind reeled from the discovery that Jayce Kincaid was gone. Her brother had been right about one thing:

this man's capture was proving more difficult than anyone she'd ever known.

Thoughts of Stanley brought to mind the
letter she'd just posted to him. She had told
him that plans were delayed but moving
along well and she was certain to soon have
Jayce in custody. Now she had no idea of
how long it might be.

They would have to return to pick up
Jayce and Leah and transport them to Last
Chance Creek, she surmised. That would at
least get her back to Nome. Perhaps she
could send a letter to Stanley to have the
Pinkerton men transported to Nome to
await her arrival. While there, she could
work something out to take Jayce into custody.

She relaxed a bit. Surely this would be the
answer. Until now there had been no time to
get anyone else in place to assist her. But
two and a half months was enough time for
Stanley to work out the details to send a
dozen men to her aid.

Jacob and his men pushed off and
climbed into the boat. Helaina was unpre-
pared for the rocking motion as they made
their way out toward the Bering Sea. The
men's long powerful strokes took them

quickly away from the shore and into the deeper waters. She gripped the side of the skin boat and held on tightly. What if they were to capsize? The boats hardly seemed a match for the long journey ahead of them.

"Are you certain we're quite safe?" she asked Jacob.

He grunted as he pulled the oar through the water. "As safe as anyone ever is out here. This is God's country, and He alone holds the future." He smiled for a moment, and then an expression crossed his face that suggested he just remembered something important. "But you don't believe in God—do you, Mrs. Beecham?" He shrugged. "So I'm not sure what or who you think holds your future."

He turned his attention back to the water, leaving Helaina once again infuriated with his snide mannerisms. The boat heaved hard to the right, causing Helaina to retighten her grip. Her gaze fell to the inside of the boat. It was nothing more than a wooden frame with skins lashed around it. She felt her stomach churn and knew without a doubt that she was going to be sick.

"You're turning green, Mrs. Beecham. Are

you given over to seasickness?" Jacob called.

Helaina's only answer was to lose her lunch over the side of the boat. She dampened her handkerchief in the sea and wiped her mouth before glancing up. Jacob's look of concern surprised her.

"Are you feeling any better?" He seemed to genuinely care.

"I had no idea it would be this rough," she said honestly. The fight had been taken completely out of her. The boat seemed to settle a bit but not enough. She fought back a wave of nausea.

"You might actually feel better if you lie down. Adjust things as you need," he said, then turned his attention back to the job at hand.

Helaina wasn't in the mood for an argument. She pulled her bag close and used it for a pillow. Lying down did help a bit. She closed her eyes and pulled her arm up over her face to shield the intense sun. This was going to cost the Pinkertons more than usual, she decided then and there.

Jacob watched Helaina as she struggled to get comfortable. He felt sorry for her. He had never figured the spitfire woman would fall victim to the rolling waves. Lying there as she was now, she looked almost child-like—innocent and harmless.

What are you after? Why are you here?

The questions haunted him over and over. Jayce swore he didn't know her from the past. He had no idea of where she'd come from, but he planned to find out. He would send telegrams once in Ketchikan and see if he might get information from some of his friends. Meanwhile, Jacob planned to keep her too busy to be trouble to any of them. If she wanted an Alaskan adventure—he'd give her one she'd not soon forget.

Chapter Sixteen

"What do you call this?" Helaina asked, wrinkling her nose at the food in front of her.

"We call it supper," Jacob replied. "It's actually pretty good—you should try it before turning it down."

"What is it?" She picked at the chunks of meat.

"It's seal meat in its own oil."

She frowned and pushed it away. "Don't we have anything else? Something fresh, perhaps?"

"I got some fish," Kimik said proudly. "You want a piece?"

She nodded enthusiastically. "Yes, I'd like that very much."

Kimik pulled out a newly caught fish and held up his knife. "How big you want?"

Helaina looked at the fish and then at Jacob. "Isn't he going to cook it?"

"I doubt it."

"You mean he plans to eat it raw?"

Jacob nodded and rubbed his chin. "Since he doesn't plan to cook it, that would be my guess."

She gave him a look of complete disgust. "I can't eat raw fish."

"You could cook yourself a piece over the fire," Jacob suggested. "Shouldn't take too long."

"And how would I do that? I don't see any pans or utensils."

Jacob held up a willow branch. "You could use this. Spear it through and hold it over the fire."

"But that stick isn't sanitary. I have no idea what's been on it." She crinkled her nose, as if imagining all the possibilities.

"Suit yourself, Mrs. Beecham."

"This is impossible," she said, picking up her plate. "What about the supplies you're taking with us? Aren't there some kind of canned goods we could open?"

"You gonna buy them?"

"I'll happily pay for a decent meal." She tossed the tin pan in Jacob's direction. "What do you have?"

"I have some canned milk, sugar, flour, beans, canned and dried, and—"

"Open some beans. At least that way I can heat them here by the fire."

Jacob shrugged and got to his feet. "Shall I run you a tab or will you pay in cash?"

She quickly found her bag and fished around until she came up with several bills. "Start my account with this," she said rather snidely.

Jacob noted she'd given him a considerable amount of money. He tried not to react with too much interest and went to find her can of beans. She was already proving to be difficult; the episode of seasickness had only been the start. After that she'd complained about needing to stop for a chance to relieve herself, then wondered if there wasn't some way to apply shade to her section of the boat, and finally questioned Jacob as to whether they'd travel all night.

And now she was turning her nose up at the food. It wasn't a good way to get started.

He returned with the beans and tossed the can to her. She looked at it for a moment, then put her hand on her hip. "Do you have something with which to open this?"

He rolled his eyes, hoping to show her just how deep his exasperation ran. "Give it here." He rummaged in his bag and produced a can opener. He made short work of the lid and bent it back without severing it completely from the rest of the can.

"Anything else?" he asked, handing her the beans.

She put the can next to the fire. "A spoon would be nice."

He looked into her blue eyes and crossed his arms. "I'm sure a spoon would be very nice, but I don't have one. I only have the can opener because Leah told me we needed one for the house. Sorry."

"Very well."

She squared her shoulders and assessed the situation without another word. After a few minutes she took up her handkerchief and pulled the can back from the fire. Gingerly touching the metal, she found it to be sufficiently cool, then worked to bend the can lid back as far as possible. To Jacob's surprise, she then lifted the beans to her lips as if drinking from a glass. She'd need to be careful, Jacob thought, or she'd cut her lips for sure.

The men had chosen to sit away from Jacob and Helaina. They seemed to understand that they'd not have the same camaraderie with this new white woman that they'd shared over the years with Leah. Jacob figured it was just as well. Helaina's caustic nature was not something he would have wished on his enemy, much less his friends.

"Don't you ever miss civilization?" Helaina asked without warning.

Jacob thought about her question for a moment. He remembered a time when Denver had been his home. The city had seemed overwhelming, even terrifying. He hated the noise most of all, not to mention the rudeness of people who seemed always to be in a big hurry.

"If you mean big cities full of people and racket, then no," he said softly, "I don't miss it."

"But what about the innovations—the

changes? The world is not as you left it when you came to hide away up here."

He looked at her oddly. She had such a strange way of looking at life. Her words were always something of an accusation. "What do you mean 'hide away up here'? I didn't come here to hide. I first came to the Yukon with my father. I stayed up north because I love it. There's something about this country that reaches deep inside a man. I honestly never thought it would happen to me. There was a time, in fact, that I planned to leave as soon as I had the means."

"But what about automobiles and aeroplanes?"

"What about wars and financial failures?"

She cocked her head to one side and studied him for a moment. "Is that really all you think of when you think of America and the wonders of our time?"

"I don't know. I understand that there are great inventions coming to light every day. I realize doctors are learning new ways to help people, and that travel is improving in speed and quality. Still, I know that there are problems."

"Such as?" She dropped the sarcastic

overtone to her voice to add, "I'd really like to know how you see it."

Jacob leaned back on his elbows and stretched his legs out beside the fire. "Sometimes I get the newspapers from Seattle or elsewhere. The ship captains bring them or the missionaries carry them back from their trips. I see the complications of life in big cities within the pages. There seems to be a great deal of crime and hunger, yet no one really knows anyone well enough to care. Vast populations of strangers are content to wander through life with no concern or compassion for anyone but themselves."

Helaina frowned and toyed with the can. "The crime is bad, certainly, but the legal authorities are doing what they can to right the wrongs of the world."

"But isn't there something more than just righting wrongs? What about changing hearts? What about turning people from wrong and teaching them to care for one another?"

"And how would you propose to do that?"

Jacob sat up again. "With God, of course. The hearts and minds of people can only be changed when they understand that there is something—someone—to change for. It's the hopelessness that causes them to break the law. It's that which also kills them."

"Or they get killed by other people," Helaina admitted. "Like my family."

"Your situation is a good example. I can't comprehend why your folks and husband were murdered, but I can guess that there was a hopelessness deep inside the man or men who took their lives. There always is. Even when something else motivates the actions."

"Like what?"

"Greed. I once found myself accused of a murder because of someone else's greed."

Helaina perked up at this. Jacob saw that he held her interest completely as she asked, "Tell me about it?"

Jacob shrugged and put a piece of driftwood on the fire. "I had a good friend, Gump Lindquist, who was looking for gold. He'd found some too. He'd also found trouble in the form of a man who came looking for something that didn't belong to him. It's a long story, but the man was someone I'd known from before. He killed the old man as a way of getting to me—threatening me so that I'd help him. But when the ruckus caught the attention of other people—witnesses—the man fled and I was accused of murder."

"But you didn't do it?" she asked.

"No, I didn't do it," Jacob replied, remembering those horrible days. He'd honestly thought they'd hang him, and all because of what Cec Blackabee had done.

"How did you prove it? Was there a trial?"

"Like I said, it's a long story. My guardians were faithful to believe me and to not give up on exposing the truth. The authorities caught the man, even as he confessed what he'd done. Of course, he didn't know the law was standing outside the door listening in. My point is the man who killed my friend was consumed in his own hopelessness. He was overcome with greed and desired gold more than he valued human life."

"And you think God could have changed this hopelessness?"

"He changed it for me. Sitting in that jail, not even seventeen years old, I was sure they were going to hang me. I thought God didn't care. Here I'd trusted Him and He'd let this happen to me . . . let my friend die."

Helaina's face contorted, as if the comment caused her pain. She quickly lowered her focus to the can of beans. "And didn't He?" she murmured.

"No. God didn't just let Gump die, and He certainly didn't desert me. Sometimes the desperation of the moment causes us to feel as though God is far away—that He doesn't care. That's the hopelessness of the world creeping in."

"I really find all of this to be nonsense," Helaina declared, seeming to compose herself once again. It was as if a mask of steel fell into place. "People make choices and do as they will. They are driven by certain motives, I will allow you that. But their choices have consequences and bad choices must be punished. You were fortunate that your friends were able to uncover the truth. But had they not, the law would have had no choice but to hang you."

"That's a rather calloused, coldhearted way of looking at things, isn't it?"

"Not at all. Justice is often mistaken for being cruel, but it's only fair that people pay for their wrongdoings."

The words seemed to come from deep in Helaina's heart. This surprised Jacob. He'd never heard a woman talk with quite so much conviction for punishment. "What of mercy?" he asked.

"Mercy? Mercy has no place in the law. The law is the law. It is written and easily interpreted in order to keep our societies from falling into disorder," she said emphatically.

"I think you're wrong, Mrs. Beecham. I think mercy plays an important role in the law and its interpretation. I think that you can't just see our world in hues of black or white. We are all individual and very human in nature."

"Meaning what?"

"Meaning that we fail. We make mistakes. Sometimes we trust the wrong person and sometimes we're just in the wrong place at the wrong time. If there were no mercy for situations like that, what would happen to people who are innocently accused? Could you really live with the idea of our legal system putting people to death simply because they appeared to be guilty? Does your heart not cry out for mercy and truth?"

"My heart cries out for justice, Mr. Barringer. Only that. Justice is the key to our society maintaining order. Therefore, justice is more important than your mercy."

———

"There they are!" Leah declared, pointing down the dock to where Karen and Adrik Ivankov stood. Karen, still tall and slender, looked very much as she had the last time Leah had seen her. She smiled and waved enthusiastically at Leah. Adrik, a man who had always seemed larger than life to Leah, did likewise. "Hurry, Jayce." She left him to carry the bags and ran to where the couple awaited her.

Leah fell into Karen's arms and hugged her close. Karen was the only mother Leah had known for nearly twenty years. It was so good to be with her again. Leah wondered now why she'd delayed so long in coming.

"I can't believe you're really here," Karen whispered against Leah's ear. "I've missed you so much."

"I know. I've missed you too. It's been so long."

"And you've brought Mr. Kincaid back with you, I see." Karen and Leah looked to where Adrik and Jayce were in conversation several feet away.

"I really had no choice. He showed up on

the shore when I was ready to leave, and Jacob announced that he would accompany me."

Karen turned her focus back on Leah. "What's wrong with that?"

Leah smiled. Karen's once-vibrant red hair was laced now with gray, but her eyes were as keen as ever. There would be no hiding the story from Karen, not that Leah really wanted to. "It's complicated, to say the least," she began. "You remember how I felt about Jayce back when I still lived here with you?"

"Yes," Karen said, nodding. "And how you still feel about him."

Leah nodded and sobered. "Yes."

"But he still doesn't feel that way about you?"

"I think not," Leah said with a heavy sigh. "Yet he's everywhere. He's in my thoughts and in my heart, and now he's here . . . at least for now. He tells me he has business elsewhere. So I don't imagine he'll stay here long."

"Would it matter if he did?"

Leah looked at Karen. "I'm not sure. Sometimes I get the feeling he would like a second chance. I know that sounds crazy, because just as soon as I think that way, he does something or says something that proves to me he can't possibly want that. So while on one hand I wish he would stay and allow us to start over in our friendship, on the other I just wish he would go."

"I've just invited Jayce to stay with us for a while," Adrik announced as they joined the women. "He said yes."

Leah looked to Karen and shrugged. "See what I mean?"

Karen grinned. "I do indeed. But unlike you, I think it matters a great deal more than you'll admit. I think once you let it all settle in, you'll be glad he's staying."

———

Jayce was glad for the invitation to remain with the Ivankovs. Ketchikan was a beautiful city set against impressive hills—mountains, some might say, although he'd seen much bigger. The Ivankov home was nestled deep in the forest, secluded from the harbor and the worries of town life. Here a man could lose himself by traveling days and days into the deep, dark woods. He liked that idea. He loved the solitude.

Standing in the seclusion of heady pine

and fir, the light fading ever so slightly over-head, Jayce found the canopy of tall trees to be a welcoming comfort. They seemed almost to hide him away—shelter him from harm.

"I thought I saw you out here," Adrik said as he stalked up the path.

Adrik was a big bear of a man. Part Russian and part Tlingit Indian, he immediately dwarfed any other person around him. The only person who had never shown him fear, at least as far as Jayce had witnessed, was Karen. Even now Jayce felt rather unnerved by the man.

"I love the quiet. The stillness of the forest is almost too much to bear," Jayce admitted, trying to forget his uneasiness. "It's such a contrast to other places in this terri-tory. So rich and green here, compared to the barren scrub and brush willows of the Arctic."

"It's all that rain and rich soil," Adrik told him. He looked at Jayce and smiled. "Has it changed much in ten years?"

"It's hard to believe I've been gone that long, but, no, it hasn't changed all that much. There are some things I noticed at the docks, but here . . . it seems almost eternally the same."

"Some things don't show the wear of time as much. People do, but not everything does."

The comment made Jayce a bit uneasy, and he quickly thought of what he might say to change the subject. "I've heard that we have approval for a railroad to be built from Seward to Fairbanks," he finally said.

"Yes. There's been a lot of controversy over it. Some people want to develop the land and others don't."

"Where do you stand?"

Adrik looked heavenward for a moment. "I see good on both sides. I hate to think of the land being spoiled—abused. I'm not sure the things that the government hopes to accomplish can ever be realized for this area, and it worries me to wonder how far they will go to be right."

"Right about what?"

"Right about their vision for the territory. You know they are already talking about pushing for statehood next year."

"I had heard that," Jayce admitted.

"Well, a lot of folks in the government think Alaska is the answer to troubles in the

States. They think once we get statehood, they can promote moving people here and lessening the population of large cities. I don't think people will be inclined to move here, however, without more incentive than a railroad and thirty-seven cents a day to labor on its creation."

"You may be right. Still, I see exploration and innovation to be beneficial. I love this territory and think it would serve us well to develop some of the cities and areas between them, but I wouldn't want to see it spoiled, and like you I do have my fears."

"Some people just don't see a good thing when they have it."

They stood in silence for several minutes. Jayce felt there was something Adrik wanted to say, but he wasn't at all certain what that might be. He felt a bit uncomfortable waiting for the older man to address him but held his tongue.

Finally Adrik did speak. He turned toward Jayce and the serious expression he held immediately set the stage. "You know you're welcome here. You're a good man, and I'm pleased to hear you've set your life right with the Lord."

"But?"

Adrik smiled. "You're a man who likes to get right to the heart of things, I see."

"Might as well. I figure you have something to say, and I've no reason to keep you from it."

Adrik nodded. "I'd like to know what your plans are."

"My plans?"

Adrik nodded again. "For Leah."

Chapter Seventeen

Jacob looked at the ledger and then to Helaina. They had been back in Last Chance for nearly three weeks, and she still couldn't comprehend the way Leah kept books.

"I don't understand how to figure out what the furs or trade items are worth," Helaina admitted. "I don't know if a new pair of mukluks are worth two cases of milk, a bag of sugar, and a coil of rope. How would I know that?"

"You don't have to know it. Leah can figure it all up later and then reconcile it with the villagers. Don't turn people away just because you don't understand the system. Qavlunaq said you yelled at her. It upset her and she came to me in confusion."

"They all hate me," Helaina retorted. "They are meanspirited and vicious. I don't see why you even bother to help them."

Jacob frowned. He considered what to say to her for several moments while Helaina paced back and forth in a huff. "They don't hate you. . . . They just don't understand you. You have to see it through their eyes."

"Why can't they try to see it through my eyes?"

"Because you're in *their* territory, living off the fat of *their* land."

"Literally. Who in the world ever decided that eating whale blubber and seal fat was a good thing to do?"

Jacob shook his head. She was by far and away the most difficult person he'd ever known. "It's what's available to them, Helaina." He'd long since dropped calling her Mrs. Beecham, even though calling her by her first name seemed somehow unwise. He couldn't really say why. Up here, everyone went by their first name, but using hers seemed to imply an intimacy that did not exist.

She stopped and looked at him hard. "Can you honestly say you prefer this life to something else you might have in a real town—in a civilized state?"

Jacob closed the ledger book. "Are you trying to convince me to leave? Is that your plan?"

She composed herself and pushed back an errant strand of blond hair. "I have no plan. I simply asked you a question. You seem quite content here in this isolated, remote village, yet so many things are missing."

"Such as?"

"Real bathrooms. Electricity. Telephones." She plopped herself down on a stool behind the counter. "There's a whole different world out there. A world that's developed and changed while this place just stays the same. It's probably always been like this— and probably always will be."

"But what's wrong with that? Why must everything evolve into something else?"

She looked at him in complete exasperation. "For the betterment of mankind. Can you not see that?"

"I see problems in the south, just like we have problems in the north. There is good with the bad in both places. I don't see that we have to be a replica of the States just because we're a territory."

She sighed and gazed, unblinking, at the wall behind him. "I didn't expect you to comprehend my thoughts. I don't even understand it myself . . . not completely. It's just this place—the isolation and the negative way the people see me—well, it's all so hard. I don't even feel like myself anymore. Nothing here is familiar or right."

It was the first time Jacob felt truly sorry for her. "Look, I know this must be hard, but better you figure it out like this than to have found yourself stuck at the top of the world. It's even more foreign there."

She shook her head. "I would have survived. You don't know me. I would have gotten by. I can't help that I miss my life. I miss the food and the comfort."

"What? You haven't found comfort in our luxurious home?" he asked, grinning.

Helaina actually smiled at this. "The bathing facilities leave much to be desired."

"A bowl of lukewarm water has always served me well enough," Jacob teased.

"Look," she began, "I'm sorry to be so frustrated and ill-tempered. This hasn't really turned out the way I'd hoped. I'm lousy with the dogs and can't seem to make sense of the store."

"And you're used to being a woman who easily picks up her duties and does them well—aren't you?"

She glared at Jacob, and for a moment he thought she might get angry. Then just as quickly her expression softened. "I am."

"So you're completely out of place in this situation, but that doesn't have to be a bad thing. You're learning new ways, and you are getting better at all of it. Even the dogs. You just have to show them who's boss, and frankly, you've never appeared to have any trouble with that in the past." He smiled again, hoping she wouldn't take offense.

"So where do we go from here?"

"Well, I think it would benefit us both if I go clean up and you get supper ready. I really do appreciate having you prepare the meals. That leaves me free for other tasks."

"It seems the least I can do, given the fact that you've had to leave your home on my account."

"It wouldn't be proper for me to share the

place with you," Jacob countered. "Taking up residence together up here constitutes marriage. We don't want to give anyone the wrong impression. Besides, the weather has been fine and the dog shed is comfortable enough."

"It still seems unfair, but I am grateful for what you've done. Ayoona showed me how to make a stew with squirrel earlier in the day. It's been simmering since this afternoon."

"That sounds wonderful. I hope she gave you some of those wild potatoes."

"She did. There are some other things in there that I'm not entirely familiar with, but when she had me brave a taste, I had to admit it was quite good."

"I'm sure it is." He headed for the door. "Just put the ledger away for now. We'll talk about it later and see if we can work out an easier system. For now, I'm going to clean up. I'm starved. Oh, will there be biscuits?"

She laughed. "Aren't there always? I've never met a man who liked biscuits as much as you do."

"Doughnuts." He said the word firmly as if it should mean something to Helaina. At her look of confusion, he added, "That's one thing I really miss from civilization, as you call it. My mother used to make the best doughnuts."

"Maybe I can find a recipe," Helaina offered.

"That would be really nice."

He left her there and headed off to clean up. He thought it very kind of her to offer to make doughnuts, but still he wondered whether or not she'd ever adjust to life in Alaska. He was glad for her sake that she'd not made the trip north with the team on the *Homestead.* She would never have made it. It only made him wonder again—why? Why had she signed up for such a project? *She hates the north—hates the isolation and the cold. So why did she want to be on the* Homestead?

Her lies in Nome came back to haunt him. She was clearly here to bide her time. But why? What was her interest in Jayce? What could compel a woman of her social caliber to follow him to the wilds of Alaska—for that was what she had done. Jayce had told him that Helaina was a last-minute addition to the team—one that had been frowned upon by everyone. Even the captain seemed unhappy about it, but he would say nothing on the matter.

Now she was here, and Jacob knew she was miserable. She didn't fit in with the natives, and she resented the Kjellmanns and their beliefs. At least she managed to put that aside and join them on Sundays for church, however. He thought she did this more out of desperation for some semblance of normalcy than for any desire to learn about God's Word. Still, she had shown interest in his devotions at night. They had even settled into a strange sort of ritual where he would take up the Bible as the meal concluded each evening. He would always read from the Scriptures and sometimes they would discuss what the meaning was and why it should matter to them in this day and age.

Jacob had to give her credit. Helaina had been open to the interpretations and understandings that he shared. She sometimes argued what she saw to be foolishness, but just as often she would ponder passages and ask him questions the following day. This had caused him to start praying for her. Whereas before he could see no reason why he should be saddled with this strange, angry woman, now he wondered if the Lord hadn't brought her into his life for the purpose of sharing Jesus.

After cleaning up, Jacob grabbed his Bible and headed back to the house. He could almost taste the squirrel stew. A smile crossed his face. He'd have to reward Ayoona for her help with Helaina.

They ate in relative silence that evening. Jacob could tell Helaina had a great deal on her mind, and for once he found that he'd really like to know what it was that troubled her. He was on his second bowl of stew, still contemplating how he might approach the matter, when he heard her heave a heavy sigh.

Jacob just decided to wade into the conversation, come what may. "You seem to be carrying the weight of the world. You aren't still worried about those ledgers, are you?"

"No," she said, pushing back her bowl. She stared at the table and said nothing more.

Jacob pushed ahead. "Can you not talk about what's bothering you?"

She looked up. "Do you honestly care?"

Her question took Jacob by surprise. His

answer startled him even more. "Yes. Yes, I care. I wouldn't have asked you if I didn't."

"Do you remember our trip here from Nome?"

Jacob laughed. "How could I not?"

She smiled. "I know I was a burden. But do you remember our conversation about hopelessness and mercy?"

"Of course, I remember. It's only been a few weeks."

She leaned forward and folded her hands together atop the table. "I've thought about some of the things you said. Then last night you read from Matthew, and I've been troubled by it ever since."

"Why?" He took up his Bible and opened to the eighteenth chapter of Matthew. "Tell me and we can discuss it."

"Can we read it again?"

"Sure." He drew his finger down the chapter until he came to the twenty-third verse. " 'Therefore is the kingdom of heaven likened unto a certain king, which would take account of his servants. And when he had begun to reckon, one was brought unto him, which owed him ten thousand talents. But forasmuch as he had not to pay, his lord commanded him to be sold and his wife, and children, and all that he had, and payment to be made.' "

"That was the law then, correct?" Helaina asked.

Jacob looked up. "I suppose it must have been."

"So the king did nothing wrong in seeking justice. The man owed him and couldn't pay him. The king had a right to receive his due pay."

"I can agree with that. The man owed a debt." He looked back to the Bible. "Should I go on?"

"Yes. Please."

He found his place. " 'The servant therefore fell down, and worshipped him, saying, "Lord, have patience with me, and I will pay thee all." Then the lord of that servant was moved with compassion, and loosed him, and forgave him the debt.' "

"But he wasn't obligated to do so," Helaina said, stopping Jacob from going further. "The law said that he should pay his debt."

"Correct. The king showed mercy. The servant begged for more time. The king was moved by his circumstance and let him go."

"But the law clearly was on the side of the king. A debt was owed."

"And the king forgave that debt."

"Please read on," she said, her brows knitting together.

" 'But the same servant went out, and found one of his fellowservants, which owed him an hundred pence: and he laid hands on him, and took him by the throat, saying, "Pay me that thou owest." And his fellowservant fell down at his feet and besought him, saying, "Have patience with me, and I will pay thee all." And he would not: but went and cast him into prison, till he should pay the debt.' "

"He did nothing wrong," Helaina said, her tone quite troubled. "The man was entitled to be paid back. Just because the king forgave his debt, that shouldn't imply that the man is obligated to forgive someone else's debt. If you owed me twenty dollars and John owed you twenty dollars, and I told you to forget about paying me back, it shouldn't obligate you to forgive John's debt. The situation in this verse is confusing to me. It was a legal loan—a binding agreement."

"But the man was in the same position as

his fellow servant," Jacob replied. "He didn't have the money to pay him at that time. The man never came to him and said, 'I won't pay you.' He simply asked for more time. Who knows what the agreement might have been between the two men. Maybe it was such that the man had lent the money saying, 'Pay me back when you can.' "

Helaina considered these words for a moment. "But it was the servant's right to put the man in prison. Just as it was the king's right to put the servant in prison. The law is the law."

"But mercy is greater than the law."

"That cannot be!" she snapped, and for the first time there seemed to be real anger in her voice. "Nothing is above the law."

Jacob looked at her for a moment. "Do you not see this story for what it is really about? Let me finish the chapter." He found his place quickly and continued. " 'So when his fellowservants saw what was done, they were very sorry, and came and told unto their lord all that was done. Then his lord, after that he had called him, said unto him, O thou wicked servant, I forgave thee all that debt, because thou desiredst me: Shouldest not thou also have had compassion on thy fellowservant, even as I had pity on thee? And his lord was wroth, and delivered him to the tormentors, till he should pay all that was due unto him. So likewise shall my heavenly Father do also unto you, if ye from your hearts forgive not every one his brother their trespasses.' "

"That isn't right," Helaina said, leaning back and crossing her arms. "It's not just."

Jacob shook his head. "How is it not just?"

"The man was under no obligation to forgive the debt owed him just because the king had forgiven him. That makes no sense to me. The man owed a debt and was responsible to pay back that debt. Why should the servant be obligated—forced to break a contract with another—just because his contract had been cancelled out?"

"He should have desired to do it. Mercy had been given him. Do you know what that's like? Because I do. Remember I told you about being in jail—accused of a murder I didn't commit? When I was let go, I knew what true mercy was for the first time in my life. I didn't get to go free because of anything I'd done. I had no say in the matter. My friends went out and found a way to prove the truth—that was the only reason I was set free."

"But you weren't guilty. You owed no debt. This man owed a debt, and I do not understand why, just because one person forgives, another is forced to also do likewise. God makes no sense to me in this— especially when that chapter concludes to say that I must forgive everyone—no matter the guilt or the crime."

Jacob closed the Bible and tried to think of a way in which he might convince her. Sometimes the Bible offered difficult truths. Obviously this was one of those times for Helaina. At least she hadn't walked away from it or put it aside. She had mulled over this Scripture for over a day. There must be a reason.

"You're not a very forgiving person, are you, Helaina?" He wanted to take the words back the minute they were out of his mouth. He couldn't believe he'd actually spoken them aloud.

"I forgive those who deserve to be forgiven," she said.

A thought came to mind. "And who really deserves to be forgiven?"

She seemed to consider this for a moment. "Well, I suppose no one. If they break the law—they must pay the penalty. They don't deserve to get out of whatever punishment is given."

"So do you believe forgiveness should be based on merit?"

"I don't know that I would find that to be true either," she admitted.

He nodded, feeling certain she would say something like this. "Who then merits forgiveness? Is it the person who is truly sorry? Is it the person who made a mistake? Is it the person who simply didn't realize the crime?"

"Ignorance of the law is no excuse," she replied, sounding more like her old self.

"So if it is left up to you, no one deserves to be forgiven." He paused for a moment, then smiled. "Which I happen to agree with. No one deserves it. No one really earns it or merits it."

"Then what of this passage?" She was back to being confused.

"This passage is not just about forgiveness," Jacob said. He gazed deep into her blue eyes, hoping to somehow understand the pain that he saw there. "It's about mercy—compassion. Neither man deserved forgiveness. The law was clearly in favor of the man to whom the money was owed. God wants us to understand that the law is clearly in His favor. We do not deserve forgiveness because of anything we've done to merit it. But God in His compassion shows mercy on us . . . and . . . He forgives. He's asked for us to do the same."

"Threatened us to do the same, you mean." Her words were laced with bitterness.

"But, Helaina, if the love of God is in you—if you know that blessed wonder of being shown mercy—believe me, you'll desire to show mercy in return. You'll want to forgive . . . because in doing so, you'll know God's heart just that much better. You'll feel His presence in that very action of forgiveness."

"I've never needed anyone's forgiveness. I keep the law," she said firmly and added, "I don't compromise it."

"The Lord doesn't compromise the law or do away with it. He found a way to satisfy it through Christ. He loves the law because the law reflects His holiness—His perfection. He doesn't want you to forsake the law, but rather to understand the need for mercy . . . because you're wrong, Helaina. You *have* needed someone's forgiveness—you need *His* forgiveness. Because without it you will face an eternity separated from Him."

She held his gaze but said nothing. He could see that she still felt confused, but the time had come for him to let her make her choice. He prayed for her silently as he gathered his things. "The stew was perfect. Thank you for a wonderful dinner." He started to leave, then remembered something.

"I nearly forgot to tell you. I'll be leaving for Nook tomorrow."

"Nook? Where is that?"

"It's a town up north. Nook is the native name; they call it Teller now. I'm delivering some young dogs. I should only be a few days, but you can never tell how things will go. We're taking the pups by water, and they don't always appreciate that mode of transportation. John will look after the dogs while I'm gone, so you won't have to worry about that—although it would be good practice for you."

"Couldn't I go with you? You know I'm not

much use around here," Helaina said, her voice sounding almost desperate.

"No, there won't be room for even one more person. Besides, I won't be gone that long. You'll do fine. Keep the store going and keep track of what people bring in to trade. We'll figure it up later. For the most part, they know what things are worth. They are honest and good people. You won't have any trouble from them."

———

Helaina spent a restless night contemplating the Bible verses she'd discussed with Jacob and facing the uncertain discomfort of his departure. She finally gave up trying to sleep about the time she heard the dogs start to bark and yip. This was a sure sign that Jacob was up. No doubt, as he gathered the dogs he would take to Nook, the other animals would be miserable— whining and howling their displeasure.

She felt like whining and howling her own displeasure. "How can he just leave me here? No one here cares whether I live or die."

Helaina got up and dressed quickly. She wondered if she should make Jacob breakfast or if he'd take off before she would even have a chance to make anything decent. Looking around the room in complete dejection, she realized that she would miss Jacob. She hadn't thought about Robert in days—maybe weeks. Truth be told, she hadn't even thought about Stanley or Jayce or the job she'd come north to accomplish.

"What's wrong with me?"

And then it came to her. Her interest in Jacob had taken a new form . . . and the thought terrified her. *This can't be. I cannot let myself care about him—nor let him care about me.*

"It's wrong," she murmured. "It's all gone very wrong."

Chapter Eighteen

Helaina heard that the revenue cutter *Bear* was in the harbor and that they were off-loading mail and other supplies for the village. Jacob had been expecting a supply of goods for the store, but Helaina had no idea if she would need to pay for it or arrange for the things to be brought to the store. Much to her relief, however, John appeared with a couple of envelopes and the announcement that he and some of the other men would be delivering several boxes for the store. His dark eyes seemed to watch her intently—almost as if he expected her to do something wrong. She felt they all watched her this way, and she hated it.

"Thank you, John," she told him in a clipped tone.

He nodded and handed the envelopes over. "I'll be back."

Helaina looked at the mail and realized one of the letters was for her. The other was marked *Urgent* and addressed to Jacob. The return address suggested it had come from the captain of the *Homestead.* This seemed very strange, given the man was supposed to be somewhere in the Arctic, where Helaina knew there would be no mail service.

She opened her own letter and read the contents. The expedition association in Vancouver had written her to acknowledge that Jayce Kincaid had indeed been with them for a considerable time in 1914 and into very early 1915. He was not a man given to long periods away from the job; in fact, he was just the opposite, often working over the weekend and well past the hours others put in. They further added that his service had been invaluable to them, and they hoped that he would be available to join them again soon.

Closing the letter, Helaina tried to digest the information and make sense of it. She knew for a fact that Jayce had been in England working at the British Museum in 1914. At least a man calling himself Jayce Kincaid had been there. She thought it might be important to write to Stanley and let him know of this news. Maybe her brother could lend some kind of insight to the situation.

Since John had still not returned, Helaina looked at the other letter in her hand. The word *urgent* caused her to contemplate whether she should just open the letter. What if someone were in trouble and needed Jacob's immediate attention? Obviously it was important, or the captain would never have sent it. She decided to open it and risk Jacob's ire.

Dear Mr. Barringer,

Our expedition has run into trouble, as you may have already heard. There has been sickness and problems with the ship, and we found it necessary to return home to make repairs and reconsider our next move. It is a great disappointment to us all.

The urgency of this letter is to let you know that we want to secure your help immediately for our next journey. We are already making plans and would like to have your pledge for next year, along with your help in the planning. Your friend Mr. Kincaid has been an invaluable help with the dogs, and we are grateful that he managed to catch up with the crew.

Helaina stopped and reread this portion of the letter several times. What in the world was the captain talking about? Jayce hadn't caught up with the crew. He was with Leah Barringer. Or was he? Had Jacob lied to her? When Leah went to Ketchikan, had Jayce made his way on the revenue cutter north to rendezvous with the *Homestead*?

Her anger rose with each suggested thought. *I've been duped somehow. Jayce probably realized who I was. I don't know how he could have, but he must have figured it out. Then, instead of making a scene or trying to do me in, he headed out—back to the expedition—knowing I wouldn't be able to join him.*

The sound of the men coming down the

stairs drew her attention back to the moment. She quickly folded the letter and stuffed it back in the envelope. She'd have to figure out later what to do.

John and the others brought in a dozen boxes and stacked them in the front room. "Thank you for your help," she told them as they made their way to the door.

"You are welcome," John replied.

She thought about her situation and called after him, "John, is anyone making their way to Nome?"

He paused and turned. "Nome? No. We hunt whale tomorrow. Most of the village will move up the coast. The women are picking berries and other things, and they will trap squirrels and rabbits."

"Then I'll be here alone?" Helaina asked, terrified by the thought.

"The Kjellmanns will be here. A few others."

Helaina nodded, and John must have taken this for her approval because he quickly left without another word. Jacob had said nothing to her about the village taking a nomadic trek north. Who would care for the dogs? Jacob had said that John would be responsible.

She ran up the stairs and outside, hoping to stop John in time to question him. He was nowhere to be found, however. Looking around her, Helaina felt a deep sense of loneliness. *I am at the top of the world and all alone. Stanley is safe and comfortable in his office in Washington, and I am here being made a fool of by a dangerous fugitive.*

In her heart, she wished Jacob were there. *If he were here,* she thought, *I could question him about the letter and Jayce.* But even as the thought came, Helaina knew such a thing would be difficult. How could she question Jacob without giving away her interest in Jayce? And if he saw that interest, would he understand? Would he be on the side of the law?

"He's a Christian," she whispered. "He knows the honorable and right thing is to obey the law and do good. He would surely understand that my desire is only to aid in the capture of a dangerous criminal."

But Jayce was his friend. And friendships tended to make people look at matters differently. She really had few choices. When Jacob returned she would give him the letter and apologize for opening it, then maybe make some side comment about thinking that Jayce was with Leah in Ketchikan.

She smiled to herself. That wouldn't seem so strange. After all, Jacob had told her they were together. It shouldn't seem out of place for her to ask about something like that. It was just a matter of curiosity.

———

Jayce worked at sharpening his knife in the quiet of the day. Leah had gone with Adrik and the children into Ketchikan, while Jayce had opted to remain behind and tend to other things. Karen, too, had stayed. She had told him that she intended to bake bread and that the first loaf would be ready around lunchtime. The invitation was then extended to join her for the noon meal. Jayce could hardly say no to that.

He rhythmically ran the knife's blade against the sharpening stone. There was something comfortable, almost soothing, in the familiarity of this action. It was something he'd known since childhood, even though he'd been raised in the city with plenty of wealth and servants who could sharpen the knives.

His father had been an outdoorsman who

loved hunting, often taking his sons with him. Jayce had found great pleasure in the wilderness lands of upstate New York and Canada, and as the years went by, often it was just him and his father. Those were special times. Times in which Jayce learned to be a man.

His father often told Jayce that God could be found in all of creation. *"When a man looks at a snowcapped mountain or a frothing, wild ocean, he should remember that the Creator of the universe masterminded all of this and more."* Jayce remembered the words as if it were only yesterday that he heard them. He'd had very little appreciation of them as a young man.

His father had often talked of Seward's Folly—the Alaskan Territory—especially after gold was found. He and Jayce had even planned a trip; not for the gold, but for the opportunity of seeing such a place. When his father died Jayce set aside the plans, but after his mother died, he headed west.

Seeing that it was nearly noon, Jayce pushed aside thoughts of the past and decided to check and see if lunch was ready. Already he could smell the heavenly scent of fresh bread. It was a treat he didn't often get. He put away his knife and walked to the log house. Karen smiled broadly at him as he came through the door.

"I thought perhaps I'd have to call you, but then I opened one of the kitchen windows and let the aroma of the bread do the job."

"It did the job well," Jayce admitted. "I must say this is a real treat."

"Come sit here," she said, pulling out a chair. "I have everything ready."

Jayce did as he was instructed as Karen brought a bowl of chicken and dumplings to the table. "Adrik was able to get some chickens last week. We've been enjoying them ever since, although Christopher believes we should keep them as pets."

"Sounds like a typical kid," Jayce said.

Karen turned to retrieve a pot of coffee. "He's not yet ten, but he thinks he's twenty. He has picked up a hefty portion of adventurous nature from both Adrik and myself." She poured Jayce a cup of the steaming liquid, then did likewise for herself.

"I remember being that age. I was just thinking about it, in fact. My father used to take me hunting. I think it taught me a passion for the wilderness. I'll be sorry when we populate the world so much that there aren't any more areas of wilderness."

"That would be sad indeed," Karen said, taking a seat across from Jayce. "Would you say grace?"

Jayce nodded and offered a simple prayer of thanks. "This smells heavenly. I haven't had a meal like this in some time."

Karen brought a plate of freshly sliced bread to the table. "Here, it's still warm."

Jayce took a piece and popped a bite of it in his mouth. The taste was incredible. "Mmmm," he said as he chewed.

"I seem to remember that your father and mother are both passed on. Is that right?"

Jayce nodded. "Yes. My mother had died right before I came north the first time. My father passed away several years before her. It was hard. My entire family seemed to disintegrate the day my father was buried."

Karen's expression was compassionate. "What happened?"

"My siblings were not wise with what my father left behind. They went through the money as if it were a never-ending supply. After they went through what he'd left them, they began to tap into what was endowed to my mother. Before I knew it—long before she'd confide in me as to what had happened—it was necessary to sell her house."

"How sad."

"It truly was. My mother and father had once been esteemed in the neighborhood. By the time my mother died, however, her society friends had long since fallen away."

"Then they weren't really friends at all," Karen said quite matter-of-factly.

"True enough, but that only caused it to hurt all the more."

"So, Jayce . . . will you be with us long?" Karen asked, the tone of her voice adding weight to the seemingly simple question.

Jayce could not help but think of Leah and of Adrik asking him what his plans were for her. Though he had sought her attention, so far Leah had gone out of her way to make sure they had no time alone. He wondered if she was afraid of him—afraid of what he might say. Just as he feared the words he felt compelled to share with Karen.

"I don't know where to start," he said softly. His heart was in great turmoil. "Adrik has asked me what my plans are—what my plans for Leah might be. I told him honestly that I didn't know. I wasn't sure how she felt anymore, and I wasn't sure what to do with the feelings I had."

"And what are those feelings, Jayce?"

He drew a deep breath. "I would . . . that is . . . I . . . well, I care deeply for her. I could now see taking her for a wife—even though I couldn't see it back then."

"Do you love her?"

"I think I do." He shook his head. "No. I know I love her."

Karen's smile broadened. "And have you prayed for direction?"

"I have to admit, I pray and then I tend to find myself caught up in other thoughts. I hurt her so much; I know that well. I was shocked to find her still so bitter about the past. I figured she'd long forgotten me. I had seen her as a child and that her feelings were those of a child."

Karen crossed her arms and leaned back in the chair. "But now you see it differently?"

"Yes. I realize she knew her heart and mind quite well, even then. I suppose because I knew myself to be so unsettled at that age, I couldn't believe anyone else would have the necessary maturity in order to make important decisions."

"This territory is unlike the settled cities of

the United States," Karen said thoughtfully. "There are few second chances here. People grow up fast under the midnight sun."

"I know that to be true now. I just need to know if second chances ever happen."

Karen drew a deep breath. "They are rare. But they do happen."

"Mama!"

Karen's attention was immediately drawn away. "That would be Christopher. He always outruns his father in getting home." She got to her feet. "Pray about it, Jayce. Second chances are always possible when God is in the middle of the matter. He is a God of second chances."

———

Jayce took Karen's advice to heart. He began to pray fervently for direction where Leah was concerned. At the same time, he watched Leah interact with her family. She seemed so happy to be a part of something bigger than herself. For the first time, he knew without a doubt that he wanted a wife and children. He could only hope that it wasn't too late to have such a future with Leah Barringer.

"Are you wanting to be alone?" he asked,

coming upon Leah as she sat by the creek that ran behind the cabin.

"No. You're welcome to join me."

He took a seat on the ground beside her. "I remember how much I enjoyed this place. It holds a lot of pleasant memories."

"Yes," she barely breathed the word.

"Leah," he said, pausing to think of how he wanted to word his next thought, "what do you want . . . what are your plans for the future?"

She looked at him oddly, then returned her gaze to the creek. "I don't know. I'd like to have a husband and family, but apparently God hasn't seen that in His plans for me." She grew quiet, as if embarrassed. "I'm sorry," she said, shaking her head. "I shouldn't have said that."

"Why? Can't you be honest with me?"

"Given our past, Jayce, I don't know that I can . . . well . . . it isn't a matter of honesty, but I just don't feel like discussing it with you."

"I wish you would."

A gentle breeze brought with it the scent of rain. Leah shifted to her knees, as if to get up. Instead, she remained for the moment.

"I've talked to Karen about going to Seattle."

"Seattle? But why?"

She sighed as though the thought was almost too much to bear. "She has family there. I might be able to stay with them."

"For what purpose?" Jayce asked. He couldn't begin to understand why she would want to do such a thing.

"Because I want a husband and children," she said firmly and looked at him squarely for the first time. "There are more possibilities for me to find such things . . . in Seattle."

She got to her feet then. "Like I said, I shouldn't be talking to you about any of this."

She walked away, heading past the cabin. Jayce thought about going after her, but it almost felt that an unseen hand held him in place.

Seattle? She'd really leave for Seattle?

His thoughts jumbled and twisted in his mind. He thought she loved Alaska. He needed for her to love Alaska, because if he were to marry her . . . The thought trailed off, and Jayce realized he was practically holding his breath.

He had to convince her to stay. He had to prove to her that the things she said to him ten years ago weren't in vain. He loved her. He knew that now . . . now that he faced losing her again.

Chapter Nineteen

"What do you mean you opened my letter?" Jacob asked, looking at the torn envelope. "This wasn't yours."

"I know," Helaina said, sounding somewhat put off. "I thought it was important."

"Important to meddle in my affairs?" Jacob barely contained his anger. "You above all people should know better."

"Why do you say that? I was just trying to help, and you make it sound like I've committed some sort of crime."

"You have." He looked at her hard. "You're the one who's such a stickler for the letter of the law. You broke the law. You took something that didn't belong to you."

"I didn't take it," she protested. "I only opened it. I didn't try to keep it from you or use it to my own advantage." She looked away at this point, and Jacob couldn't help but wonder what she had thought to gain by reading his mail.

"You shouldn't have done it."

She turned quickly. Jacob was surprised to find that her face was quite flushed. She seemed genuinely embarrassed, but her actions gave him cause for consideration. He had long wondered how he might convince her that her hard attitude—her unyielding, unmerciful heart—was wrong.

"I suppose you want to hear that I'm sorry," she finally said.

"It doesn't matter if you are sorry. A thief is always sorry when he or she is caught."

"I'm not a thief!" She began to pace, as was often her way when upset. "I saw that the letter was marked urgent and that it was from the captain of the *Homestead*. I thought perhaps in your absence, I could help."

"It doesn't matter. You broke the law. My

mail was a private matter between me and the captain."

She exhaled loudly, paused for a moment, then continued to pace. "I don't understand why you're so upset about this. It's not like I tried to hide the letter or keep it from you. You've read it for yourself. You have all the information you now need."

"Yes. That much is true. But since you are a woman of the law, you should face some penalty for breaking the law."

In exasperation she came at him. "This is complete nonsense."

"No. No, it's not. If we went to Nome and I presented my case to the authorities there, told them of how you tampered with my mail, there would be consequences."

Helaina looked more upset than ever. He wondered for a moment if the authorities in Nome could somehow expose her real purpose for being in Alaska.

Helaina crossed her arms and lifted her jaw ever so slightly. "Why are you being so hard about this?"

"Why are you hard about the law?"

Jacob could see her expression change. She seemed to finally understand where he was coming from. "This is such a small offense," she argued. Her tone suggested a sense of defeat.

"So the penalty will probably be fairly small," he countered. "Unless of course the judge wishes to make an example out of you. They do that, you know. I once saw a situation where a woman stole meat for her child. The boy was dying and without food would surely not last another day. The times were hard and she did wrong."

"She should have gone to someone and begged if necessary," Helaina said, seeming to gather her strength. "There is always another way to deal with a difficult situation."

"The judge apparently thought so too. He sentenced her to three months of labor in the jail. She had no one to watch her son, so he took the boy from her and put him in the orphanage. The child died there a week later. He refused to eat because he wanted his mother."

Helaina grimaced. "It wasn't the judge's fault. The mother did wrong."

"And so have you," Jacob said, trying to sound as stern as possible. "I want you to pack your things. I'm taking you to Nome—to the authorities there."

"What? This is ridiculous!" She came to him and took hold of his arm. "I can't believe you would do this."

"But the law is the law, and I am entitled to justice."

Helaina's expression contorted. It was almost as if Jacob could see every confused emotion as it played itself in her mind. "Can't we work this out?" she asked.

She dropped her hold, and Jacob crossed his arms and stared at her with what he hoped was a fierce scowl. "But you deserve to go before the law."

"I do," she said with a sigh. "I know what I did was wrong. I shouldn't have opened your letter, but it . . ." She fell silent and drew a deep breath. "I am without excuse. I did wrong."

"And you deserve to face your consequences."

She met Jacob's gaze. Suddenly he thought she seemed much younger—so frightened and unsure of herself. "I know what I deserve."

"Then there really isn't a question of what should be done. Is there?" He didn't wait for an answer but turned instead to take up his coat. "I can't trust you."

He pulled on his jacket and looked at her for a moment. She stood before him, speechless. He could see that she'd reached the end of her understanding for the situation. She didn't understand the need to seek forgiveness, because in her mind she'd never done anything bad enough to need forgiving.

"Enough of this," he said, feeling rather sad for her. "I won't make you go to Nome. I forgive you. And though the law is the law, and I have every right to seek satisfaction against you—I waive that right. Let's not speak of the letter again."

He saw her shoulders slump forward in relief, yet still she had no words. "This, Helaina, this is mercy. Remember how it feels . . . because chances are better than not that someone, someday, will need mercy from you."

————

Helaina stared at the ceiling long after she'd gone to bed. Her earlier encounter with Jacob had left her emotions raw and her heart uncertain. He had terrified her . . .

made her realize that he held her life—her secret—in his hands. He could have forced her to Nome, where she would have had to take at least the judge into her confidence. Who knew if that would have allowed her to get off—to go unpunished for her actions.

She rolled over and pulled the pillow to her chest. Hugging it close, she realized that Jacob had helped her to see something startling about herself. It scared her—and made her more uneasy than she'd been in a long, long time.

Unable to sleep, she got to her feet and lit the lamp. "I can't understand any of this. God demands justice himself. I've heard enough sermons to know that."

She went to where Jacob had left his Bible and picked it up, contemplating the well-worn book for several minutes. With a deep breath, she took it to the table and sat down, then drew the lamp closer and opened it. The page read *Micah* at the top. She had never heard of this person, or perhaps it was a place. Scanning down, however, her gaze rested on the eighth verse of the sixth chapter.

"He hath shewed thee, O man, what is good; and what doth the Lord require of

thee, but to do justly, and to love mercy, and to walk humbly with thy God."

Helaina trembled at the words. She read them again. Do justly . . . love mercy. God seemed to suggest the two walked hand in hand. But how? She pondered the words, desperate to understand. How could one seek to do justly and love mercy at the same time? It made no sense to her. Surely one would cancel out the other. You could hardly hold people justly responsible for their actions and show mercy. Could you?

"But Jacob just did that with me," she whispered. "He held me responsible—he made me account for my wrongdoing. Then he showed me mercy. I deserved much worse."

She closed the Bible and leaned back. Could it really be that there were times when the law was not to be the focus as much as leniency . . . mercy . . . forgiveness?

She had never felt the need to seek forgiveness from anyone. Not in all of her life—not in the way Jacob suggested that all of mankind needed. Yet Jacob had made her feel a sense of desperation—a sense of need that she couldn't even begin to understand. And not only that; she wanted Jacob to no longer be angry with her. She cared about what he felt—what he thought. She very much wanted his mercy . . . even though she didn't deserve it.

Chapter Twenty

SEPTEMBER 1915

The summer had passed quickly for Leah. She longed for her home in Last Chance, but at the same time she knew she'd miss her family here in Ketchikan. Jayce had been in and out of her world. For a time he had been there with them, then he'd taken off for parts unknown. Leah couldn't help but wonder what he was doing, but she tried not to care too much. She knew something had changed, but she couldn't put her finger on what flickered between them . . . at least not without rekindling a hope that Leah had long tried hard to suppress.

Letters from Jacob told of the frustrations

and difficulties he'd had with Helaina Beecham. The woman had at first seemed so angry regarding any mention of God and the Bible. But over the weeks and given the isolation, Helaina had attended church services and appeared to be quite interested in some of the topics. Jacob himself was surprised by her poignant and educated questions. He thought in time her heart might actually be changed to see God as a loving Creator, rather than a stern, unyielding judge.

Jacob also wrote of the village. The hunts had been excellent; fishing had been so good that they had been able to dry a huge supply for winter. Some of the people liked to bury the fish and dig it up for later use. Leah had never been able to get used to this type of eating. To her, the salmon or cod was rotten, whereas the Eskimo people saw it as a delicacy.

But always Leah's thoughts returned to Jayce. He had promised to return in time to head back to Nome with her. He'd also indicated that he'd like to talk to her about something important but that he would wait until they left for home.

"I can't believe you're already leaving,"

Karen said, holding Leah's clean blouses. "I pressed these, but no doubt after you travel with them, they'll have to be pressed again."

"We're heading into winter at home. The temperatures will be dropping, and before long the snows and ice will seal us in our village," Leah said, smiling. "I'll be wearing so many layers by then that no one will ever see these blouses." The hand-me-downs from Karen were appreciated but were not the most practical for life in Last Chance Creek.

Leah took the clothes and packed them in a small trunk Adrik had given her. There were many other things to take as well. Books were a real treasure, and Karen had given her several to wile away the hours through the long winter months. Adrik had included some items Jacob had requested, and another crate was packed with all kinds of canned goods from Karen and Leah's efforts. It would be a real treat in the village, and Leah already knew she would share generously.

"I hope you won't wait as long to come visit us next time," Karen began. "I know the

Lord has put you in that place for a reason, but I miss you and our long talks."

"I do too. Writing you takes some of that longing away, but it isn't the same."

"Who knows? Maybe they'll run us a telephone line from Last Chance to Ketchikan someday," Karen teased. "Wouldn't that be something?"

"Well, if they can run a train line from Seward to Fairbanks, I would think a phone line across the interior won't be far behind."

"Maybe they'll put a train line in as well. Then you could just hop on board and be here in a couple of days."

Leah tried to imagine for a moment what that might be like. "Do you suppose they'll actually ever accomplish something like that?"

"It's impossible to say. Adrik tells me that there are all sorts of plans in the works. They're already pushing for statehood, you know. They plan to propose it to the Congress as soon as possible."

"It doesn't seem very likely that anyone would care if we became a state or not. Most people think we're nothing but ice up here. I heard that from Jayce."

"What else has he said?" Karen asked.

The look on her face suggested an antici-
pated answer.

"Why? What have you heard?"

Karen shook her head. "Oh no you don't.
I asked first."

Leah closed the lid on her case and tried
to act as though she hadn't thought every
day about Jayce and what he might say to
her once they were alone on the ship home.
"He says he wants to talk to me—when
we're alone."

"About what?"

"He didn't say. He said it was important,
but that he didn't want to interfere with my
time visiting family. Then he's kept himself
kind of busy and out of the way."

"I wasn't going to say anything . . ." Karen
began. "Oh, I really shouldn't say anything
at all." She turned and walked to the window. Lifting back the curtain, she continued. "I guess what I will say is that Jayce
has come a long way. He knows the truth of
who God is—that He's real and not just
some figurehead out there. Jayce cares
about this land—almost as much as Adrik."
She let the curtain fall back into place and
crossed her arms as she met Leah's gaze.

"I think Jayce regrets the past. I hope

you'll both put aside what happened back then and start anew."

"But how does someone just put the past away like that? Especially when the past has been your constant companion for so many years?" Leah questioned.

"I would start with God," Karen said frankly. "He's the only one who can help you let go of your regret and bitterness. He's the only one who will help you make sense of this."

———

Leah thought about Karen's words for days, and even as she boarded the steamer, *Orion's Belt,* Leah contemplated what her former guardian meant by all that she'd said.

"You seem awfully quiet," Jayce said, frowning. "I suppose this is very hard for you."

Leah felt almost startled by his words. She didn't know quite what to say. "I'll miss them—but I miss my home in Last Chance too."

"So you've decided to stay in Alaska?"

"How could I not? There's just something about this place." She smiled and waved to her family on shore. "Everywhere I go it's different; the land is so vast and so unpredictable. I'd actually like to see every inch of this territory." She looked at him and laughed at the stunned look on his face. "Does that shock you so much?"

"Shock me?" He shook his head. "No, not really shock. It's more like a pleasant surprise."

"But why should it be a surprise? I've made no secret about loving Alaska."

"But what of going husband hunting in Seattle? I heard they could be bought on the docks, just like many other things," he teased.

Leah forced herself to rest in God's peace rather than focus on how nice Jayce looked—his dark hair, a little longer than usual, blowing in the gentle breeze. "I'm trying hard to let the Lord lead me," she finally admitted. "But I've never been good at that kind of thing. I'm much too impatient."

"You? I find that hard to believe. You're the most patient person I've ever met. Look at the way you took such good care of me when I had the leg injury. Even now, when my leg pains me, you slow down your pace and walk at my speed. Don't think I haven't noticed."

She smiled and leaned against the railing, pleased that he'd been aware of this act of kindness. Karen had long ago suggested that Leah display only a gentle and loving spirit when dealing with Jayce. In changing her heart in this way, Leah had to admit she felt better about herself and about Jayce. It hadn't been easy, but over the weeks in Ketchikan, Leah had tried her best to just be friends with Jayce and enjoy his company. She had no idea of what might happen in the future, but she wanted to remember the summer of 1915 as one of peace and joy.

That night after supper, Leah thought perhaps Jayce could talk to her about whatever it was he wanted to say. But instead they passed a quiet evening reading in the salon before heading to their individual cabins.

After weaving in and out of a dozen or so islands, they finally docked in Sitka. Leah thought Jayce might talk to her here as they enjoyed a short time on shore, but he never did. Leah sensed he was nervous, and that only served to make her edgy. She thought maybe he wanted to ensure that she wouldn't resort to her old self—dealing with him in a vile, ill-tempered manner, since he planned to live in Last Chance Creek for the winter.

The ship departed Sitka that evening and pushed out into the ocean. It wouldn't dock again until Seward, where the ship would deliver workers for the railroad project.

"Leah?"

It was Jayce. He'd found her at the rail, shivering as she watched the endless waters of the Pacific. "It's getting late. I wasn't sure where you were. You know it's not all that safe to venture around on your own."

"You forget, Jayce, that I'm used to taking care of myself. Jacob is often gone, and I've learned to be independent and capable." She tried not to sound challenging or smug, but she could tell by the way Jayce shrugged that she'd probably said the wrong thing.

"I'm ready to go in," she added with a smile. "It's getting colder."

"There's also quite a squall line on the horizon. Captain thinks we're in for stormy weather."

"Then we should probably get below. I wouldn't want to be responsible for keeping you out and losing you overboard," she teased.

He grinned and took hold of her elbow. "I maintain that you do not have much confidence in me or my abilities."

Leah started to give him a sassy retort, then paused. She looked up at him and realized he was watching her quite intently. Their faces were only inches away, so it seemed only natural that he should close the distance and kiss her.

It felt like something from one of her dreams, and Leah closed her eyes and prayed that she might never awaken. This was her first and only real kiss, and she wanted to memorize every moment of it. She didn't even realize that she'd put her arms around Jayce's neck until he pulled back and whispered, "I wasn't expecting that kind of reception."

She felt her face grow hot, and she quickly jumped back. "I'm . . . I didn't . . . oh . . ." The words died in her throat. What had she done?

He chuckled. "I didn't mind that kind of reception, if that's what has you worried."

She licked her bottom lip, then chewed on it nervously. *What should I say? What can I do? I don't want to appear wanton. Oh, what must he think of me? If he calls me a child or tells me I'm too young . . .*

"Leah?"

She looked up and met his sweet, gentle face. His dark eyes seemed to pierce her through to the heart. "What?" She barely breathed the word.

"I'm not sorry for kissing you. I hope you're not sorry either."

He said nothing more, and Leah, in her state of shock, couldn't make words form in her mouth. Instead, she allowed Jayce to lead her below. Once he was assured she was safely inside with the door locked, he called good-night and left her there.

For several minutes, all Leah could do was stare dumbly at the door. What had just happened? Better still, when might it happen again?

———

Leah awoke to a horrible pitching of the boat. She sat up in bed, nearly being dumped from her mattress as she struggled to balance herself.

The storm!

Jayce had said there was a storm headed

their way. She had an inside cabin, so there was no window from which to observe the situation. She pulled the blanket up around her neck and wondered if they were in any danger. She hoped the weather might pass them quickly and the rocking abate.

For hours she felt the ship fight the waves. Nausea washed over her, but Leah had never been one given to seasickness and refused to succumb to the situation. For a moment, she thought of going to find Jayce. He would be able to tell her if they were in any real danger. Would he be angry? she wondered. Surely it was nothing more than a simple storm, and soon it would pass and all would be well again.

The room seemed to close in, however, as Leah waited in the darkness. *What should I do?* The ship heaved hard to the right, tossing Leah from the mattress. She landed on the floor with a thud, her hip stinging from the fall. She tried to pull herself up, but then the ship slammed down recklessly to the left. Without hope of control, Leah fell hard against the frame of the bed, this time hitting her head.

A knock sounded at her door, but Leah felt unable to rise to answer it. To her surprise the door opened and Jayce entered the room. "Are you okay?" he asked, rushing to her side.

"I think so. I hit my head, but I'm not seeing stars or anything." She let him help her up. They could barely balance against the pitching of the ship. "What's happening? Why are you here?" She felt her breath quicken as she realized he was holding her quite close.

"Listen, Leah, the truth is, we're in trouble. The ship's captain has called for help from every able-bodied man. We're taking on water."

She swallowed hard. "We're sinking?"

"Not if I can help it." He leaned down and kissed her hard. "Leah, I love you."

The words refused to register. She looked at him, dumbfounded. She longed to say something, but, what if his words were simply borne of fear? Perhaps he was just responding to the threat of the storm.

"Don't look at me that way," he said with a laugh. "You look absolutely disgusted with me. I know I've made a lot of mistakes, Leah, but this could be the last chance I have to tell you how I feel."

"I'm not disgusted," she managed to say.

"I . . . I don't know what I am. But I'm sure it has nothing to do with disgust."

He kissed her again, then guided her hand to the metal frame of the bed. "Hold tight." She wrapped her fingers around the piece and did as he told her.

"I have to go, but I didn't want to leave without letting you know how I feel. I've been a fool, Leah. I know that now. I wish I'd known it ten years ago."

She felt her senses regroup. "I knew it ten years ago," she said, trying hard not to sound frightened.

He smiled. "But that's because you're smarter than me." The ship seemed to groan beneath them. "Look, I have to go. Stay here unless they call to abandon the ship."

"Do you think they will?"

"I don't know how bad the damage is. I know we're in trouble, but I'm hoping we can turn it around. Get dressed and make sure your things are ready in case we have to leave quickly. And, Leah?"

"What?" She felt her knees begin to shake violently.

"Pray."

With that he crossed the room and left,

leaving her door open to the passageway. Mindless of the exposure, Leah fought against the motion to pull on her sealskin pants over woolen tights. They would keep her warm against the ocean air, should they have to seek shelter in a lifeboat.

"Father, please stop the storm. Send it away from us and calm the seas. Oh, help us, Father," she prayed as she began layering her clothes. She had already been wearing a long woolen undershirt that Karen had made for her. She added a blouse over this and a kuspuk to top the blouse. She had no heavy parka, for Jacob had promised to bring that to Nome when he met her there. She couldn't help but wonder if she would be warm enough should they have to leave the ship.

To her surprise, Leah began to realize that the pitching had lessened. She breathed a sigh of relief. The storm was passing. That had to be good. Perhaps the danger had passed. "Thank you, God," she whispered.

Most of her things had been packed into crates and stored in the hold, but what little remained in the cabin she quickly packed in her small bag. As a last thought, she took up the box of matches on the nightstand

and stuck them in her mukluks as she
pulled the heavy boots on over her wool
socks. They might have need of them later,
and Jacob had taught her there was never
such a thing as a useless item in the
Alaskan Territory.

But just as Leah felt that things were improving, people began to run amuck in the
passageway. She heard their shouts and
their frightened cries.

"I have to get my children!"

"Where's my key? I have to get my things
from the cabin!"

"No, sir! Leave everything. There won't be
room in the lifeboats."

Lifeboats? Leah felt her feet freeze in
place. It was impossible to tell, but she
thought she heard a man crying, "Abandon
ship! Abandon ship!"

She moved to the door and tried to step
out, only to be pushed back inside by a
heavyset man who appeared to have the
cabin across from hers.

"What's happening?" she asked.

"Didn't you hear? We're sinking. We're to
abandon ship now!" the man said before
disappearing into his room.

Leah went back to the bed where she'd left her bag. If the man had been correct, she would need to leave her things. She quickly took off the kuspuk and opened her bag. She took out another blouse and pulled it on over the first one. Replacing the kuspuk, she then took up three pairs of heavy wool socks and stuffed them into the top of her pants. The rest could be left behind—along with all the wonderful things she had in the hold.

She felt a sort of listing to the right as she hurried to the hall. People were frantic, nearly throwing each other to the floor as they fought to get topside. Leah avoided them as best she could but found herself slammed against the wall more than once.

"We must get to the lifeboats," a woman sobbed as she pushed past Leah. "We have to or we'll die." She looked Leah in the eyes just long enough to reflect the terror in her heart.

"We cannot panic," Leah said, trying to help the woman to the stairs. "We must be brave."

The woman seemed to absorb this for a moment and finally nodded. "We must be brave." She continued to murmur this over and over as they made their way along the passage.

Leah focused on each step as they fell into line behind the other people making their way to the top. In her mind, Leah cared only about one thing. Where was Jayce? Had he already abandoned ship?

"No, he would have come for me," she murmured.

"Where will we go?" another passenger questioned from behind her. "We're in the middle of the ocean. Who will find us here?"

Other people began to comment on this—each one more terrified than the one before. She prayed for them silently. *Please, Lord, calm their spirits.*

A strong beefy-armed man reached out to pull her up the last two steps. "Come on, miss. Make your way to the port side. We don't want another *Titanic* on our hands. Come on, folks, there's plenty of lifeboats for everybody. Make your way down."

Leah thought of the luxury liner that had sunk only three years earlier after hitting an iceberg. The tragic loss of life had been overwhelming. When she and Jacob had finally heard about the horrific ordeal, it was already old news. Now she might very well live through another Titanic situation.

"Get on down there, lady. There are boats waiting to be lowered."

She searched the decks for any sign of Jayce. He had to be there! He had to be somewhere! She broke away from the pressing stream of people who were rushing to reach safety.

"Jayce!" she called over and over. Her façade of calm fell away. "Jayce, where are you?"

But with everyone else screaming and calling the names of their loved ones, Leah knew it was hopeless. She might never see him again. The thought chilled her to the bone and frightened her more than the idea of setting into the ocean in nothing but a small lifeboat.

She might lose him again. Only this time—it would be forever.

Chapter Twenty-one

Jayce searched the deck for Leah and could find no sign of her. A few of the men were loading into boats where women sat in numb silence, while down in the water, lifeboats were splaying out on the still-choppy waters. Jayce felt bad for the passengers. They were terrified, and with good reason. He hurried to help two of the crew who struggled with the winch to lower one of the boats. The people in the boat were screaming as the mechanism lowered them in a lopsided manner. If the crewmen continued, they'd spill them all into the Pacific.

"Let me help," Jayce said, pushing one of the young men out of his way.

"It's stuck," the sailor said.

Jayce gave the handle a good kick, then pushed with all his might. The winch gave way, and the boat lowered in an even manner.

Jayce glanced up and caught a fleeting sight of a woman. He craned his neck to see around the sailor. It was Leah! He called to her and she stopped in midstep. As she turned, he could see the abject terror in her expression. Hurrying through the remaining men, he reached her and glanced at his watch. "Three minutes."

"What?" she asked, embracing him. "I couldn't find you."

"Well, you have now. Only we have to hurry. The boiler is going to blow this ship sky-high. We need to get to a boat." He glanced left and saw a boat being lowered with only two women. "Come on, hurry."

They ran for the side, and Jayce quickly called to the sailors. "Stop! Two more." The men seemed nervously irritated but waited for Jayce and Leah to board. "Hurry!" Jayce said, motioning to the men. "Then join us. We'll wait for you."

The men lowered them in record speed. They hit the water hard, nearly spilling the old woman at the far side of the boat. She cried out, but held fast to the side with one hand, while gripping what appeared to be a native-made bowl with the other. Jayce could do nothing to help her, and Leah was already trying to comfort the other woman, who was grabbing at her chest and moaning.

"We have to put on life jackets," Jayce called. "They're in the storage box."

Leah went to work to retrieve them. They were wrapped in a canvas-type tarp and looked fairly new. Jayce breathed a sigh of relief at this. He'd heard stories of life jackets that were no good to anyone because of their age and poor craftsmanship.

Leah helped the sick woman, whom they'd learned was named Bethel, into her jacket, but the old woman flatly refused to put hers on. "It's too confining. I know how to swim."

Jayce didn't have the heart to tell her that the cold temperatures of the water would be more likely to claim her life than the water itself.

Jayce looked at his watch. They were

nearly out of time—the boiler would blow soon. He pulled on his own life jacket as Leah secured hers, and then he took up oars. "Leah, get the other oars—we have to get out of here." She did as he told her as he looked back up to the men who'd helped them. "Jump for it. We'll pick you up."

There were two other lifeboats nearby. The men on these encouraged the crew as well. "Jump! Jump! We're right here. We have blankets. Jump!"

Jayce watched as several sailors did just that. They hit the icy waters and disappeared into the darkness. Jayce watched for them to reappear. One by one, like bobbers on a fishing line, they came up—fighting and thrashing against the icy cold. Two of the men were quickly picked up by one of the other boats, but none of the sailors were close enough for Jayce to reach.

"Leah, let's row in this direction." He pointed the way, then began to put his back into it. Leah did likewise. They had moved out maybe twenty yards when the first explosion nearly capsized them.

"Keep rowing, Leah. Keep rowing. We have to get away from the ship."

They did their best, but Jayce knew it

wouldn't be easy to escape harm. When the second, more deadly explosion came only seconds later, they were pummeled with fiery debris. Jayce kept rowing. He felt something bite into his neck and arms while pieces of the ship came down like rain.

The fire lit up the night, and around them Jayce could see boats fighting to get away from the doomed ship. They were in the midst of utter chaos. No one was paying attention to anyone else; they were only thinking of survival.

Jayce saw a man floating in the water face down. He stopped rowing and motioned for Leah to help him. They reached over the side together and tried to pull the man to safety. Then Jayce's worst fears were confirmed as they rolled the man over. "He's dead, Leah," he said. "Let him go."

"Oh," Bethel moaned behind Leah. "I'm dying."

Jayce looked at the woman. She seemed to be gasping for breath, while beyond her the other old lady had apparently succumbed to her fears and fainted. The cherished bowl lay at her feet, surprisingly in one piece.

The fire was dying away as the ship continued to sink. Here and there fiery debris floated on the water, temporarily lighting their way. It would only be a matter of minutes until they were in darkness once again. Jayce felt the hopelessness of their situation settle on his shoulders. What were they to do now?

Leah turned to help Bethel. "Just rest. The worst is over now. Don't worry your heart anymore."

The woman's tear-stained face haunted Jayce. "I have a daughter in Nome. If I don't make it . . ."

"Shh, you'll make it," Leah encouraged.

"But if I don't, please let her know what happened to me. Her name is Caroline Rivers."

Jayce watched Leah comfort the woman. Her tenderness to this stranger caused Jayce to only love Leah more. Dr. Cox in Nome had said she was a great healer, and Jayce could understand why. Leah had a natural heart for making others feel better.

"Jayce, I think the other passenger is dead."

He shook off his thoughts. "What?"

Leah's expression was stricken. "She's

taken a blow to her head. The piece is still there. She's dead."

Bethel began to sob. "We're all doomed. God have mercy on us."

"Come on, Leah. We need to row and catch up with the others," Jayce said, still not certain what should be done.

Leah grabbed up the oar and positioned herself to row. It was the only thing they could do, Jayce reasoned. There were no other options.

Jacob awoke with a start. He didn't know why, but he immediately thought of Leah. He sat up and listened. He had been help-ing Anamiaq cut thick bricks of tundra sod. The man was adding an addition onto his small house since they were to have an-other baby.

"Leah?" Jacob said aloud. He could have sworn he'd heard her call him. His uneasi-ness grew. Something was wrong.

He lit a lantern and checked his watch. It was three in the morning. He yawned and tried to figure out what was wrong. Leah was traveling back by ship. Jacob had planned to leave for Nome the next day.

Had something happened? Was she all right?

He tried to lie back down and sleep, but it was impossible. He got up and left the tent, checking on the few dogs he'd brought with him. He and Anamiaq had planned to get the sod cut, then wait to transport it until they could bring out the dogsled teams. It wouldn't be long, given the recent weather. The dogs seemed fine, but they, too, were restless.

"Something wrong?" Anamiaq called out from the tent.

"I don't know. I have a bad feeling about Leah, and I can't seem to shake it. I don't know why, but I just feel like she's in trouble."

————

The heavy cloud coverage and fog obscured the sun and kept Jayce wondering where they were. They had lost track of the other lifeboats sometime in the night, and now they were on their own. Jayce constantly consulted his compass, hoping to get them back to the closest shore, but he figured them to be quite a ways out. He tried to calculate just how many miles out from

Sitka they might have been, but the storm had wreaked havoc with any accurate measurements. They were tossed about all over the ocean; they could be closer or they might be farther away. It was impossible to tell without some sort of landmark.

"I wish we had something I could give to Bethel," Leah said as the woman slept. "I'm afraid for her."

"I know. Look, there's another problem here," Jayce said, glancing at the dead woman at the opposite end. "We'll have to . . . well . . . you know . . . let her go," he said hesitantly. "I don't know where we are or how long it will be before we find help. It's not good for us to carry her body around."

"We don't even know who she is. Bethel doesn't know her. She has nothing on her that identifies where she's from or who she is," Leah protested.

"I know, and I'm sorry." He knew she understood, but he also knew how difficult this situation had become. It could be days before they were rescued.

"It's starting to rain again," Leah said, looking heavenward. "Give me the tarp. I'll see if we can't save some of the water to drink. It won't taste pleasant, but it will keep us alive."

Jayce helped her to accomplish setting up a kind of protection for them, while positioning the tarp to allow for water to run into the dead woman's bowl. This was their only hope for fresh water.

The rain poured steadily for over an hour and showed no signs of letting up. While Bethel slept, Jayce carefully made his way to the dead woman. With Leah's help, they lifted her body over the side and released her to a watery grave. Jayce felt they should say something. "We should pray," he told Leah as the body disappeared in the waves.

"That would be good," she replied, tears in her eyes. "At least God knows who she is."

Jayce bowed his head. "Lord, you know each of us here, just as Leah mentioned that you know this woman. Receive her into your kingdom, Lord. Give her family peace of mind when they hear of her passing." He paused and tried to think of what else he might say in this small, impromptu funeral. "Please guide our way home . . . show us what to do to survive. Keep us from fear, Lord. Draw us near to you. Amen."

"Amen," Leah murmured. "Come on, get back under the tarp or we'll be completely drenched." They huddled together, clutching the edges of the canvas as they sought refuge beneath its canopy.

"We need to keep pushing east," Jayce finally said. "We know we'll find land either east or north, but east is our better bet. We weren't that far out—not so far that we can't catch the current and make it back with a little work."

Leah nodded. "I trust you to know what's best."

He smiled. "Since when?"

She raised a brow and studied him for a moment. "Since you told me you loved me. That caused me to realize you were finally making sense."

"I do love you, you know—that wasn't just spoken out of the horror of the moment."

Leah looked away and shrugged. "I had thought of that."

He turned her back to face him. "Then don't. Because it isn't true. I love you. I knew it back in Ketchikan. No, I knew it the moment I saw you in Last Chance—when you welcomed me home."

"I thought you were Jacob." She frowned. "Poor Jacob. He'll be frantic when news of this reaches him."

Jayce hadn't really thought of how this might affect anyone else. "Your family in Ketchikan will hear of it too."

"They'll all be sick with worry." She shook her head. "I can only pray God gives them peace of mind. They know us. They know our strength. Surely they will have some hope that we will keep each other alive."

Jayce nodded. "I would think so. Especially since they know your determination."

Hours later, as the night came upon them, Leah wasn't at all sure her determination was worth much. She hated to admit her fears to Jayce, but the truth was, this was the scariest thing she'd ever endured. She felt comforted only by her continued prayers and the fact that Jayce seemed so self-assured and confident of getting them to land.

Bethel wasn't doing well at all, and all

three of them were suffering from exposure, thirst, and hunger. As the seas calmed, Leah huddled in close to Bethel and tried to keep the woman warm. The tarp offered very little protection, but it was better than nothing. Jayce was tired, and Leah knew it would do none of them any good if he grew ill from lack of sleep. At the same time, she knew they couldn't just drift aimlessly all night. They might lose any chance for finding their way if they didn't stay alert and watchful.

"You need rest," Leah told Jayce as she sat up. "I can row awhile."

"Go ahead and sleep. I'll need your help soon enough."

"You've been at this all day."

"I've rested off and on. Look, I think we're getting closer. You rest, and then you can take over in a few hours."

She nodded and repositioned herself beside Bethel. The woman stirred and asked, "Have we arrived?"

Leah patted her arm. "Not yet, Bethel. Just sleep."

Leah dozed off to the rhythmic movement of the boat. She dreamed of being a young girl and of listening to a Sunday school lesson about Jesus walking on the water. Even in her dream she wished she might have that same ability. *Then,* she thought, *I could walk to land.*

Chapter Twenty-two

From the moment they set foot in Nome, Jacob knew the truth. *Orion's Belt* had been scheduled into Nome in three days time, but word had already come that the ship had met with problems in the Pacific. No one had heard from *Orion's Belt* since she left Sitka Sound.

"The passengers are probably safe," Helaina tried to encourage. "There have been a great many changes in the rules and laws surrounding safety on ships. Ever since the *Titanic* . . ."

Jacob scowled at her. "This is Alaska, not the civilized world, as you so often like to point out. Rules are often overlooked up here."

"But those ships travel south as well," Helaina protested. "They would have to follow regulations or risk extremely high fines. When the *Titanic* went down—"

"I don't want to hear about this! I have to figure out what to do now." Jacob paced the dock for a moment. "I'm going to Sitka," he finally said. "I'm taking the first available ship. If there are any still coming into Nome." He knew this would be the most difficult thing. There were fewer and fewer ships willing to risk getting stuck in the frozen north.

"I'll come with you."

He turned and found Helaina looking at him quite earnestly. That she would join him on this search for Leah and Jayce touched him deeply. "You don't need to do that," he said softly, "but you are kind to offer."

She shook her head, bits of blond hair pulling away from the haphazard bun she'd secured only minutes before they'd come into town. "You shouldn't go alone. This is a difficult enough situation when you have someone at your side to help bear the load. I won't let you do this by yourself."

Jacob saw her determination. He wouldn't try to stop her. He still didn't know who she really was or why she'd come north, but there was no doubt she felt sympathy for his situation. She might even feel some sense of responsibility, given she'd stepped into Leah's shoes for the past few months.

"All right. We'll go together. I don't know how long we'll be gone, though. If you need to make your way back to the expedition headquarters, I'll understand. If we haven't found Leah and Jayce, however, I'll have to say no to helping Captain Latimore until I figure out what's happened."

"I'm sure he'll understand that, Jacob. Your family should come first."

Helaina waited impatiently for Jacob to return with their tickets to Sitka. She was angry with herself for pretending to care about Jacob's situation, while at the same time she knew it wasn't entirely a façade. She didn't want him to face the possibility of his sister's death by himself, yet she was really more interested in knowing the fate of Jayce Kincaid. Jacob had already told her that Leah's letter mentioned she and Jayce would return together on the ship *Orion's*

Belt out of Ketchikan. This had intrigued Helaina, who was still trying to figure out how it was that Jayce could have been north with Captain Latimore, while also being in Ketchikan with Leah. She had just about convinced herself that there were two men—both using the name Jayce Kincaid. But which was the real one—who was the criminal that she sought? She had wanted to ask Jacob about the matter, but she feared bringing up the fact that she'd opened and read his letter. And besides, she couldn't be sure what side he might take if he knew the truth of why she'd come to Alaska.

Helaina sighed. She would just have to ponder the matter alone.

Kincaid had never been photographed, but the man who had tried to kill her brother was the spitting image of the man she'd known as Jayce Kincaid. She'd even written to Stanley on the subject. His reply was simply *Bring him back.*

"We can't leave until the day after tomorrow," Jacob said in frustration. "I tried everything, but there's nothing. We're lucky to get this one—it's a freighter headed to

Seattle. We can get off partway and try to get a ship headed to Sitka after that.

"There aren't as many ships coming north—pretty soon there won't be any. The weather has been much worse than usual, and everyone thinks it's going to be a real danger to keep sending ships up here. The days are slipping away fast, and before you know it the ice will keep captains from risking their livelihood."

"I heard ships often come here and dock out in the unfrozen portions of sea. Then people are sledded across the frozen water to Nome," Helaina said, looking out across the gray waters.

"True enough, but nothing is ever predictable. Sometimes the ships can make it through and sometimes they can't. Eventually the risk is too great and they wait for spring. So many elements are in play. But it doesn't matter. We'll leave when we can. If there isn't a ship home, John and Oopick will see to our things and the dogs. Nothing is as important as knowing whether Leah and Jayce are safe."

"But, Jacob," she said, hesitant to bring up the subject, "what if . . . well . . . what if you don't find them? Ships go down all the time and lives are lost and never accounted for." Helaina had already been struggling with this thought. If they had no account of Jayce's death, she would always wonder if he hadn't just slipped away again.

Jacob looked at her for a moment, and the anger shone clear in his eyes. "You always have to look on the bad side of everything, don't you? If you would just stop trying to be God in your own life, you might realize He has the ability to bring things around right."

Jacob stalked off down the street, leaving Helaina to watch after him in frustrated silence. She wanted to call after him or even run after him and tell him how wrong he was. She wanted to declare for all around that she didn't always think the worst. But instead, Jacob's words about God troubled her more than her desire to have the last word.

He'd accused her of trying to be God in her own life. How ridiculous, she thought. How silly to imagine that anyone would attempt to take on a job like that. But in refusing God's direction in her life, she supposed there was a certain element of truth in what Jacob said. And for reasons beyond her ability to understand just yet, that bothered her more than she could explain.

———

Leah awoke to stillness. Absolute stillness. There was no wind—no rocking motion. Startled, she sat up to find they had actually beached on land. She thought for a moment that she might be dreaming.

Heavy clouds overhead began to sprinkle down rain. Leah looked for Jayce, but couldn't find him anywhere. More startling was the fact that Bethel was missing. Had she passed on during the night? Had Jayce simply slipped her body into the sea to keep from causing Leah to endure another funeral?

A sort of panic welled up in her. "Jayce!"

She got to her feet and realized that the boat was empty of their few supplies, including the tarp. "Jayce!"

Then she saw him. He came bounding out of the woods, waving his arms. "I'm here. It's all right. I'm here."

She ran to him as rain began to fall in earnest. "I thought I'd lost you," she cried against his neck. "Oh, where were you?"

"Putting the finishing touches on our

shelter. I just got Bethel secured and was coming back for you. Come on, we're getting wet."

Leah let him lead her into the forest of spruce and alder. "Bethel's all right, then?"

"She's resting again. I think she's just suffered such a shock that it's been hard on her heart. Watch your step here." He helped her over some fallen trees.

"Yes, I thought that too. Perhaps I can find some plants here to help her." Leah looked around the shore. "Where are we, by the way?"

"I'm not sure, but I'm thinking it might be Baranof Island."

"Then we'd not be far from Sitka," she said, looking as far down the shore as her eyes could see.

"If it is Baranof, we're probably well away from Sitka. Probably the south end of the island. I was here for a time eight or so years ago. It looks somewhat familiar to me, but I can't be sure."

"Well, at least it's land," Leah said. "That's fine with me. I know how to survive here. Out there," she said, motioning back toward the water, "is another story."

They came upon the small camp. He'd

done well, Leah thought. He'd placed them in a protected area where large rocks created a natural wall and willows made it easy to implement the tarp to make a shelter. She shed her life jacket and tossed it inside.

"Bethel, how are you feeling?" Leah asked as she crawled under the canvas.

"I'm better, but so very weary. I feel as though I haven't eaten in months."

"We plan to rectify that situation soon," Leah said. "I can make a trap and set it out to catch us something to eat. Plus there are all sorts of berries on this island. They are probably very picked over by the wildlife and natives, but we'll find food. You'll see."

Jayce smiled at her. "I knew we were in good hands," he said teasingly.

Bethel eased back on her bed of spruce boughs, using her life jacket for a pillow. "I can rest now, knowing that we're all safe."

The rain poured down but there was no wind, and for this Leah was very grateful. She looked around the little camp and found Jayce had tried to secure what few things they had. The water pot was there, half full with rainwater, and Jayce had shed his coat to let it dry over another stack of boughs.

"So how are we set for supplies? I see you must have a knife, because you've cut down the branches," she said, meeting his gaze.

"I have a knife, a compass, a comb, some money, and a belt. And, of course, my clothes," Jayce said. "Not really much to speak of."

"At least we have a knife. That means a lot," Leah said, reaching into her mukluks. "And we have these." She took out the matches and held them up.

"You brilliant girl," Jayce said, a grin spreading across his face. "Now we can keep warm."

"And cook food," Leah added. "If we catch some."

"We'll find something. I'll see to that."

"One thing we can get relatively soon is fish," Leah said. "If you make a circle of rocks on the tide floor, stack them high, but not so high as to be out of the water when the tide is in, we can trap fish. When the tide comes in, the fish will collect in the trap, and when the tide goes back out, they will be unable to swim over the rocks."

He got up and took his coat. "I can get to

work on that right now. The tide is out and the rain isn't so bad as to keep me from accomplishing the job. Can you build a fire?"

"Yes. I can do that. Bethel will be resting anyway," Leah said, noting that the old woman was already snoring.

They each went to their separate tasks. Leah knew how to dig out dried kindling from beneath the heavy forest ground covering. Here she also found logs, dried and brittle from years of hidden neglect. Before long, she had a fire blazing between an opening in the canvas and the rocky outcropping. The smoke climbed the wall of stone and was smothered in the rain.

Jayce returned just as Bethel was awaking. Leah couldn't help but giggle at the sight of him with his rolled up wool trousers. He carried his boots and socks in hand. "I hope that works. I'm soaked to the bone, and my feet and legs are frozen. If we don't get any fish, it won't be for lack of effort."

"Could I have a drink?" Bethel asked.

"Certainly. Here, let me help you sit up," Leah offered. Jayce took up the little pottery bowl and handed it to Leah. "We all have to share one vessel, I'm sorry to say. But after what we've all come through, I'm sure this is the least of our worries."

Bethel drank her fill, then let Leah help her reposition in order to sit up for a while. Leaning back against the rock, Bethel offered them both a smile. "I have lived through worse, but not much."

"Where are you from, Bethel?" Jayce asked, settling down to warm himself by the fire.

"I was actually born and raised in California. Then I married a man of God who desired to come north to preach the gospel to the natives of this new territory. We lived most of our life near Prince of Wales and Kotzebue."

"I know that area well," Leah replied. "I live in Last Chance Creek, not far from Cape Woolley. My brother and I often go to that area to trade and collect furs."

"Why, we were practically neighbors," Bethel said with a nod.

"Is your husband still living?" Jayce asked.

"I'm sorry to say I lost him last year. We had just celebrated our fiftieth wedding anniversary not but the day before." Tears came to the old woman's eyes. "I'm afraid it is still difficult to talk about. I miss him a great deal."

Leah patted the woman's arm. "You needn't cause yourself pain on our account. Tell us instead about your life as a missionary. How fascinating that must have been. When did you go north?"

Bethel composed herself a bit and then spoke. "We married in 1864. The Civil War was going on, and people were fighting bitterly in the east. In California, gold fever and other problems consumed the minds of men. My husband suggested we get involved with ministering to the poor souls who came to pan for gold only to lose everything, including the shirt off their backs. We spent a time in California and Nevada, but it was never what my husband really wanted. One day in the late 1870s he came in to me. He had heard about a man who was setting up schools and missions in Alaska. Have you heard of Sheldon Jackson?"

"Of course," Leah said. The man had been responsible for starting many missions and schools in her area as well. There had also been an interesting experiment with introducing reindeer stations that had caused quite a stir among the natives.

"Dr. Jackson encouraged us to come to Sitka first, and then he persuaded us to go west to Teller and the other places I mentioned."

"So you've been in Alaska all these years," Leah said, shaking her head. "You've seen the gold rushes come and go but have remained to outlive the sensation of it all."

"True enough," Bethel replied. "We raised three lovely girls up there. Caroline is the oldest. She loved the land and remained, whereas the others went south. I was just returning from a trip to see them. That's why I was on the ship."

"We were heading home too," Leah said, unable to keep the longing from her voice. "My brother and I have lived in Last Chance for over ten years."

"Do you know the Kjellmann's, then?" Bethel asked.

"They are dear friends. Emma is like the sister I never had," Leah admitted.

"What do you do there?"

"In the past, my brother ran the mail in the winter. He was awarded the contract for several smaller villages, but this year he decided to forego it."

Bethel looked to Jayce, asking, "But why would you do that? What else will you do for a job?"

Jayce laughed. "I'm not her brother, but I think I can speak for him. He's been asked to help with an Arctic exploration. I was to be a part of that as well. I think Jacob plans to put things in order so that he can attempt that trip next year."

"We also run a trading post of sorts," Leah threw out. "We'll still have that, and Jacob will no doubt have to run for supplies throughout the winter."

Bethel seemed to consider this a moment, then turned back to Jayce. "If you aren't the brother, then who are you?"

"I hope to be the husband," he said, throwing a wink at Leah. "I haven't asked her yet, but I'm working up to it."

Bethel laughed. "I promise not to say a word."

Leah looked at Jayce in dumbfounded silence. Surely he hadn't just said what she thought he'd said. *Did he just say that he planned to marry me?*

Her heart pounded in her ears, blocking

out Bethel and Jayce's conversation. After all they'd been through—all the pain and years of absence—had Jayce really just proposed in his roundabout way?

Chapter Twenty-three

"What do you mean we can't go out and search?" Jacob asked a man at the Sitka docks. "I'm willing to pay you good money."

Their trip from Nome hadn't been easy or fast, and now he was feeling the stress of not knowing if Leah and Jayce had survived. There had been no word. Bodies had been recovered, but identifying them was difficult. Jacob had gone to the makeshift morgue to see if any of them were Leah or Jayce. To his relief, they weren't among the dead, but that relief was short-lived.

"Look around you, mister," the older man declared. "This weather ain't right for being on the water. I know you're worried. Other folks here are worried as well. We'll go when things calm down."

Jacob knew the man was right. The ocean was pitching and roiling; he'd never have attempted such a sea at home. The chill in the air offered him no comfort as he thought of Leah being lost out there on the water—or worse. He tried not to think of all the possibilities.

For several moments he just stood staring at the angry gray waters. Somewhere out there, he fervently believed, Leah and Jayce were struggling to survive . . . and he couldn't help them. It had been nearly two weeks since *Orion's Belt* went down. How could he not know what had happened? How could he just stand idly by and wait?

When he came back to the hotel, Helaina was there to meet him. "What happened? Any word?"

"No," Jacob said. "The weather has made it impossible to search. Short of those boats that made it into various ports, there haven't been reports of other survivors. They aren't finding any more bodies. The search has pretty much been called off."

"I'm sorry, Jacob."

They sat down in the lobby of the hotel and said nothing for several minutes. Jacob didn't like the feeling of helplessness that washed over him. He had fought so hard to get this far, and now there was nothing he could do but wait.

"Have you had any word from your family?" Helaina prompted.

"Adrik is searching with some of the men from his area. He plans to work his way up the island coast and then in Sitka after that. He thought we could work together." Jacob stared off into space. Leah was smart and very capable. Jayce too. If they'd made it to a lifeboat, they would be capable of surviving. He was sure of it. He prayed for them— for all the passengers of *Orion's Belt*—but it didn't feel like enough.

"So where is God in all of this?" Helaina's tone told him that she wasn't merely trying to stir up trouble; she really wanted answers. Answers Jacob wasn't sure he could come up with.

"Sometimes it's hard to understand why things like this happen," Jacob said, trying to relax in the chair. "I know I've questioned God several times in my life, and I always see the answer later, or else God gives me a peace about it. Like when my ma died. I didn't see any good purpose in that, but later, I realized she'd always been kind of fragile and weak. She might have lived on like that and my pa would never have been able to endure it. I figure he would have left all of us—not because he didn't care about us, but because he wouldn't have been able to watch my ma die day by day. That would have broken my mother's heart. At least she died feeling loved and cared about."

"I still see no good reason for my parents and husband to be murdered. I know you say there is probably a good reason— something God wants to teach me in all of this—but I don't see it. Those kinds of lessons are cruel. Like now."

Jacob looked at her for a moment. She really was a beautiful woman. "Answers to our questions aren't always real clear—and frankly, I've learned that even when I know the whys and hows, it doesn't stop me from hurting."

"But it might help me stop reliving it," Helaina said in a distant voice. "Sometimes I imagine their final moments—even though I wasn't there physically. I read the reports and demanded all the details until the police were so tired of me they simply gave in. It was gruesome, and sometimes I wish I'd heeded their warning and left well enough alone."

"Did they ever catch the men who committed the murders?" Jacob asked.

"Yes, but it didn't help as much as I'd hoped. I had thought that once they were caught and tried, convicted, and punished, that my life would go on—that I would feel satisfied."

"But you didn't?"

"No. Well, my life went on, but the feeling of satisfaction was absent. No matter that the men were in jail—my family was still dead."

"That's why revenge never works."

"But I wasn't just seeking revenge. I wanted justice."

"There you go with justice again. I don't think you even understand the word. Justice suggests impartiality, and you show no signs of that."

She glared at him. "Justice is what our legal system is about—it's what this country was founded on. It's all I want in life—it's what I fight for." Jacob thought for a moment she might get up and leave, but instead she composed herself and squared her shoulders. "This isn't about me or justice—it's about Leah and Mr. Kincaid."

"I can't do anything about them right now, except pray—which I have been doing ever since we heard about the ship going down. But I think we need to go back to the issue at hand, and the point is, often people mistake revenge for justice. They think they'll feel better if they can see their offenders behind bars or even put to death. But it doesn't change the fact that they are hurting. I've found that offering mercy and forgiveness frees me from much of that pain. It also helps me to find a new direction for my life."

Helaina's voice took on a raw edge. "As I've said before, people who break the law deserve to face the penalty. Mercy is a matter left up to the courts. I will never understand your beliefs that people should just get off free and clear because they ask to be forgiven."

"Well, forgiveness is something we do on our part. We have control of forgiveness— whether we'll give it or withhold it. I can forgive the man who steals from me, but the court might still sentence him to time in jail.

You could choose to forgive the men who murdered your family, but they would still need to pay the penalty for their crime."

"I could never forgive them," Helaina said bitterly. "And don't bring up that story from the Bible again. Just because God has decided to forgive mankind their sins if they accept His Son, doesn't mean that I should have to forgive as well. I cannot agree with that. It's just not that simple."

"I never said it was simple," Jacob replied. "Forgiveness is a decided effort. It doesn't come easy for most."

"I would venture to say it doesn't come to most . . . period."

Jacob fell silent. Helaina's pain was visible in her expression. He'd certainly never meant to hurt her, but at the same time, he believed God had put the two of them together for a reason. "Why did you come to Alaska? Honestly."

The pain left her face as a look of surprise seemed to cause her to tense. "You know why I came. You know all about the expedition."

"And I know you said that you wanted to make your husband proud, but I get the feeling there's more to it than that. I've al-

ways been rather good at discerning people, and you have hidden motives, Helaina.
I've known that from the start, but I didn't
want to say anything."

Her face flushed crimson at this comment. "I don't know what you're talking
about."

"But you do. I can see that now, more
than ever. If you can't be honest with me,
then I'd just as soon you not come back to
Last Chance. I hate lies, and now I feel confident that you are lying to me."

Helaina cleared her throat nervously.
"Look . . . that is. . . . you simply do not
need to pry into my life. I've done nothing
but honor the agreement we had. I've
learned to handle the dogs to the best of my
ability. I ran your store and kept your house,
again because of the agreement. I upheld
my part of the bargain and gave you no reason to distrust me."

"You lied about the expedition. That much
I already know." He looked at her hard, hoping she might feel intimidated.

"You're just upset because of Leah,"
Helaina said, crossing her arms. She was
wearing one of her southern outfits, as Jacob called them. A blue wool skirt and

jacket with a high-collared white blouse. She looked every bit the prim and proper lady.

"I am upset about Leah, but that isn't marring my judgment in the least. There was never a second summer expedition planned. The first expedition was in trouble, and they had to cancel and turn back by the middle of June."

"But the plan . . . prior to that trouble . . . before they cancelled their exploration, was to have a second expedition," Helaina said hesitantly.

"That's a lie, Helaina."

She said nothing, but Jacob could see she was uncomfortable. He almost felt sorry for her. Almost. "Helaina, there was no telegraph service in either Nome or St. Michael when you suggested you'd received word from the expedition association. Service was out—I know because I wanted to send a telegram. There was also not enough time for you to have received a post or letter, because there hadn't been a mail ship in for days when you suggested having heard from the group. I believe you made it up to serve some ulterior purpose. What I want to know is, why? Why were you so determined to get Jayce Kincaid to Seattle?"

Helaina stood up. "I don't have to take this. I will not sit here and be accused like some common criminal."

"It's a sin to lie. You know that, right? It's one of the Ten Commandments."

"The commandment you refer to states, 'Thou shalt not bear false witness against your neighbor,' " Helaina said angrily. "I did not bear false witness against anyone." With that she stormed off.

Jacob watched after her for several minutes. He had no more answers than when he'd started, but at least now she knew that he suspected her. It would be interesting to see what she did from this point.

———

Jayce and Leah struggled to row the lifeboat up the coast toward what they hoped would be Sitka. Leah thought she had never been so tired. She tried hard to keep up with Jayce's rhythm but knew it was impossible.

Bethel rested but was fully awake. She had continued to improve after several days of rest. Leah had found some plants to ease Bethel's condition, but the quality had been rather poor due to the onset of the cold weather. They had also been fortunate to gather enough fish to eat well. Eating something substantial had given them all renewed hope and energy, and now they were anxious to move on. By all calculations they had been missing for just over two weeks, and they knew that their families were probably frantic.

"We'll rest in just a few more minutes," Jayce promised.

"That would . . . be good," she gasped out, her arms burning from the strain.

Jayce seemed only then to realize how tired she was. "I guess we could rest now," he said. "I didn't realize how hard I was pushing you. I'm sorry."

"It's all right. I don't want our families to worry any longer than they have to. We've already been gone too long."

"I know the delay was due to me," Bethel said apologetically.

"We were all exhausted," Jayce answered. "I couldn't have gone on without food and water. None of us could have. Besides, the weather caused us trouble more times than not. It isn't a good time of the year to travel in Alaska."

"I know Jacob will understand," Leah replied, still trying to regain her wind. "Karen and Adrik too. They will all say we did the right thing in renewing our strength, waiting out the weather, and making sure Bethel had a chance to recover."

"My heart has always been weak. I suppose this will be my last trip of any consequence."

"Maybe your family will come to you now," Leah said smiling.

Bethel nodded, then seemed to think of something else. "I know Leah has a brother, but have you any siblings, Mr. Kincaid?"

Jayce frowned. "I do. I have an older sister and brother, as well as a younger brother. Well, he's younger, but not by much. See, we're twins."

"How unusual. That must have been interesting growing up."

"Especially since Chase insists on getting himself into trouble at every turn."

Leah looked at Jayce and shook her head. "I didn't know you had a twin."

"Well, it never seemed important to bring up. We're as different as night and day, even though we're identical in appearance. My biggest trouble is that Chase insists on blaming me for everything wrong in his life. He even blames me that he's the youngest. We have a rather unusual situation in fact. I was born at 11:57 P.M. on December 31st, in the year 1882. Chase was born at 12:04 A.M. on January 1st, 1883. We're twins born in entirely different years."

"That is quite interesting," Bethel declared. "But I thought twins had an unusual sense of connection. You two were never close?"

"Never. He hated me from the beginning. He blamed me for the trouble he had in school—for the problems he caused our parents. He even blamed me for the death of our mother."

"Why?" Leah couldn't imagine why a brother would act in such a way. "Why would he do that?"

Jayce began rowing again. "When my father died, my siblings went through their inheritances and then started taking what they could from our mother. My mother was rather naïve and gave generously to anyone who asked. By the time I realized what they were doing, she was nearly destitute. She had accumulated debts, and we had to sell her home in order to satisfy her bankers.

Losing everything that reminded her of our father was more than she could bear. She was also distraught over the fact that Chase had gotten himself in trouble, and there was no money with which to bail him out. She grew quite sick with worry about him being in jail."

"And how does Chase figure that to be your fault?" Leah asked.

Jayce's face darkened. "Because I had the money to get him out, and I wouldn't do it. I knew he'd run if I did. I tried to reason with our mother and explain that jail was the best place for him—at least he'd be out of trouble there. But that wasn't the way she saw it, for Chase made certain her thoughts were in conflict with mine. He would send her horrible letters telling her how awful his conditions were and how badly people treated him. Mother pleaded with me to help him. I finally told her that I would take her to the jail and let her see the situation for herself."

"And did she go?" Bethel asked.

"Yes," Jayce said, looking past them as though he could see it all being played out in the skies overhead. "I took her there and she saw him . . . saw that he was living quite well, playing cards with the guards and eating high on the hog. When he realized what I'd done, Chase was livid. He rushed at me with the intention of killing me—at least I believe that was his plan. The guards had to pull him off, while our mother screamed for everyone to stop. I took her home, and she went to her bed, never again to get out."

"So Chase blames you for revealing the truth to her?" Leah asked.

"And for that truth taking her life."

"That is a sad story, indeed," Bethel said, clucking sympathetically. "What of your older siblings?"

"They blamed me as well. I was our father's favorite, and they hated me for that, seeking in turn to destroy my standing with our mother—although she thought equally well of each of us. It never bothered her to realize her children had taken advantage of her—or that she had given up everything she owned so that they would have whatever they wanted. She loved us all—right up to the end."

Bethel shifted and sat up to stretch her body. "A mother's love—the most precious of all earthly commodities. You cannot buy it or sell it, yet everyone desires it. Oh my! Look!"

Leah scanned the shores in the direction Bethel pointed. A dozen or so Tlingit Indians stood on the beach watching them. Leah stood. The boat rocked wildly, but she maintained her balance. "We need your help," she called in their native tongue. "Our ship sank, and we are trying to get to Sitka." She looked to Jayce and saw the relief in his expression. "We're saved. They'll know how to help."

———

Helaina paced her room in maddening steps. How dare he! How dare he accuse her of lying? She didn't care that it was true; she only felt that he had no right to interfere in her job. Now he would tell Jayce—if they found him at all—and her plans to talk him into heading to Seattle would be ruined. *Not that I have any real idea for getting Jayce there anyway,* she thought.

Not long after they'd arrived in Sitka, she had wired her brother with her concerns of whether Kincaid was even living. An hour ago she had added to the previous missives and told her brother that Jacob Barringer was suspicious of her—that he was now a real threat. Helaina hoped Stanley might offer her some insight or suggestion as to how to resolve it all.

Helaina had also mentioned her concerns about Jayce not being the right man. She had proof that suggested he'd been in two places at once. Not only with her information related to England, when Jayce supposedly stole from the British Museum, but also the situation with the *Homestead* and Jayce's supposed help with the dogs. The only answer was that there had to be someone who resembled Jayce. Perhaps a brother—maybe a cousin or someone else.

"The man I saw in Nome did not fit the patterns and attitudes of the man my brother wrote about. Jayce Kincaid seemed quite helpful and good. He showed no signs of breaking the law or of taking advantage of other people. Plus, he couldn't have been on the expeditions as Captain Latimore suggested. Jayce spent the summer with Leah," she said aloud, trying to organize her thoughts. "It just didn't make sense, unless there was another person."

She had shared these concerns with Stanley as well. Now she would just have to wait for some kind of direction from her brother.

A knock sounded on her door, and Helaina nearly jumped a foot. It came again, only this time harder and louder. "Open up, Mrs. Beecham."

Helaina recognized Jacob's voice and hurried to do as he said. "What's wrong? Have you had word?"

"No. They brought in a couple of bodies about an hour ago, but neither of them was Leah or Jayce. However, the weather has settled, and I'm going out in search of them."

"I'll change my clothes."

"You're staying here," Jacob replied without room for argument. "I just wanted to let you know where I'll be." He turned to leave, and Helaina followed him into the hallway.

"How can you just leave me here? I came to help you."

"I don't trust your help." With that he stormed off.

Helaina hurried to change her clothes. She might still catch him at the dock. She didn't want him going to hunt for Jayce and Leah without her. He would no doubt warn

Jayce about her, and then the man probably wouldn't even return to Sitka.

Another knock sounded at her door. She smiled, anticipating his return. She sauntered to the door feeling rather triumphant.

She opened the door. "I thought you were . . ." It wasn't Jacob.

"I have a telegram for you," the young man declared. "In fact, I have three telegrams for you."

Helaina frowned. "Very well." She went to get her purse.

"I never saw anyone get three telegrams at once."

"Well, it's really none of your concern," she snapped, knowing she was losing precious time. She dismissed the boy quickly and opened the messages.

They were all from her brother, and he was not happy.

Get JK to Seattle. STOP. Use law in Sitka. STOP. I will notify. STOP.

The next one was just as insistent.

JK is a killer. STOP. Do not worry about his innocence or guilt. STOP. We have all the proof we need. STOP. Get him to Seattle. STOP.

The final one was more of the same.

Have wired the law in Sitka. STOP. They will assist. STOP. If JK is living take to Seattle immediately. STOP. Team will aid you there. STOP.

Helaina tossed the telegrams into the trash and grabbed her coat. She had to try to reach Jacob before he left town. If he reached Jayce first, there would be no hope of taking him in without a fight.

Chapter Twenty-four

Jacob felt the crushing weight of defeat as their boat made its way to the docks in Sitka. He noted that the steamer *Victoria* was in the harbor and wondered if she might be heading to Nome. Soon no one would be risking a trip there.

Jacob sighed. The *Victoria* couldn't help him even if they were headed in the right direction. He still didn't know where Leah was. He had been out on the water for nearly forty-eight hours and hadn't found anything. It was as if the sea had swallowed up all evidence of *Orion's Belt* and her passengers.

"Will we go out again tomorrow?"

He looked at Helaina, not in the least happy to have her on board. She had come only moments before the ship's owner cast off and insisted she be allowed to help with the search. When she stood her ground and refused to leave the deck, Jacob finally relented but told her she was on her own. He wanted nothing more to do with her.

Even now he walked to the other side of the deck, anxious to be rid of Helaina. There were few things he despised as much as lying. The fact that she was caught in her lies and still continued to perpetuate them bothered him even more. Even on this journey she tried to explain away what had happened in Nome by telling Jacob that he'd misunderstood her meaning when she'd said that she'd gotten word about the expedition. She claimed she'd known that a second expedition was being planned even before coming to Nome.

Jacob was not swayed. He called her a liar and asked that she leave him alone. She had for a time, but then, like a bad penny, she just kept turning up.

"Jacob, please listen to me," Helaina now said, as she came up from behind him.

He clenched his jaw to keep from saying something he'd regret. He refused to play her game of words.

"Jacob, I know you're angry, but you don't understand—maybe you never will, but I'm not the person you think I am."

He drew a deep breath and continued gazing out at the Pacific. They'd soon dock and he'd be rid of her. For now, however, he'd have to ignore her pleading and hope that she got tired of trying to convince him of her innocence. He turned to her. "When we get back to the hotel, I want you to gather your things and get out." He looked out upon the water again.

"Jacob, I have to have a place to stay."

"Then pay for it yourself. I'll talk to the manager."

"I always intended to pay for the room anyway," Helaina answered in a rather defensive tone. "I have never asked you to pay for my needs."

"The *Victoria* is here. I'd just as soon see you book passage and leave. I don't need your help here."

"Jacob, you're being unreasonable," she protested. "I thought Christians were supposed to be forgiving and not judge without hearing the truth."

That got under his skin. Jacob turned slowly and narrowed his eyes. "I know the truth. I was in Nome, remember."

"But you don't know everything," Helaina said, her tone pleading. "Look, this is far more important than you know. There are things I cannot tell you." She gave an exasperated sigh. "I know it looks bad, but in a few days you'll understand. Just trust me until then. Don't say anything about this, and I swear I'll give you a thorough explanation."

"I don't want your explanations, and I certainly do not intend to spend any more time with you. My sister may be dead. My friend too. I don't have any interest in your stories or excuses."

"You're such a hypocrite," she said, putting her hands on her waist. "You are just as unforgiving as I am. But the difference here is that I don't claim to be a Christian or to value what the Bible says. You do."

She walked to the other side of the boat and sat down on a crate. Jacob refused to be troubled by her words. He knew she only hoped to rile him into arguing with her. He didn't understand what she hoped to gain by this, however. It wasn't like he could do anything about the lies she'd told, other than expose them. What seemed truly changed, however, was that she appeared for once to care what he thought.

As soon as the ship was tied off, Jacob exited without even looking to see what Helaina was doing. Hurrying up the dock, his heart nearly stopped when he found Adrik Ivankov waiting for him with several Tlingit natives.

"Is she dead?" he asked, his heart nearly breaking. His chest tightened and he couldn't breathe.

Adrik broke into a grin. "Not when I left her at the hotel."

Jacob closed his eyes and let the truth settle over him. "How . . . where . . . ?"

"We've been searching since word came to Ketchikan. These men and others have been helping." He motioned to the Tlingits. "We went out in a dozen boats and searched the beaches of nearby islands. We found her and Jayce and an elderly woman that they rescued. They were in one of the lifeboats and were trying to find their way to Sitka. Doing pretty well at it too."

"Jayce and Leah are alive?" Helaina asked, coming to join them.

Adrik looked at her oddly. "Yes, they are. Who are you, if you don't mind my asking?"

She extended her hand. "Mrs. Helaina Beecham."

"Adrik Ivankov." He shook her hand briefly. "The hotel was full, but when they told me Jacob had two rooms registered to his name, I knew he wouldn't mind our imposition. I've put Leah in one room, and Jayce in the other."

"Where are you staying, Adrik?"

"We have a camp down near the beach," Adrik told them.

Helaina seemed anxious to get back to the room. "I'd love to see them both, and I know Jacob longs to see for himself that Leah is safe. Let's go to the hotel." She pushed past Adrik and made her way up the street.

"Leah told me quite a bit about that one," Adrik said as he and Jacob followed after.

"She's up to something, but I really don't know what it's all about. I've caught her in several lies and had honestly thought she'd changed, but as soon as we got here and the focus was on finding Jayce, she started in again."

"Why does she want to find Jayce?"

Jacob shrugged. "I don't know. She's tried several times to get him to go to Seattle with her. I don't know what it's all about, but I've had a gut full. I've told her to get away from us. Now that we have Leah and Jayce safe, I plan to be rid of her for good."

"Will you come and stay with us awhile in Ketchikan?"

"Not if we're going to make it back before we're frozen out. As it is, we'll probably have to borrow a dog team and hike out for home once we reach Nome. There's just no telling. I know we can't afford to delay."

"I understand. Sure is good to see you, though." He put his arm around Jacob's shoulder.

"You too, Adrik. I wish I could have come and stayed for a visit, but there was too much work to be done this summer."

The older man scratched his bearded chin. "Just don't forget that life is about more than work. You need a little rest and fun now and then." He grinned and slapped Jacob's back. "Wouldn't hurt you to find a wife either."

Jacob smiled. "Maybe you could get one of the shamans to make me a potion. My natural charm and good looks don't seem to be doing the trick."

"Those only work on Tlingit people—they're much too powerful for the likes of you." He winked at Jacob and laughed.

By now they'd reached the hotel. Jacob dashed up the stairs to the rooms he and Helaina had taken. He went to the open door of Helaina's room. The two women were talking rapidly—both smiling.

"Leah!"

She turned to him and shrugged. "We took the long way home."

He crossed the distance and embraced her close. "Thank God you're safe."

"We were just talking about what happened," Helaina offered. "The ship actually blew up."

Leah and Jacob separated. "I know that," Jacob retorted.

"You seem to know a lot of things," Jayce announced from the door. "You all are making quite a ruckus over here. A man can't even get some much-needed sleep."

"Jayce, it's good to see you," Jacob said,

going to his friend. "I can't imagine what you must have gone through."

"It wasn't easy, but your sister is quite ingenious. She had us eating well and living high off the land. That girl can dig for clams like no one I've ever seen, and the crabs she managed to cook for us had legs as big around as a dog's."

Leah rolled her eyes. "He exaggerates."

"Have you been here long?" Jacob asked.

"No," Adrik replied. "Just got in about thirty minutes prior to you. We got the older woman to the hospital. I hadn't even had a chance to let the authorities know they were alive."

"I could do that," Helaina offered.

Everyone looked at her for a moment, but it was Jacob who replied in a clipped tone. "I'm sure that would be a good idea. You go ahead. We're going to dinner. I'm starved."

"Well, you can go to dinner," Jayce replied. "I was just about to have a bath. Hot water and everything. Then I'm going to sleep in a real bed with real sheets."

"We are pretty dirty," Leah said, looking down at her clothes.

"Doesn't matter," Jacob replied. "I'm hungry and dirty. I wanna eat first."

Adrik laughed and headed for the door. "Then it's my treat. I know just the place. They won't care how dirty you are, and if you fall asleep in your grub, they'll just move you out of the way and bring the next person in."

Jacob let Leah go ahead of him to the door, completely ignoring Helaina. "Sounds perfect."

"You're welcome to come too, Mrs. Beecham," Adrik called.

Helaina seemed to consider it for a moment, then shook her head. "No, I'm not that hungry. You go ahead. It's only right that you have some time with your family."

Helaina knew she would have to act fast. Despite being dirty, she slipped into her regular clothes and hurried out of the hotel in search of the local law offices. They seemed to know all about her when she arrived.

"Got a telegram from a man in Washington, D.C. He says you're helping the Pinkerton Agency to apprehend a dangerous criminal."

"That's all true," Helaina said, nodding.

"He was on *Orion's Belt* when it went down. I feared he might be dead, but he's returned to Sitka, and I need your help in apprehending him."

"Well, we can certainly do that," the man in charge declared. "What do you propose to do with him after we apprehend him?"

"I need to get him to Seattle as soon as possible. I'll have to book passage on the first available ship."

"The *Victoria* is here right now," a red-headed man threw out. He was haphazardly cleaning his pistol, making Helaina more than a little nervous.

"That's right," the older man declared. "The *Victoria* is headed to Seattle tonight. In just a couple of hours, in fact."

"I must be on that ship with Jayce Kincaid," Helaina said, realizing it would work the best for all parties concerned. If she could get him on that ship and out of town before Jacob and Leah realized what was happening, she could be assured of victory.

"Brett can run you down some tickets. You have the funds?"

Helaina nodded and opened her purse. "I believe this will cover it." She gave him several large bills. The boy put aside the gun and got to his feet.

"You take this money and get her two tickets. Make sure they don't put her in the hold. She needs a decent cabin—got it?"

"Sure, Walt. I ain't stupid."

"Well, that remains to be seen," Walt answered. "After you get the tickets, you go to the ship and make sure they don't pull out early. We'll be there directly." The young man ran out the door, whistling all the way.

"Well, little lady, I don't understand a country that allows its women to be arresting dangerous criminals, but I guess I have no say in the matter." He took up his hat and motioned her to the door. "After you."

"But we'll need more men. This is a dangerous, crafty, deceptive criminal. He's killed two men and wounded a third."

"Lady, I can handle him. Don't worry your pretty head about it." He reached to the wall and grabbed up some handcuffs and leg irons.

"But—"

He frowned at her, and for a moment Helaina was worried he'd changed his mind about helping her. Finally he asked, "Are we going or not?"

She nodded. "Very well. But I warned you."

Helaina felt as if her heart might pound right out of her chest. The end of her long ordeal was in sight. She would soon have Jayce Kincaid captured and on his way to Seattle. Then she could go home.

But even as she made her way to the hotel, there was a sense of unrest in her soul. Jacob despised her, and she longed to set the record straight with him. She wanted very much for him to know the truth, especially since he accused her so often of keeping it from him. Maybe she would write him a letter once she was back home.

"He's in the room at the top of the stairs," Helaina explained. "After we apprehend him, I'll need to gather my things. I don't have very much, so it will only take a minute."

"I can handle it," the man replied. He had a determined look on his face as he shifted the irons to his left hand and pulled out a revolver with his right hand.

He motioned Helaina to stand back as they reached the last step. He went to the door and knocked loudly, then stepped to the side. For a moment Helaina froze in place, then quickly jumped to the opposite side of the door. When no one came to answer the knock, she feared Jayce might have changed his mind and left for dinner.

The man knocked again, this time harder. There was some sort of reply from inside, but Helaina couldn't really tell what the muffled words were. She stiffened, pulling herself back against the wall.

"What's the matter, Jacob, forget your key?" Jayce asked as he opened the door. He yawned, then startled to realize there was a gun in his face. His eyes widened as Walt pushed the revolver closer.

"Now you raise those hands nice and easy, mister."

"What's this about? Are you robbing me, 'cause if you are, you're out of luck. I have nothing. I was one of those folks who was on *Orion's Belt* when it went down."

"I know who you are, Mr. Kincaid. Now don't cause me any trouble. I'm the law in this town, and I don't take well to folks who cause trouble."

Helaina stepped out as he managed to handcuff Jayce. She saw the look of surprise change to confusion as Jayce's eyes narrowed. "What is this about, Helaina?"

"I'm working for the Pinkerton Agency in Washington, D.C., Mr. Kincaid. You might remember a little scuffle you had with my brother on the back of a B&O Railroad car. You threw him off."

"You've got the wrong man." Jayce looked to the man who was even now checking his pockets for weapons. "She's got the wrong person."

"I have evidence that suggests otherwise," Helaina said, trying hard not to remember her own concerns about this case. Stanley was firm on what was to be done, so she pulled out the drawing of Jayce and unfolded it for him to see. "I was told to apprehend a man named Jayce Kincaid, who also fit this description."

"Looks just like you, mister," Walt declared.

"I'm telling you it isn't me," Jayce protested, trying to twist away from Walt. The older man held him fast.

Helaina put the picture back into her pocket. "You are under arrest for the death of two men, also agents, as well as for multiple theft and assault charges."

Jayce shook his head. "I've never even been to Washington, D.C. I'm telling you

this is wrong. I'm not the man you're looking for."

"That's what they all say," the officer declared. He snapped the leg irons into place
and straightened. "Come along, Mr. Kincaid. You have a ship waiting for you."

"I can't just leave without saying some-
thing to Jacob and Leah." He looked to
Helaina for help. "Please, you know what
I'm saying. I have to talk to them."

"I'm sorry," she said, her voice nothing
more than a whisper. "We have to go."

"You'd best collect your things, Mrs. Beecham."

Helaina couldn't shake the feeling that
this was all suddenly very wrong. "Yes, I'll
go right now."

She hurried to the room next door and
pulled the key from her purse. It was difficult
to see in the darkened room. She went to
the chair where she'd left her smallest traveling bag containing her personal items as
well as her only other traveling outfit. Taking
this up, she thought about her Eskimo
clothes and decided against taking them.
She'd have no need of them at home.

She rejoined the men and followed them

down the stairs. Jayce protested every step of the way, alternating between pleading for Helaina's mercy and arguing his innocence.

"Helaina, I don't know why you're doing this. I don't know why you think me guilty of these things. I didn't do it. I'm telling you, I've never been to Washington, D.C."

She refused to even speak to him about the situation. Her conscience already bothered her more than she'd admit. There were too many inconsistencies, and she didn't know how to rectify the situation except to take Jayce back to stand trial. Then, surely if he was telling the truth, there would be evidence to support this and he would go free. If not . . . he would hang.

She swallowed hard at this thought. *What if we're wrong and he does hang? What if he can't get evidence in time?* She looked at Jayce as he hung his head. He wasn't fighting them—he wasn't even really trying to cause them any problems. It was definitely a surprise, given the other times the man had been arrested he'd turned ugly on his captors.

He hardly seemed like a killer. But then again, few killers looked as she had expected them to look. Especially the men who killed her family. They were hardly more than boys. Desperate boys. She shuddered. They had hanged, and Jayce Kincaid would hang as well. It was the price for his crimes.

Chapter Twenty-five

Leah carefully balanced a plate of food for Jayce as they made their way back to the hotel. Darkness obscured the mountains and shadows hung ominously, then disappeared as patches of fog moved over the town. A sense of foreboding washed over her, but Leah tried not to think about it. Right now she was blessed to be safe and reunited with her family.

She smoothed the red checkered napkin over the plate and smiled. Jayce had been so exhausted, but Leah knew when he awoke, he'd be starved. The restaurant had prepared a nice plate with meatloaf and potatoes. There was even a piece of apple pie. Her heart nearly burst with happiness. It had taken ten years and a shipwreck, but Jayce had finally told her he loved her. God had brought him back to her, and now they would plan a life together.

"I just wish I could figure it all out," Jacob told Adrik. "I suppose we'll never know for sure what Helaina's been up to. Especially now that we'll be heading home to Last Chance. I told her she wasn't to join us."

"You can hardly keep her from showing up in the village," Adrik replied.

"You know how the people of those villages are. If a stranger shows up, they handle them with great caution, but if someone known shows up and others speak against them, they'll be turned away. She won't be able to survive the winter there without friends."

"It would probably be good to explain that to her before she tags along."

"I will."

They climbed the steps to their room, and Adrik suppressed a yawn. "I don't know why I'm following you. I need to be gettin' back to my camp. I'll come see you in morning, and we'll discuss your plans." He started to turn and head back down the stairs.

"That's strange," Jacob said. "The door to my room is open." He looked inside. The hall light revealed that Jayce was gone.

"Maybe Jayce went out for something to eat and didn't think to close the door," Adrik offered.

Leah felt her heart skip a beat. She glanced to the door of her own room. "Let me check my room."

She handed Adrik the plate and went to her door—it was locked. She used her key, and when she stepped into the room, a terrible feeling washed over her. There was no sign of Helaina, and her bag was missing.

"Anything?" Jacob asked as he came to the door.

"Helaina's gone—her bag's gone too. She left this," Leah said, holding up Helaina's sealskin pants and kuspuk.

"Well, maybe they went to supper together." Adrik balanced the plate in his left hand and pulled out his watch with his right. "It's getting late. Why don't we wait and see if they show up."

"She's done something," Jacob declared. "I know she has. She's planned all along to get to Jayce, but for what reasons I can only guess."

Leah's stomach churned in a most unpleasant way. "What are you saying?"

"I'm saying that Helaina has had an agenda ever since meeting up with us in Nome. I don't know what it's all about or why she's after Jayce, but there's something she wants bad enough to risk everybody's anger and a whole lot of danger."

"But what could that be?" Leah asked. "Do you suppose she's in love with him?"

"No. That honestly never crossed my mind," Jacob said. Leah's face must have shown the relief she felt, because he quickly added, "And it wouldn't matter if she were in love. I know Jayce loves you. There's no doubting that."

"Well, we may just be wrong on all accounts," Adrik reminded them. "I say let's wait and see what happens."

"But it's nearly nine o'clock," Leah said. "If we wait much longer we won't be able to ask anyone about them."

"Who do you propose we ask?" Jacob said, shaking his head.

Leah had no idea. She heard the sorrowful blast of a ship's whistle, and she couldn't help but think of *Orion's Belt* and the accident that took the lives of so many people. She had thought she and Jayce had survived for a reason—a reason that clearly involved a future together. Now she wasn't so sure. What if Jayce had deserted her? What if all of his words of love and devotion were just given because of the situation they were in? She bit her lip to keep from crying.

"I need to clean up," she told her brother. "Why don't you two wait in Jacob's room? I'll come over when I'm done."

"Bath is at the end of the hall," Jacob told her.

His words barely registered. The exhaustion of her ordeal began to overpower her. All Leah wanted was to run and hide and have a good cry.

As soon as Jacob and Adrik pulled the door closed, she let the tears come. A deep sob broke from her throat. "I can't understand any of this, Lord. I suppose it's silly to be worried already, but something's wrong. I just know it. I felt it even when Helaina showed up earlier. I could see in her eyes that she was watching Jayce with new purpose. I should have warned him. I shouldn't have left him alone."

She went to find her things, tears blinding her eyes. There had to be an answer—a reason for the things that were happening. Leah reached for her bundle of clothes Adrik had given her.

On the floor she saw a piece of paper. It seemed unimportant, but at the same time it beckoned her attention. She bent over to pick it up and noticed there were two other pieces in the trash can. They were telegrams. Taking all three in hand, Leah read the words addressed to Mrs. Helaina Beecham.

Leah read the words aloud. " 'JK is a killer. STOP. Do not worry about his innocence or guilt. STOP. We have all the proof we need. STOP. Get him to Seattle. . . .' " She looked at the other cables and felt a wave of dizziness overcome her. What in the world was this all about? Who was JK?

Jayce Kincaid.

She hurried to Jacob's room and pounded on the door until he opened it. "Look!" She thrust the telegrams into her brother's hands.

"What is it?"

"These are telegrams addressed to Helaina. Jacob, she's taken Jayce away.

She thinks he's a killer. Apparently someone else does too."

Jacob read the cables and handed them over to Adrik one by one. "I knew she had something going on. At least it explains her continued desire to get Jayce to Seattle."

"But what's this about him being a killer and not worrying about his guilt or innocence?" Adrik asked.

Jacob met Leah's eyes. "I don't know. I do know that Jayce Kincaid is no killer. I'd be willing to stake my life on that."

Adrik handed the paper back to Jacob. "It says the local law authorities are supposed to be helping her. My guess is that she has Jayce down at the jail. Why don't we get on down there and see for ourselves what this ruckus is all about."

"That's a good idea," Leah said, already heading out the door.

A million thoughts rushed through her head. Who was Jayce supposed to have killed, and why was Helaina involved in his capture? Had she really come to Alaska with the purpose of finding Jayce in order to take him back to Seattle?

"Hold up, Leah. You don't even know where you're going," Jacob called to her.

She stopped just outside the hotel, the fog much thicker now. At least Adrik would know where they were going. "It doesn't make sense," she said as the men joined her. "None of it. Why would the authorities send a woman to capture a man they believed was a killer?"

"That's a good question," Adrik replied, leading the way to the jail. "One that we'll hopefully get to ask her in just a minute."

Leah felt a surge of energy as anger encased her mind. She would tell Helaina Beecham what an awful person she was to force an innocent man to jail—a man who had just been rescued from a horrible ordeal. *The thought of that woman lying in wait at my home, just to capture Jayce, makes me want to throttle her.*

Adrik went into the jail first, with Jacob and Leah right behind him. Jacob put his arm out to keep Leah from rushing ahead. "Let Adrik handle it," he whispered.

"What can I do for you?" a large man asked. He leaned back in his chair and watched the three of them with a wary expression.

"I'm Adrik Ivankov. I'm wondering if you can tell me if Jayce Kincaid is here."

The man got to his feet. He was nearly as big as Adrik and didn't seem at all intimidated, as many people were when encountering the big man. "What do you want with him?"

"He's our friend!" Leah declared. "We just got back after nearly losing our lives on the *Orion's Belt.*" Jacob held her tight. It was the only thing that kept Leah from charging the man.

"Well, your friend is in a world of trouble, missy. He's been arrested for murder."

Leah lunged forward, but Jacob held her securely. "He didn't do anything of the kind. Jayce Kincaid is no killer."

"The authorities in Washington, D.C., say otherwise. They've charged him with the death of their people. We received a cable earlier in the day asking us to assist the Pinkertons in his arrest."

"Pinkertons? Here?" Adrik questioned. "Who?"

"Mrs. Beecham," the man replied. "Not that I approve of women in such lines of duty, but it came all official. We helped her apprehend Kincaid earlier tonight."

"I want to see him," Leah said.

The man shook his head. "He's not here. He's on his way to Seattle."

"How? When?" She was terrified.

The man looked at them and crossed his arms. "Mrs. Beecham took him out of here on the *Victoria*. It just left the sound a few minutes ago. They're bound for Seattle with the last of the summer tourists."

Leah turned to Jacob and Adrik. "We have to do something!"

"I don't know what we can do," Jacob replied. "There isn't another ship available— at least not another steamer."

"Please, Adrik, we have to figure a way. Couldn't we get a message to the ship?"

"You people don't seem to understand. The Pinkertons were hired to take this man back for trial. You aren't going to stop that, and you sure aren't going to interfere with the *Victoria's* schedule. I'll arrest you myself on charges of obstructing justice."

"Justice," Jacob muttered. "That's what this is all about."

"What?" Leah turned to him. "What are you saying?"

"Helaina has this idea of what justice is. She believes that criminals should be meted out their full due without thought or consideration of the circumstance. She's without any compassion. She believes the law is the law, and there's no room for further consideration."

"She seems a good, law-abiding citizen."

Jacob turned to the officer. "She's angry and vengeful, and I intend to see her stopped."

———

Hours later the trio sat rather dumbfounded in Jacob's room. They had worn themselves out trying to figure what their next step should be.

"I think we can send a cable to Seattle," Adrik said. "We can contact the authorities there and suggest Helaina has the wrong man."

Jacob shook his head; his shoulders slumped in defeat as much as exhaustion. "But they'll want some sort of proof, and we don't have anything to offer."

"I think the man Helaina really wants is Jayce's twin brother, Chase," Leah said without warning.

Jacob looked at her. She was serious.

"What are you talking about? Jayce has a twin?"

"Yes!" She suddenly seemed to regain her strength. "He told us about him while we were trying to get to Sitka. Me and Mrs. Wilkerson. He told us that he had a brother named Chase—that he was born just a few minutes after Jayce and that they are identical in appearance. Jayce said that his brother was always getting into trouble. That has to be the answer!"

"It could very well explain an awful lot," Adrik said, nodding. "But would that offer enough proof to the police?"

"I don't know, but I believe we have to try. Jayce said that Chase has been causing him trouble for years. The man even blames Jayce for the death of their mother, although she died because she was heartbroken over the misdeeds of Chase and the loss of her home and husband."

Jacob listened to every word, but he still found Leah's story difficult to believe. *And if I don't believe it—how can I expect the authorities to accept it as truth?* He blew out a heavy breath. "Look, I don't see how this is going to matter to the police. We can tell them whatever we want, but we can't prove any of it. I can't prove Jayce has an identical twin brother. I can't prove he has any family at all."

"We have to try," Leah said, tears forming in her eyes. "They mean to see him dead. They'll hang him for murdering those two agents. We have to find a way to help him, Jacob. We need to go to Seattle."

Chapter Twenty-six

Jayce couldn't figure out what Helaina had planned next. She seemed quite nervous about the entire matter of docking in Seattle. Two burly sailors appeared at their cabin when the passengers were notified they could begin debarking. Jayce looked at the men, wondering if they were going to be the ones to escort him straight to jail.

"Look, my plans have changed," Helaina told Jayce. "There are a half-dozen Pinkertons waiting to take you from me when we set foot in Seattle. However, I would rather they not do that just yet."

Jayce sized up the men and then looked

to Helaina again. "Why are you telling me this?"

Helaina pinned her hat securely and looked at the two sailors. "I will leave with the other passengers, and then I'd like for you to bring him along when the crew leaves the ship. I'll secure a carriage and meet you at the end of the docks. You said it would be about an hour—is that correct?"

"Yes, ma'am," the older of the two answered. "We'll have him to you in an hour or less."

"Very well. I'll go along now with the rest of the passengers." She turned to Jayce and met his curious expression. "If you want a chance to prove your innocence, then cooperate with me in this. These men have been paid well to see you do not slip away from my charge." With that she left, not even giving Jayce a chance to answer.

He looked at the two men. "So she paid you well, eh?"

"Very well." It was the same man who'd answered earlier. "She said you might try to promise us the moon, but that you didn't have a cent to your name."

"Well, she's right—at least I don't have a

cent on me. I actually do have money in the bank. If you're open to negotiations . . . ?"

The men glanced at each other, then returned their gaze back to Jayce. "Sorry. We gave the lady our word. Besides, she has the law on her side. We don't plan to get on the wrong side of the law. She told us that if you escaped she'd put us in jail."

Jayce nodded. "No doubt she would. Well, fear not. I intend to go along with this plan of hers for the time being." And he spoke the truth. Just the fact that she was willing to consider him as innocent seemed worth the gamble.

An hour later the men delivered Jayce to Helaina. Her nervousness was palpable; she kept scanning the docks and motioning for the men to hurry. Finally Jayce was seated opposite her in the cab.

"What are you doing?" Jayce demanded as Helaina leaned over to unlock his leg irons. "I thought I was under arrest."

"You are," Helaina replied. "I just have some final paper work to get, and that may take a bit of time. Until then, we aren't leaving." She tossed the irons into her bag, then leaned back against the seat.

"So you're going to leave me in handcuffs

indefinitely? These aren't exactly comfortable, you know. And I could use a bath and a shave."

Helaina stared out the window. It was obvious that she had a lot on her mind. And why not? Jayce had hounded her all the way from Sitka to Seattle. He told her about his brother, and while she had seemed notably surprised at this turn of events, she had refused to comment on the possibilities.

"I have a right to a lawyer," he now told her. "I want one now."

"No," she replied in a curt manner.

"You have no right to hold me against my will this way."

Helaina finally looked at him. "I have a warrant for your arrest. I can do as I please. I have legal authority by way of my association with the Pinkertons."

"Look, you have to believe me, Mrs. Beecham. I'm not guilty of these crimes. I have people in Vancouver who will testify to my being there during the times you've suggested I was elsewhere committing crimes. I've already told you that my brother Chase has been in constant trouble since the day he was born. He's been in and out of jails.

Get in touch with the New York City police. They can tell you all about my brother."

Jayce looked at her for a reply. She seemed lost in her thoughts. Perhaps at last she was finally beginning to consider his innocence. "I'd like to help you catch my brother. The truth is, I saw him in Last Chance in June, just before the dog attack sent me to Nome."

She frowned. "The captain of the *Homestead* said you were with them in the Arctic prior to the time they had to leave because of sickness and other problems."

"But you know that I wasn't there," Jayce replied. "I was with Leah in Ketchikan, where I also have witnesses. I also took a trip to Juneau and have witnesses there as well."

"There's just no way to prove that you aren't the one responsible for killing those agents," Helaina said, shaking her head.

"If I can prove by the dates to have been somewhere else, then you would have to concede my innocence."

The cab stopped in front of the elegant Sorrento Hotel. Jayce could see it was a large, respectable place tailored in an Italian style. "How are you going to account for dragging me through the lobby in these?" He held up his manacled hands.

"We will drape my cloak over your arms," Helaina replied.

"And if I refuse to cooperate?"

She looked at him for a moment. "You don't have to cooperate. I can call the authorities and have you escorted to Washington, D.C., tonight. My brother will take his information against you and see you hanged. Or you can do what I tell you to do, and I'll continue checking out your story. It's that simple."

"But if I leave for Washington tonight, the authorities will also have to check out my story."

"Not necessarily, Mr. Kincaid. You see, I'm the only one who has found evidence of discrepancies that might show you to be innocent. Stanley might not be as likely to look into them."

"So you believe me?" Jayce felt a wave of hope.

Helaina shook her head. "I don't know what to believe. I do know that it isn't a simple matter any longer. I once thought it was very clear—thought I understood what I needed to do. But now it's different."

"I appreciate whatever mercy you might extend."

She frowned. "This isn't about mercy. It's about justice."

"How do you figure that?"

"Justice is seeing the right man punished for the crimes he's committed. That's all this is—nothing more."

The Sorrento stood as a remarkable tribute to the architect's desire to blend the warmth and luxury of Italy with the growing desire for elegance in Seattle. Jayce noted the dark mahogany walls. It almost seemed as though they had stepped into a men's club. Even the leather wing-backed chairs lent credence to this thought. Helaina seemed unimpressed. At least she made no comment.

They checked into the hotel as Mr. and Mrs. Beecham. Helaina explained to Jayce in a hushed voice that she wanted no trouble from the appearance of her, a widowed woman, sharing a room with a single man. Jayce heard her request a suite with a separate bedroom. She also demanded the bedroom have no windows. The clerk seemed rather confused by her stipulation, but he found exactly what she needed and concluded by asking her to have her husband sign the register.

She looked to Jayce as if expecting him to use this as an excuse to draw attention. Instead, he shook his head. "I'd prefer she sign."

He then looked away as if bored and indifferent with the entire process. Jayce heard the clerk mutter in a thoroughly annoyed manner.

"It's all right," Helaina declared. "My husband can be a bit eccentric. You must forgive him."

Jayce looked back to find her signing the register. The clerk then handed her the key and summoned a bellman. "Take their bags to room 212."

"We only have one small bag," Helaina said, smiling. "We can manage it ourselves."

The clerk rolled his eyes. "Very well."

They climbed the stairs to the second floor in silence. Jayce wanted to ask Helaina detailed questions about her plans, but he figured she would never reveal anything to him unless it suited her purpose. For now he'd give her the idea that he was cooperating, but if he felt things were getting out of hand, then he'd have to do otherwise. There was only one thing he would insist on.

Once they were secure in the hotel room, he tossed the cloak aside and faced Helaina. "You know that I could overpower you."

She looked at him for a moment and nodded. "No doubt."

"But I want you to understand and believe in my innocence. I want your help to clear my name. In return, I will stay here for a time. But I have two demands of my own."

"And what would they be, Mr. Kincaid?"

"I want a lawyer, and I want to write a letter to Leah. She's not going to understand my disappearance, and I won't have her misunderstanding this situation. I love that woman. I plan to marry her, and not you or the entire Pinkerton Agency is going to stop me."

She pulled off her hat and tossed it to a nearby writing desk. "I cannot allow you a lawyer at this time. If we involve anyone else—anyone—it will only jeopardize my ability to learn the truth."

"A lawyer could get to information you'd have no right to," Jayce protested.

"You are very naïve, Mr. Kincaid. I've been doing this for a long time. I have my connections and my processes for getting things done. I am willing to learn the truth about this and see your brother rightfully take your place. However, you must yield this to me. I need time. As it is, my brother is going to be livid. I took you off that ship right under the nose of a half-dozen Pinkerton agents. I couldn't see letting them take you, however, without at least trying to prove your claims one way or another. If I get you a lawyer, you'll have to go to jail and sit in a cell. Is that what you want?"

Jayce looked around him. The room was comfortably situated with a sofa and several chairs, a writing desk, and a luxurious fireplace. The bedroom door was closed, so he had no way to know what that room held. He had to admit a grand hotel room was better than a cell any day. "I suppose I can wait it out for a while. Will you in return trust me to be without these?" He held up his cuffed hands. "After all, we've already established that it wouldn't take much for me to overpower you—even manacled."

She considered this for a moment, then went to her purse. Producing the key, she

drew a deep breath. "I hope you will not dis-
appoint my trust, Mr. Kincaid. If you do anything to cause me difficulty, I will end my
quest to prove the truth."

"I understand. If it helps at all, I give you
my word that I'll remain here as you attempt
to get your proof."

"Very well." She unlocked the cuffs and
tucked the key in her pocket. "As for the letter," she said, crossing the room to open the
bedroom door. "I suppose it will do no
harm. I didn't want Leah or Jacob hurt in
this situation. I know Jacob believes me to
be a horrible liar, but I had my job to do."

"And that justifies telling lies?"

She reddened a bit at this. "Yes. Yes, I believe that I should use whatever means necessary to put evil criminals behind bars."

"Does that include breaking the law yourself—as you're doing now?"

She grew angry. "I'm doing this to help
you. You'd do well to remember that. Believe me, I don't understand my own choice
in this. It's all because of Jacob and the
nonsense he tried to feed me about justice
and mercy. If not for that, I'd just forget
about the discrepancies and turn you over
to the authorities. Furthermore, I'll let you

write your letter, but for now this bedroom is your cell. I need to lock you in there to ensure that you won't escape while I'm out trying to gather information."

Jayce shrugged and walked to the door. Inside he could see a huge plush bed. "Suit yourself. I could use the sleep. Just make sure I have what I need to write that letter."

She went to the desk and took out paper and ink. "This should serve your purpose."

Jayce went into the room and waited for her to bring him the items. He stood at the far side of the bed so as not to unnerve her. Helaina placed the articles on the bed. "You should be able to use the nightstand for a table. I'll be back in a few hours. I'll bring you something to eat and drink at that time."

"All right. You have my promise that I won't try to leave."

She met his gaze. There was something almost sad in her expression. She seemed troubled and confused. Jayce figured it was an inner war—a battle within her that she'd never had to confront before. Apparently Jacob had given her cause to see the flaws in her logic. Jayce silently thanked God for this, because he was certain had Jacob not planted those seeds of doubt, he'd even now be on a train bound for Washington and a hangman's noose.

Helaina penned her words carefully. The telegram would cost her a precious amount of money, but she didn't care. She'd already requested more money from her bank in New York; after all, the Sorrento was far from inexpensive.

Stanley. Send me the fingerprint file for Jayce Kincaid. I believe he is inno-cent and the prints will prove this. Send a courier as soon as possible to the Sorrento Hotel in Seattle. Please don't be angry with me. I just learned Kincaid has an identical twin brother named Chase. We need to be certain which brother committed the crimes. Helaina.

She reread the words several times and afterward handed the paper to the tele-graph operator. "I need this to be sent im-mediately. Here's the address."

The man looked over the message and nodded. "There's an extra charge for rush delivery."

"I don't care. This is a matter of life and death."

He looked at her oddly and nodded. "Okay, but it won't be cheap."

"It's already costing me everything," she murmured.

———

Leah settled down onto a pallet beside her brother. She would have laughed at her circumstance had it not been such a grave situation. The only transportation they could get to Seattle was aboard a freighter. There were no cabins or beds to be had. Just a quiet corner in the hold.

"We'll never get there in time," Jacob said. His voice was so full of regret that Leah instantly felt sorry for him.

"So much has happened to bring us to this place, Jacob. I know it isn't what either of us planned. We have to trust that God has everything in His hands."

"But what can we possibly hope to accomplish?" Jacob refused to look at her. "Leah, we're days behind them, and obviously Helaina had plans to be aided once she arrived in Seattle. Jayce is probably already gone."

"I know that's a possibility," Leah agreed, "but I don't feel like it's the reality. Besides, Karen promised to help. Her nephew is a private investigator in Seattle. Adrik has wired him, and he'll already be on the job before we arrive. God willing, he will have even found Helaina and Jayce and kept them from leaving Seattle. Remember, he has many friends to call upon for assistance."

"I know you're right. There is hope. There is always hope. I'm just . . . well . . . I guess I don't know what to think. Helaina told me there was more to her than what I thought, and I couldn't begin to guess the half of it."

"I think we have to put aside those kind of concerns and just focus on the future. I'm terrified for Jayce, but I know my fear will do him no good. He'll need us now more than ever. I don't intend to give up my husband without a fight."

Jacob turned and smiled. "You aren't married yet."

"No, but my reputation is ruined just the same. After all, we spent all of that time alone . . . Well, Mrs. Wilkerson was there, but she was very sick," Leah said with a grin.

"Did you get to see her before we left?"

"Yes. She's doing better, but the doctor fears her heart is very damaged. She must always take it easy—lots of bed rest," Leah recounted. "I hope to see her in Nome when we return. It was her daughter's desire to get her back before the winter closed in."

"Wish we could be doing the same. I'm telling you, Leah, the thought of a city like Seattle unnerves me. I don't have any desire to go there, and we have no way of knowing what we'll encounter or how long it will take. I'll probably have to get some kind of job if it drags on too long."

"With a city that size, there is bound to be plenty of work. But don't worry about that just yet. Like Karen said, we can stay with her sister or one of the other relatives for a while. If things look like they will go on for a lengthy time, then we can reconsider what to do." She paused for a moment and grew thoughtful. "There's also another possibility."

"What's that?"

"Once we make it to Seattle and I'm safely in the care of Karen's family, you could return to Nome. There are more opportunities to get to Nome out of Seattle than Sitka or Ketchikan."

"I won't desert you. I won't desert Jayce either. I don't have to be happy about the circumstance to honor my commitment."

Four days later they docked in Seattle. Leah had never been so glad to see land in all her life. She wanted to run from the ship but comported herself in a ladylike manner down the gangplank. She wore a woolen skirt and coat, compliments of Karen. It felt rather strange to wear a dress after so many years, but at least she didn't feel too out of place.

The good thing about taking a freighter to Seattle was that they didn't have to endure the swarming crowds of a passenger liner. This made it much easier to spot the man who was to meet them.

"You must be Timothy Rogers," Leah said as a man approached them. He wore a stylish blue suit that complemented his tall, lean body and curly red hair.

He tipped his hat. "I am. Aunt Karen said you'd be arriving on the freighter, but I thought surely she was jesting." He looked beyond Leah to Jacob. "It's good to finally meet you both. My aunt has spoken of you as though you were her own children."

"In many ways, we were," Jacob admitted. "She has been a mother to us both."

Leah nodded but quickly changed the subject. "Tell me, have you any news of Jayce and Mrs. Beecham? Have you found them? Are they still here?"

Timothy smiled. "Indeed they are. I put my men to work immediately, and we searched every hotel in the downtown area. They are staying nearby, registered as Mr. and Mrs. Beecham. I've had them under surveillance now for days. He never leaves the hotel—the maid said he's always in the bedroom and the door is locked. Mrs. Beecham, however, has made some interesting trips."

"Such as?" Leah asked, casting a quick glance to Jacob before refocusing on Timothy.

"Such as wiring the Pinkerton agency in Washington, D.C., for a fingerprint file on Jayce Kincaid. It seems our gal is starting to doubt his guilt. She snuck him off the ship right under the noses of the agents her brother had sent to arrest Kincaid. It infuriated her brother, who sent a wire back telling her to forego this nonsense of worrying about whether or not Kincaid was the right man and that he was sending his men to arrest Jayce immediately. To which she sent the message that if he didn't help her and cooperate, she would disappear into the city until she had better answers."

"She cares about whether or not he's guilty," Jacob murmured.

"Yes, isn't that a change?" Leah said, catching Jacob's gaze. "Perhaps there's hope for Mrs. Beecham. Maybe she's learned that truth is more important than the letter of the law."

"And maybe she's finally learned what mercy is all about," Jacob said with a hint of a smile forming on his lips.

Chapter Twenty-seven

Helaina had finally convinced Stanley to send the fingerprint files by courier. She breathed a sigh of relief and headed into the hotel. The past few days were beginning to take their toll. Jayce had been a well-behaved prisoner, but his attitude and actions only caused her more guilt and frustration.

I never would have worried about any of this before. Jacob Barringer has been a thorn in my side with his talk of mercy and compassion. Now I have Stanley angry and have jeopardized an important case . . . all in the name of mercy.

She made her way upstairs to the shared

suite. For days she'd been sleeping on the sofa, and it had proved to be most inadequate. She longed for a bed but knew that it was better to keep Jayce imprisoned in the bedroom, rather than allow him free-range of the suite.

Unlocking the door to her room, she had nothing on her mind but to rest and rethink the information she'd gathered over the summer. But a roomful of people caused her to realize her plans were for naught.

"Mrs. Beecham."

Jacob stood by the windows and watched, as if waiting for her to do something dramatic. Beside him stood a tall, red-headed man. Jayce sat on the sofa along with Leah, while a fourth man sat at the writing desk.

"What's going on?" Helaina asked.

"We might ask you the same thing," Jacob retorted. "You kidnap a man in the dead of night and have the nerve to ask *us* what's going on?"

Helaina squared her shoulders. "I have a warrant for his arrest."

"So why isn't he in a jail, Mrs. Beecham?" the man at the desk questioned. He stood and came to where she stood.

"And who are you, sir?"

"Magnus Carlson, attorney-at-law. I now represent Mr. Kincaid."

Helaina eyed the man for a moment. He wasn't all that tall, and he carried an extra fifty pounds or more, but there was a certain presence to him. His pudgy face sported gold-rimmed glasses, from behind which icy blue eyes watched her every move.

"I see." She looked to Jayce. "I thought we had an agreement."

"I didn't bring them here," Jayce replied. "They found me."

"Might I inquire as to how you located us?" Helaina posed the question to Jacob.

"A private detective was hired by cable the night you left," Jacob replied. "He's been on the case ever since and brought us here to set Jayce free."

"I'm sorry, but that isn't possible," Helaina stated. She opened her purse. "I have the papers right here that entitle me to capture and arrest Mr. Kincaid."

"Then why hasn't he been properly remanded to the local authorities?" Carlson asked.

Helaina looked to Jayce. "Haven't you already told them this?"

"He has given his side of it," Carlson replied, "but we'd like to hear yours. This man's rights have been violated. Whether you have a warrant or not, he has constitutional rights."

"Yes," Helaina replied. "I'm very aware of that." She drew a deep breath. "There have been many discrepancies in this case. I chose this path to save Mr. Kincaid the drudgery of a jail cell while I researched and received the information I felt would help either convict or clear him."

"What exactly are the charges against Mr. Kincaid?"

Helaina looked around the room. "Why don't we sit down? This will take a while." She took her place in a wing-backed chair and smoothed the skirt of her new plum-colored traveling suit. Taking off her gloves, Helaina draped them across her lap while the others took their places.

Jacob joined Leah and Jayce on the sofa, while the other two men took up the remaining chairs. Helaina felt almost relieved to finally be able to explain to Jacob, but at the same time she could see the anger in his expression. He would never believe her.

There would never be anything she could say to win his approval.

"Earlier this year my brother, Stanley, a Pinkerton man in Washington, D.C., captured a man calling himself Jayce Kincaid. The man was responsible for the death of two Pinkerton agents, as well as a theft of goods at the British Museum in London. There were other charges of thefts and assaults as well. Stanley took the man into custody and boarded a train for Washington, D.C. On the way, Mr. Kincaid managed to free himself from his handcuffs. When Stanley realized what had happened, they fought. Eventually, the fight took them out on the open platform of this private car. Mr. Kincaid was a powerful man whose larger size gave him advantage against my brother. After throwing several punches that nearly rendered my brother unconscious, Mr. Kincaid threw Stanley from the train. This resulted in Stanley being severely injured."

"I'm quite sorry for your brother, Mrs. Beecham, but how could he be certain that this man was the responsible party?"

Helaina opened her purse and pulled out the folded sketch. "Stanley had this drawing made." She handed it to Carlson and waited while he passed it along to the others. "Kincaid had never been photographed by the authorities, and this was the only thing we had to identify him. This and a set of fingerprints taken from the train car."

"Fingerprints?" Leah questioned.

"Each person has a unique design of swirls and ridges on their fingers," Helaina explained. "No two are alike." She looked at Jayce. "Even in the case of twins—although I have heard of twins having prints that were alike, but reversed in order."

"So the fingerprints will prove that Jayce wasn't the one on the train," Leah stated, her voice sounding quite excited.

"That is my hope," Helaina said honestly. "I've had a hard time convincing my brother to send a courier with the file, but I believe he is finally willing to do this."

"You cannot just hold this man against his will in the meantime," Carlson said. "You do realize I could have you before a judge on this matter."

Helaina swallowed hard. This whole case had caused her nothing but problems from the beginning, and now it threatened to cause her grief with the law. The law that she so thoroughly respected. "I suppose I do, but I hope you will also see the problem in my turning Mr. Kincaid over to the police. If I do that, the Pinkerton men my brother sent here will simply take him into custody and put him on the first train back to the Capitol. He won't have a chance to prove his case before they throw him into jail to await a trial. I had hoped to have the proof needed, by obtaining the print files, prior to acting further on this matter."

"But why, Mrs. Beecham? If you had a job to do, why did you delay in doing it?"

"Yes, please tell us about that, Helaina," Jacob said rather snidely. "You were trying to find ways to force Jayce back to Seattle from the first day we met you."

She grew uncomfortable under his scrutiny. "It is true that I had a job to do. I thought the evidence against Jayce Kincaid was strong enough to prove his guilt. But that changed. Other things came to light . . . situations developed that I couldn't just ignore."

"For example?" Carlson asked.

Helaina thought back to all that had transpired and began to list off the events that gave her cause to doubt. "I suppose it all culminated for me when I read a letter to Jacob from the captain of the *Homestead.*" She glanced briefly at Jacob. "He mentioned how helpful Jayce had been on their short-lived expedition north. I knew Jayce was in Ketchikan with Leah. But, at the same time, here was a reputable man praising Mr. Kincaid's help with the dogs in the Arctic. I knew something had to be wrong."

"You must release this man until you have solid proof that allows you to arrest him. You cannot expect to keep him locked here in this hotel like some sort of animal."

"But if I release him, he will probably escape," Helaina replied. She was already convinced for herself that Jayce was innocent. But she had to, for the sake of Stanley's reputation and her own, prove that the fingerprints were not a match. "If Jayce leaves before I can check his fingerprints against the recorded prints, I will face serious problems."

"I won't leave, Helaina. I want to be proven innocent. As much as you want to know the truth, I want it more," Jayce said, his expression quite serious. "I have no reason to flee. I know what those prints will tell you."

"I don't know what should be done," Helaina finally admitted. "The file won't arrive by courier for a week or more."

"I have a suggestion," the redheaded man spoke up. He smiled at Helaina. "I'm Timothy Rogers, the private investigator who helped the Barringers—actually we're family." He turned and smiled at Leah. This caused her to nod.

"Anyway, I have a suggestion that might help all parties concerned. I can see that Mrs. Beecham has actually, out of the goodness of her heart, not imposed jail or the possibility of being sent east on Mr. Kincaid. She is trying to learn the truth in the hopes of knowing one way or the other if Jayce Kincaid was responsible for the deaths of other people. This is a critical issue. We cannot expect her to simply feel at ease in setting a possible killer free."

"Granted, Mr. Rogers, but there are laws to abide by. The law makes it very clear how these things are to be handled," Carlson said.

"And the law is the law," Jacob muttered, staring at Helaina with an unyielding gaze.

"That aside," Timothy continued, "I believe I have a solution. Since this should take no more than a week or two, I would like to offer my home. I have a large house with plenty of space for everyone. There is no Mrs. Rogers to be put off by my bringing home unplanned house guests, although my housekeeper might fret a bit."

"That is a very generous offer, Mr. Rogers," Helaina said. "But I'm not sure how that solves the situation."

"My thought, Mrs. Beecham, is that with everyone under the same roof, all parties may find the situation more agreeable. Mr. Kincaid will feel less like a prisoner. He has given his word that he has no plans to flee and desires the same thing you do. The Barringers are obviously interested in helping see Mr. Kincaid set free, so they are not planning to go until this thing is settled. And for you, the benefit would not only be peace of mind, but less strain on your budget. This hotel is quite expensive and my house is free."

"What say you, Mr. Kincaid? Would this meet with your approval?" Carlson asked.

"I would be willing to stay with Mr. Rogers. I'm even willing, for the sake of giving Mrs. Beecham peace of mind, to remain on the grounds until the proof is delivered and I am absolved of these charges. It would be my act of good faith, in return for hers."

Helaina knew they were all waiting for her to answer. "I suppose," she said after giving it only a moment of thought, "that this would be a better solution."

"Very well," Magnus Carlson said, getting to his feet. "Let us move our affairs to Mr. Rogers' house."

Helaina saw the others nod in agreement. All seemed pleased with the outcome—except Jacob. He continued to look at her as though she had been responsible for killing the agents herself. His contempt was evident, and for reasons that completely eluded Helaina, it very nearly broke her heart.

———

"But I think she's genuinely sorry for the things she's done," Leah protested.

Jacob had refused to hear a single argument in favor of Helaina. "I don't care how sorry she is—look at how she's treated everyone. Look at what she's done to cause problems for you and Jayce. Doesn't that bother you in the least?"

Leah looked at him and nodded. "It bothered me at first. You know how I worried about what she was up to—only I figured it to be some romantic notion. It never even occurred to me that she could be some kind of bounty hunter. But, Jacob, you can't just hold a grudge against her. It will hurt you more than it will her."

Jacob crossed his arms and shook his head. "I don't want to deal with her at all—ever again. Let her get her proof and then get out of our lives."

"But she needs your forgiveness."

He jumped up from the chair at this. "Hmph. She's never done anything to deserve it."

Leah laughed. "Jacob Barringer, listen to yourself. Since when do we offer forgiveness because someone deserves it?"

Jacob remembered the conversation he'd had with Helaina where he'd told her no one deserved forgiveness. He was trying to teach her about mercy, and now that she'd actually practiced a little of it, he was willing to condemn her without hearing another word.

"Just go talk to her," Leah said, coming to

his side. "You more than anyone knows what it is to be shown mercy. Helaina merely wanted to capture the man who so brutally wounded her brother. She had the evidence and word of the Pinkertons, and she was doing an honorable job. We cannot hold that against her."

Jacob knew Leah was right, but it was hard to admit it. "I suppose I can hear her out, but I have no desire to be her friend."

"I don't see any reason why you have to be her friend," Leah countered. "But you have the power to give her peace of mind, to show her real mercy . . . the very thing you've desired for her to learn."

He felt a sense of calm wash over himself as he made up his mind to seek Helaina out. "I'll talk to her. I can't promise anything more."

"Then I'll pray for you, Jacob." Leah reached out and touched her brother's face. "Just as you prayed for me."

Deciding it was best to get the matter over with, Jacob headed to the door. "You'd better pray hard, then. I have a feeling I'm going to need extra help with this one."

Helaina sat reading quietly in the front parlor when she heard someone clear his throat from the doorway. Looking up, she saw Jacob. Her heart picked up pace a bit as she closed her book. "Yes?"

He seemed uneasy. "I came here to . . . well . . . I want to be fair and hear you out."

Helaina felt hope surge within. "Truly?"

He walked into the room in a rather aloof manner. "I wouldn't be here if I didn't intend to hear what you have to say."

She'd tried so hard to talk to him prior to this that for a moment Helaina thought she might be dreaming. She suddenly felt very guarded. "I suppose you should sit down. Confession sometimes takes a while," she said with the slightest hint of a smile.

Jacob did as she suggested, sitting on the edge of the green brocade chair opposite her. "I'm sitting."

She nodded. "Well, you know from our conversation at the hotel that I came into this case at the request of my brother. It seemed every time one of the Pinkerton men got close to Kincaid, he either ran or hurt someone. It was decided that Kincaid would never suspect a woman. I was encouraged to use whatever means necessary to get Jayce into a position where agents could come in and arrest him and take him into custody.

"There were eyewitness accounts and descriptions of the man who was a thief and a murderer. The proof seemed very solid, Jacob, or my brother would never have sent me."

"But the proof was wrong. There were other issues to consider."

"Yes, issues that no one had any idea existed. Who would ever suspect an identical twin?" she asked. "There was no information or background on who this man really was or where he was from. When I heard Jayce's story on the way to Seattle, everything finally made sense. You see, I had written to the exploration association in Vancouver, and they had confirmed Jayce's employment during the same time he was supposedly committing crimes on the east coast. It didn't make sense at the time, so I continued to dig.

"When I read the letter from Captain Latimore—the one I opened in your absence . . ."

"How could I forget?" His tone was still very guarded and edged with anger.

"As I said, when I read the captain's praises for Jayce Kincaid's help with the dogs, nothing made sense. I knew he wasn't on that expedition—well, at first I thought he might have figured out who I was and that he had given me the slip. But when I knew for a fact that Jayce was with Leah in Ketchikan, it changed everything. I knew that he couldn't be two places at the same time. I even wrote to my brother to suggest that something was wrong and that perhaps we needed to look into whether or not Jayce had a family member who was using his name—taking his identity."

"So why did you take Jayce from Sitka? If you were confident that you had the wrong man, why bring him here?"

She frowned. How could she hope to make him understand her turmoil? She wanted only to see justice served and Stanley's reputation restored. She wanted a killer behind bars, but she also wanted to make certain the man she put there was truly the right one.

"I know you have no reason to believe me. I did lie to you before, and for that I am sorry and hope you . . . well . . . that you . . . might . . . forgive me," Helaina stammered.

She hurried on. "But I also need for you to understand that my brother was firm on what I was to do. He wanted Jayce brought to Seattle, and I didn't want to let him down. He's all I have left."

"Why didn't you just tell us that? Why all the sneaking around and secrecy?"

"Because Jayce is your friend. You wouldn't have believed me," Helaina said, getting rather angry. "I did my job, and at first I really didn't care what anyone else thought."

"At first?"

Helaina nodded and tried to restrain her emotions. "I honestly didn't care about your feelings or anyone else's when I first came to Nome. I was already unhappy because I'd lost the opportunity to capture Jayce in Seattle. But now . . . now I see how this wild chase has come about solely to teach me several things."

"What sort of things?"

She tried to figure out how best to word it. The last thing she needed was for Jacob to believe she was merely trying to sell him a bill of goods. She wanted—needed—him to believe her.

"You started talking about your faith,

about your trust in God. You started telling me—showing me—about mercy and compassion. These were things I definitely didn't understand. I'm not sure I understand them even now. After all, the balance seems at odds to me. I'm breaking the law and disappointing my brother by not just taking Jayce to the Pinkerton agents and turning him over. I deserve to face the consequences for my actions, but at the same time, I want to make certain Jayce is really the guilty party before sending him off to my brother. I suppose you would say that is mercy. For me, however, it's this battle of duties and beliefs that I've never had to face before now."

Jacob seemed to relax and his expression softened. "Sometimes it's hard to understand how the balance works. Everyone struggles."

"Even you?" she asked with a bit of an awkward laugh. "You seem to have it all under control."

"I'm struggling now," Jacob said softly. "I'm fighting my own war right this minute—with you."

She cocked her head to the side. "How so?"

"I know you want my forgiveness, but frankly, Helaina, I don't want to give it. I don't want to extend mercy to you. Why? Because you have hurt me—hurt my friends and loved ones. However, I know what the Bible says about forgiveness and about my part in practicing such a thing. And even though you don't believe in following the Bible's teachings, I do. Therefore the responsibility comes back on my shoulders."

"I'm not saying that you don't have a right to be angry, Jacob. Because I truly believe you are entitled to that. I did lie. It was wrong, and yet I justified it as being necessary because of my job. Just know that my intention was not to hurt you."

"But whether that was your intention or not—it happened nevertheless."

"I know." She looked away, feeling so uncertain of what she was about to say. "You've taught me to look at life differently, Jacob. I still don't know what to believe or not believe about God, but on the issue of mercy, I have to admit to having a new perspective. I know you cannot begin to appreciate the ramifications of this, but it has changed my entire life. A few months back I would never have questioned Jayce's guilt.

In fact, his innocence or guilt would simply have been the responsibility of someone else—not me. And if that truth wasn't proven, I was still able to distance myself and not care whether the outcome was good or bad. I had done my job. Now, however, I find myself questioning everything. I tell myself, despite the complications, I cannot send an innocent man to his death. I know that no one else cares to learn the truth in this matter as much as I do—they are angry at what they believe has been done to men of their own fellowship." She looked past Jacob, no longer seeing him. "Months ago, I wouldn't have defied my brother and the agency, and I certainly wouldn't have cared if you gave me your forgiveness." She paused and drew a deep breath before adding, "But I care now."

For several moments neither one said another word, then Jacob surprised her by getting to his feet. "This isn't easy for me, but at least I think I can understand this all a little better than before. I've treated you badly, even knowing that I was wrong for doing so. I guess what I'm trying to say is that I forgive you." He frowned and looked away. He seemed to wrestle with his own emotions, something Helaina thought quite unusual. Finally he added, "I hope you'll forgive me as well."

Helaina had not expected this or the sudden release of desire—need—from within her heart. Tears came to her eyes. She didn't understand what was happening to her, but the relief was so great that she couldn't do anything for a moment. He had asked for her forgiveness, when all the while she had been desperate for his.

"I forgive you," she whispered, hardly able to make the words form. She bowed her head and struggled to regain her composure. When she finally looked up, Jacob had already moved to the door. He watched her with a strange but guarded look on his face.

"Thank you," he said, then abruptly left the room.

Helaina buried her face in her hands and sobbed. *I don't understand any of this. What is happening to me . . . and why should his opinion matter so much?*

Chapter Twenty-eight

"The city is quite intimidating," Helaina said as Leah accompanied her on a shopping trip. "It's the noise you usually have to get used to."

"And all the people. There are people everywhere." Leah looked at the swarming mass of humankind and shook her head. How could so many people live together in one place? The noise was oppressive. There didn't seem to be a single moment of silence.

"It does take a certain kind of person to endure it," Helaina replied. "But don't you find the choices to be far superior here?"

Leah considered this for a moment. "The numerous choices are almost as bad as getting used to the numerous people. I've lived a much simpler life in Alaska. Still, it's been a very good life." She pulled her woolen cape closer as raindrops began to fall. "I suppose I could say that I would rather not have the extra choices."

"But why? Wasn't it quite the adventure yesterday as we searched for new clothes? You look quite handsome in that afternoon suit."

"But Jacob and I have never spent our money foolishly. This outfit will only serve its purpose down here. And if we have our way about it, we won't stay here any longer once Jayce is cleared of your charges and set free."

Helaina grimaced. "They aren't my charges, and I'm sorry you and your brother equate them as such."

Leah heard the regret in her voice and took compassion on the woman. "I'm sorry; I meant nothing by that."

"I know," Helaina replied, motioning to a storefront. "Here's the place I want."

"A stationery store?" Leah noted that they

advertised the largest inventory of writing supplies. "Why here?"

"I need quality paper and ink in order to make a good image of Jayce's fingerprints. We'll take prints from Jayce and then compare them when the courier finally brings the copies from Washington."

"And that will be the end of it?" Leah questioned. "Once you are able to prove that the prints are different, Jayce will be free to go?"

"Yes, I suppose he will be free," Helaina replied. "I'm hoping, however, he might help us in obtaining the true culprit. I need for Jayce to help me find Chase."

"You want Jayce to turn against his own brother?"

Helaina opened the door to the store and stepped inside. Leah was right on her heels. She couldn't imagine that the woman really expected any cooperation out of Jayce after all she'd done to him.

"Do you?" Leah reached out to halt Helaina in her steps. "I mean, you've put us all through a great deal. How can you possibly believe we'll just stay here and help you? I think that's asking entirely too much."

Helaina turned and looked at her as

though Leah were being quite unreasonable. "You do want to see a murderer behind bars—don't you?"

"Not if it means having to stay here and force Jayce to hunt down his brother. That's the Pinkertons' job or the duty of the authorities. It isn't our responsibility."

"But you cannot think to just leave."

"You cannot think to make us stay." Leah shook her head. "You must know the pain we've endured. We simply want to return home and be done with this chapter of our lives. We need for God to heal the sorrows and pains of the past and look to the future."

"So you'll just leave when we get the proof?" Helaina questioned. "You won't help me at all?"

Leah shook her head. "I for one intend to go home."

"But how is that in accordance to what you believe?"

"What do you mean?"

Helaina pulled Leah to one corner of the store as another woman came into the shop. "The Bible is full of verses about helping those in need. There are verses—I've read them myself—that speak to bearing one another's burdens, to helping those who ask for it. What of that?"

Leah shook her head. "I can't speak for the others, Helaina. You'll have to take that up with them. I just wouldn't count on any of us remaining here once the truth is known. Jayce has already given you more information than he would otherwise have to give. He's told you all about his brother and where he last saw him. I cannot imagine he owes you more than that."

———

Jayce watched Leah from the parlor entryway for several minutes. She looked so different in her new clothes. She was as radiant and beautiful as he'd ever seen her, but also so completely out of place. As she studied the newspaper, Jayce could see the information there did not set well. No doubt she found news of the ongoing war to be very disturbing.

Jayce smiled to himself. He decided to put an end to her worries and give her something more positive to think on. He'd been waiting for just the right moment to speak to her about marriage.

He sauntered into the room, still limping

ever so slightly from the dog wound. "Alone at last."

Leah smiled and put the paper aside. "Where are the others?"

"I heard Mrs. Beecham say she was going out for a time. Jacob and Timothy are deep in a conversation about the affairs of the world." He settled down on the sofa and reached out to take hold of her hand. "I think we should talk."

"I agree." She shifted her weight to face him. "What would you like to talk about?"

"Well, the obvious topic that comes to mind is us. Of course, if you have another subject more near and dear to your heart . . ."

Leah covered his hand with hers. "I suppose that will suffice."

Just then the front doorbell rang. Leah looked to Jayce. "Do you think the courier has arrived?"

"I certainly hope so." He got up and headed for the foyer. He turned abruptly. "I suppose our conversation will have to wait a little longer."

Leah followed behind, sounding quite disappointed. "I suppose so."

Jayce arrived just behind the butler. The

man admitted their guest and nearly jumped a foot when he realized Jayce was standing right beside him.

"Sorry, sir. I did not see you there. This is Captain Latimore."

"Yes, I know the man well," Jayce said, extending his hand. "I see you got my letter."

"Indeed, I did. Mr. Kincaid, I'm glad you got in touch. You said Mr. Barringer was here as well?"

"Yes." He turned to Leah. "Have you two met?"

Leah nodded. "I met the captain in Last Chance—when you were injured."

"It's good to see you again, Miss Barringer."

"Leah, if you'll excuse us for a time, Jacob and I have business with the captain."

"Of course. Let me know if you need anything." She turned and headed back to the parlor.

Jayce smiled at the captain. "Why don't you come with me? I'll take you to Jacob and we can talk." Jayce led the way to Timothy's study. Knocking on the open door, he looked in expectantly. "We have a guest."

The men looked up, but it was Timothy

who welcomed them in. "Come join us. We
are always up for a guest."

"Captain Latimore," Jacob said, getting
to his feet. "I'm glad to see you. This is our
host and dear friend, Timothy Rogers."

The two men shook hands, then Timothy
motioned to the butler. "Bring us coffee and
something to eat. I'm sure we could all use
a bit of something to tide us over until supper."

"How is your family, Captain? Did your
wife enjoy the Arctic?" Jacob asked.

"I'm afraid the expedition was difficult for
Regina to endure. Our son had just turned
three, so he could not accompany us. She
missed him fiercely. But of course you
would remember that," he said, turning to
Jayce.

"Captain, I wasn't with you. You mentioned my presence in a letter to Jacob, but
that wound I suffered from the dogs kept
me from joining you."

The captain looked stunned. "Then who
was the man calling himself Jayce Kincaid?
He was identical to you."

"I know. I believe it was my brother
Chase—my twin. Although I'm uncertain as

to how he knew I was expected on the *Homestead.*"

"How strange," the captain said, shaking his head. "As I recall he showed up in Kotzebue. We were there trying to arrange native help. One of the men saw him and recognized him. After that he assumed your role without question. At times he seemed uncertain, fumbled around a bit, but I attributed that to your injury. I rarely spoke to him face-to-face, but when we talked, he answered as though he were you."

"I'm sure he did. He has always had a habit of pretending to be me. I hope he caused no trouble."

"None at all. That's why I was encouraged to ask for your return next year." The captain seemed troubled by this new turn of events. "I would still like for you to join us . . . since I know you studied and planned for the trip. Your geological skills would be much needed." He turned to Jacob. "Your dog handling skills will also be needed."

"You were speaking of your wife and her difficult time on the trip," Jacob interjected, seeming to sense the need to change the focus. "Will she accompany you next year?"

"No, I'm sorry to say she won't be able to, but I'm happy to announce we are expecting our second child in April."

"Congratulations," Jayce offered. "It's a troubling time for our world, but children are always a blessing."

"We were just discussing some of the war's conflicts. The Germans seem to have decided it would be in their best interests to play fair," Timothy said. "What say you, Captain?"

"I have had great concern about the affairs of this country. I worry that we will somehow be dragged into this matter, and that is really why I'm here today. I have no problem in interesting men in exploration—especially when it comes to the areas of the Arctic. Since the trouble with the *Karluk* and others, there has been a fascination for defeating the frozen north—taming the untamable, if you will. Even the army has approached me with interests for a mutual expedition, but they'd like for it to remain a secret. No sense stirring up the rest of the country in wondering what they're up to."

"What exactly are they up to?" Jacob asked.

"They believe this war will escalate. They

desire that we be prepared to ward off possible invasions. Russia is having all kinds of trouble. They are fighting amongst themselves. It's the opinion of my government contacts that Russia may well go into a full civil war. If that happens, we may find them coming across the strait to attack or try to reclaim parts of Alaska. Many believe the sale was completely unfair, you know."

"But surely they know it would mean war with America if they were to attack Alaska," Jayce replied. "Fair or unfair, the deal was signed and paid for. The territory belongs to us."

"Exactly," the captain agreed. "However, it doesn't mean there won't be those who aren't motivated to change the situation."

Jayce considered this for a moment. If the captain's thoughts were correct, it could mean a great deal of danger to those living in the Seward Peninsula, so close to the Russian people. "So the army wants to form an expedition for what purpose exactly?"

"I'm not entirely sure of their complete objective, but the main one would be for the purpose of devising strategic locations for defense. They would want to explore the entire coastal region of the western boundaries of Alaska."

Jacob shifted to the edge of his chair. "And what would be your focus in this effort?"

The captain smiled. "I am still of a mind to explore for the purpose of seeing it all and knowing what else might be made of it. If there is potential for the military, then there is potential for towns and cities as well."

Jayce shook his head. "That land is raw and inhospitable. Life in the Arctic and along the Bering Sea is not an easy one. There isn't enough vegetation there to support large numbers of people, and planting additional crops simply won't work. This is not a good area of the world to raise food."

"Nor to build houses or roads," Jacob added. "The ground is permanently frozen just inches from the surface. Much of the area becomes impassable bogs and marshlands in the summer months as the top of this ground thaws. In the winter, the only travel by land is done with snowshoes and dogsleds. You won't get automobiles to pass over the frozen tundra with any degree of success."

Latimore frowned. "I thought you to be

men of vision. You know that where there is a dream for such things, men will also figure out how to accomplish those dreams. I intend to be a part of that, and I would like you two to join my team."

"So you will definitely make another attempt at the north next year?" Jayce questioned.

"Yes, and we might even set up a winter camp in order to endure the elements and figure out what might be done to minimize the dangers and problems, with the hope of expanding villages already in place to become larger settlements—even cities."

"I've lived winters in the north," Jacob replied. "It's not for the faint of heart. One of the biggest things you're forgetting, besides the cold, is the darkness. For a great many weeks, we lose the sun all together. How do you propose to maintain cities in complete darkness? There simply won't be enough wood, coal or kerosene to keep things warm and lighted. There won't be flowing rivers for power stations so that you can string electricity in these proposed towns."

"Not to mention that the endless hours of darkness are even harder on a person than the summer's endless hours of light. It takes a special kind of person to live in the north," Jayce added.

"So you would defeat my project before it even starts?" the captain asked.

"Not at all," Jayce replied. "We would just suggest you be realistic."

"I think the men make good arguments," Timothy declared, "but I, for one, would be quite supportive of such a project. I think our pioneering grandparents and great-grandparents might never have settled this far west had they been unwilling to take risks. But there should also be a balance of caution."

Latimore nodded, rubbing his dark beard. "I completely agree. However, I will point out, if we don't go—someone else will. There have already been multiple trips to the Arctic by other teams. Some have not fared well, and others have. You have men talking all along the lyceum circuits about their exploits in the Alaskan wilderness. The passion is there, my friends. It's just a matter of figuring out who will go and then how to raise the funds to undertake such a project."

"I would definitely be interested," Jayce admitted. "But there are things about my life

that have changed. I intend to take a wife."
He looked at Jacob and grinned. "Although
I haven't exactly had a chance to ask her
yet."

"My first comment on that news is, congratulations," the captain replied, smiling.
"And my second is, bring her along. We will
have jobs for women as well as men. We
plan to seek the help of the natives again—
hopefully with better success this time. But
we could always use a good seamstress."

"I'm sure Leah would love the adventure,"
Jacob admitted, "but while her sewing abilities are first rate, she's also a skilled
healer."

"Wonderful! We could probably never
hope to secure a doctor on such a trip, but
if your sister is capable in this area, we
would be quite well settled."

"How soon will you begin to assemble
your men?" Jayce asked.

"I'm already at the task. That's why I'm
here today. I can use a geologist and a man
to handle the dog teams."

"I don't suppose you'll need a private detective," Timothy said, grinning, "but what
of an investor?"

Latimore smiled. "There is always need for those, kind sir."

———

After refusing to stay for supper, Latimore took his leave. Leah then found herself in the middle of an animated table conversation concerning next year's expedition. Helaina, however, seemed quite unhappy with the topic.

"I see nothing of value in this; after all, there is a war going on in Europe. The expense is rather frivolous," she told them. "You could do your country a better service by helping me capture the killer who murders in your name."

Jayce looked at her and shook her head. "I never sought a career in the law. I'm sure there are plenty of men who would be happy to help you, but I'm not one of them."

"Leah said it would be your plan to head back to Alaska as soon as your name was cleared. I can't help but say that this a disappointment to me." She sliced into the beef and took a bite.

"Enough of a disappointment to keep you from clearing my name?" Jayce asked quite seriously. Every eye turned to Helaina, and they all waited for her answer.

She swallowed and seemed to consider the matter for a moment. "I wouldn't do that. I would never hold an innocent man just because he refused to assist me. I'm sorry you would believe that of me."

"But you've said in the past that you would do just about anything to get your man." Jacob looked at her hard. "Why would this not be an option?"

"Because it wouldn't be just," Helaina said, pushing back her plate. "But neither is it just for you to leave a guilty man at large."

"I've already given you all of the information I can," Jayce said, getting up from the table. Leah could see the anger in his eyes. "I've told you about my brother and the places I know him to go. I've told you about the company he keeps. I owe you nothing. Now if you'll excuse me."

"But wait! You would be the one person who might get close to him without arousing suspicions."

"How callous you are," Jacob interjected. "You honestly expect a man to turn traitor to his own family?"

"If his brother is guilty as he suggests,

then yes, I do. It's the law. It's only right. Would you not turn your sister in if she committed murder right before your very eyes?"

Jayce only shook his head and stalked from the room.

Leah got up. "If you'll excuse me, I should go to him."

She left the room without another word. Helaina's insensitivity to Jayce's pain truly irritated Leah, but there was little she could say that she hadn't already said.

"Jayce? Are you all right?"

She found him in the front room, standing by the fireplace. He turned at the sound of her. "Do you think I should stay? Am I wrong?"

Leah went to him. "No. I think it's an unreasonable request."

"But what if he kills again, Leah? What if he kills someone, and I could have stopped him?"

"You don't know that you could stop him," Leah argued. "You don't know where he is, and there's no guarantee that you could ever find him. Like you told me once, when he wants to disappear, he disappears."

She could see the pain in his expression,

knowing the war being fought in his heart was not one with an easy resolution. Someone would get hurt in this situation—no matter which side won out.

"Leah."

The way he spoke her name sounded almost like a plea. She put her hand to his shoulder and smiled. "I'm here for you, Jayce. I've always been here for you."

He took her in his arms and crushed her against him. "I love you. I think I always have." He paused, then added in a hushed whisper, "Marry me, Leah. Please marry me."

Chapter Twenty-nine

Climbing the stairs to Mr. Rogers' house, Helaina paused at the sound of laughter coming from the front room. No doubt Jacob and Leah and Jayce were all caught up in an animated discussion. Helaina bit her lower lip and wondered if perhaps she should just come in through the back entry. At least then she wouldn't have to make the obligatory greetings and spend time in small talk with people she knew would rather she simply disappear from their lives.

The door opened, to her surprise. "Good afternoon, madam," the butler said in his stately manner. "Would you care for tea?"

SUMMER *of the* MIDNIGHT SUN 493

He helped her with her coat and hat. "No thank you," Helaina replied. "I believe I'll just go upstairs and have a rest."

She crossed the highly polished oak floors, her heels clicking rhythmically as she passed the parlor door. Against her will she looked inside the room. Leah met her gaze and waved.

"How are you, Helaina? I've not seen you all day."

Helaina knew she had no choice but to pause. "I had to tend to business this morning. I've been back and forth, actually. I still have no word about the courier."

"Come join us," Leah suggested. "We were just talking about our wedding."

"Will it be soon?"

"Yes. Jayce and I are to be married before we return to Alaska."

The men seemed rather hesitant to join in the conversation. Helaina sensed their indifference at her appearance. "That's wonderful news. Congratulations," she said half-heartedly.

"Timothy is helping us to arrange things through his minister." Leah smiled at Jayce and added, "It will just be a small private service."

"I'm sure it will be lovely."

"We were also discussing our plans for next summer. We all plan to be involved in the expedition," Leah said. "I never would have believed it, but Captain Latimore said one thing they definitely could have used on this last expedition was a skilled seamstress. I can fit that bill easily. Not only that, but I can act as nurse to the expedition members."

"She is very good with a needle," Jacob finally joined in. "She can stitch up garments or men."

Helaina smiled, but an overwhelming emptiness inside threatened to consume her. "I'm glad for all of you. Now, if you'll excuse me." The men seemed relieved, but Leah appeared to be trying hard to make Helaina feel included.

"Are you certain you can't stay?"

"I'm afraid I'm quite tired. Thank you for the invitation, but perhaps I will see you at dinner." She edged toward the door the entire time. "Good day."

She headed upstairs, nearly running the remaining distance to her room. Closing the door behind her, Helaina felt hot tears stream down her cheeks. She felt so displaced. "What's wrong with me? I'm acting like a fool."

But inside, she felt as though her world were falling apart. Nothing fit anymore. She longed for something she couldn't even identify. In fact, when she thought of Jayce and Leah and Jacob just now, she knew they had something that she desired. Their companionship was so rich—so intimate. Yet it wasn't that alone that left Helaina feeling so empty.

"What is it? What do they have? What is it that I want?"

She moved to her window and pulled back the lacy curtains. Her room looked out on the backyard, and there she found Leah and Jayce walking hand in hand. From time to time Leah would look up and smile or laugh at something Jayce had said. While Jayce . . . Jayce seemed perfectly content to be imprisoned with the woman he loved.

"He must be innocent," Helaina reasoned. "His conscience is too clear. There is no anxiety in his heart. There can't be any guilt."

She let the curtain fall back in place. "But how can he know such peace?"

She thought immediately of Mrs. Hayworth. The older woman would have given her a motherly pat on the arm and said, "There. There. Chaos in life is given by the father of chaos, whereas peace comes from God alone. It's a special kind of peace that changes night into day and storm into calm."

Helaina sat down on the edge of her bed. "I don't know how God can offer peace when He allows such a world of conflict and hurt to go unchecked—unreined." She shook her head. "He cannot care about me."

———

"Leah, why did you fall in love with me?" Jayce asked as they walked in Timothy's fading gardens. "I mean back then—when we first met. What made you so certain that I was the man you would want to take as a husband?"

Leah shrugged. "There was no one thing. If anything, there was one thing that made it impossible for us to be together. Well . . ." She paused and smiled. "There were two things. One was you."

"Of course," he said, nodding. "I must have been crazy."

Her smile broadened. "The other was God."

"How so?" He enjoyed the warmth of her ungloved hand in his. How small and fragile Leah seemed at times—like now. But he knew her to be fully capable of taking care of herself—of enduring great trials.

"I knew I couldn't marry you unless you loved God. See, all of my life the people around me had encouraged me to love God and to put Him first. When I finally ended up in Ketchikan with Karen and Adrik, I came to understand the difference in a marriage where God was put first. I contrasted it against my parents, who had a great deal of love for each other but didn't have that common ground.

"My father was never happy. He was always restless. Always looking for some way to get rich and make his family comfortable. And in this pursuit, he knew nothing but failure and misery."

"What about your mother?"

"She was a godly woman, her only desire that her children seek God's purpose for their lives. As she lay dying, she didn't fear for herself or worry about the end. She cared only for us—that our hearts might be made right with the Lord so that she could one day see us again in heaven."

Jayce put his arm around Leah's shoulders. "She no doubt loved you deeply."

"She did, and that kept me going, even after she was gone."

"I know what you're talking about when you speak of how different Karen and Adrik's life was in contrast to others. See, my parents were God-fearing, church-attending, generous people. But their religion seemed rather shallow at times. When hard times came or something bad touched our lives, they were just as weak and frightened as people who had no place to go—no one to trust," Jayce said sadly. "I never saw them possess the kind of restful spirit that I saw in Karen and Adrik."

"That was what most impressed me," Leah said. "No matter how bad things got, they were always able to rest in the Lord. When you rejected me, Karen encouraged me to find peace in God. She told me over and over how God had a special plan for my life, and that I should never desire for anything but His perfect will. She reminded me that if I belonged to Him and sought to do things His way, I would always know the kind of peace that the Bible evidenced, even when things around me were falling apart."

"I can't begin to imagine the pain I caused you," Jayce admitted. He looked into her eyes as he pulled her around to face him. "I know it doesn't mean much, but I wish I could go back and relive those moments. I wish I knew then what I know now."

Leah put her hand to his cheek. "Jayce, I never thought I'd ever say this, but you were right to walk away. I was too young. I didn't know my own heart. I can't even believe I'm saying this now." She shook her head. "I was very immature. For all I'd been through, I was still very focused on myself. When something bad happened, I always weighed it in light of how it affected me—not others. I needed to learn a great deal before I was ready to be your wife. Sorry it took me ten years."

He grinned. "Are you sure two people who have a history of such poor choices can make a future together—a good future?"

"As long as we put God first," Leah said quite seriously. "And seek His will no matter our own desires."

"I know you're right. The wisdom of God's Word is definitely in that answer. I will try to be a good and godly man, Leah. But I know I'm flawed. I know there are serious problems in my heart—especially where Chase and my other siblings are concerned. Helaina Beecham doesn't understand how much I would like to see Chase punished for what he's done to me. She doesn't know how easy it would be for me to say yes to her request for me to help her."

"If that's what God wants you to do," Leah said softly, "then do it. I won't stand in the way."

"But I can't say that it is what God wants. Oh, He wants Chase to stop killing and stealing. He would also no doubt want Chase to pay for what he's done. But I can't discern if God is calling me to make it my campaign to hunt him down. I'm not certain about anything regarding Chase, except that this situation cannot be easily settled. I'm afraid it would only end in the death of one, or both, of us."

———

It was quite early in the morning, but Helaina found sleep impossible. Glancing at the clock, she knew that no one, save maybe the cook, would even be stirring at this unreasonable hour. She dressed quickly and made her way downstairs, hoping that the noise of her door opening and closing wouldn't awaken anyone else.

She had planned to make her way to what Timothy called the music room. The room was small and quiet, containing a piano that, as far as she knew, no one in the household could even play.

There were two chairs positioned in front of the window. They faced each other and yet gave the occupant ample view to the outside world. Helaina liked it here best. Early mornings were a peaceful time of day, and peace was what she desperately craved. She took a seat in a rather unladylike fashion, curling up in the chair with her legs tucked securely under her.

"Are you hiding out?"

Jacob's voice nearly sent her flying from the chair to do just that. Helaina quickly repositioned herself, her blond hair settling loose around her shoulders. "What are you doing up? It's quite early, you know."

He crossed the room and stared down at

her for a moment. "I might ask you the same thing."

She looked away and shrugged. "I couldn't sleep."

"Seems to me you can't sleep a lot these days. You're up well into the night and then awake equally early in the morning—usually before sunrise."

"How would you know that?" She tried hard to sound as if his observations didn't matter.

"I know more than that. You're losing weight. You've hardly been eating this past week."

"That's none of your concern."

Jacob took a seat and crossed his legs out in front of him. He looked quite re-laxed—almost as though he intended to be there for some time. "I know something isn't right. I've tried to ignore it, but God keeps bringing it back to my attention. This morn-ing I woke up about the time you started stirring, and I knew I was supposed to come down here and speak with you."

"How could you know that? Did God sud-denly appear to you?" she asked snidely. His calm unnerved her, and Helaina didn't like that feeling at all.

"I suppose He did, in a sense." Jacob crossed his arms. "I know you're quite unhappy. I know you wish for this situation to be over with—for Jayce's brother to be found and put to trial for all his sins. But I think there's something else. Something you aren't even allowing yourself to realize."

"Who are you to suggest such things?" She narrowed her eyes. "I know you said you forgave me, but why come to me now, all tender and caring? You are a hypocrite."

"I treated you badly. That much is true. You see, God has always allowed me both the blessing and curse of being able to pretty well know a person from a first meeting."

"What do you mean?"

"I mean I can tell if they have good or bad intentions. A preacher once told me it's called discernment. It's a gift of God."

"And when you met me, you knew I was evil—right from the start."

"No, not evil. I knew you were up to something—something you weren't admitting. I knew there was more than happenstance that had brought us together. You came with a purpose—an agenda."

"True enough, but it's easy to say that

now. Now that the truth is known to everyone."

Jacob nodded. "I suppose it would take
something else to make you realize that
God honestly cares enough about you to
send someone into your life who could help
you find your way back to Him. Something
that no one else could possibly know."

"Like what?" There was no way she could
believe this game of his. God might know
everything that went on, but He didn't care
about it, and He certainly didn't share that
information with anyone else. Why should
He?

"I've been praying for you for some time
now," Jacob began, "and every time I pray
for you, one word keeps coming to mind."

"And what would that be?"

He met her gaze and didn't even blink.
"Guilt."

She swallowed hard and tried not to react. "Guilt? You must be crazy."

"Am I?"

She wanted only to get up and pace the
room, but she knew this would be a dead
giveaway to how close to the truth he'd
struck. "If you're so confident that I'm consumed with guilt—and if God is the one giv-

ing you the information, then by all means share what you know."

Jacob drew a deep breath. "I believe you feel consumed with guilt because of the death of your parents and husband. I think you blame yourself."

She began to tremble. "Why . . . why . . . would I blame myself?" She didn't want to hear his answer, but at the same time she had to.

"Because maybe you were the intended victim? Because you should have been with them—died with them . . . died instead of them."

Helaina felt as though she couldn't breathe. She'd never told anyone how she felt about those things. About the truth of how the original kidnapping plot had been intended for her and her alone. She suddenly felt dizzy—her vision began to blur.

"Helaina. Helaina."

She could hear him calling her name, but she couldn't respond. She couldn't see him.

"Helaina, wake up."

She finally struggled against the grip of darkness and opened her eyes. Jacob stood over her chair, gently patting her face. "I . . . what . . ." She drew a deep breath.

Jacob's words came rushing back to her. There was no pretense of defense left in her. She looked into his eyes, feeling as though he could see every secret in her heart. Surely the only way he could have known these things was because God had allowed him to know them. But why?

"I'm all right," she told him. She straightened and stared down at her shaking hands. "Anyone could have guessed about the guilt," she said in a voice barely audible.

"I suppose so," Jacob admitted, retaking his seat.

"But," she continued, "only a couple of people knew that the original plot was intended for me." She looked up against her will. "It should have been me."

"But it wasn't, and you find that impossible to live with. Don't you?"

She nodded very slowly. "I went to Europe on a whim. Robert couldn't get away, but I wanted very much to go shopping and to see friends. I talked my mother into taking over my responsibilities to host a charity event for the children's orphanage. It should have been me."

"But God had other plans, Helaina," Jacob said matter-of-factly.

"I know, and I hated Him for it. How could He be so cruel as to take those I loved and leave me behind? How could He allow those men to kill them? I don't understand that at all." She felt the tears begin to fall. "Robert was the love of my life. My mother was my best friend. And my father . . . well . . . he represented security to me well before I even knew Robert existed. They were there one day and then they were gone, and all because some amateur group of thugs decided they could best make a living by kidnapping me."

"What happened to make them kill your family?"

She could hear the confession of the youngest member of the group. "They got scared when there turned out to be three people in the carriage instead of one. Robert charged the men, and they fired their guns without regard. They were terrified, for they had no plan for what to do past stealing me away and demanding money." She wiped her eyes with the back of her sleeve. "I thought I would die when I heard the news."

"I think I know how that feels. When I got

word about my father's death, it was unbearable."

"I felt so consumed with guilt. Because Stanley was working with the Pinkertons, I was given access to everything related to the file. I even saw photographs that I never should have seen. Pictures that never leave my memory."

"So you got involved with the law in order to ease that guilt?"

She looked at him and nodded. There was both a relief and a sensation of awe that he knew her so well. Could this really be because God had told him? "Every time I helped put a criminal behind bars, I felt a little bit of guilt slip away. I figured if I did enough—if I got enough people—then the hurt would stop and the emptiness would disappear. But it never has."

"And it never will," Jacob said. "Not that way. Only God can fill that empty place. Only God knows how much you hurt—how guilty you feel. Their death wasn't your fault, but you're carrying it as though it were, as though if you carry it long enough you might somehow bring them back to life."

She flew out of the chair and headed straight at him. She wanted to slap him—to silence him. "You don't understand. You can't understand. I have to do something. I have to right the wrong."

He jumped back in defense, then reached out and took hold of her wrists. Helaina crumpled to her knees in front of him. "You can't make anything right, Helaina. You can't change what has happened."

"Then why go on?" She looked up at him as he edged forward. "Why live—why try?"

"It wasn't your time to go, Helaina. God has another purpose—another plan for you. I don't know why your loved ones had to die, but I know that the injustice grieved God's heart just as much as it grieved yours."

"Why didn't He stop it? Why, Jacob? If He cares so much, why does He allow all this evil in the world? All this pain?"

"I don't have answers for that. We live in a fallen world and men will make bad choices—they will sin without regard to God or man. Why it has to be that way, I really don't understand either. But I do know that God has not left us as orphans. He promises to be with us always."

Helaina composed herself. She pulled away from Jacob and got to her feet. "I've heard those answers before. But they make no sense. God is supposed to be all-powerful and all-knowing. It makes no sense that He allows these things to happen to good people." She smoothed her skirt and wiped her face. "If you'll excuse me."

"I will," Jacob said as she moved to the door. "But I won't stop praying for you. God won't let me."

The words burrowed into her heart. She didn't want to admit that Jacob's concern touched her. "Do what you will," she murmured. "I don't believe it will help, but you do what you like."

———

Later that day the courier arrived from Washington, D.C. To Helaina's surprise, he turned out to be her very annoyed, very angry brother.

"I can't believe you're doing this. You know better. I've brought my men with me. They're waiting to take Jayce Kincaid into custody."

Helaina stood her ground. "No, Stanley. Not until we compare those prints."

"Helaina."

"No. I know without a doubt that this man

is innocent. I want the prints as proof. I have his fingerprints all ready for the comparison. You cannot send an innocent man to prison or to be hanged. You would never forgive yourself."

Stanley calmed a bit at this. "Very well. I can't believe you're doing this, but since I have no choice, let's get the job done." He took a folder from his case. "Here they are."

Helaina nodded. "Come with me into the library."

"Where's Kincaid?"

She smiled over her shoulder. "In the library."

She saw her brother's reaction when he came into the room and stood face-to-face with Jayce Kincaid. For a moment his scowl deepened and his hands balled into fists.

"Kincaid," he muttered.

"I don't have the pleasure of knowing you, sir."

Stanley stiffened. His eyes narrowed as he stepped closer. He seemed to be searching Jayce's face—almost as if looking for proof. Helaina saw Stanley's expression change. "You aren't the right man. You look like him—but you're not him." There was a sense of awe in his tone.

Helaina looked at her brother curiously. "Why are you saying that now?"

"I cut the man who threw me from the train. I cut him deep across the left eye. It bled so badly that his blood covered me as well. It would have left a considerable scar." He shook his head. "You look just like him."

Helaina spread the prints atop the table and drew out a magnifying glass that Timothy provided. She looked at the set that she'd made. The ridges and lines were nearly committed to memory. Then taking the glass to the pages her brother had provided, she could finally prove the truth she'd known since leaving Alaska.

"They don't match," she whispered and looked up to meet Jayce's face. "Jayce Kincaid is an innocent man."

Chapter Thirty

Jayce felt a profound sense of relief with those six words. Though he'd known the prints wouldn't match, to have legitimate proof of his innocence was almost overwhelming.

"But if it's not you . . . then who is it?" Stanley asked.

"My brother Chase Kincaid is probably responsible," Jayce replied. "He is my identical twin."

"Which is what I've been telling you since I arrived in Seattle," Helaina declared.

"Yes, yes. I remember well your list of discrepancies, though I'd disregarded them until now. Has Chase a record?" Stanley asked.

"He has served time, but overall, he's done a remarkable job of not getting caught. He has a long list of friends who are happy to help him in his endeavors because Chase has always been generous with money," Jayce answered.

"What is his goal, do you think?" Helaina asked. "For example, why steal from the British Museum?"

Jayce shrugged. "My guess is that he needed money first and foremost. Second, I would imagine that, rather than simply steal from someone's home or from individuals, my brother saw real excitement in taking things from the prestigious British Museum. He was always in pursuit of a good thrill. And of course, the chance to taint my name would add to the benefits."

Stanley seemed to consider this for a moment. "So where is he now? Do you have any idea?"

"Not really," Jayce admitted. "However, we might know someone who can give us some information. Captain Latimore is here in town. He is the man we spoke of earlier, who captained the ship Chase was on earlier this summer. The expedition met with problems and ended their trip early. Latimore can at least tell us where he parted company with Chase."

Stanley nodded. "Very well. How do we reach this Captain Latimore?"

"I've already sent for him," Helaina said with a smile. "We figured that he might prove helpful."

Stanley squared his shoulders and eyed Jayce. He shook his head as if he still couldn't believe his eyes. "I must say, the resemblance is uncanny. Had I not been assured that my cut left its mark and had the fingerprints not proved your identity, I would have seen you hanged."

"Captain Latimore has arrived," the butler announced.

The group turned to await the captain. Jayce both dreaded and looked forward to what the man might have to say; his own gut ached as he struggled over his dilemma with Chase. If he refused to turn Chase over to the law, he was allowing a vicious criminal to go free. But if he saw to Chase's capture, he was turning over his own flesh and blood to die.

"Captain Latimore," Helaina said in greeting. "Thank you for coming."

"You said it was urgent," the man replied. He looked to the group and nodded. "I came as soon as I could."

Jayce stepped forward. "We need some information regarding my brother Chase and his affairs while with you onboard *Homestead*."

The captain nodded. "I'll give you whatever I can."

Leah reached out for Jayce's hand, and he felt strengthened by her support. She had never once doubted him. Neither had Jacob. This thought gave him courage to face what he knew must be done.

"Captain, my name is Stanley Curtis. I'm a Pinkerton agent. I live in Washington, D.C., and have been on the trail of a dangerous criminal for some time. We had thought the man to be Jayce Kincaid but have since learned that it is probably his twin brother, Chase. I understand you had opportunity to employ Chase this summer."

The captain rubbed his beard for a moment. "I did employ the man—thought he was Jayce. We had met a couple of times prior, and the man seemed exactly as I remembered Jayce. I had no reason to doubt him when he agreed that he was Jayce Kincaid."

"Did the man in question have a scar over his left eye?" Stanley asked.

The captain seemed excited at this question. "Yes. Yes, he did. Although I hadn't really thought about it until now. It was positioned just above the eyebrow on the left side. The scar was not that old; it hadn't faded as a scar will over time."

"Yes," Stanley said, looking to Jayce. "It must be him."

"So what do we do now?" Jayce asked in return.

"Sir, when did you last see Chase Kincaid?" Stanley questioned.

The captain considered this question for a moment. "When the expedition broke company, we returned the natives to Kotzebue, but Chase asked to be taken to Nome. The rest of the crew returned to the States or to Vancouver."

"You left Chase in Nome?"

Latimore nodded. "Yes. I believe that would have been in early August. He told me he planned to spend the winter there."

"So he may still be there," Jayce said. He

exchanged a brief glance with Leah before letting go of her hand and getting to his feet. "We'll have to return to Nome as soon as possible."

"Why would Chase Kincaid remain in Nome?" Stanley didn't sound at all like he believed this possibility.

"He must think it best to lay low and hide out for a time. He might have even gotten wind of what was happening with your search and how you were after me," Jayce said.

"That's impossible," Helaina replied. "I was very careful with my investigation."

"True enough, but I wouldn't trust that he counts himself safe for the time."

"Does he know much about Alaska— about survival up there?" Stanley asked.

"I wouldn't have thought so," Jayce began, "but then, I wouldn't have expected him to handle the dog teams like a professional. Captain Latimore said he was quite proficient with the teams."

"Well, he was clumsy at first, but he quickly recovered and then took on real proficiency. We were well into the northern reaches of the Arctic where the ice never thaws. Some of the team had discussed staying throughout the winter. We had plans to locate one of the Canadian islands for this purpose when we started having so much trouble. But Mr. Kincaid was perfectly capable with the dogs and even volunteered to be one of those who stayed behind."

Jayce knew it was his brother's way of thwarting the law. "I'm going to Nome," he stated firmly. "If he's there, I will capture him and take him to the authorities."

"I'll send my men with you," Stanley said. "I have at least two who won't mind the trip and have no family to hold them back."

"I'm going too," Helaina suddenly declared. "It was my job to catch him—I don't intend to fail at this mission."

Jayce intervened. "No. You cannot go. Chase is too dangerous. He'd have no regard for the fact that you're a woman."

"He's right," Stanley added, "this is too dangerous."

"It wasn't too dangerous when you sent me out here five months ago," Helaina remarked.

Though Jayce sensed her anger, he couldn't let her go along with them—not after realizing the extent of his brother's ruthlessness. "It wouldn't be right, Helaina. Chase may already be onto you. If he's heard about a woman hunting me down, then your cover will be no good. You won't be safe."

"Besides, you had your chance at this," Stanley said firmly. "You figured out that Jayce wasn't the right man. That doesn't make you a failure at this mission. You succeeded in saving an innocent person from the gallows."

"But it's not enough," Helaina replied. "I want to see the right man caught. I want to be the one to capture him."

Jayce shook his head. "It doesn't matter who catches him. It only matters that he be caught."

Helaina said nothing, but Jayce knew she was seething. He hoped she might learn to trust him again, as she had before, when she'd needed him to remain her prisoner.

"So we need to book tickets to Nome," Jacob said, shaking his head. "That won't be easy. The season is nearly over and most captains are going to be unwilling to risk their ships and the lives of their crew."

"It's not impossible, though," Latimore

stated. "I could probably be persuaded to help."

As Latimore, Jacob, and Stanley circled together to make plans, Jayce felt more confused than ever. He believed he was doing the right thing, but his conviction troubled him more and more. Chase was in Nome. Chase, the murderer—the thief. *But he's also my brother.* Jayce felt as though his heart were torn in two.

Helaina fumed over being excluded from the upcoming trip. She had worked hard on this job, and now Stanley wanted to keep her from being a part of actually apprehending the right man. It infuriated her.

She sat at the music room window staring out at the pouring rain. There had to be a way to maintain her role in this situation. She knew herself to be a woman of means, not only financially, but mentally. She had often come up with crafty, witty plans for catching criminals. So why couldn't she take charge now and make it all work to her benefit? Chase Kincaid might have heard of a woman's involvement, but it was doubtful he'd recognize her. Jayce and her brother were simply being too careful.

"I know you don't agree with my decision," Stanley said from the doorway to the music room. "I hope in time, however, that you will see it as sensible."

Helaina knew in that moment she had to be cautious. If she was to be successful in managing to maintain a role in the capture of Chase Kincaid, she would have to convince Stanley that she had given up her part. "I'm just disappointed," she finally replied. "I know it's possible that Chase could know about me, but I doubt that he does. I understand your fears for me, but at the same time I hope you understand how very much I wanted to be a part of the team that caught Chase."

"I know. I know how disappointing it is because I'd like to be a part of that group myself," he said, crossing the room to where she sat. "No one wants this man behind bars more than I do."

She sighed, knowing he had a valid point. He had suffered far more embarrassment and physical pain than she had. "I know, Stanley. He wronged you, and you have a right to see him taken—to take him yourself."

"I'm sorry that I ever got you tangled up in

this. I knew at the time I assigned it to you that it was dangerous. I suppose to my way of thinking, if I couldn't be there to get Kincaid—you were the next best choice."

Helaina understood. "So do you intend to leave for Washington right away?"

"Yes. Probably tomorrow or the next day, although it might be nice to see something of Seattle. This is my first time here—probably my only time. Perhaps you could show me something of the town and then we can head back to Washington together."

Helaina hadn't counted on that. She forced a smile. "But of course. That would be wonderful. We could spend the travel time catching up on things. Do you already have the tickets?"

"No."

She got to her feet. "The trip home will be taxing, so you should rest. I'll go get tickets; I am quite familiar with the station, as I've been there several times." At least that much was true. Helaina had gone there every day this last week checking on the courier.

"Thank you. That would be great."

She kissed him on the cheek. "Then I'd best get to work. I'll see about the tickets,

and after I return we can go out into the city.
I know several wonderful restaurants. The
seafood is incredible here."

Stanley smiled. "I think I would like that
very much."

Helaina headed to her room to change
her clothes. She threw her day dress on the
bed and took up a lightweight blouse of
white lawn. The simple lines and high neck
matched her desire to appear businesslike
and less the vulnerable female. She then
chose a dark brown wool suit—her plainest
and least feminine article of clothing.
Though the war crinolines with their full bell
skirts and wide-collared bodices were more
popular, Helaina could not get used to the
shorter skirt lengths. Why, some fashions
were edging up as much as eight inches
from the floor. It seemed rather scan-
dalous—just asking for unwanted attention.

She looked in the mirror, pleased. She
had business to tend to. Business at the
station where she would buy her brother's
ticket home, and business at the docks
where she would hopefully book passage to
Nome. Passage she hoped would get her
there before the others.

Chapter Thirty-one

Leah stood beside the fireplace in the front parlor. She wore a beautiful white muslin creation that Jacob had insisted she buy for the occasion. "A woman only marries once," he told her. "She should have something beautiful to call her own and to always remember the day by."

I'll have no trouble remembering this day, she thought. Her stomach churned as she waited for the minister to finish complimenting Timothy on his house and get to the job at hand.

"I was glad to see that the rain had stopped," the older man said as he took up his Bible. "It's always a pity to have rain on a wedding day—not that I believe in the wives' tales of rain representing the number of tears a bride will cry during her years of marriage." He laughed as though even suggesting such a thing was completely out of place.

"We were glad to see it stop as well," Jayce said, coming to stand beside Leah. He winked at her. "You are beautiful. More beautiful than I could have ever imagined."

Leah felt her cheeks grow hot. "I feel rather silly," she whispered. "It would have been more appropriate to wear sealskin and mukluks."

He laughed and took her hand in his. "You'll be wearing them again soon enough. But it does my heart good to know that you still desire that kind of life after living in the comfort of this lovely home."

She looked into his eyes. "The only home I desire is the one we share together. I really don't care where it is—so long as you are there and happy."

"I feel the same way."

"Shall we begin?" the pastor asked.

"Posthaste," Jacob declared, surprising them all. "Let's not waste any more time."

"Helaina and Stanley never came back?" Leah asked as her brother and Timothy took their places as witnesses to the wedding. The butler, cook, and housekeeper had also come to join the festivities at Timothy's request.

"No," Jayce said. "When I told them the wedding was to be this afternoon, Stanley informed me that he and Helaina had plans. I think they both felt out of place."

Leah nodded. "Then let's start." She turned to the pastor and smiled. "I've waited ten years for this."

Jayce pulled her close against his side. "And I have waited a lifetime."

The wedding proceeded in the simplicity and joy that Leah had always imagined. She could hardly believe that, after all this time, God had brought about her dreams. So many years had been spent in the bleak hopelessness that the one man she dearly loved would never love her. Now all of that had changed.

"Will you, Leah, have this man, Jayce, to be your lawfully wedded husband?"

The words blurred in her ears. *Of course I will have him.* She trembled as she gazed up to meet Jayce's face. *I will have him and love him forever and always.*

———

"You know," Stanley said as they allowed the cab to drive them through Seattle, "I'm sorry I doubted your intuition about Kincaid."

"It really wasn't intuition," Helaina replied. "I can't say for sure what it was. Jacob Barringer kept talking to me about mercy and compassion. I told him I believed in justice, and he accused me of seeking nothing but revenge."

"Sometimes I think we do seek revenge. I know I have felt that way about Kincaid. I wanted him to pay for not only what he did to me, but what he did to my fellow agents. I know it's better to remain at a distance when dealing with these criminals, but I couldn't help it."

"Still, the law is the law," Helaina replied. "I've always felt confident that, in serving the purpose of the law, mercy was unimportant. I suppose this case has changed my mind somewhat. But I'm still uncertain as to how the two are reconciled without someone paying a steep price."

She considered her next question carefully. "Stan, what are your thoughts on God?"

"What in the world causes you to ask something like that?" he replied. "God is God. What else can I say?"

"Do you see a need for Him in your life? Have you ever thought to turn your life over to Him?"

"In what way?"

She shrugged. "I'm not completely certain. Jacob and Leah, and even Kincaid— they are all Christians. But not just the kind of people who go to church on Sunday, making sure they're seen by all the right people. These people really believe in God—in doing what He wants them to do. They read their Bibles every day, and when people are troubled and hurting, they talk about things from that Bible. They use Scriptures to help each other overcome difficulties."

"Some people need that kind of crutch," Stanley answered. "I suppose I see nothing wrong with it, but neither do I feel a need for it."

"So you've never felt the need to turn your life over to God?"

Stanley strained to see something out the window, then eased back against the leather upholstery. He looked at Helaina and shook his head. "No. I believe man has to make his own way in the world. We alone are responsible for our actions. We can't be blaming things on supernatural beings—be they divine or evil."

"Then God plays no part in your life?"

"I've never really considered it, to tell you the truth. Why would He care about me?"

"Jacob says He cares about all of us. That He showed us mercy even before we existed on this earth and sent His Son to die for us."

"I've heard all of that, but I think it rather pretentious to imagine that God would sacrifice His Son for us lowly sinners. Why would He do that? Why not just make everything right with the snap of His finger?" Stanley smiled. "If God has fingers."

He shook his head. "No, I'm confident that man controls his own path. He must. He must make choices good or bad. When he makes bad ones, then I get involved."

Helaina had heard it all before, but in the back of her mind she was confused. She had hoped in hearing it again that her convictions might be reestablished. But instead, Stanley's words only troubled her more. Because in spite of Stanley's assurance in his theories and thoughts, Jacob Barringer seemed far more confident of a truth that was not of his own making.

———

"These are the men I promised you," Stanley said. He turned to introduce the larger of the two first. "This is Big Butch Bradford. He's been in the service of the Pinkertons for nearly ten years. He's a good man to have in your corner."

Leah watched as her brother and Jayce shook hands with Big Butch. The man's thick barrel chest and broad shoulders reminded her of Adrik Ivankov.

"And this is Sam Wiseford, and the name is quite appropriate. He is very wise—too smart for his own good. He'll be a good asset to you. He's only been with the Pinkertons for a year, but he's already distinguished himself several times."

Leah thought the man looked too young to even be allowed a job as a Pinkerton. He was athletic in appearance with sandy brown hair that fell in a boyish manner across his face. She smiled when he realized she'd been watching him. He blushed furiously.

"Where's Helaina? We'll be late if she isn't ready," Stanley said.

Leah looked around the room, realizing for the first time that Helaina hadn't joined them. "I'm sure she's just packing last-minute things. Let me go see if I can lend her a hand."

Leah heard Stanley grunt an approval and continue talking about his men and what their duties were to be. Leah could hardly contain her joy at returning to Alaska. She missed the summer in her village and now longed for her friends and little house. She particularly missed Ayoona and Emma.

"Helaina?" she called from outside the woman's closed door. "Helaina, Stanley says you must hurry. Can I help you pack?"

She knocked when there was no reply and found that the door was open. Looking inside, Leah called again. "Helaina, are you here?"

There was no sound. Leah went into the room and looked around—all of Helaina's things were gone, and there was no sign of the woman anywhere. Leah noticed a folded piece of paper on the nightstand and saw a name on the outside. *Stanley.* The script was flowery and feminine, no doubt from Helaina. Leah got a strange feeling that trouble was on the horizon. She hurried downstairs and held out the note to Stanley.

"I found this, but it appears Helaina is gone."

"Gone?" Jacob asked. "Gone where?"

Stanley read the note and growled. "Gone to Alaska. The foolish ninny has bribed passage on a freighter bound north. She left last night."

Jayce looked to Leah. "She's gone after my brother."

"She's gone to get herself killed, is what she's done," Jacob declared, his anger evident. "I can't believe she'd put herself in harm's way like this."

"Oh, she thrives on it," Stanley replied in disgust. "I can't begin to tell you how many times she's done things like this."

"So what do we do now?" Jayce asked.

"We don't have a lot of choices. Captain Latimore won't be ready for another two days," Leah replied. "I think we'll simply have to try to catch up with her before she finds trouble."

"I'll find her—I promise you that," Jacob told Stanley. "We'll do what we can to keep her out of trouble, but knowing your sister, she'll probably attract it to herself like a magnet to metal."

Stanley shifted his weight. "I wish I could come with you, but I'm needed in Washington. My supervisor wasn't happy I even came here."

Stanley handed him a card. "Here's the address where I can be reached. Please let me know as soon as possible if she's all right. Then send her home. Hog-tie her if need be."

"I doubt we'll get her out of Alaska until next spring. We'll be lucky if we can just get ourselves into Nome without great difficulty," Jacob said, taking the card. "But I assure you we will get there."

Later, Leah found Jacob in the music room. He hadn't seemed himself for days, and she chalked it up to him being out of his element. But after seeing his reaction to Helaina's secret departure, Leah couldn't help but wonder if there wasn't something more to this.

"Are you all right?" she asked her brother.

"I'm about as mad as a person can be with Mrs. Beecham."

"She's really managed to . . . well . . . attract your attention."

"I'd like to give her some attention all right. She wouldn't like it, of course."

"Jacob, what's this all about? Why are you so upset with Helaina? Sure, she's thrown the wool over our eyes and set herself up for trouble, but she's a grown woman. She's done jobs like this before. Why torment yourself over her getting to Nome first?"

"Because if she gets there first, she just may get herself killed. Jayce has told me that once his brother feels threatened, he'll stop at nothing to be rid of the threat. He wouldn't think twice about killing Helaina."

"I wouldn't want to see her come to harm either, Jacob. I didn't mean to sound calloused. I just think your feelings for her are stronger than you'd like to admit."

Jacob looked at her oddly for a moment, then let out a heavy sigh. "I fear she's in trouble. She used to have her firm belief in the law and justice to drive her through times of peril. But I've been talking to her about the Lord's mercy and compassion.

It's given her a lot to think about, and I know she's troubled by it. I'm afraid it might affect her judgment in dealing with Chase Kincaid."

"But you did nothing wrong, Jacob. You shared God's truth with her. That's what we're supposed to do. She still has to make her own choice. If she decides against choosing God, it won't be your fault any more than it will be to your credit if she does choose Him."

"I know all of that, but . . . well . . . I feel that before she had an inner strength that made her fearless and capable of dealing with desperate situations. I'm not sure she still has that. She's doubting herself now, which is good on one hand but may end her life on the other."

Leah began to see his reasoning. "I think I understand. But even in knowing this, we are helpless to do anything but pray. And you know even better than I do that prayer is our most powerful tool." She took hold of Jacob's hands and squeezed them tight. "Jacob, you need to stop feeling guilty and use that energy to pray."

He nodded. "I know."

Leah could see that she'd accomplish

nothing more in talk. She would pray for Jacob and trust God to guide his heart. So many times in life they'd done this for each other. . . . It had never failed her.

Chapter Thirty-two

The rocking motion of the *Homestead* nearly sent Leah from the bed. In fact, had Jayce not held on to her tight, she might have found herself sleeping on the floor.

"The weather is getting rougher," she said, snuggling against her husband.

Jayce pulled her close and murmured sleepily. "Soon we'll be home and we won't have to worry about it."

"But there's a lot to do before we get home. I hope you know how proud I am of your decision."

Leah looked up as Jayce opened his eyes. "Having you at my side gives me a strength I don't think I would have otherwise had. I feel so mixed in my decision. On one hand, he has to be stopped. He's a killer and seems to have no regard for anyone. But he's also my brother."

"I know. I kept thinking to myself: how would I respond if this were Jacob?"

"But there's a difference. You and Jacob grew up close to each other. You cared for each other and stuck it out together. Chase has avoided me since we were five. He's always gone his own way and has spent most of his life blaming others for his problems."

"Well, I'm proud of you for not hating him. You've treated him well, considering how he acted toward your mother—not to mention others."

"Not always. When I saw him in Last Chance this summer, I hid from him. I was so stunned to find him there. I figured he would only cause me trouble. I would like to know how he learned of my whereabouts, but I suppose he'll never tell me."

Leah sighed and placed her head on her husband's shoulder. "I never thought I'd say this, but I'm homesick."

"Your taste of big-city life and fancy

clothes didn't change your mind about remaining in Alaska?"

She laughed. "Just like it changed your
mind? After all, you got to sleep in a plush
bed in a warm house with servants. You
never once had to hunt or look for wood to
fuel your stove."

Jayce kissed the top of her head. "I'm at
home wherever you are," he whispered. "I
just never realized it until now."

———

Jacob knew Captain Latimore was deeply
worried about his ship. They'd reached
Nome, but the waters had roughened considerably, and now early ice was threatening
to keep the ship from returning to Seattle.

After overseeing the last of the loads being taken into Nome, Jacob went to meet
with the captain. "It seems to me," Jacob
told him, "that unless you are hard-pressed
for a return on your money, you should
leave that in our hands. We can arrange sale
of the goods and collect the money for you.
Of course, it might be spring before you see
it." He grinned.

"I'm agreeable to you handling the procedure and keeping ten percent of my share for your troubles."

Jacob reached out and shook hands with the captain. "Consider it done."

"Then we will endeavor to leave as soon as possible. Pray for us to make it safely back."

"I will. Oh, and they tell me there are a group of passengers who have asked if you will allow them to return with you. A couple of them are hoping to get to San Francisco, but most are content to get to Seattle."

"I would be glad to do so. It hardly seems like a sound business decision to return empty."

Jacob looked down the shoreline. "I'll let them know they should talk to you. You can settle on the cost of passage and such." He shook hands once again with the captain. "I'll see you in June."

Jacob went about the business of arranging for the sale of the goods. It took some time to manage the account and inform the proper authorities of how they might contact him and arrange the sales.

"I'll take all the canned goods you have," a merchant told Jacob as he checked his invoices. "Of course, with all the trouble of late, we might see a lot of people leave this town, and I'll be left holding the goods."

"What kind of trouble?" Jacob asked, counting the remaining inventory.

"Didn't you hear? We just had a double murder and a kidnapping. Two of our deputies were gunned down—ambushed. A lady who'd just arrived in town was taken hostage by the madman."

Jacob looked up. "Was the woman's name Beecham?"

"I don't recall. I just know it's scared a good many people. Maybe not bad enough to leave Nome, but bad just the same."

Jacob tried to focus on the transaction but found it impossible. "Look. Here are the tallies." He showed the man his papers. "I can let you have all of this."

"I'll take it. Come by in the morning, and I'll have a draft for you."

Jacob nodded. "I'll do that."

With business concluded and his heart full of dread, Jacob hurried into town to find Leah and Jayce. When he caught up with them at the hotel, there was no doubting they'd already heard the news.

"A woman's been taken hostage," Leah

said in a hushed voice. "The police chief was injured and two men were killed."

"So what do we do?" Jacob asked Jayce.

"We were just heading over to the jail. The Pinkerton men are already there. I want to talk to the police chief and see what insight he can offer. I'm sure the offender was Chase, although I suppose I could be wrong. Fights and killings go on all the time up here."

"But kidnappings don't," Jacob nearly growled. "I just know that ninny got herself taken hostage."

Jayce and Leah exchanged a look and nodded. "We do too," Jayce replied.

The police chief confirmed their fears. "We were approached by Mrs. Beecham two days ago. She showed us her documentation and discussed the situation at length. She said it was imperative that we catch Chase Kincaid as soon as possible."

"So what happened after that?"

"Well, we helped her find the man. He was calling himself Jayce Kincaid. Mrs. Beecham said this was normal procedure for him." Jayce nodded and sighed. The chief continued. "He seemed to have a penchant for playing cards, so I arranged a game with a couple of my deputies. There were also a couple of other townsmen in on it too. Mrs. Beecham insisted on being involved as well."

"I'll bet she did," Jacob muttered.

The police chief shrugged. "There didn't seem to be any harm in letting her at least be there. I figured she could identify the man. We set it up in the hotel lobby last night—gaming goes on there all the time."

"So what went wrong?" Jayce asked.

"Kincaid seemed to know what was going on." He looked hard at Jayce. "I've never met twins before. It's almost spooky."

Jayce nodded. "In more ways than you know."

The chief seemed mesmerized for a moment, then continued his story. "Like I said, Kincaid seemed to know what we were up to. It was like someone had given him the information for the entire plan. We let the game play out for most of the night. Thought he'd be drunk and tired by the time we jumped him. But instead, he seemed just as fresh as when he'd sat down.

"A couple of the guys left the game. They cut their losses and exited the hotel, as did I, to maintain a position from the street.

Pretty soon it was just my men and Mrs. Beecham. She was sitting close to the front of the room reading a book. When my men decided the time was right, they went into action. But Kincaid was two steps ahead of them. He shot them both on the spot—dead on, right through the heart. That brought the hotel owner running. Kincaid winged him and sent him diving for cover. Mrs. Beecham, however, was not to be undone. She pulled a derringer and pointed it right at Kincaid's head. According to the hotel owner, the man didn't seem at all disturbed by this. In fact, as he handed over his gun, he smiled at her."

Jacob barely held his temper. He felt a rage burning inside that he couldn't even begin to explain. Maybe he did care for Helaina more than he should. Maybe she had somehow wormed her way under his skin.

"Well, Mrs. Beecham thought she'd march him to jail holding that derringer on him. Kincaid pretended to go along with it at first. I was in the street, trying to position myself to catch him when he came out. But when I called to him, it distracted Mrs. Beecham and Kincaid took control of her gun and grabbed her as a shield."

"And then what?" Jacob sounded more demanding than he'd intended. "Where did he take her?"

"I'm really not sure. There was a bit of a crowd gathering in the streets by this time, and Kincaid threatened to kill anyone who followed. I tried to talk him into letting her go, but he ended up shooting me in the foot as a warning. He took off with Mrs. Beecham and disappeared into the darkness. Wounded as I was, I had to let him go—at least momentarily. I knew I'd need to put together a posse of men to go after Kincaid, and that was going to take some time."

"Did you ever go after him? I mean if this just happened last night, what's going on now?" one of the Pinkerton men asked.

"No one wants to get involved. Kincaid was so brazen and callous, they fear for their lives. I've asked around, but nobody has seen a thing. I can't just up and leave Nome to go hunting him down—not with my foot like this. I've put the word out that he's out there and dangerous. I've given his description and the description of the woman to people coming in and out of town and sent information out on the telegraph, but you know how slowly things happen in Alaska. You can't expect that we'd know something this soon."

"I'll go after them," Jacob said, getting to his feet. "People don't just disappear. There have to be clues—tracks."

"I'll go too. It's my brother on the loose."

"You aren't leaving me behind," Leah told them.

"That's where you're wrong," Jayce said firmly. "I can't have you risking your life out there. You need to stay here or arrange to get back to Last Chance. Those are the only options you have."

"He's right, Leah. You can't be in the middle of this."

"But you can?" she asked her brother.

"We're going too," Sam declared.

Jacob shook his head. "No. You'll just slow us down. Wait here and then you can take him from us when we return."

"Wait a minute," the police chief called out. "If you two are serious about going after that man, I should deputize you both. That way anything you have to do will be in the name of the law."

The law. Jacob would have laughed at

that comment had it not been such a serious situation. Helaina and her love of the law had gotten them all into this situation to begin with.

"That's fine by me," Jayce said, standing.

Jacob came back to the chief's desk. "Me too. Let's just get it over with so we can be on our way." He glanced at Leah. She gave him a glaring look that told him this matter was far from settled.

The police chief swore them both in. "I wish I could give you a file full of information, but like I said, nobody is saying a word. I think they're all running scared."

"That's all right," Jacob said, once again moving toward the door. "I'll find out what I need to know."

"You do know," the chief called out, "he's to be taken dead or alive."

Jacob turned and met Jayce's tight-jawed expression. His friend's eyes had darkened to almost black. "We'll bring him back however he chooses. If he cooperates, then he'll be alive," Jayce murmured.

Jacob had never felt sorrier for anyone. He couldn't imagine the pain this new situation had caused his friend. How could a man hunt down his own brother—knowing that it might well end the life of one or the other?

They walked in silence toward the restaurant to eat and make plans. The weight of the world seemed upon all three, and Jacob knew that somehow he and Jayce still had to convince Leah to remain behind.

They sat down to a table and ordered coffee and roast beef sandwiches. Jacob toyed with his knife as he waited for Leah to offer her protests. When he looked up, however, she was doing the one thing he hadn't expected—she was crying.

He looked to Jayce, feeling helpless against her tears. "I can go alone," he offered.

"No." Jayce put his hand out and took hold of Leah's arm. "I think Leah understands the seriousness of this situation. She's had time to think about it."

"That doesn't change the fact that I don't want you going out there without me. What if one of you gets hurt? You know I'm good at tending injuries."

"And what if you're the one who gets injured?" Jayce asked.

"Or what if one of us gets injured because

we had to worry about you?" Jacob questioned.

Leah met his gaze and seemed to calm a bit. "I hadn't thought of it that way."

"You know if you're out there, you'll be our first concern. I would constantly be wondering where you were and how you figured in to the situation. What I can't bear to think about is Chase taking two hostages."

Leah looked to the table as the waitress brought their order. Jacob smiled at the woman. "How are you, Sally?"

She smiled shyly. "I'm good. Be better soon. I'm getting married."

"Congratulations," Jacob offered, taking the plate she held out. "I hope he's a good man."

She nodded. "Sure. He's plenty good."

She finished serving them, then disappeared into the back room. Jacob offered a blessing on the food and then started to eat. He'd barely taken a bite when Leah spoke.

"All right. I'll go home. I don't want to stay here in Nome indefinitely. If you can get word to John or someone in our village to come and help me, then I'll wait here for them."

"Maybe you could stay and help the doctor again until John can get here," Jayce suggested. "That way you'd have a safe place to stay and you'd feel useful all at the same time."

Leah nodded. "But then I want to go home."

He smiled and touched her cheek. "I know you do. I want to go there too."

"No worse than I do," Jacob added. He reached across the small table to touch Leah's hand. "Thank you for understanding. I couldn't bear it if something happened to you."

"I do understand. But sometimes, understanding isn't enough to calm your heart."

————

Leah watched her brother and husband prepare to leave Nome. They were packing as if for a hunt, only this time they were hunting man instead of bear or seal. She felt a sense of dread—almost panic. What if they were killed like the other two deputies? What if she never saw them again . . . never knew what happened?

She tried to reason that someone had to go—that Helaina couldn't be left in the hands of such a ruthless man. But in her heart, she wished it could be someone else.

Oh, Father, please keep them safe. Please bring them back to me. I love them so much. I need them with me. The prayer did little to calm her spirit.

"I've arranged to get word to John," Jacob told her. "A couple of natives are headed to Prince of Wales. They can drop off word on the way. As soon as he can, I'm sure he'll be here to help you get home. There's a load of goods I set aside from what we brought up from Seattle. Take those back with you."

Leah nodded and hugged him close. "Please be careful, Jacob. I'm so afraid for you."

He kissed her forehead and pulled back. "It's all in God's hands. You know that. If it's my time, it won't matter if I'm hunting down Chase Kincaid or resting in my bed."

She knew this was true, but it didn't help matters. Jacob picked up a large rifle and slung it over his shoulder. "You need to have faith, little sister. I'll see you soon."

He left Leah alone with Jayce. This good-bye was even harder. She looked at her husband and felt the tears well in her eyes. She hadn't wanted to cry. She didn't want to burden either Jayce or Jacob with her tears.

" 'The Lord is my portion, saith my soul; therefore will I hope in him. The Lord is good unto them that wait for him, to the soul that seeketh him. It is good that a man should both hope and quietly wait for the salvation of the Lord,' " she whispered.

Jayce nodded. "Lamentations, chapter three."

She smiled. "I've often taken comfort in those verses."

"As have I."

She rushed into his arms. "I love you, Jayce. I cannot bear the thought of losing you. I know I told you how proud I was of your willingness to help in this, but now I wish you'd both just refuse and go home with me."

"I know. I wish I could. For your sake and the sake of our future, I wish I could walk away. But it's because of you and our future that I *must* go after Chase and see this thing end, once and for all."

"I know." The words were barely audible as Leah buried her face against his neck.

He pulled back slightly and lifted her face to meet his gaze. " 'The Lord is my portion, saith my soul; therefore will I hope in him. The Lord is good unto them that wait for him, to the soul that seeketh him.' " He stroked her chin with his thumb. "Hope in Him, Leah. Wait for Him. He's never let you down."

She nodded. "I know. He brought you back to me when it seemed impossible to ever hope that such a thing could happen."

"He never punishes obedience. Remember that too. We are seeking to be obedient, Leah. God will honor that and see us through. You . . . me . . . Jacob . . . even Helaina and Chase. The Lord has a plan. We have to trust Him for the outcome."

She felt her strength renew. "Yes. I will wait for Him. I will wait for the Lord's salvation."

Jayce kissed her passionately, his warm mouth claiming hers in a way that promised forever. She cherished that brief moment and could have cried when he dropped his hold and walked away. He joined Jacob in the street as a new snow started to fall.

Leah knew he wouldn't look back. He couldn't look back and leave her. With all the strength she could muster, Leah closed the door and walked back to her room in the hotel. The Lord had given him to her after years of loneliness and regret. The Lord would hold Jayce safely in His hand now. She had to believe that—to trust that.

She thought of another portion of Scripture in the third chapter of Lamentations. Quoting it from memory, she smiled at the assurance it offered.

" 'It is of the Lord's mercies that we are not consumed, because his compassions fail not.' " She straightened her shoulders and drew in a deep breath. " 'They are new every morning: great is thy faithfulness.' "

She smiled and wrapped her arms around her body. A peace settled over her that defied the situation. God was faithful. He would see to her—no matter what. No matter her lack of understanding or the madness of the moment.

"You were faithful yesterday . . . and today, Lord." She raised her arms to the ceiling in an act of praise. "I know you will be faithful tomorrow and the next day . . . and forever."

TRACIE PETERSON is a popular speaker and bestselling author who has written more than seventy books, both historical and contemporary fiction. Tracie and her family make their home in Montana.